"Th...
The inva...

"UFO?" the President said. "Why do you call it that?"

"Unidentified Flying Object, sir," said General Ashcroft, who stood stiffly at attention to one side of the President's desk. "A term invented in a proposed Air Force project called Blue Book. We decided not to fund their investigations. It was pure silliness."

"The fact is, Mr. President, we should have kept watching the skies. But no one ever thought."

Jimmy sighed, "And now it's too late to change the world."

"It may not be too late," President Dole said. "Not strictly speaking, anyway. You see, Mr. Andrews, you're not the only crackpot we keep on the payroll. Another one of my pie-in-the-sky geniuses, a Dr. Hawking, claims to have concocted a time machine. His strange quantum theories, his speculations about time and wormholes, have made him a laughingstock among his peers—but if he says the time machine will work, then I'm willing to give it a shot. Preferably before those aliens launch their weapons."

"A time machine!" Jimmy could not keep the delight out of his voice. "And you want to send me back to . . . change history? Alter key events, do whatever I can to ensure that science fiction becomes popular?"

"And let's not forget the fact," Ashcroft interrupted, "that in our current crisis, you are completely expendable."

—from "Mundane Lane"
by Kevin J. Anderson

TIME TWISTERS

EDITED BY
Jean Rabe
and Martin H. Greenberg

DAW BOOKS, INC.
DONALD A. WOLLHEIM, FOUNDER
375 Hudson Street, New York, NY 10014

ELIZABETH R. WOLLHEIM
SHEILA E. GILBERT
PUBLISHERS
http://www.dawbooks.com

First Printing, January 2007
1 2 3 4 5 6 7 8 9

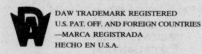

DAW TRADEMARK REGISTERED
U.S. PAT. OFF. AND FOREIGN COUNTRIES
—MARCA REGISTRADA
HECHO EN U.S.A.

PRINTED IN THE U.S.A.

ACKNOWLEDGMENTS

Introduction copyright © 2007 by Jean Rabe.

"Pruning the Tree," copyright © 2007 by Christopher T. Pierson.

"Occupation Duty," copyright © 2007 by Harry Turtledove.

"Mundane Lane," copyright © 2007 by WordFire, Inc.

"The Power and the Glory," copyright © 2007 by Robert E. Vardeman.

"Voices," copyright © 2007 by Jackie Cassada.

"Downtown Knight," copyright © 2007 by James M. Ward.

"Parsley Sage, Rosemary, and Time," copyright © 2007 by Jon L. Breen.

"A Better Place," copyright © 2007 by Linda P. Baker.

"Chaos Theory," copyright © 2007 by Stephen Leigh.

"The Man in Cell 91," copyright © 2007 by Gene DeWeese.

"Oyer and Terminer," copyright © 2007 by Joe Masdon.

"Standing Still," copyright © 2007 by Donald J. Bingle.

"One Rainy Day in Paris," copyright © 2007 by Skip and Penny Williams.

"Try and Try Again," copyright © 2007 by Pierce Askegren.

"Yeshua's Choice," copyright © 2007 by Nancy Virginia Varian.

"Three Power Play," copyright © 2007 by Wes Nicholson.

"One Time Around?" copyright © 2007 by John Helfers.

TABLE OF CONTENTS

INTRODUCTION

Jean Rabe

Time is the fire in which we burn.
—*Gene Roddenberry*

Time . . . we never seem to have enough of it, do we? We're usually always running out.

We're late for this or that.

We flunk time management courses.

We grow old too quickly.

Occasionally, there's too much of it—when in hurricanes, floods, wars, and other disasters we pray for the clock to speed ahead so things can be resolved and made better.

But more often than not, we always want more time, one more day on the calendar.

Ah, time—what if it could be tweaked? What if forces could manipulate it so that presidents might not be assassinated or space travel might be avoided? What if the outcome of wars could be finessed? What if villains and heroes could be plucked from one time-line and placed in another?

1

What if and what if.

The notion of time travel stirs our imaginations.

Time has been the object of novels, movies, college courses, games, and this anthology. It is the subject of classic quotes by famous folks:

Time and the hour run through the roughest day—William Shakespeare

The only reason for time is so that everything doesn't happen at once—Albert Einstein

Time only seems to matter when it's running out—Peter Strup

We must use time as a tool, not as a crutch—John Fitzgerald Kennedy

There is time for everything—Thomas Edison

Time is what we want most, but what we use worst—William Penn

All great achievements require time—Maya Angelou

The time you enjoy wasting is not wasted time—Bertrand Russell

Tempus fugit (time flies)—Ovid (Publius Ovidius Naso)

Time flies like the wind. Fruit flies like bananas—Groucho Marx

Lost time is never found again—Benjamin Franklin

It was the best of times, it was the worst of times—Charles Dickens

Time certainly changes in each of these tales from some of the best voices in science fiction and fantasy. The master of alternate history, Harry Turtledove, takes us upcountry from Gaza with his story. Kevin J. Anderson considers time . . . and space . . . in his stroll down Mundane Lane. James M. Ward lets an influential family play with time. And Gene DeWeese, Nancy Varian, and Jackie Cassada mix time and religion. Linda Baker takes us to the future, Robert Vardeman takes us to Tesla's lab, and John Helfers takes us home.

If you've a little time on your hands, settle yourself into a favorite easy chair, put your feet up, and delve into *Time Twisters*.

It won't be time wasted.

Good reading,
Jean Rabe

PRUNING THE TREE

Chris Pierson

I saw it happen. Right in front of me. It's still sinking in.

The cars came around the corner, into the plaza.
Open-tops, a convoy of them, like you see on TV. The
people were smiling and waving. It was a beautiful
day, sunny, warm, the smell of fresh-cut grass in the
air. Not bad for November—part of why I moved
down here. Everyone was shouting his name, waving
signs and flags. Women *cried* to see him. Men stood
proud. I felt it, too. That was the way he was, the way
we always wanted a president to be, really. Not like
the other guy, sweating on TV during the debates,
always looking like he was up to something. Thank
God *he* lost.

And his wife . . . man, what a beautiful woman. I'm
not the kind of guy who uses words like poise, but
yeah, she had it. They even made the governor look
good, sitting next to them. I was proud to be an American that day.

For a while.

They came around the corner. It gets hazy after
that. They came around the corner, into the plaza . . .
hang on, give me a moment. It's still a little hard to
talk about.

4

Some people say they saw puffs of smoke, but they can't agree about where they were. Behind the hill, up in one of the buildings . . . I heard one guy say Secret Security did it, which sounds like bull to me, but I don't know. I'm not sure what to believe any more. You'll see why.

I didn't see where the shots came from. I just saw him grab his throat, like he was having trouble breathing. Then the back of his head blew up. I saw his wife trying to help him, but I fought in the war. I know when a man's hurt, and when he's dead. He couldn't be helped.

They'd killed President Clayton.

I hear the cops caught a guy. Communist, they say. Had three names—they always have three names, don't they? John Wilkes Booth with Lincoln. Alan Harvey Emory with Hoover. Now this guy, this Gary Robert Anderson. I dunno, maybe the news just likes to use their middle names to make it sound more serious. Like Jim Clayton getting killed isn't serious enough.

They caught the shooter in a movie theater, of all places. Watching a show. Yeah, that's where I'd go, if I'd just shot the President's head off. A lot of people don't think he's the guy. I guess we'll find out, soon enough. Soon enough. I don't think it was the Soviets behind it, myself—Morchenko and his boys are still supposed to be our friends, last I heard. I think it was Himmler's lot. They're still pissed that Clayton named Leibowitz his vice-president. Now we've got ourselves a real-life Jew in charge, running all forty-six states. There's gonna be another war now, just you wait. Probably by summer. They'll try to invade Britain again, and this time they'll have Spain on their side. We'll have to help Churchill out of a jam again. Leibowitz won't sit by. *President* Leibowitz. Still sounds weird, but it's only been a couple weeks.

There's gonna be another war. World War Three. If we're still here.

If any of it's still here.

Because I know something, and you're not going to believe it when I tell you. Something that makes Jim Clayton getting shot look like *nothing*. You probably won't believe me. Hell, *I* wouldn't believe me, and I'm me. But I gotta tell someone. I can take it if you laugh. I just need you to listen.

All right. Here goes.

Like I said, I was down in Jackson the day Clayton got shot. I watched him go down, saw the flecks of blood on his wife's face, the bits of skull on the trunk of that open-top Tucker he was riding in. Jesus, I'll be having nightmares about that till I die. If I die. If I last that long.

Sorry, I'm getting ahead of myself.

After the shots, the motorcade took off. Men in dark suits and sunglasses everywhere. One pointed a gun in my face, then moved on. No one knew what the hell was going on, not the people, not the cops, not the Feds. Everybody scattered. We all thought we might be next, like a presidential assassin would stick around to pop random civilians. We weren't thinking straight. And I'm not proud to say it: I ran. Ran crying, even before they broke out the tear gas and fire-hoses to quell the riots. I just had to get away. It was chaos.

I made it half a mile before the adrenaline started to fade. I don't even remember most of that. I was in a part of town I didn't know too well. I've only lived in the area three months, and I stay home with my wife most evenings. Christ, my wife. She hasn't stopped crying over Clayton. The woman cries in her *sleep*.

I don't have the heart to tell her the other thing.

There was a bar there, and the door was open. I thought, yeah, I could use a drink right now, so I went in. The place was close to empty—just a couple of coloreds at one of the tables in the back. Colored bartender, too. *That* part of town. I got nothing against them, though—I'm pro-Full Rights—so I sat down, ordered a drink. They had Kraft on tap. I got a shot, too. Good whiskey, from Lower Canada. Smooth going down.

The TV was going. Ben Lambert, old stone-face from FBC news, was on, and *he* was crying and saying Clayton had been pronounced dead at 2:43 PM, Monday, November 14, 1966. May God rest his soul. I watched a bit of it, but it didn't say much new. No one seemed to know what was happening. I let it fuzz out, ordered another shot, and nursed my beer. I didn't even see the bartender when he went over and shut the door. I just heard it when he shot the bolt.

I set down my beer, looked around. The other coloreds had gotten up too, and were closing the windows. One went and turned off the television. I stood up, getting scared for the first time. I thought these people might be some of King's Avengers, looking for a white man to hang from a tree. Shit, I *liked* Martin Luther King. I broke my radio when I heard he'd died when that nut blew up that bus in Memphis. That lunatic had three names too, but damned if I can remember the middle one. Dick Something Nixon.

"What the hell is this?" I asked.

"Easy now, mate," the bartender said. He didn't sound like any colored I'd heard in the South. Fellow sounded like he came from overseas. British? Australian? I never found out.

"Easy?" I asked. "You're not gonna make pale fruit out of me?"

The guy frowned, like he'd never heard the phrase before. "Pale what?"

"White lynching," said one of the others, an older woman with the same accent. "I read about it in Cimino's last report. Happened all over the South in this fork."

"It was going on in last fork I was in," said the third colored. *He* sounded more normal, but he wasn't from these parts. Minnesota, maybe. That weird, sorta-Swedish accent. Coulda been Upper Canadian, I suppose. "It's why they sent us, instead of Nelson's crew. We're safer here."

"Look!" I snapped. "Would someone just tell me what's going on?"

"Easy," the bartender said again. "We ain't gonna hurt you. We just want to ask you some questions."

"See," said the woman, "we're kind of lost."

"Why don't you sit down," said the bartender. He held out a hand. "I'm Paul. Paul Clayton."

That put a shock through me. "Like the President," I said, shaking his hand.

"Who?" he asked.

The woman rolled her eyes. "The President, Paul. Just got shot. Weren't you paying attention to the tube?"

"Oh," the bartender said. "Yeah, him. Sorry."

"Jesus," said the other guy, the Canadian-sounding one. He headed toward the front door. "I'll keep watch. You two handle the Q&A."

"My name's Emma Truman," said the woman. "Also like the President."

I frowned. "I don't remember a President Truman."

They all looked at one another. Paul grinned, then shook his head.

"Doesn't matter," said Emma. "Over by the door, that's Tom Mansfield. What's your name?"

"Jeff," I said. "Jeff Wilcox."

"Pleased to meet you, Jeff."

"Look," I said. "I'm not sure what's going on. The President's been dead for an hour, and now you three abduct me. This is weird, you know?"

"Honey," said Emma, her eyes very serious, "I've *seen* weird. This is nothing."

And left it there.

"This ain't an abduction, mate," Paul said. "It's more of a . . . detainment. You're safe, don't worry.

We just need some help. Like Emma said, we're lost. We need to get our bearings."

"Lost?" I asked. "You *work* here."

"Will you sit down?"

Paul's voice didn't change much, but there was a tightness to it that scared me a little. And for the first time, I saw the bulge under the sweater he had on. Christ, I thought, he's got a gun.

I sat down.

"Thanks," Emma said. "Just a few minutes, and we're out of your hair. Promise. What do you do for a living, Jeff?"

"I work over at Davis High. I'm a history teacher."

The guy by the door, Tom, broke out laughing. Paul cracked a smile too. I think I even saw a flicker in Emma's eye. "That's . . . convenient," she said.

"You get the day off because the President was in town?" asked Paul. "This president with the same name as me?"

"Yeah," I said. "It was going to be a big thing for the students. Most of them came into town with their families. A lot of them were probably there when . . . oh, man." I hung my head. It was really starting to sink in.

"It's rough, I know," Paul said. "You wish you could go back and change things. Make it like it never happened."

"Yeah," I said. "That's exactly it."

Emma scowled. "That's a bad wish, Jeff. You don't know how bad."

I looked at her, hard. "That's about the fifteenth really weird thing you've said since I met you, Emma."

"It won't be the last. What are you doing?"

I'd pulled out a cigarette, had the match out. "Smoke?"

"They still do that in this fork, Emma," said Paul, and waved a hand at me. "Good on you, mate. Go ahead."

I lit up. The smoke calmed my nerves a little. "You keep mentioning forks," I said. "What's that about?"

They looked at each other. Emma shrugged. "Don't see the harm in telling you," she said. "But we go first, all right?"

I was pretty sure she had a gun too, so I nodded.

"Okay," said Paul. He pulled out a pad of paper and a pen. "Quick quiz, mate. About history, so this should be easy. First question—is America at war right now?"

"Of course," I said. "In Korea. We've been over there since 1951."

"Korea," said Paul. "Hm. Good, that's a start. Against the communists?"

I blinked. "Are you kidding me?"

Paul stopped writing. He didn't look happy. "Maybe . . ."

"Jeff," Emma asked, leaning in. "Who are we fighting in Korea?"

"The Japs," I said. "Who else?"

"Ah, shit," said Tom from the door. "It's one of *those*."

"I thought we'd dealt with that tangle," said Emma.

"We did," Paul said. "Wang's crew, a while back. Something must have re-tangled it."

I sighed, taking another drag. "I suppose I'll figure out what a 'tangle' is later, too."

"Probably," said Paul. "What happened at the end of World War Two, Jeff? Who won?"

Seriously. He asked that.

"Nobody *won*," I said. "Hitler took most of Europe, but we kept him out of England, and Trotsky's Reds pushed him back before he could storm Moscow. It was the same with the Japs. They kept some parts of Asia, we took back others. Then they dropped a nuke on Kauai."

"Nuke . . . on . . . Kauai," said Paul, writing fast, his eyebrows rising.

"America had nuclear weapons too, though, right?" asked Emma.

"Yes," I said. "Enough to hit Okinawa, then threaten to drop more on Tokyo and Berlin. But the Nazis had them too, and so did the Reds. Hence the truce."

"Four-way cold war," said Paul, impressed. "That's a new one."

It went on from there. I stopped thinking it was a joke pretty quick. These guys really didn't seem to know much about history. I mean, they had it all wrong. They'd never heard about half the presidents, they didn't know that Lenin named Trotsky his successor over in Russia—they asked about some guy named Stalin, whoever *that* is. They seemed to think there was some kind of economic depression, back in the '20s. They thought Canada was still one country instead of three, that the Italians were Germany's allies during the war instead of ours, and that there was this place called Vietnam, somewhere in the Greater Jap Empire. I think they even mentioned America having fifty-one states, at one point. It was by far the strangest hour of my life—and this is on the same day Clayton got killed.

Then it got stranger.

"Fine, then," Paul said, taking a puff of his smoke and coughing a little. He'd bummed one from me; so had Tom. Emma was completely appalled. It was pretty obvious that neither of them had smoked before, and while Tom had turned green and put his out right away, Paul was enjoying his, kind of like I'd enjoyed sneaking my first beer when I was twelve. "World War One. How did it start?"

"Archduke Ferdinand got shot. A Serb did it, named Gavrilo Princip. Only two names—he was one of the rare ones."

Paul stopped writing and gave Emma a look. She raised an eyebrow. I thought they wanted more, so I kept going.

"I think it would have happened anyway, though—most of Europe was just waiting for a reason at the time. The Russians—"

"That's all right, Jeff," Emma said, as Paul closed his notebook and put it away. "Was the president at the time Woodrow Wilson?"

"Yes," I said.

"How long did he stay in power?"

"Until 1916," I said. "Then John Gavin beat him when he was up for reelection."

"There it is," said Tom.

"We got our divergence," Paul said.

Emma held up a hand, stopping them. "What happened at the end of the war?"

"Gavin got us involved right away," I said. "That was the platform he ran on—helping friends in their time of need. Bulgaria surrendered early. We drove the Germans and Austrians back, and they capitulated in the summer of 1917. The Ottomans held out for most of another year, but that was more of a footnote, really."

"There . . . it . . . is," Tom said again, peering out the window. "We've got what we need, Em. We should go. There's police coming—they're probably looking for the guy shot this Clayton."

"Yeah," said Emma, standing up. "Paul, go down and get the pod warm. We'll be along."

"On it," said Paul. He stubbed out his cigarette. "Thanks for the smoke. It was . . . interesting." He clapped me on the arm, then headed toward the stairs that led down to the bar's basement.

The others started getting ready to go. "Thank you for your help, Jeff," Emma said, all business. "You got us pointed in the right direction."

"Hold on," I said, reaching out to grab her arm.

As I did, I heard a click, and glanced across the bar. Tom had drawn his gun. It didn't look like any weapon I'd ever seen. It was sleeker, made of what looked like ceramic, with a red light on top. But none of that matters with guns, really. What matters is the hole in the end, and whether it's pointed at you. Tom's was.

"Get back from her," he said.

"Whoa," I said, raising my hands and stepping away from Emma.

She shook her head, her eyes locking with mine. "Put it away, Tom. You think a history teacher's going to take me hostage? Besides, he's unarmed. You saw the scan when he came in."

Tom pursed his lips, giving her a look that said *you never know*. But he holstered his gun under his jacket anyway. She was definitely the one in charge. It seemed weird, watching a woman order armed men around.

"I'm sorry," I said. "I didn't mean to startle you."

"Don't worry about it," Emma replied. "Besides, it's my fault. I promised you answers."

"We don't have a lot of time," Tom said, looking outside again.

Emma turned back to me. "I'm sorry, Jeff. I'll have to make this quick." She paused, her brow furrowing. "You ever read science fiction? Any H.G. Wells?"

"Sure," I said. "*War of the Worlds*. Fellow made a radio show of it, caused a riot."

"Yeah," Emma said. "I'm talking about another story, though. *The Time Machine*."

It all went click then. I stared at them. "You're telling me you're from the future?" Because they sure didn't look like they were from the past.

Emma nodded. "A hundred and fifty years from now. Or rather, *not* from now. You see, time's kind of like a tree. It's constantly forking into different branches. In one time, the French come to the colonies' aid during the revolution, and you get America. In another they don't, and you get something else. In one, D-Day works out fine. In another, the Germans find out in advance, and it turns into a bloodbath."

"What's D-Day?" I asked.

"Never mind. What I'm telling you is, the world I grew up in lay in a different fork from yours. Or so we thought, anyway. It's more complicated than that."

"You can *change* a fork, by messing with shit in the past," Tom put in.

I blinked at them. "You mean, if you went back, say, and stopped that bomber from killing Hitler in '47, everything now would be different?"

Tom snickered.

"Uh, yeah," Emma said. "Something like that. So you can see how what we do got very, very dangerous. Fortunately, people understood it was a bad idea to go back and mess with history, so the powers that be worked out an arrangement. A temporal détente."

"Yeah, *that* worked," muttered Tom.

Emma shrugged. "It did, for a while. But then something went wrong. One day the world woke up, and nothing was the same. The Soviet Union was still around, but America had broken up. Most of Europe was a radioactive wasteland. It was a mess."

I'd been nodding up till now. Now I squinted at her, dragging on my cigarette. It had burned down, so I put it out. "How did anyone know things had changed?" I asked. "I mean, the world they knew must have been normal to them, right?"

"It was," Emma said. "But some of us were out in the flow when it happened. When we came home, everything was different. My parents never even met, and Tom's and Paul's never *existed*. Don't try to think about how that's possible, it only hurts. I don't know the answers. I just know that our world's gone, and we don't know why."

"Terrorists," Tom muttered.

Emma waggled her hand. "It could have been a lot of things. An accident. Some country broke the treaty. None of us were sure. But we didn't like the world as it was, so we got the hell out, and came back to fix things."

"Ah," I said. "That's why you wanted to know about history. You need to find out where things changed."

"Yes. So we can change them back."

"And you think it has something to do with President Gavin."

She shrugged. "Maybe it does, maybe it doesn't. It's not the first thing we've fixed. Every time we think we've set things right, the divergence shifts further back. We first thought this whole thing started because someone tried to stop some buildings being blown up in 2001. Now the fork happens almost a whole century earlier. All I know is, there was no John Gavin in *our* election in 1916, and Wilson got re-elected. So that's where we're headed."

"Sounds like someone's one step ahead of you. Or behind, I guess."

"No shit," said Tom, chuckling. "I'm telling you, Em, it's terrorists."

"Whatever it is," she said, rolling her eyes, "we've got other teams searching the flow for the cause. Paul, Tom and I, we're strictly recon and containment. We fix time when it breaks."

There was a hammering outside, and shouting. Men were pounding on the door of the barber shop next door. Tom looked out and sucked a breath through his teeth. "Out of time, Em. School's out," he said, drawing his gun once more. "We've gotta go."

Emma looked at me. I looked at her. "One more question," I asked. "When you go back to 1916—when you make sure Wilson wins—what happens to *this*?" I waved at everything, all around.

Really meaning, what happens to *me*.

She shook her head. "I don't know. This world will probably still exist somewhere, in another fork. Maybe in a lot of them. But as for *this* fork, things will change. You'll wake up one day, and everything will be different. But that could happen anyway, if whoever's causing the trouble goes back and, say, makes sure Custer survives Little Big Horn. It's probably inevitable, so you'd best make peace with it."

The noise next door stopped. I could hear footsteps crunching on gravel.

"Out," Tom said. "*Now.*"

Emma nodded, then leaned in and kissed me on the cheek. I remember she smelled like rain.

"Good-bye, Jeff," she said. "And thanks."

With that, she turned and went downstairs after Paul. Tom followed, stopping only to point at the floor, his eyes heart-attack serious. *Stay here.*

Part of me wanted to ask if I could go with them, but I stayed. They had guns, I didn't. And I belong here. Or now. Both.

About thirty seconds before the cops came knocking, I heard a sound from the basement: first a hum, then a noise like someone had torn a big piece of sheet-metal in two. I felt a charge in the air, like before a thunderstorm, and there was the stink of ozone. The hairs on my arms stood up. My watch stopped, and hasn't worked since. The TV flashed white, then went dark and started to smoke.

When the police came in, I was the only person left in the place. I thought I'd have some explaining to do, but they didn't care about a white guy alone in a colored bar. They were looking for the guy who shot Clayton. They figured out I wasn't him, so they went on.

And I walked home, wishing the whole way that I'd told Emma I didn't know who the hell Custer was.

Like I said, believe me or don't. Makes no difference to me.

Jesus, even I don't know if I buy it. But I've made peace, like Emma said. I'm ready for the change. One day I might wake up, and we'll be at war with this Vietnam place, and the Nazis won't exist any more, and the president will be some guy from Texas named

Johnson. Or one day I might wake up, and I'll be living in Confederate States of America.

Or one day, I might not wake up at all. My grandfather fought in World War One, after all. God knows what happened to him before the divergence. The more I think about it, the more I'm sure that's the truth. It's why they didn't care that they told me all their secrets. Emma even said it: *don't see the harm*. It's been fifty years since John Gavin was elected. A lot will change if he isn't.

Yeah, that's probably it. I only exist right now because things went wrong, somewhere in the past. Any time now, I might just . . . disappear.

And so might you.

OCCUPATION DUTY

Harry Turtledove

Pheidas wasn't thrilled about going upcountry from Gaza—who would have been? But when you were a nineteen-year-old conscript serving out your term, nobody gave a curse about whether you were thrilled. You were there to do what other people told you— and on the double, soldier!

He got into the armored personnel carrier with all the enthusiasm of someone climbing into his own coffin. None of the other young Philistinians climbing aboard looked any happier than he did. The reason wasn't hard to figure: there was a small—but not nearly small enough—chance they were doing exactly that.

The last man in slammed the clamshell doors at the rear. The big diesel engine rumbled to life. "Next stop, Hierosolyma," the sergeant said.

"Oh, boy," said Pheidas' buddy Antenor.

He spoke softly, but Sergeant Dryops heard him anyway. "You better hope Hierosolyma's our next stop, kid," the noncom said. "If we stop before we get there, it's on account of we've got trouble with the Moabites. You want trouble with the stinking ragheads? You want trouble with them on their terms?"

Antenor shook his head to show he didn't. That

18

wasn't going to be good enough. Before Pheidas could say as much, Dryops beat him to the punch.

"*You want trouble with them on their terms?*" he yelled.

"No, Sergeant," Antenor said loudly. Dryops nodded, mollified. And Antenor's reply not only took care of military courtesy, it was also the gods' truth. The Moabites caused too much trouble any which way. As far as they were concerned, their rightful border was the beach washed by the Inner Sea. The Philistinians? Invaders. Interlopers. Never mind that they'd been on the land for more than three thousand years. In the history-crowded Middle East, that wasn't long enough.

They don't even believe in Dagon, Pheidas thought as the APC clattered north and east, one of a long string of armored fighting vehicles. It wasn't that he wanted the miserable Moabites worshiping the same god he did. If that didn't ruin the divine neighborhood, he didn't know what would. But too many Moabites didn't believe Dagon *was* a god. Some thought he was a demon; others denied he was there at all. They felt the same way about the other Philistinian deities, too.

Antenor's mind must have been running in the same direction as Pheidas', for he said: "They're jealous of us. They've always been jealous of us."

"Sure," Pheidas said. You learned that in school. Right from the beginning, the Philistinians had been more progressive than the tribes of the interior. They were the ones who'd first learned how to work iron, and they'd done their best to keep the hill tribes from finding out how to do it. Some things didn't change much. The Moabites were still backward, but there were an awful lot of them, and they didn't mind a bit if they died in the service of their own grim tribal gods.

Around Gaza, the land was green and fertile. The Philistinians always had a knack for making the desert bloom. That was why so many nasty neighbors had coveted their country, almost from the very beginning.

Pheidas nudged Antenor. "Hey!" he said.

"What?" Antenor had been about to light a cigarette. He looked annoyed at getting interrupted.

"You were good in school. What was the name of that guy Lord Goliath knocked off?"

"Oh. Him." Antenor frowned, trying to remember. After a moment, he did—he *had* been good in school. "Tabitas, that's what. Tabitas of the Evraioi."

"*That's* right!" Pheidas nodded. He couldn't have come up with it himself, but he knew it as soon as he heard it. "Crazy, isn't it? Here we are all these years later, going off to do the same cursed job all over again."

"Miserable mountain rats don't go away," Sergeant Dryops said. "They want to make *us* go away, but that ain't gonna happen, either." He paused. "Is it?"

"No, Sergeant!" This time, all the troopers in the APC sang out as loud as they could. Once bitten, twice raucous. Dryops not only nodded, he even smiled a little. Pheidas wondered if the world would end. It didn't. The world was a tough old place.

As he peered out from time to time through the firing port by his head, Pheidas watched it get tougher, too. The people of the hills and the people of the coast had been enemies since the days of Goliath and Tabitas, maybe longer. Sometimes it seemed the landscapes were enemies, too.

Things went from green to brown as soon as the land started climbing and getting rougher—as soon as it went from a place where more Philistinians lived to one were there were more Moabites. Chickens and goats and skinny stray dogs roamed the streets of Moabite villages. The houses and shops looked a million years old despite their rust-streaked corrugated iron roofs. Pheidas wouldn't have wanted to drive any of the ancient, beat-up cars. The sun blasted everything with the force of a tactical nuke.

Spray-painted squiggles in the pothook Moabite script marred whitewashed walls. Pheidas could read it. Learning enough Moabite to get by was part of basic training. PHILS OUT! was the most common graffiti. Pheidas didn't mind that one so much. He didn't like the Moabites any better than they liked his people. He would have been happy to stay out if his commanders hadn't told him to go in.

But then he saw one that said CHEMOSH CUTS OFF DAGON'S SCALY TAIL! Chemosh was the Moabites' favorite god. For lots of them, he was the only tribal god. A few even said he was the only god, period. You really had to watch out for fanatics like that. They were the kind who turned terrorist.

The scrawl that really raised his hackles, though, was THE SWORD BUDDHA AND THE FOUR WITH CHEMOSH! The Turks of Babylon were newcomers to these parts; they'd brought the Sword Buddha down off the steppe hardly more than a thousand years ago. But Aluzza, Allat, Manah, and Hubal had been worshiped in Arabia for a very long time. And Babylon and Arabia were both swimming in oil, which these days counted for even more than the strength of their gods.

Sergeant Dryops saw that one, too. He muttered into his gray-streaked red mustache. Pheidas couldn't make out all of what he said. From what he *could* understand, he was surprised the steel by Dryops' head didn't melt.

"We've got friends, too," the veteran noncom said when his language grew a little less incandescent. "The Ellenes in Syria don't like the Moabites any better than we do. And they *really* don't like the Turks."

That made Pheidas feel a little better—until Antenor went and spoiled it by saying: "They don't have much oil, though."

Dryops looked at him as if he'd found him on the sole of his marching boot. "Blood's thicker than oil, by the gods," he growled.

Antenor didn't say anything at all. His silence seemed more devastating than speech. There *were* ties between Philistinians and Ellenes, yes. But they were ancient.

Some of the Philistinians' ancestors had come from Crete before settling on the mainland here. But the languages now were as different as Galatian and Irish—more different, maybe, because they'd been separate longer. And Babylon outweighed Syria about three to one.

A couple of Moabite men in headcloths and white cotton robes—good cover against the sun—scowled at the armored column as it clattered past. Scowls were basically honest. As long as nobody did anything more than scowl . . . Pheidas could look out through the firing port instead of shooting through it. That suited him fine.

It wasn't far from Gaza to Hierosolyma, not as the crow flew. But a crow didn't fly back through the years, and Pheidas felt he'd fallen into a different century when his convoy rolled into the hill town. Gaza was a city of steel and glass and reinforced concrete, a city that looked across the Inner Sea to the whole wide world. Hierosolyma, hidden in the hills, was built of golden limestone and wood and brick, and looked as if it had been there forever. Had it seemed very different when the Turks sacked it, when the Romans wrecked it, when Philip of Macedon besieged the Persian garrison there, or when Lord Goliath took it away from the Evraioi? Pheidas had his doubts.

Men in robes and women in long, baggy dresses only made the impression of age stronger. Some of the men did wear modern shirts and trousers, but none of the women—none—chose the skimpy, clinging styles that were all the rage down by the sea. As far as girl-watching went, it would be a barren time.

But it wouldn't be dull. Graffiti on whitewashed walls was thicker and fiercer here than it had been in the villages to the southwest. Philistinian soldiers with assault rifles patrolled the narrow, twisting streets. They never traveled in parties smaller than four; the Moabites had assault rifles, too, and other, nastier, toys, and used them whenever they figured they could get away with it.

The APC rattled past a couple of firebombed buildings. A wine bottle full of gasoline with a cloth wick was a low-tech weapon, which didn't mean it wasn't effective. Then Pheidas stopped worrying about gasoline bombs, because something a demon of a lot bigger went off much too close. The APC swayed and shook and almost flipped over. Then it stopped so suddenly, it pitched all the soldiers in the fighting compartment into a heap.

"*Get* off me, Dagon damn you!" Sergeant Dryops shouted. "Open the doors and pile out. Somebody's gonna need help."

As usual, a man with a loud voice and a clear notion of what he wanted stood a good chance of getting it. The soldiers unscrambled themselves. Antenor opened the doors at the back of the carrier. The men jumped out, weapons at the ready.

"Gods!" Pheidas exclaimed. He ran forward, boots thudding on cobblestones that might have known the scritch of hobnailed Roman marching sandals.

Someone had driven a car into the Philistinian column—a car with a bomb inside. Then he'd set it off. The car was nothing but twisted steel and flames, with thick black smoke rising from it. Mixed with the chemical stinks was one that held a certain ghastly appeal—it smelled like burnt roast pork. Pheidas' stomach did a slow lurch: that wasn't pork burning.

The murder bomber hadn't just blown himself up. That would have been too much to hope for. He'd wrecked a Philistinian command car almost as thoroughly as the one that carried the bomb. Pheidas didn't think anybody in there could be alive. And the blast had overturned an APC and set it on fire. Burned and wounded Philistinian soldiers came stumbling out of it.

"Anybody left inside?" Pheidas shouted. He wouldn't have left a Moabite to cook in there. . . . Well, right this minute, maybe he would.

"Did the driver get away?" asked a soldier bleeding from a cut on the forehead.

"We'll find out." Pheidas and Antenor both dashed around the burning chassis to see. The driver's compartment was separate from the one where the soldiers sat, and had its own escape hatches.

If the driver hadn't got out—and it didn't look as if he had—he never would now. The APC's front end had taken the brunt of the blast. With the best will in the world, try to force your way through those flames and you'd end up like one of the babies the Phoenicians up the coast fed to the fires in the old days—and, some people whispered, even now.

A shriek behind Pheidas made him whirl, rifle at the ready. A Moabite woman lay on the ground, blood pouring from a gash in her thigh. Part of Pheidas hoped she would just bleed out. But that wasn't how he'd been trained. He ran over and yanked up her dress so he could bandage the gash.

"What are you doing to her?" The question came in harsh, guttural Moabite. "Why are you putting hands on her?"

Pheidas glanced up. The Moabite standing over him couldn't have been more than a couple of years older than he was. The fellow had a gash under one eye, but he didn't know or care. He seemed to think Pheidas would drop his pants and start humping the wounded woman any second now.

"I'm going to fix her leg if I can," Pheidas answered, using Moabite herself. Speaking the language always made him feel he had a mouth full of rocks. "If you know first aid, you do it instead."

"Not me. Not me, by Chemosh's white beard!" The young Moabite backed away. "You better not do anything dirty to her, that's all."

"Are you crazy?" Pheidas said, and then he forgot

about the kid. He had to tie off a bleeder. He'd learned how to do that, but he'd never actually done it before. He thanked Dagon that he didn't lose his lunch. He pinned the wound closed, gave the woman a pain shot, and put a bandage around everything. When he finished, his hands were covered with blood. He wiped them on her dress. It was already so bloody, a little more gore wouldn't matter.

Only then did he look up and see that the young Moabite was still watching him. "You did what you said," the fellow admitted.

Wearily, Pheidas pointed to the burning wreck of the car the murder bomber had driven. "A Philistinian didn't do that to her," he said. "A Moabite did. One of your people, not one of mine."

"If you weren't occupying us, we wouldn't have to do things like that," the Moabite answered.

"If we weren't occupying you, you'd throw us into the sea," Pheidas said.

"You deserve it. You came from the sea. You should go back into it," the Moabite said. "If Dagon is so wonderful, he can take care of you there."

Pheidas swung his assault rifle so it almost bore on the young man. He wasn't especially devout—most Philistinians weren't these days—but he wasn't about to let this fellow mock him. "I didn't say anything about your god," he growled, sounding as much like Sergeant Dryops as he could. "Keep your mouth shut about mine."

"You can't say anything bad about Chemosh," the young man said. "Chemosh is a true god. Chemosh is *the* true god."

Fanaticism rang in his voice, though he would probably just have called it pride. Pheidas gestured with the rifle. "Get lost, punk, or you'll be sorry."

"Ha! You fear the glory of Chemosh! You know Dagon is nothing but a dead statue!" But the Moabite backed off. Unlike the murder bomber, he didn't have the stuff of martyrs in him—right this minute, anyhow.

Another Moabite came up to Pheidas. This one wore somber business clothes under a headscarf. "I am a physician," he said in accented but understandable Philistinian. "I will care for the woman now. Thank you for what you did."

"You're welcome," Pheidas said. "Help the soldiers, too, please. Some of them need it more than she does."

The Moabite doctor hesitated. "I would rather not," he said at last. "Nothing personal, but I could find myself in a dangerous position if it were discovered that I had done such a thing."

"Your own people would kill you, you mean," Pheidas said.

"Yes." The physician nodded. "Unfortunately, that is exactly what I mean."

Pheidas felt like pounding his head on the slates of the sidewalk in despair. "How are we both supposed to live on this land when you feel that way?"

"When one of us is gone, the other will live on this land," the Moabite replied. Pheidas knew exactly what he meant. *When you Philistinians are gone, we will live on it.*

Sandbagged machinegun nests, barbed wire, and concrete barriers to thwart murder bombers in cars surrounded the Philistinian barracks in Hierosolyma. Pheidas didn't feel particularly safe even after he dumped his pack by a cot. Too easy to set up a mortar on a roof or in the courtyard of a house and lob a few bombs this way. You could disassemble the thing and hide it long before anybody found you.

"All the comforts of home," Antenor said, looking around at the dismal place.

"Sure, if you live in a jail," Pheidas said.

Antenor laughed, for all the world as if he were kidding. "This whole country's a jail," he said. "We're stuck in it, and so are the cursed Moabites."

"We're occupying this part of it," Pheidas said. "If

the Moabites ever get the upper hand, they'll massacre us."

"They say their god says we deserve it." Antenor's raised eyebrow told what he thought of that.

"Chemosh is king!" Pheidas said in Moabite—a phrase any Philistinian had heard often enough to understand, regardless of whether he knew another word of the language. He returned to his own tongue for a two-word editorial: "Stinking fanatics."

"They are," Antenor agreed glumly. "It gives them an advantage. They really believe in the fight while we . . . just kind of go on."

As usual, Sergeant Dryops heard everything that mattered. "I'll tell you what I believe in," he rasped. "I believe in not letting one of those ragheads drygulch me on account of I got careless—or on account of I got too trusting. Some dogs shouldn't get even one bite."

"Heh." Pheidas knew his laugh sounded nervous. Like Arabs and Aramaeans and Phoenicians, Moabites had little use for dogs. Call one of them a son of a bitch and you made an enemy—quite possibly a murderous enemy—for life.

Dryops understood why Pheidas was jumpy. "None of those mangy hounds in here," he said. "Cursed well better not be, anyhow." He laughed.

"The way those people—all those peoples—feel about dogs is enough to make you anti-Semitic," Antenor said. After three thousand years on the Middle Eastern mainland, Philistinians had a good deal of Semitic blood in them, too. Pheidas found himself nodding all the same.

"I don't give a rat's ass how they feel about dogs," Sergeant Dryops said. "But when they want to murder me . . . that, I don't like."

He didn't need to feel sure he had Dagon's power behind him. His boundless scorn for the Moabites was plenty to keep him going.

*   *   *

Along with half his squad, Pheidas tramped the narrow, winding streets of Hierosolyma. His eyes went this way, that way, every which way. He registered all the windows, all the balconies, all the rooftops. Every time a Moabite drew near, he tensed. Did the man have a murder belt full of explosives and nails laced around his middle? Was the woman carrying grenades?

Moabite men called names, in their language and in Philistinian. Some of what they said made *dog* and *son of a bitch* seem like endearments. In civilian life, Pheidas might have tried to kill someone for insults like that. As a soldier, he had to keep his finger off the trigger. Even sticks and stones weren't reason enough to open up. So the high command insisted, anyhow.

But the high command wasn't out there. Soldiers— ordinary human beings—were. Somebody a couple of blocks from Pheidas got hit by a rock and an insult at the same time. He did what he would have done if he were still a civilian. A few seconds later, a young Moabite writhed in the street, blood pouring from his head and his chest.

When Pheidas heard the burst of automatic-weapon fire, the muzzle of his own rifle automatically swung toward the sound. But the screams and shouts and curses that followed weren't close enough to give him any targets. They got louder instead of softer, though. "That's trouble," he said.

"Better believe it," Antenor said.

Then there were more bangs. These came from the Novgorodian assault rifles terrorists used all over the world. More Philistinian guns barked in reply.

Pheidas had heard plenty. "Come on!" he shouted, and ran toward the sound of the firing. His squad-mates pounded after him.

"Maybe . . . we can keep . . . the riot . . . from starting," Antenor panted as he ran.

It was already too late. "Death to the Philistinians!"

somebody yelled from a second-story window. A wine bottle with a flaming wick flew out and smashed on the cobbles in the street. Flame splashed out in a five-cubit circle. Pheidas sidestepped like a dancer. Behind him, one of the other Philistinian soldiers chucked a grenade through the window from which the incendiary had come. A shriek rang out hard on the heels of the boom. The soldier nodded in grim satisfaction and ran on.

A couple of Philistinians were down. So were more than a couple of Moabites. Pheidas smelled blood and fear. Some of the fear was bound to be his own. Two bullets snapped past his head. He dove into the nearest doorway. When he saw somebody in a headscarf, he fired at him.

The man went down, clutching at his side. "Mesha! My Mesha!" a woman screeched, and then: "Murder!"

More and more Moabites converged on the flashpoint. So many of them carried weapons, Pheidas wondered if they weren't waiting for a moment like this. Philistinian soldiers ran toward trouble, too, as they'd been trained. When rocks and firebombs and gunfire met them, they answered with gunfire of their own.

An APC awkwardly turned a tight corner. Its heavy machine gun and bulletproof sides let it dominate the field—or would have, if a Moabite hadn't set it on fire with another bottle full of gasoline. Some of the Philistinians inside managed to get out. Pheidas didn't think all of them did.

"Chemosh is king!" The cry rose again and again, ever louder. So did another one: "Death to Dagon!"

Pheidas peered out from the doorway. Somebody in a dun-colored uniform like his was down. A Moabite with a Novgorodian rifle drew a bead on the wounded Philistinian from no more than three cubits away. Pheidas shot the Moabite in the back. He threw out his arms as he toppled, the rifle flying from his

hands. Pheidas ran to his countryman. The Philistinian
had a big chunk blown out of one calf. "Hurts," he
said as Pheidas dragged him back to cover.

"I bet it does." Pheidas gave him a shot and band-
aged the wound. He was glad he'd replenished his aid
kit after helping the Moabite woman. He wasn't so
glad he'd helped her, not any more.

"Death to Dagon!" the Moabites howled. "Chemosh is king!"

Another Moabite with a rifle ran out to try to help
his friend the way Pheidas had helped the wounded
Philistinian. Pheidas shot him, too. He'd never fired
his own weapon in anger until this morning. One of
these days, he would have to try to figure out what it
all meant. Now he just wanted to stay alive.

"What a mess." Thanks to the shot, the wounded
Philistinian sounded dreamy, not tormented.

"Man, you can say that again," Pheidas said. "The
Arabs in Amman will be screaming about what we
did to their little Semite brothers. So will the Phoenicians, and the Turks in Babylon. We'll be lucky if we
don't wind up in another real war."

"Yeah." The wounded man didn't seem to care.
That was the drug talking—the drug and the fact that
he wouldn't be doing any more fighting for a while
no matter what.

An ambulance rolled up, lights flashing and sirens
wailing. The Moabites threw rocks at it even though
it had the Green Waves painted on the doors. They
didn't recognize that symbol of mercy; their ambu-
lances, like most in the Middle East, used the Green
Sun instead. Parthians used the Green Lion, while
most of the world preferred the Green Hammer.

Pheidas waved to the ambulance driver, who
stopped the vehicle. A couple of medics got out and
picked up the man who'd been shot. They both had
pistols on their hips. Medics were supposed to be non-
combatants, but the Moabites didn't care about leav-

ing them alone, so they protected themselves as best they could.

The ambulance screamed away. "Over here!" somebody shouted in Philistinian. "Quick!"

Pheidas caught the slight guttural accent. "Sit tight! He's a fraud!" he yelled. What did the Moabites have waiting? Snipers? A machine gun? Grenades?

A tank fired. The boom of the cannon and the blam of the bursting shell came almost too close together to separate into two noises. Screams followed a moment later. Pheidas hoped some of them came from the Moabite who'd tried to trap his buddies.

"You all right?" That was Antenor's voice.

"So far, yeah. You?" Pheidas called back.

"I'm not bleeding, anyway," his friend said. "Don't know what the demon I'm supposed to do, though."

"Stay alive. Shoot the ragheads if they get too close. What else is there?" Pheidas said.

"There should be something." Antenor sounded desperately unhappy. Pheidas hoped he wouldn't think too much. If you did, you were liable to give the bad guys a chance to punch your ticket when you could have punched theirs instead.

To them, of course, you were the bad guys. The Moabites were surer they were right than Pheidas' own folk were. *Now who's thinking too much?* Pheidas wondered.

"To me! To me!" That was an unmistakable Philistinian voice. Pheidas dashed out of the doorway. He sprayed a quick burst to make any Moabites in the neighborhood keep their heads down. The Philistinian shouted again. He was inside a grocery. Pheidas ran over and jumped through the blown-out front window.

"What's up?" he asked, flopping down flat.

The Philistinian who'd called wore a captain's three dragons on each shoulder strap. "I've got a captive here, and I want to make sure we get him out in one piece," he answered, keeping his rifle trained on a plump, most dejected-looking man. "I think he's one of those Sword Buddha maniacs from Babylon, here to stir up the Moabites."

"Great," Pheidas said, peering out to make sure nobody was getting ready to rush the grocery.

"My name is Chemoshyatti," the man said in flawless Moabite. "I have run this grocery for years. By my god, Philistinian, you mistake me."

"My left one," the captain said. "I found the tracts in your register's cash drawer." He didn't turn his head away from Chemoshyatti, but addressed his next words to Pheidas: "The usual garbage."

"Uh-huh," Pheidas said. In the Middle Kingdom and Southeast Asia, Buddhism was a peaceful faith. But the variant the Turks brought down off the steppe preached that nirvana came through killing foes. You didn't even have to be a Buddhist yourself to gain it if you took enough enemies with you. Babylonia fostered terrorists as far as its acolytes could reach.

Antenor and another Philistinian soldier warily approached the grocery. Pheidas raised up enough to let them see him in helmet and uniform, then ducked down again. The captain urged them on, saying, "Now we've got enough men to make sure we can get this guy to the people who need to ask him questions."

That wouldn't be much fun, not for the fellow who had to do the answering. Chemoshyatti, or whatever his real name was, must have decided the same thing. One second, he stood there looking innocent and sorry for himself. The next, he flung himself across the five or six cubits that separated him from the Philistinian officer. He was good; nothing gave the move away until he made it.

But the captain was good, too. He hadn't let the man he'd caught come too close, and he hadn't let the fellow's nondescript appearance lull him. Before the grocer who said he was a Moabite could reach him, the captain squeezed off a neat four-round burst, just the way he'd learned to do it in basic. The rounds stitched across the plump man's chest. The captain side-stepped. Chemoshyatti crashed down and didn't get up.

He choked out a few words that weren't Moabite: "*Om mani . . . padme hum.*" Then he slumped over, dead. A latrine stink filled the grocery as his bowels let go.

"Sword Buddhist, sure as demons from the after-world," the captain said grimly.

"Why don't they leave us alone?" Pheidas said. "The Moabites would be bad enough without the Turks stirring them up."

"That's what the Turks live for, though," the officer said. "Maybe we'll have to pay some more unofficial calls on Babylon." Philistinian planes had wrecked a Babylonian nuclear pile a few years back; the idea of Sword Buddhists with atomic bombs gave politicians all over the world the galloping jimjams. None of the big powers wanted to do anything about it, though, for fear of offending others and starting the war they wanted to head off. The Philistinians, in a tradition that dated back to the days of Crete, took the bull by the horns. Babylonian bosses often came down with sudden and unexplained cases of loss of life, too. Officially, Philistinia denied everything. But the captain hadn't talked about anything official.

He scooped out the propaganda pamphlets he'd mentioned. They were of the usual sort, preaching the glories of murder and martyrdom in punchy text and bright pictures. One headline grabbed Pheidas' eyes and didn't want to let go. *CHEMOSH WANTS PHI-LISTINIANS DEAD!* it screamed.

"Know what I heard, sir?" Pheidas said.

"What's that?" the captain asked.

"That there are Sword Buddhists in Philistinia, too. They want to get us to murder Moabites. They don't care who kills who, as long as somebody's killing somebody."

"I've heard the same thing. You wouldn't want to

think that kind of nonsense could take hold in modern, educated people, but it does, curse it. It does."
The captain scowled. "I'll bet some of them get driven round the bend because of the things the Moabites do."

"Wouldn't be surprised," Pheidas nodded. Another burst of gunfire not far away made him spin back toward the window, but he decided halfway through the motion that the shooting wasn't close enough to be dangerous. He went on, "And the ragheads say the same thing about us. How did it all get started? How do we make it stop?"

"It goes back to the days when we first came to Philistinia," the captain said, "all those years ago. Maybe it'd be different now if things were different back then. I don't know. I don't know how to get off the wheel, either, any more than anybody else does. And as long as we're on it, we'd better keep winning."

"Yes, sir," Pheidas said.

MUNDANE LANE

Kevin J. Anderson

No one would have believed in the last years of the twentieth century that human affairs were being watched from the vast, dark reaches of space. No one even considered the possibility that alien minds immeasurably superior to our own might regard this Earth with plans to invade.

No one even considered such a crazy idea, because in the last years of the twentieth century the genre of imaginative fiction had been forgotten. The very idea of a space program had died away from lack of interest before the first man could be shot into orbit. The Soviets had tried to launch a satellite called *Sputnik*, but the rocket blew up on the Cosmodrome launchpad; the Communist Party members who had advocated the appalling waste of money were sentenced to a gulag. No one in the US or USSR ever suggested the idea again. The people of Earth were far too busy with their own problems to waste time with silly flights of fancy.

Thus, when the giant alien motherships loomed above Earth's cities, the members of the human race—certainly doomed—looked up at the astounding vessels and simply could not comprehend what was about to happen. . . .

*   *   *

In his cramped basement office of a Washington think tank four blocks from the White House, Jimmy Andrews sat in his creaking government-issue chair. The walls were thick cinderblock painted a heavy seafoam green, a shade that some bureaucrat had chosen as the perfect color for all civil servants to enjoy.

Jimmy nudged thick black-rimmed glasses up on his nose and carefully opened the brittle yellowing pages of another issue of *Amazing Stories*. Copies of the long-vanished science fiction magazines were increasingly hard to find; very few had been printed before paper shortages in World War II killed the magazines entirely.

As a sure sign of wasteful government spending, Jimmy was paid to read the absurd pulp magazines for "ideas," a job that many considered ridiculous. Now he eagerly devoured yet another story about metal men, master-minds of Mars, and mole creatures that lived beneath the Earth's crust. The prose was rather awkward (even a fan like Jimmy could admit that), but the ideas—ah, the ideas!

On his desk, the red phone rang. He was so startled he knocked the fragile issue of *Amazing Stories* off the desktop. The red phone? Jimmy stared while it rang a second time. Until now, he had thought the phone was a mere prop. He used it as a paperweight.

Jimmy grabbed the phone on the third ring. It wouldn't do to let whoever called on the red phone think he was gossiping at the water cooler. "Hello? Um, I mean, Jimmy Andrews's desk. Um, I mean, Office of Unlikely Possibilities. May I help you?"

"This is General Ashcroft," a gruff voice said. "Get your sorry self to the Oval Office—and I mean now! President Dole wants to see you immediately."

"P-P-President Dole?"

"My spy cameras better show you *running* over here instead of walking, Andrews!" On the other end of the line, the red phone went dead.

Jimmy bolted out of the office. Panting and sweating, he scuttled down the sidewalk, bumping into pedestrians who seemed frozen into awestruck statues. Why wouldn't they get out of the way? Then he glanced upward—and saw an enormous saucer hovering over the Capitol building, its shadow large enough to cover ten square blocks.

"The aliens really came!" he gasped. "The invasion fleet is really here."

A police officer pointed to the sky. "What is that? Some new aircraft? Never seen anything like it."

"Must be the Russians," said another man on the sidewalk. "It's gotta be the Russians."

The cop scowled at him. "Of course it's the Russians. Who else could it possibly be?"

Jimmy was about to explain the real alternative, when he remembered General Ashcroft's impatience, and he began to run again.

The Oval Office was the stuff of legend, but not such imaginative legends as an invasion from space. Jimmy came to a halt, barely catching his breath. Today of all days he wished he had worn a suit and a tie, but he didn't have a professional wardrobe like his fellow staff workers. His faded blue T-shirt was too tight over a potbelly that was the result of spending his lunch hours reading instead of jogging along the Potomac.

Fortunately, President Dole was too preoccupied to notice Jimmy's clothes. Dole put his one good arm on the polished wood of the desk and leaned forward, beetling his heavy brows. "So, Mr. Andrews, I'm told you're one of the only people left in the world who reads crazy sci-fi stuff. Now it's time to earn back the salary that people said we were wasting on you. You're part of a think tank, Mr. Andrews. I expect you to do some thinking for us."

"Yes, Mr. President. How can I help? I've already seen the UFO."

"UFO?" the President said. "Why do you call it that?"

"Unidentified Flying Object, sir," said General Ashcroft, who stood stiffly at attention to one side of the President's desk. "A term invented in a proposed Air Force project called Blue Book. We decided not to fund their investigations. It was pure silliness."

Jimmy nearly choked. "Pure silliness? Excuse me, sir, but did I not notice a giant alien spacecraft overhead? Maybe if the Air Force had studied UFOs, we'd have had some warning!"

"That's enough, gentlemen." President Dole cut them off. "If anyone else read that science fiction stuff, we might have done some planning, but who in the world imagined there could be aliens out in space? Flying saucers that might want to invade the Earth? Inconceivable!"

"Actually, many people thought of it, Mr. President," Jimmy said, standing proud. "A man named H.G. Wells wrote a book about an invasion from Mars back in 1898. It's been long out of print, however. Even a century ago readers thought it was pure silliness."

"The fact is, Mr. President," General Ashcroft said, "we should have kept watching the skies. But no one ever thought."

Jimmy sighed, "And now it's too late to change the world."

"It may not be too late," President Dole said. "Not strictly speaking, anyway. You see, Mr. Andrews, you're not the only crackpot we keep on the payroll. Another one of my pie-in-the-sky geniuses, a Dr. Hawking, claims to have concocted a time machine. His strange quantum theories, his speculations about time and wormholes, have made him a laughingstock among his peers—but if he says the time machine will work, then I'm willing to give it a shot." Dole glanced toward the ceiling of the Oval Office. "Preferably before those aliens launch their weapons."

"A time machine!" Jimmy could not keep the delight out of his voice. "And you want to send me back to . . . change history? Alter key events, do whatever I can to ensure that science fiction becomes popular? Yes, I see, we have to change our entire social mindset. Science fiction could inspire our scientists, give them new ideas. Yes, that would work!" He began to talk faster and faster. "If we can imagine the possibility of a threat from space, then it only follows that someone will imagine defenses against it. And the only way we can do that is by going back, oh . . . half a century, giving a few people the proper nudge. Editors, writers, fans, filmmakers. Science fiction can flourish instead of fade away!" He bowed. "And I understand why you've picked me to go, Mr. President. I'm the right man for the job."

"And let's not forget the fact," Ashcroft interrupted, "that in our current crisis, you are completely expendable."

It was 1961, and Jimmy Andrews promised to make it a *different* year than the one in which he had been born.

With his quantum time machine, Dr. Hawking had glimpsed other timelines, spotting what he called cruxpoints where the futures had changed. While Jimmy and the scientist hunched together in the government laboratory, plotting and planning, the aliens had issued a dire statement that sounded like a thunderbolt: Every human should prepare to die.

By that time, Jimmy and Dr. Hawking had identified three important cruxpoints. He looked into the scientist's droopy eyes and thin skeletal face that had been wasted by ALS. Speaking through his voice synthesizer, Hawking pointed out, "You have to go before the invaders obliterate my time machine."

Jimmy said, "These three points will have to be enough." He gathered his notes, put together a disguise with frantic assistance from the White House, and then, feeling as if every cell in his body had turned into fizzing foam from a shaken can of warm soda pop, he had arrived back here. 1961.

Wearing a plaid sport coat and snappy Panama hat, he carried a case of catalogs and brochures in keeping with his persona as an auto parts salesman. He stood under the neon sign of a bar in downtown Manhattan known to be a frequent haunt of authors meeting their agents.

He looked around in the dim light, smelled cigarette smoke and old beer. Two men sat on stools pulled up to the dark wood of the bar; the meeting seemed somber, not celebratory. The one with the large, bushy beard was immediately recognizable; the other, unfamiliar man had a full tumbler of Scotch in his hand, which he sipped vigorously.

Jimmy came close enough to eavesdrop as the man with the Scotch said consolingly, "I tell you, Frank, we've tried everywhere. Twenty rejection letters. Nobody understands what you're trying to do. And sci-fi novels can't be more than sixty thousand words long. Nobody will read something as massive as what you've written—four hundred pages!"

"But this novel is my masterpiece, Lurton. Do you know how many years I've worked on it?"

"Nobody said it isn't impressive, Frank." Lurton sipped his Scotch again. "In fact, you're a genius. Even *I* don't understand half of what you put in that book, all those strange words. One editor said that nobody could read through the first hundred pages without getting confused and annoyed."

"James Joyce probably had the same problems with *Finnegans Wake*," the bearded man grumbled. "I absolutely believe people will read an imaginative and thought-provoking book, if anybody has the guts to publish it."

"Remember your audience, Frank. There are few enough readers for sci-fi as it is, and most of them are twelve- to fifteen-year-old boys."

"That's why Paul Atreides is a fifteen-year-old boy."
Frank was clearly starting to get angry.

"But a desert planet with giant sandworms and
some sort of addictive drug? *Drugs*, Frank? And what
is all this religious guff? Give us bug-eyed monsters
and scantily clad women. Your female character
doesn't even scream when she sees a sandworm! Nobody'll believe that."

"I believe in this *book*, Lurton. Bev believes in it,
too, and if you can't support what I want to do, then
you don't have any business being my agent."

It was time for Jimmy to barge in before things got
out of hand. "Excuse me, gentlemen. Are you by any
chance Frank Herbert, the author?"

The bearded man looked surprised. "You've heard
of me?"

"Certainly! I loved your first novel, *The Dragon in
the Sea*. I certainly hope you're working on something
new. It's been quite some time."

"And I have quite a novel . . . but no publisher."
His large beard swallowed up his downturned lips.

"We've exhausted all the possibilities," Lurton
said—Lurton Blasingame, the agent. "As I was just
explaining to my client, every possible publisher has
turned down the manuscript. It's time to move on."

Jimmy swung his sample case up onto the bar.
"Could I offer an idea? I'm an auto parts salesman.
Have you heard of Chilton Books? They print auto-
repair manuals, the best in the business. You could
send Mr. Herbert's manuscript there."

Lurton finished his Scotch. "It would be nonsense
to send a huge sci-fi novel to a publisher of auto-repair
manuals. Thanks for the suggestion anyway."

Jimmy pressed the issue. "Wait a minute, it may
not be such a strange possibility. At our recent conference, the Chilton editor, Sterling Lanier, told me he's
a science fiction fan. He said that he wanted to publish
something unusual, and not just the same old manuals."

Frank Herbert had a gleam in his eyes. "Why not

give it a try, Lurton? Maybe we could change the title to *How to Repair Your Ornithopter.*"

"You realize, Frank, this is the longest of long shots."

"Maybe this man Lanier won't be constrained by the rigid thinking of his fiction house peers," Frank said. "Maybe he can market it to an audience other than twelve-year-old boys. I'm sure it'll be a big seller."

Lurton remained skeptical. "All right, but I warn you, Frank, this is the last time. If Chilton Books doesn't go for it, I don't think *Dune World* will ever be published."

Frank extended his hand to shake Jimmy's. "I appreciate the thought, mister. Could we buy you a drink?"

Jimmy desperately wanted to stay, but he shook his head. "I'm very sorry. I don't have the time."

Attendance at the 1968 World Science Fiction Convention was abysmally low, the smallest turnout yet for one of the annual gatherings. Originally scheduled for the posh Claremont Hotel in Oakland, California, the venue had been changed to the Rodeo Motel in downtown Emeryville. In Jimmy's timeline, this would be the last such gathering before fandom collapsed as an organized entity. In his day there were no longer any science fiction conventions at all.

He wandered through the motel, poking his head in the various panels held in small meeting rooms, the minimally crowded autograph sessions with a few old writers from the pulp magazine days. He was thrilled to find others who had read every issue of *Amazing* and *Astounding*. In all his adult years, Jimmy had met only a couple of like-minded souls who didn't consider him weird or immature to be reading "that strange spaceman stuff."

This tiny World Science Fiction Convention had gathered the few remaining readers who didn't mind being identified with the genre. By his guess, only a hundred or so people were there, most of them gloomy because of the recent news that the television show *Star Trek* had just been cancelled. When it aired, *Star Trek* was seen as not one small step, but a giant leap for science fiction, with intelligent and thought-provoking episodes (along with a pointy-eared alien and very short skirts on the female crewmembers).

Jimmy found a few fans sitting in the lobby, some of them dressed in costumes, others trading battered out-of-print books, all of them grumbling about the show's cancellation. "There's simply nothing we can do," said one brown-haired woman with glasses who sat on a sofa, putting her chin in her hands. "I loved *Star Trek*. I even met Mr. Roddenberry at the Hugo ceremony last year."

"We know, Bjo."

"They'll probably replace *Star Trek* with another doctor show," groaned a beanpole-thin young man wearing a floppy Three Musketeers hat. "But what can you do? We're not studio executives."

Jimmy took a seat on the floor next to the fans. "You could write a letter."

"What good would one letter do?" asked the woman named Bjo.

"Not just one letter—why not a whole campaign? There are at least a hundred people gathered right here at this motel. It would be a start. Then you could all tell your friends. There must be other fans in the world."

"A few," said the man in the Three Musketeers hat.

Bjo seemed delighted to have something to hold onto. "I'll do it for *Star Trek*. I'll write a letter. In fact, I'll write a sample letter and mimeograph it so everybody has a starting point. You'll all write to the studio, won't you?" It didn't sound like a question. "It's time we stop hiding. As fans, we shouldn't be ashamed of what we enjoy to read or watch."

The skinny man said, "We're embarrassed because we feel so alone."

"Then we need to get organized," Bjo said. "Even

though the pulp magazines died, a couple of fan publications managed to survive. They've got mailing lists. They've got friends. It'll be a genuine letter-writing campaign. We'll bury Paramount with letters demanding that *Star Trek* be given another chance!"

"How can you think that'll work, Bjo? It's never been done before."

She leaned forward. "Isn't that what science fiction's about? Imagining things that other people consider impossible?"

"This could be really important." Jimmy clutched his hands together earnestly. "By putting together a letter-writing campaign, you'll light a fire under fandom again. If we win this battle, then everybody in Hollywood will realize that we have power after all."

"Sounds even more far-fetched than something written by Edgar Rice Burroughs," said a quiet, chubby young man who had been dozing against the corner of the lobby sofa.

"I like ERB!" a woman next to him snapped, then her expression softened. "I didn't know anybody still read him. Do you prefer John Carter of Mars or Carson of Venus?"

"We all prefer *Star Trek.*" Bjo got to her feet. Jimmy could see that she was going to take charge. This movement was in her hands now. If she could get *Star Trek* renewed for one year, if she could organize fandom and prove there was a strong audience for science fiction, it would certainly get the ball rolling.

"We don't have much time," Bjo said.

"None of us does," Jimmy admitted.

He longed to stay with the fans and meet some of his favorite old authors, but he had far more important things to do. Saving the human race had to take precedent over the dealers' room.

Jimmy pedaled his bicycle on the MGM Studio lot, gawking at the standing sets like a tourist. He was dressed as a script runner, but the papers in his bicycle basket were all blank. Timing now had to be impeccable.

He headed toward the main building just as a young man with dark hair and a neat beard emerged, shoulders slumped, his gaze downward. The cloud over his head was like a billboard announcing that he'd had another defeat.

Pedaling furiously, Jimmy brought the bike over to the sidewalk, skidded to a stop, and jingled his bell, startling the man. "Excuse me! You're Mr. Lucas, aren't you? George Lucas? I loved your student film."

The bearded man looked at him. "My student film? You mean the futuristic one?"

"Yes, *THX 1138*. I especially loved the robot policemen."

Lucas heaved a heavy sigh. "The only thing of mine anybody seems to know is *American Graffiti*. I swear their attention span is only two months long." He forced an unconvincing smile. "What can you do? *American Graffiti* earned a lot of money, but now that I want to make something different and dear to my heart, I keep getting turned down."

"What are you trying to do, Mr. Lucas?"

"When I was a kid growing up in Modesto, I used to read comic books and pulp science fiction magazines." He turned and looked at Jimmy. "I'm willing to bet there's a whole generation who'd love to see an ambitious movie with interesting special effects, not just giant rubber monsters on strings. Unfortunately, studios aren't willing to bet on it. I've pitched and pitched my new movie, *The Star Wars*. They can't imagine giving me the budget I want—ten million dollars!—to make a sci-fi movie they 'know' won't make money."

"Oh, I bet it could be one of the biggest money-makers of all time."

"I appreciate the sentiment, but even I'm not that naïve." Lucas shook his head. "Why am I talking to a script runner about this?"

"Because I'll listen," Jimmy said. "I love science fiction, too."

"Great, then I'll have an audience of one if I make *The Star Wars*. I'm trying to do a really big science fiction movie, but the execs don't see what I see, no matter how I describe it to them."

Jimmy pounced with his suggestion. "A picture's worth a thousand words, Mr. Lucas—and film is a visual medium. Instead of just giving a verbal pitch, maybe . . . bring some illustrations. Do you know any artists who can paint something spectacular and imaginative? Give them a real eye-full of what they're going to be investing in. That could make all the difference."

Lucas raised his eyebrows. "I do have a friend who works at Boeing painting pictures of new aircraft designs, Ralph McQuarrie. I've seen him doodle and play with ideas. Maybe I should give him my movie treatment, commission him to do a set of paintings of my alien landscapes, strange ships, creatures, and characters." Now the man stood taller, his shoulders square with new confidence. "That just might do it! I was about to cancel my pitch at Twentieth-Century Fox because I didn't think I had a chance. Ralph can do some paintings for me in time." Already intent, deeply focused, Lucas hurried off after saying a curt goodbye.

Sitting on his bicycle, Jimmy watched the man go. This was the last cruxpoint he and Dr. Hawking had been able to select. He hoped he had done enough, sparked enough imagination, fertilized a field that would bear fruit beyond mundane concerns. If he succeeded, there would be an entire cultural shift, a social mindset that made mankind think forward, look to the skies, and boldly go where no man had gone before.

Maybe that version of Earth would have a chance against an alien invasion, since Jimmy's original Earth had no chance at all. When the time machine activated again, he didn't know what kind of world he was going back to.

*   *   *

When the marauding invasion fleet cruised into the solar system, they scanned Earth broadcasts. The alien subcommander had been hoping for easy pickings. The economics of conquering planet after planet simply did not allow for a long, drawn-out siege against vigorous resistance.

"Such a fertile world," the subcommander said. "We have made no prior contact with this . . . Earth?"

"They have never seen us, have no reason to expect us," said the strategic advisor, lifting a tentacle. "We have enough ships to intimidate them, though we cannot sustain a long battle."

"They will crumble easily," predicted the subcommander.

"Excuse me," said the communications officer. "I have deconstructed their broadcasts and tapped into their library databases. I found a disturbing cultural trend. It seems these humans have been anticipating something like us for the past century. Observe." He played clips of movies he had plucked from the cacophony of transmissions.

"The inhabitants of Earth have a popular entertainment category called science fiction. Their best-selling novel in the genre describes a harsh desert planet and a vigorous resistance against a large galactic empire similar to our own. One of their longest running and most successful televised entertainment series concerns their own exploration and expansion into the galaxy. Among their most lucrative filmed entertainments is tellingly titled *Star Wars*, filled with images of spectacular space battles. Subcommander, if even a fraction of these images is true, our fleet stands no chance."

"So these humans are ready for us. Somehow they were forewarned." After a few long and silent moments, the subcommander turned to his strategic advisor. "Do you concur?"

The advisor looked extremely troubled. "Given this

information, Subcommander, I cannot recommend that we proceed. We do not have the military capability to withstand a protracted resistance."

The subcommander growled, then nodded. He could not afford another failure. He was sure to be executed this time unless he easily and inexpensively conquered a new world. If these creatures could imagine such things for *entertainment*, how much more prepared must their military be!

"Very well, target another solar system," he said. "There will be plenty of others to choose from. Let us go find an unimaginative race instead."

Note: Frank Herbert's *Dune*, the best-selling science fiction novel of all time, was rejected more than twenty times before it was finally published by a company that produced auto-repair manuals.

Star Trek was originally cancelled after only two seasons, until a group of science fiction fans led by Bjo Trimble launched a massive letter-writing campaign such as the networks had never before seen, and the show was renewed.

Even after the success of his film *American Graffitti*, George Lucas could not find a studio willing to invest in his science fiction movie *Star Wars*. However, when he commissioned his artist friend Ralph McQuarrie to paint extravagant scenes from the proposed movie, 20th Century Fox immediately picked up the project.

THE POWER AND THE GLORY

Robert E. Vardeman

Other workers leaned on their shovels, taking a break from the stifling heat. But Nikolai Tesla did not. He continued moving dirt from the trench to the pile beside it, in spite of being the slightest of the men. Tall, whipcord thin, his black hair glued itself to his head with sweat. Now and then he tossed his head to keep the sweat from burning his fever-bright dark eyes.

"Nikolai," complained the man next to him, "you're showing us up. Slow down. The foreman'll want us all to work as hard as you—and he *still* won't pay us shit."

The Austro-Hungarian looked up. A slight sneer came to his thin lips.

"We are near Pearl Street, aren't we?"

"Suppose so. What's the difference? This is still just a hole in the ground no matter where we put it." Anotoly Berzgi edged closer and looked at Tesla. He shook his head. The man worked like a machine, but no machine ever had such an intense look or produced such a torrent of ideas. Twice Tesla had tinkered with construction equipment and increased the amount of work they could do. And with a shovel in his hand, he worked tirelessly, in spite of the humid New York summer.

"That's Edison's headquarters. Where he has his direct current generators."

"What? Oh, the electricity?"

"He cheated me," Tesla said, his voice crackling with emotion. "I worked for a year improving his generator designs, and he cheated me out of fifty thousand."

"How much?"

"Fifty thousand dollars. I came to America because the French subsidiary of an Edison company cheated me. I thought it would be different here. But it is not. Edison cheats, no matter what continent his company occupies."

"What could you do for the great Edison that would be worth so much?" Berzgi stared at Tesla. The amount was incredible, more than a man could earn in a lifetime of digging ditches.

"He hired me to improve his DC equipment. I tried to convince him that alternating current was better, but he scoffed," Tesla said, his tone clipped and precise. "He goes on to electrocute animals when I have a chance to sell my AC generators to Westinghouse."

"Westinghouse?" said Berzgi.

"The inventor who died in the air brake accident," said Tesla. He wiped away sweat and shook his head sadly. "Westinghouse had vision and saw the elegance of my designs. Together, we were going to harness Niagara Falls and send power throughout the entire state of New York!"

Berzgi tried not to snicker. Such a thing was impossible. The great Edison had to place his generators every mile to keep the electricity flowing. He sighed. How nice it would be to read his letters from the old country by electric bulb rather than the guttering candle he had bought for a penny from old Grania. He could not afford coal oil, and with what he was being paid for digging trenches he never would.

"A great man, Westinghouse. I went to his funeral,"

Tesla said. "He left this world too soon." Tesla hesitated and Berzgi thought a tear formed at the corner of one dark eye. "Like my brother Dane. He, too, was a genius, unlike me. I work hard every hour of the day to come to even half of those men's brilliance."

Berzgi saw a change come over Tesla. He somehow grew in stature, though slight, as if coming to a momentous decision.

"I cannot develop alternating current without the money Westinghouse offered me, and with his death, his company has been sold." Tesla spat. "To Edison."

"Git off yer shovels. I ain't payin' ya to lollygag!" The foreman bustled up and down the line, hounding his tired, sweaty laborers back to work.

"Tonight," Berzgi said. "Come with me. We will have a drink and talk."

"Of the old country?" scoffed Tesla. "I have work to do."

"Work? What do you do? I have a second job in a laundry."

"I invent," Tesla said, drawing himself up even more and looking down his roman nose at his comrade, dark black eyes intense. "And I have found an even more effective way of powering the world. I tap into the magnetic field of the planet itself!"

Berzgi shook his head and shrugged. He didn't know what Tesla meant, but it intrigued him.

"Can you show me?"

"You do not want a drink?" Tesla grinned as he joshed his coworker. It was the first time all day Berzgi had seen the serious man smile.

"I do."

"Then bring what you drink to my laboratory and I will show you how I intend to give everyone free power—and without Edison's disagreeable power lines dangling everywhere you look!"

Tesla lifted his shovel and stabbed at the thick, waxy black cables running overhead to the Pearl Street generator. He dropped the blade to the dirt and began digging as furiously as a badger, a dust cloud rising from his industry to obscure him and his work.

Berzgi heard sizzling and hissing, followed by a cry that sounded as if someone had been seriously injured. He pushed open the heavy steel door to Tesla's laboratory in the abandoned building and peered inside. He threw up his arm to protect his face from the leaping bolts of actinic fire.

"Nikolai, are you well?" Berzgi fought down his fear and entered the huge room, littered with broken crates, dusty furniture and electrical equipment unlike anything he had ever seen in his life. His eyes widened when he saw Tesla, standing like a god, outlined in dancing electricity. Tesla wore a long, immaculate white linen lab coat and had thick black rubber gloves on, but it was the thick-lensed goggles that made him seem something more than human.

"Close the door," Tesla called. "I must not allow any of my precious power to seep out!"

"It can escape?" Berzgi considered running through the door before slamming it behind him. This place was too dangerous. Tesla's mocking laughter caused him to reconsider.

"I joke. Close the door to prevent the rats from leaving."

"You are joking again, aren't you?"

Tesla waved him forward. Berzgi had to smile when he saw how the young man's lank black hair stood on end, the ends twisting about like a living Medusa. When he reached out to point out a safe spot in the laboratory, a five-foot-long white arc of electricity leaped forth from his hand. Berzgi hesitated, then saw Tesla held a knobbed wand. This was nothing more than arcane magic—scientific magic.

"You are impressive," Berzgi said. He went to the spot on the bare concrete where Tesla had built up a low platform piled with rubber mats. He stood on them and tried not to show any fear.

"You are insulated there. Do not leave and you will be quite safe."

"What of the rats who have remained inside?" Berzgi asked.

"I often fry them for dinner," Tesla said. Berzgi wasn't able to tell if the man was still joking. "When I was much younger, I built a small windmill powered by June bugs."

"June bugs?"

"May bugs. They call them June bugs in America and I must follow my fellow citizens in this." Tesla cleared his throat as he spoke, a distant look of fond memory in his eyes. "Sixteen June bugs. All glued to the windmill to give motive power. They were remarkably efficient, working for hours to turn the rotor. The hotter it became, the harder they worked."

"A bug-powered windmill," muttered Berzgi, wondering at the man's sanity.

"It ultimately failed when a strange boy came and ate the bugs. It was then I realized we can eat anything with relish given adequate hunger. And that it is not good to power equipment with bugs."

Turning back to the vast gray metal panel studded with meters, dials and heavy switches, Tesla began to touch a control here and adjust a rheostat there like some sinister, goggled musician playing a demented concert. Berzgi felt his inner organs begin to vibrate, then what few windows remained in the old warehouse exploded. The earthquake threw him to his knees. He clung fiercely to the rubber mats, remembering what Tesla had said. Safety. Here. In spite of the rusted beams overhead beginning to buckle and plaster and dust cascade down, Berzgi stayed put.

Tesla stumbled from the temblor, braced himself against the panel, and grasped a huge power switch with both hands. Putting his back into it, he pulled the switch and plunged the warehouse into utter darkness.

"I am sorry," Tesla said, through the murk and dust now filling the warehouse. "I miscalculated the resonant frequency."

"What? What's that?" Berzgi shouted. Only then did he realize he was partially deafened from the roar caused by Tesla's equipment.

"The resonant frequency of Manhattan," Tesla said. "I fear I might have created quite a lot of damage as a result."

"You destroyed the entire island?" Berzgi dusted himself off and stood on the pillar of mats. He knew there was no longer any danger but still had to force himself to leave this island of insulated safety. He walked to stand beside Tesla.

"Don't be absurd. All I did was shake the buildings. I haven't enough power to destroy the entire island." Tesla grinned sheepishly. "Though if I had a larger generator, I might find the resonant frequency of the world and crack it open."

"The whole world?"

"It is possible, but not what I was attempting to do," Tesla said.

"What were you doing?"

"Broadcast power," the inventor said, lowering his voice to a conspiratorial whisper. "I haven't the money to build my alternating current generator—Westinghouse's death guaranteed that failure. So I went on."

"On?"

"To the next step. Radiometric power. I will do away with power cables entirely. Everyone will receive my power from a broadcast unit."

"I don't understand," Berzgi said.

"It is quite simple. I tap the magnetic power of the world itself, then broadcast it through my antenna." Tesla pointed to a heavily insulated column rising more than twenty feet that ended in a smooth copper-colored ball almost ten feet in diameter. "From here I can send my power to anyone who wants it. There will be no need for ships to carry heavy fuel. All that will be needed is a simple receiving unit and my broadcast power unit."

"No need for fuel aboard a ship? No coal? Or oil?"

"None. That space can be given over to cargo or passengers. I even envision flying machines powered by my radiometry broadcasts. My radio broadcasts," Tesla said, looking smug. "Yes, my radio waves will fill the skies and allow machines to fly and ships to sail. Why, even small conveyances like horseless carriages can be powered easily with my broadcast power."

"Who would give up their horse and buggy?" asked Berzgi.

"My radio-powered horseless conveyance would not need to be fed or groomed. If it breaks, a mechanic could fix it and no veterinarian would be required. And it would never tire. It could drive forever!"

"You would need a man to steer it." Berzgi saw Tesla turn wary and knew he had trod on sensitive areas.

"Not necessarily. My radio waves can control as well as power."

"They can do anything," Berzgi said.

"I think that is so."

"They cannot do one thing, though."

"What's that?" Tesla asked.

"Enjoy a bottle of beer. Here, my friend, I brought you one, also." Berzgi fished two brown glass bottles from his coat pockets and handed one to Tesla. "We should toast your fine demonstration of . . . almost shaking the entire island apart."

"The world," Tesla said, taking the bottle and looking at it critically. He reached into his pocket, drew out a screwdriver and deftly skewered the cork and pulled it out. As he lifted the bottle in toast, the outer door exploded inward.

Both Tesla and Berzgi swung about, spilling their beer.

"Git yer hands where we kin see 'em," came the shouted order. Four policemen trained their pistols on the pair.

"What is the meaning of this?" Tesla demanded. He handed the beer to Berzgi and then froze. The policemen cocked their pistols and obviously longed to pull the triggers.

"That's the device responsible, officers," came a querulous voice from outside. "I want him arrested!"

"Yes, sir, Mr. Edison," said an officer with lieutenant's bars on his collar. He entered the warehouse a pace ahead of the inventor. Edison pushed past him and pointed.

"That's the generator he used. He could have destroyed the entire city!"

"But all he did destroy was your—whatcha call it?—electrical turbine generator."

"That's right, Lieutenant. He did it deliberately."

"You did this?" Berzgi asked, his eyes wide. His answer came in the tiny smile dancing on Tesla's lips.

"Cuff 'im, boys," the lieutenant said, folding his arms across his barrel-chest. "Take the bastard to the Tombs."

"Where are you taking him?" asked Berzgi, pushed aside.

"Centre Street and Leonard," Tesla said, still grinning. "Edison has sent me there before."

"I'll get a lawyer," Berzgi cried. "You cannot be—"

"Shut up or we'll run you in as an accessory," Edison called. "I'll have my crew here within the hour. There won't be a stone left on this block by the end of the week."

"You can't do that!" Tesla struggled for the first time, trying to get his shackled hands around Edison's throat. "This is all I have in the world. Every penny was spent building my generator."

"Your deadly generator," Edison said haughtily. "I

am doing the city and state of New York a great favor destroying everything here. They pose a great threat to the public."

"Only to your worthless direct current generators!"

"You heard his confession, Lieutenant. Take him away!" Edison looked on with satisfaction as the police shoved Tesla from his warehouse. Berzgi watched for a moment, then picked up the cork from the beer Tesla had opened and stuffed it back into the bottle's neck. With his own bottle securely returned to his coat pocket, he left amid the clicking of the bottles and Edison's gloating laughter.

"I should have remained in jail," Tesla said, dejected. He stared at the destroyed warehouse. Not one single strand of electrical wire remained of his equipment. Edison's workmen had spent the past three days assiduously removing the equipment and then razing the building. "There is nothing for me here."

"You did not belong in jail," Berzgi said. "I had to get you out, even if it did cost one hundred dollars."

Tesla's dark eyes bored into Berzgi's.

"So much? Where did you get so much money?"

Berzgi averted his eyes, taking in the piles of brick and the lingering cloud of mortar dust from the wrecking ball. He summoned his courage and faced Tesla. The man's intent gaze had not wavered for an instant and made Berzgi feel as if he might be reduced to a smoking mound of fat.

"Not everyone thinks Edison is right."

"Westinghouse is dead. No one else will speak to me because of Edison. I went to the banker Morgan, and he refused me. I approached the War Department advisory board, but Edison has a seat on it and they denied my application for development money."

"For the death ray?"

"Death ray? Oh, that?" Tesla laughed harshly. "It was no death ray. I could build one, of course, but this—" he pointed dramatically at the rubble, "was only to inconvenience Edison and show the world how unsuitable his electrical equipment is."

"You blew out every light bulb on the circuit," Berzgi said.

"Circuit, eh? You are learning from me, is that it, Berzgi? I would hire you as an assistant, had I a laboratory."

"You say the War Department turned down your applications for money?"

"It was Edison's doing," Tesla said, waving his long-fingered hand in dismissal. "As was having me fired from my job. But finding another laborer's job will not be hard. Repaying you will be, however."

"It was not my money. Come with me, Nikolai. I want to show you something."

Tesla followed in silence, brooding. Berzgi wended his way through the maze of streets on the East Side until he came to the spot where he had been once before. He fumbled in his pocket and took out a shiny key for the new lock on the door. Berzgi took a deep breath to quiet the pounding of his pulse, inserted the key, turned and swung the door open for Tesla.

Tesla stepped inside, then stopped so fast that Berzgi ran into him. Tesla recoiled as if he had been shot.

"My hair, don't touch my hair," he said, backing off. He recovered some of his composure and pointed at the laboratory stocked with equipment. "What is this?"

"Yours, Nikolai. All yours, to do with as you see fit."

"But how is it possible?"

"You are an American citizen, but you were born in the old country. Austria-Hungary laments the loss of such a brilliant scientist," came a grating voice. "You can show your gratitude for my generosity in, as they say, 'springing you from jail' and for the use of this equipment by revealing the nature of your experiment. The one Berzgi claims was responsible for destruction of Edison's plant."

"Who are you?" Tesla faced the squarely built, mustached man, who barely came to the scientist's chin. The man wore a plain black coat, pants pressed with creases rivaling a cavalry saber's sharp blade and boots so highly polished they might have been mirrored.

"You are out of uniform," Tesla went on.

"You recognize me? Good." The man clicked his heels and bowed slightly. "Duke Leopold Gottel."

"I did not recognize you personally, but as a military man," Tesla said. "I am a *loyal* American. No matter what Edison and the War Department decide, I will not furnish weapons to a foreign power."

"Of course not, and we are not asking for that. But can you claim I represent a foreign power, when you were born in Smiljan? Your education was in Austria-Hungary and what family remains—condolences on the deaths of your beloved parents—is in our homeland."

"You rescued me from prison and will give me this to do what, then?"

"The world changes rapidly as we enter the last ten years of this aging century. Political alliances ebb and flow throughout Europe. Austria-Hungary will not be destroyed by powers, shall we say, inimical to us. You would not want to see that, would you, Herr Tesla?"

"No, of course not."

Berzgi watched the byplay and felt as if he drowned. The intent expression on Tesla's face as he stared at the banks of equipment convinced Berzgi that the scientist would relent and work for Gottel. That was good. He had been promised a huge sum of money to convince Tesla, but even as how he would spend the money came to him, Berzgi began to grow uneasy about his friend and what Gottel wanted from him.

"All we desire is a chance to use your inventions for peaceful purposes. Berzgi has mentioned how you are able to send electrical power to an airship, so that no fuel storage is required. Is this so?"

"It is," Tesla said. He stepped forward and laid his hand on the cold metal side of an equipment rack. It was as if a powerful magnet drew him to the new apparatus.

"Think of how Austria-Hungary will prosper if our fleets of dirigibles and airships can carry tons more cargo. We will become the trading power of the continent!"

"There is that benefit, yes," Tesla said distantly. Berzgi began to worry about him.

"You will do this work for the duke, then?" Berzgi asked anxiously.

"On one condition, Duke," Tesla said, as if he had not heard Berzgi.

The duke warily answered, "Most conditions can be met."

"Berzgi must be my assistant."

Berzgi stood, open mouthed. Duke Leopold laughed heartily and started to slap Tesla on the shoulder. Berzgi stopped him in time, sternly shaking his head. The flare of anger in the duke's eyes faded as he heard Tesla's words.

"A broadcast unit—for cargo airships, of course— can be built and tested by the end of the month."

"Excellent. Whatever you require, let me know. Let Berzgi know and he will tell me," Gottel said, but Tesla had pulled up a chair and faced a bank of dials and knobs.

"So much calibration needed. Who was the fool who installed such fine equipment, then did not calibrate it?"

Gottel snorted, nodded brusquely to Berzgi, then left the scientist to his work.

The heat of summer finally escaped the city, leaving behind a grudging warmth that still, yet, refused to give way to winter. Momentarily blocking the lukewarm sun, the ten-foot-long dirigible drove itself ever higher into the cloudless sky on quiet electric motors.

Tesla stood on the rooftop of his laboratory, hands clasped behind his back, staring upward.

"More power," he ordered Berzgi. "I would see how high the model can climb before the engine is out of range shuts down."

"It is at a thousand feet now, Nikolai," came Berzgi's worried voice. "We dare not go much higher."

"Higher," Tesla insisted. "It will go five times this. Ten!"

Berzgi slowly turned the rheostat, broadcasting more power to the aerial balloon. He grabbed binoculars and scanned the sky until he caught sight of the reflector-laden mini-dirigible. Even with the bright disks shining in the clear sky, he almost lost track of it.

"It is *very* high," he said anxiously. "I have lost contact with it."

"What altitude?"

Berzgi worked feverishly on the panel, then said, "Six thousand feet. The signal is too weak to supply enough electricity to keep the props turning."

"Six thousand feet," mused Tesla. He began to pace on the rooftop. Then he stopped and clapped loudly, applauding himself. "Excellent! The prototype can be scaled up to even greater distances."

"How great?"

Berzgi dropped his binoculars in surprise. He had not heard Gottel come out onto the tar-papered roof.

"Duke, I was not aware you—"

"How far can you broadcast your power, Herr Tesla?" Gottel ignored Berzgi, as he had for the past three months. This irritated Berzgi because he had recruited Tesla's talents for the duke and now was no longer necessary, except as a conduit for tidbits Tesla forgot to pass along. He had learned much and contributed to the effort. Without him, Tesla would not have progressed this much!

"There would be no trouble powering even the most dynamic electric engine, in line of sight," Tesla said. "An entire fleet could be powered from a single transmitter."

"An armada of dirigibles," the duke said, a glow coming to his eyes that worried Berzgi.

"Large ones," Tesla said. "Ones capable of carrying ten or even twenty tons of cargo."

"But only if they remain in sight of the transmitter," Gottel said. "This would require a network of transmitters."

"Is this a problem?" Tesla asked. "If you establish a cargo route between, say Vienna and Berlin or Vienna and Paris, transmitters are easily placed along the way."

"Mountaintops, towers, other elevations, increase the range," Gottel said, "but some countries might be unwilling to allow such radio broadcast units on their sovereign soil."

"I've considered this," Tesla said. He paced as he got the strange, distant expression Berzgi had come to know and dread. Tesla thought. Hard. No problem was beyond him in this state. Uneasy now, Berzgi started to stop the scientist from solving this dilemma but was too late.

"An aerial unit. Place a broadcast unit in a large dirigible and loft it. Six thousand feet? That is possible, although lower might be preferable. From this airborne laboratory can be sent radio waves in all directions. Relay units would be cheaper than actual generating units. Yes, yes, leave the generators on the ground and relay the power through a series of tethered dirigibles."

"Heavier than air flights will be possible one day soon," said Gottel.

"Think of the weight you can save using my electric motors and this," Tesla said, placing his hand on the housing of the power broadcast unit.

"A fleet of great airships that darken the sky as they fly off to . . . their missions," Gottel finished lamely.

"Off to their wars," Berzgi said under his breath.

The sun began slipping lower in the west, hidden

by taller buildings now. Tesla walked to the verge of
the roof and looked down.

"See that," he said, pointing to the light bulbs already on in the building across the street.

"They waste Edison's power," Gottel said, "turning
on their lights so early. It is still daylight."

"You don't understand," Tesla said. "Those are lit
by induction. By the same broadcast that powers that."
He looked up into the sky. The small test vehicle was
slowly spiraling downward, under Berzgi's now expert
control. In a few more minutes the hydrogen-filled dirigible would be securely moored to a pole on the roof.

"They steal your power? Our power?" asked Gottel.

"It's theirs for the taking. The radio waves are
broadcast, sent out in all directions."

"Another enem . . ." Gottel coughed to cover himself. "Another cargo dirigible could use our power?"

"Yes," Tesla said.

"That is not acceptable. Only Austro-Hungarian airships must be powered by the ground generators!"

Tesla pursed his lips, thought for a moment, then
said, "There is a possibility of 'locking' the power
broadcast."

"How is this done?"

"You could broadcast only on a specific frequency,"
Berzgi said, in spite of himself. "Your airships are
attuned to this frequency. None other would be."

"This is possible?" demanded Gottel.

"Berzgi has become quite the inventor," Tesla said.
He walked to a coop of pigeons he kept on the roof
and reached inside, letting one ride on his finger. He
looked at the bird for an uncomfortably silent minute
before speaking. "It can be done. I see the blueprints
perfectly in my mind." He stroked the pigeon's feathers, then returned it to the chicken-wire cage.

"I must have them immediately. Things on the continent require immediate use of this invention."

"Do you have an airship constructed that can accept
my relays and electric motors?"

"Half a hundred," Gottel said, his eyes burning like coals. "Give me the blueprints and they will be airborne within six weeks."

"Quite a chore," Tesla said. "The transmitters need to be built, but they are far easier to construct than the airships themselves. How large would this fleet be?"

"Fifty," the duke repeated. "Of cargo ships."

"Yes, of cargo ships," Tesla said. He walked across the roof to examine the mini-airship that had finally returned to its mooring. A quick examination of the radio controlled and powered engine caused him to nod in satisfaction.

"I will take this unit and that airship," Gottel said. "These are what you will use?"

"They are. You don't need them. Berzgi will give the plans. That is a better way of getting the information to your principals."

"You still hate Edison?"

The duke's question took Tesla by surprise.

"He is not my friend."

"You would do him harm?" the duke pressed. "He and those who support him, like the American War Department?"

"I do not wish him harm," Tesla said slowly, "but I do not wish him well, either."

"A death ray need not be aimed at him," Gottel said slyly. "It would be useful against his equipment, much as your other death ray was."

"Perhaps, yes," Tesla said, looking across the street at the burning light bulbs—powered by his broadcast unit. He snapped his fingers. Berzgi cut the power and the lights died. Gottel failed to recognize the significance of the action.

"Nikolai, I have been your friend these past months," Berzgi began. His mind tumbled over and over, turning once coherent ideas into a churning mess.

"You have found a better job. So, take it. I can pay little more. You know all my money goes into my experiments." Tesla flipped a switch and produced corona discharges throughout the laboratory.

"This death ray of yours—"

"It's not a death ray. You and Gottel must stop calling it that." He turned off the beamed energy and motioned for Berzgi to follow him to the roof where a new experiment had been set up. Berzgi followed Tesla up the steep iron stairs, every footstep clanging like a gong.

"It is Gottel," Berzgi said, rushing ahead with what amounted to reason against his homeland. "He has fooled you. He's using you to produce weapons for our country—for our old country. There is great political unrest in Europe."

"I know," Tesla said.

"You do not know, my friend. And you are my friend. A good one. I am privileged to work with you. That's not what I want to say." Berzgi made shooing motions, as if driving off flies. "There will be war in Europe soon. Prussia, the Balkans, the Austro-Hungarian Empire, all against Western Europe. The duke is building a fleet of airships to take part in that war. They will be invincible! Because of you!"

"Warships," Tesla said in an offhand manner, "cannot be invincible."

"But they are, with your inventions. The electric motors. The broadcast power. They will carry nothing but weapons. No cargo for peaceful trade, Nikolai, weapons! They will fly to an enemy city and bombard it. With your death ray, they will lay waste to the entire countryside!"

"There is no death ray," Tesla said. "If Gottel thinks I have worked on one these past months, he is wrong."

"But I have seen how you light a bulb by aiming a horn at it."

"A focusing lens, yes, a crude one to start. I have improved it over my first feeble efforts."

A pair of well-dressed men came onto the roof and stood silently.

"Who are you? Go away. No observers," Berzgi said angrily.

"Let them stay," Tesla said. "Please, Berzgi, no questions. Let them watch. Use the radio broadcast unit to get our hydrogen-filled friend aloft." Tesla ran his hand over the sleek, taut canvas skin of the mini-dirigible, as if stroking the feathers on one of his beloved pigeons.

"They should not see this," Berzgi said, hesitating to obey.

"Do it." Tesla spoke sharply, then, more gently, "Please, my friend. Turn on the broadcaster."

The unit hummed and the dirigible motor started as the radio power grew in intensity. Berzgi had become expert at spiraling the dirigible upward, applying power as needed and using the radio-controlled ailerons and rudders to keep it above the rooftop. The setting sun caught the bulging sides and turned the hydrogen-filled bag into a silver fish angling its way ever up, trying to break the bonds of the earth.

As it reached a thousand feet, Tesla went to a second unit he had installed some distance away at the edge of the roof. He made a few adjustments, then flipped a switch. Berzgi immediately let out a yelp of surprise.

"Nikolai, I have lost power! The dirigible will blow away on the wind!"

Tesla turned to the men, pointed to his unit, then said to Berzgi, "Turn off the broadcaster."

"We must reestablish contact. Without power—"

"Do it."

Berzgi angrily flipped the power switch. They would lose the dirigible! With a dying hum, the power broadcaster powered down.

"Witness," Tesla said. He fiddled a moment, bent over and aimed a long glass tube upward. As if using a rifle, he sighted along the length, then turned on another switch.

"Nikolai, the dirigible is responding again. Its prop

is turning again!" Berzgi lowered the binoculars and stared. "What have you done? Another broadcaster?"

"A power beam. A radio broadcast can be jammed. This is directed solely to the dirigible and cannot."

"A death ray?"

"Not that," Tesla said tiredly. "A power beam. I can direct my power precisely where I want, not broadcast it indiscriminately. Look at the light bulbs around us. What do you see?"

"None are lit." Berzgi craned his neck to see if the usual blazing array of light bulbs dazzled him. A few lights were turned on but only because the twilight crept upon them, not because they greedily sucked up Tesla's broadcast power.

"Precision in all things, Berzgi," Tesla said with smug satisfaction.

Berzgi furrowed his brows for a moment, then said, "Gottel has the plans for the radio transmitter."

"The broadcast power unit, yes," Tesla said. "You understand?"

"He will have a fleet of airships powered by your broadcast unit—which can be turned off by his enemies!"

"And other airships powered by *this* beam cannot be stopped in that fashion. It is not so much a death ray as a lifeline for aerial ships. American ships."

"But who are—?" Berzgi turned to confront the two silent observers, but they had disappeared.

"I owe much to my homeland. If Gottel uses the broadcast power for what he said, Austria-Hungary will grow rich from trade. If he uses it for war, he will find his dirigibles floating helplessly."

"Who were they? The men who watched us?"

"I owe much to my Fatherland, but I am an American. One is an engineer with the Army. The other is a colonel named Pershing, who has great interest in aerial devices, who can bypass Edison and those under his thumb in the War Department."

"Gottel paid for this and you are selling it to the U.S.?"

"Gottel paid for it," Tesla said, smiling, "and I am giving it to the U.S.A. After this evening's demonstration, not even Edison can block true progress."

"Wireless transmission of power," Berzgi said.

"Wireless conquest of the air," Tesla corrected. He swung his power beam around, and the dirigible obediently followed it across the sunset. "With this perfected, next I must . . ."

VOICES

Jackie Cassada

1.

She awakened in a room free from the stench of burning flesh and boiling tears. As her eyes adjusted to the soft, warm light surrounding her, she realized that she no longer felt the searing knives of fire scorching her lungs or the devouring hunger of the all-consuming flames that the Church had assured her would purify her soul.

"Sweet Jesu," she whispered. "There is no pain at all!" Not even the aches of old battles or the cramped muscles of her recent confinement intruded into the blessed sense of relief and rebirth she felt. Surely, this must be the reward of the faithful.

She sat, surprised as she did so that she was in a bed—one of softened linens and finely woven blankets, assuredly, but a bed all the same—not unlike the ones she had glimpsed in the dauphin's court. This was a bed for a noble. The coverlet slipped away, revealing her naked body.

"Of course," she said aloud, reveling in the sound of her voice that was no longer hoarse from yelling out commands to her armies or scratched from repeating her story over and over for the inquisitors.

"My clothes would have burned in the fire, leaving me clothed only in God's mercy." She fought against the impulse to cover herself; if this was her purified body, it was the body of Eve before the serpent's temptation. Therefore, it was blessed in God's sight.

For the first time, she looked at herself in a clear light, unclouded by the smoke from camp or cook fires or the oily smoke of torches in sconces outside her darkened prison cell. Her scars were gone, and her skin—when she touched her (smooth!) hands to her shoulders and her once-roughened elbows—was as soft as the youngest of babes she had cared for as a young girl in the village of Domrémy. Even her feet had lost the hard, cracked shell of tough skin that came from years of going without shoes and, later, from ill-fitting boots. Something tickled her back, below the nape of her neck, and she put her hands behind her and felt hair, long and soft, like a lady's hair after her maids had brushed and combed it. She had never been so coddled, but she had seen such lavishing of labor in the French court. She had cut her own hair when her voices told her she would have to become a soldier. She had not missed its weight until now, when she felt it again pulling at the crown of her head.

Filled with wonder and humility, the girl, not yet out of her teens, known to some as La Pucelle, to others as Jehanne d'Arc, and to more as Joan the Maid, dropped to her knees on the spotless floor, crossed her hands at her throat and bowed her head in prayer.

2.

"How long has she been kneeling like that?" the commander asked as he entered the observation room where his lieutenants were watching the latest recoveree. The two women looked at each other, some silent message passing between them, before the taller one rose to her feet.

"All morning, sir," she replied, her voice clipped and impersonal.

The commander nodded. "And you've made no attempt to communicate with her?"

Again, the look, as if neither woman wanted to take the responsibility for provoking the commander's wrath by giving him news he would rather not hear. The second woman finally stood, her blonde hair hiding part of her face as she stared at the floor.

"No, sir," she said, a slight quaver in her voice. "We thought it best to wait for you. Michael always drops the big ones on her. Catherine and Margaret are the support team."

The commander's eyes narrowed, considering the blonde woman's words. Though she always seemed reluctant to voice her thoughts, Lieutenant Fiero's skill at observation and fine detail were undeniable. He nodded his head once, in agreement.

"You're correct, Fiero," he said. "We all go in at the same time. I'll take the lead."

"Sir—"

"What is it, Sauvigne?" the commander regarded the other woman guardedly. Lieutenant Sauvigne could get under his skin with a word, sometimes merely an intonation of her voice. She never crossed the boundary between legitimate challenge and insubordination, but each time she confronted him, she managed to put him on the defensive. It was important to keep her happy, though. She was the one with the degree in medieval French history. She could also speak the French of Joan's time period and coached him and Fiero with their own mastery of the antiquated language.

"Is she ever going to be told the truth?" Sauvigne's voice held just enough restraint to sound merely inquisitive.

"That's a decision we'll make when the time comes," the commander snapped, immediately regretting both the quickness of his answer and his revelation that he had not yet made a determination. His "we" was, of course, only a courtesy. All three of them knew that he alone was calling the shots.

"The immediate question before us is whether we will be able to work with her at all," he said. "For the present, she must continue to believe that the three of us are her 'voices.' Otherwise, I'm afraid we cannot guarantee her cooperation." He turned abruptly toward the door, motioning for the women to follow him.

3.

Joan forgot her surroundings whenever she prayed. Her friends in Domrémy, her family, and, later, her beloved comrades-in-arms could never understand how she could spend so much time on her knees or lying prostrate in prayer. They did not know the joy it gave to her to open her heart to Jesu and the saints, who heard her troubles and gave her comfort, who knew her weaknesses and gave her strength, who received her love and returned it many times over. That she should hear their voices when they needed her seemed the most natural thing in the world. That they asked her to bring the dauphin to his rightful throne and drive the English out of France was little enough in return for everything they gave to her. That she should face the flames of martyrdom at the hands of her English captors was not unexpected. Her voices had told her she would die and be taken up to be with them in heaven.

This was not what she had expected heaven to be like, however. Even though carnal desires did not exist in God's kingdom, and she need not fear succumbing to temptation, she felt uncomfortable being naked for too long. She had somehow always imagined that all who entered heaven would be given robes of sanctity. Only the damned remained naked in their condemnation, the more keenly to feel the fires of Hell as it burned their flesh—much as hers had burned, though for much shorter a time than the poor damned souls in Hell.

The sound of a door opening shook Joan from the reverie that her prayers had become. She raised her head in time to see three figures bathed in light enter the room and stand before her, their arms outstretched in welcome.

She started to rise and accept their embrace, when the remembrance of her nakedness stopped her. She dared not touch them with her unclothed body; their holiness would surely destroy her. She was in their presence only by the grace and mercy of God and not through any merit on her part. Afflicted with the shame that the first parents felt when they encountered God in the garden after they had eaten of the deadly fruit, she covered herself with her hands as best as she could and waited for their judgment.

"Ave, Ioanna!" St. Michael's voice resounded with the fire of a church bell tolling the Easter Mass. "Welcome, beloved and faithful sister."

From behind him, St. Margaret and St. Catherine stepped into Joan's sight, holding between them what looked like a robe of shining cloth. Together, they clothed her in the soft fabric, winding it about her into a garment a little like the paintings of the Roman women she had seen in the homes and courts of the nobles of France.

"Merci," she murmured, feeling the comfort of modesty in the presence of these holy beings.

"Come with us," St. Michael said.

Joan responded immediately to the sound of command in his voice, following the three sanctified ones from the room and into a garden. The sweet fragrance of summer flowers filled the air around her, and Joan breathed deeply, letting the scented air flow deep into her lungs. Near the center of the garden, the flowers gave way to a clearing of fresh green grass. Three stone benches formed a semi-circle in the center of the clearing, with a small pond occupying the remainder of the circle. Michael indicated that Joan should take a seat on one of the benches. She did so, folding her hands demurely in her lap, awaiting whatever lay ahead.

Her suffering was over, and she was with God's saints in eternity. What had she to fear?

"Joan," Michael said, his deep blue eyes penetrating the new clothes, stabbing her soul with his righteous power, "we have delivered you from the fire because God is not finished with you. Once more, you must be his instrument. But where once you saved France, now you must save the earth itself."

4.

Joan fasted often during her short lifetime as a way of getting closer to God and purifying her sinful body. So she thought nothing of the hunger pangs that gnawed at her stomach as she listened for most of the day to Michael, Catherine, and Margaret explain to her the task at hand.

Michael spoke briefly about God's plan for creation, which seemed to involve something called "evolution," a concept that puzzled Joan.

"But is not the world already perfect as God created it?" she asked when Michael paused for a moment.

Michael tensed, his jaws clenching as he struggled to find a way to answer Joan's apparently simple question. Catherine stepped forward, looking at Michael for permission to field the query. He nodded, trying not to appear disturbed.

"What is perfection, but growth and change?" Catherine said. "It was God's will that you be born a helpless infant and that you grow into a woman capable of delivering France from her enemies. You grew into your perfection as God willed it. So, too, does the world grow more perfect if it is allowed to become what it was created to be. This changing and growing is what we call evolution." Catherine watched Joan's eyes as she absorbed the answer. Finally, Joan's expression cleared. Her face grew calm. Catherine continued with the story that Michael had started.

"People have become greedy for wealth and personal gain," she said. "They desire to make their fortunes by using the world's riches without taking the time to replenish them. Over many years, they have carved great wounds into the earth, wounds that cannot heal by themselves—" she paused, aware that Joan was leaning forward on the bench, drinking in the words and turning them over and over in her head. *I've said too much.*

Frantically she looked over her shoulder at Margaret, who was staring at Michael and mouthing something only she and Michael could hear. Catherine did not have to hear the words to know that Margaret was suggesting to Michael that the time had come to speak the truth. Something beeped softly at her wrist and she glanced down, surreptitiously pressing the button on her wristcomm. An urgent message flashed across the display. This time she spoke in a whisper that both Michael and Catherine could hear.

"We have no time to waste," she hissed. "There's been another incident, a volcanic eruption just off the coast of Alaska. A big one."

Michael sighed and closed his eyes. Margaret took his gesture as a signal for her to take over. She moved closer to Joan and in one swift gesture, knelt before her and took her hands in her own.

"Joan, we are not your original voices," she said. "And this is not—"

"—heaven," Joan finished. "I know that now, though I do not know what place this is."

"This place is your future," Margaret said. "We are from your future. We traveled back in time to your present and snatched you from the fire under cover of the smoke and flames."

"But my body is whole," Joan said. "Even the scars from battle are gone. How?"

Margaret allowed herself a small smile. At least Joan wasn't panicking yet.

"We have learned much about medicine and healing since you received those scars. We were able to grow new skin for you and replace your hair and eyebrows. For us, it is a natural part of our lives."

"Why is the world in danger? Is this the end of the world?" Joan's voice was calm. After all, she had grown up believing that God would eventually destroy His creation and bring all the blessed souls to Heaven to be with Him.

"It may very well be the end of the world," Margaret said, "but it is not God who is causing it. We have brought it upon ourselves, and we are the ones who must make it right."

5.

Joan learned quickly, absorbing the knowledge of nearly nine centuries of history, politics, and eco-science. As a peasant girl in Domrémy, she and her family lived close to the land, so she easily grasped the principles of cause and effect that led to the world's current state of advanced global warming, worldwide famine, a near-permanent pattern of El Niño winters and mammoth hurricane seasons. A crash course in geology and earth science helped her understand the mass tectonic shifts that caused unprecedented numbers of hurricanes and the eruptions of long dormant volcanoes. She was particularly fascinated by Michael's discussion of the development of science and the discovery of the Einstein-Hawking principle, which ultimately allowed humans to bypass the constraints of time and space and make short visits to the past. With the help of subliminal induction, she learned to speak modern French and English fluently and to carry on simple conversations in Arabic, Mandarin, Russian, Hebrew, Fulani, and Swahili. For her personal interest, she asked for a Bible, which she read almost constantly when not occupied with her grueling learning schedule. She also asked for history modules and was particularly fascinated with the history of France just after her death, though she found parts of her post-mortem story disturbing. She wept for two days when she read of the fate of Gilles de Laval, Baron de Rais.

"I failed him," she said, when Catherine asked her why she cried over such an evil man. "He believed in me and I deserted him."

"How did you desert him?" Catherine asked.

"I died," Joan replied. "I do not think he would have done those horrible things if I had lived. I would have prevented it."

"You cannot hold yourself responsible for his actions," Catherine said, but Joan shook her head emphatically.

"I am my brother's keeper," she said. "I did not keep him well enough." And nothing Catherine or Margaret or Michael said would change Joan's mind. They soon caught a glimpse of the determination and stubbornness that propelled Joan into the heart of the French army.

Joan grew angry when she read about the latter half of the twentieth century and the entirety of the twenty-first, two eras marked by a general disregard for the nations they called the "Third World" coupled with an almost manic desire to make money regardless of the expense to others or the effect on the environment. She learned how national governments were decreasing in significance in proportion to the rise of the multinational corporations with their climate-controlled biodomes that housed their employees and provided all the amenities to support a comfortable lifestyle. She read of the early space programs in the twentieth century and the early twenty-first. And of their abandonment in the middle of the twenty-first century as "inefficient and nonproductive," even when those programs were studying ways to protect the earth from

the massive asteroid strike that many scientists were
predicting before the end of the twenty-second
century.

When her three teachers thought she was ready,
they left the research complex that housed not only
the rooms in which Joan lived and studied and the
garden where she often prayed, but also the device
informally known as Hawking's Arrow. The Arrow
was named in honor of the legendary physicist's reference to "time's arrow" and its unidirectional flight
into the future.

They traveled throughout the world, visiting places
of cultural, historic, or environmental significance.
Joan saw Paris, with L'Arc de Triomphe and the Eiffel
Tower. She visited the Vatican and rode the canals of
Venice, now much smaller than it used to be due to
a rise in the water level. She toured the United States
and parts of Central and South America, charmed by
the scenic beauty, the strange animals and the strangeness of their big cities. She also visited lands plagued
by famine and disease, wartorn landscapes, burned
swathes of Amazon rainforest and land stripped of its
valuable topsoil through the process of stripmining.
Almost a year to the day from her reprieve from
death, Joan was ready to begin.

6.

Wearing clothing carefully selected to appeal to
young activists and the environmentally conscious—
hand-woven trousers, a lightweight cotton shirt and
sturdy walking shoes—the young woman who called
herself Jehanne Dark started out by speaking to select
audiences on college campuses, at Save-the-Earth ral-
lies, and fund-raising dinners for victims of the almost
daily natural disasters. Her words, delivered with the
passion of her conviction, caught fire in the hearts of
her listeners.

In the background, Michael, Margaret, and Catherine watched as their protégé quickly outstripped even their best expectations. She caught the attention of the media, and soon a camera crew followed Jehanne wherever she went. Her Campaign to Save the Earth became the hottest story in all the media formats. Her following grew, and more and more people all over the world took to heart her few basic principles:

"The world was here before you. You must respect its sanctity as if it were a holy place, for it is.

"You do not stand alone in the world. Your neighbors share it with you, and they will share your burdens if you but ask. Their poverty makes you poor. You must give to them so that you will in turn receive from them.

"The world does not need to be conquered or mastered. It needs to be healed."

Billions of people heard Jehanne exhort the multinationals to become accountable and to treat the resources that made them wealthy with respect. Little by little, a few changes became apparent. One company declared a moratorium on its deforestation of the rainforest, and planted new trees and other plants to replenish the depleted earth. Another company closed its sweatshops, redistributed its force in new, state-of-the-art workplaces, raised the minimum wage, and instituted free health care and assistance in living expenses. Armies of young people took a year off from college to work in environmentally troubled areas. Another "army" of consumers used the pressure of their buying power to force other companies to become accountable.

"We must find a way to heal the hole in the sky," she remonstrated at a rally in New York's Central Park. Almost immediately, funds appeared for studying the ozone layer. A new Global Warming conference was held in Geneva, Switzerland, with Jehanne as the keynote speaker. This time, a universal accord was adopted and signed by every attending country—and even some that did not bother to send delegates.

Toward the end of the year, the first of the letters started arriving. Initially, Michael, Margaret and Catherine read them to Joan, finding them amusing and also inferring from them that Joan's campaign was closing in on its objective. They stopped reading them when they discovered her crying uncontrollably in the garden, the latest letter clutched in her hand.

"They are calling me an alarmist," she sobbed through her tears. "They say I only want the fame, that I am a 'glory hound.'"

Catherine placed her hands on Joan's shoulders and worked the aching muscles in Joan's back, forcing her to relax a little. "These letters only mean that you are succeeding. They are running scared."

"Desperate people do desperate things," Joan said, her voice shaking with anger, hurt, and something else Catherine reluctantly identified as fear.

7.

The bullet that ended Joan's second life came during her speech at the first anniversary rally of the Campaign to Save the Earth. Joan stood tall on the outdoor podium and looked out over a sea of faces and signs proclaiming "Love the World!" "Feed the Hungry, Feed Your Soul," "Care for the Earth: It's Your Job," and other pithy slogans. In the year since she delivered her first speech, she had learned how to work a crowd, how to win their minds by securing their hearts and loyalty. Already, small signs that her agenda to heal the earth was taking effect began appearing: new growth in the rainforest, indications that the hole in the ozone layer might actually seal itself in a few years, a new understanding of the need to preserve the great predators, and a resurgence of several endangered species.

As contributions came pouring in, scientists were able to study the increasing instability of the tectonic plates and form some tentative theories on how to relieve the internal stress of the planet.

The crowd was eager to hear her speech, delivered with the simple fervor of a French peasant girl from Domrémy but expressing ideas both sophisticated and tactically sound, ideas they could latch on to. Joan gave her audience a purpose and the will to carry it out.

"I do not expect everyone of you to believe as I do, that God wills us to shepherd his creation on its journey to perfection. But I do expect you to believe in the existence of good and evil. I expect you to choose the side of good and to fight evil wherever you find it. Evil's power is destroying the earth, and only the power of good can defeat it."

A soft thud of displaced air marked the bullet's path from the gun to her abdomen, a coward's shot that lacked the finesse of the instantaneous kill from a head or heart shot. She crumpled, her hand clutching the bloody wound that opened up just below her waist. In an instant, Michael was there, followed closely by Catherine and Margaret. She lay on the ground now, gasping for breath as she tried to grab control of the pain.

"Lie still, ma cherie," Catherine whispered, "we can tend to you." She reached for the medical kit she carried with her as a para-doctor, licensed to use certain common medications in emergency situations. She pulled out a preloaded syringe. "This will take away the pain and help you relax," she said.

"No!" Joan said. "I do not want to rest yet. That will come soon enough." Her words came slowly, forced out through a wall of pain that separated her from the people hovering over her.

"Get those cameras out of here!" Michael snapped, motioning toward several reporters with their microcams who had managed to close in on the dying woman.

"Let them stay!" Joan said. "I still have something to say. Let them give my message to the world."

Margaret looked at Joan, tears already running down her cheek. She recognized the gut wound for the death sentence it was. "She's right," Margaret said. "Let her make the next few minutes mean something."

Michael took Joan's hand in his. "Are you certain?" he said, his voice cracking.

"I am."

The cameras zoomed in closer as Jehanne/Joan haltingly but with determination delivered the remainder of her speech. As her life blood seeped slowly away from a wound too massive to repair, she braced herself against the growing agony. She forced herself to remain conscious enough to finish exhorting a now utterly silent crowd to dedicate themselves to their brothers and sisters all over the world and to the preservation of the world.

"It is a worthy way to spend your life," she said. "It is a cause worth dying for."

Finally, she fell silent, lost in the final tumble toward death, yet struggling to hold on for as long as she could. Her three friends, constant companions of hers for almost two years, knelt beside her. Michael held her upper body in his arms, raising her up a little to ease her raspy breathing and letting her head rest against his chest. On either side, Margaret and Catherine held her hands and stroked her face with the tenderness of lovers, for all three had fallen in love with her soul.

All three wept silently, their faces wet with tears that would not abate.

Joan's hand suddenly gripped Catherine's. She tried to moisten her lips, now nearly bloodless. Catherine reached behind her and felt inside her kit for a wet-swab. She snapped the seal on the swab with one hand, releasing the moisture into the small sponge set on the end of a four-inch stick. She swabbed the inside of Joan's mouth and coated her lips. Joan pulled Catherine close until the blonde woman's ear was nearly touching Joan's mouth. A few seconds later, Catherine pulled away from Joan and kissed her forehead.

"It will be as you wish. I swear it," she said.

Joan's face lit up with a beatific smile then, and her eyes focused on something just beyond her friends. "Jesu!" she breathed, and surrendered her will and her soul to the inescapable sweetness of the world beyond. This time, she thought, she felt the touch of feathery wings wrap themselves around her soul.

One viewing screens all around the world, billions of people saw the martyrdom of Jehanne Dark. Watching with both fascination and horror, more than one person exclaimed, "We have murdered a saint!"

8.

Joan had a state funeral, though she was buried in a simple wooden box according to the wishes she had expressed at one time to Michael. Her death served as the final catalyst, sparking her movement to unprecedented activity. Leaders stepped forward to take her place; having seen her death in great detail, they had become fearless.

When it seemed that they could take some time away from Joan's campaign, Catherine asked Michael to activate Hawking's Arrow again.

"Are you planning on going somewhere?" he asked, a hint of a smile showing on his face, the first one since Joan's death.

"Yes," Catherine said. "You and Margaret are welcome to come along." Since knowing Joan, the formal hierarchy among the trio had broken down. They had been coworkers, military researchers attached to the Hawking machine, as well as its most experienced users. But Joan had made them friends and comrades.

"Does this have something to do with your promise to her?" Margaret asked.

Catherine nodded. She looked hesitantly at both Michael and Margaret, then took a deep breath, speaking rapidly as she exhaled. "I've been hearing her voice," she said, and waited for Michael or Margaret to rationalize the experience away. Instead, both of them looked relieved.

"So have I," said Michael.

"I have, too," echoed Margaret.

"Then you must know where we're going and what we're going to do," Catherine said.

"She thinks—thought—he could be salvaged if we snatched him before he quit the military and retired to his estates. We owe it to her to try," Margaret said.

"I agree," Michael added. "We point the arrow at 1435," he said as they made their way toward the room that housed the machine.

"Gilles de Rais," Catherine announced, "we come to you in the name of Joan the Maid."

DOWNTOWN KNIGHT

James M. Ward

"**B**eta One, this is Alpha One, do you copy? Over."
"Loud and clear Alpha One," the FBI agent responded.

"Beta One, do you have a better angle on what's coming in those twenty vehicles approaching the compound? Over." Agent Jeffers, the lead FBI agent, was sitting in the Alpha One central observation post.

Computer screens showed twenty new black Cadillacs pulling unusually large horse trailers through the main gate of the Gambino family Mafia compound.

"Negative, Alpha One, check the Gamma station. Over," The Beta FBI agent advised.

"Gamma One, this is Alpha One, do you copy? Over."

"Loud and clear Alpha One. Those twenty vehicles have come to the middle of the compound and are unloading Clydesdales from horse trailers. Over," answered the high observation post.

"Agent, repeat that, what the hell is a Clydesdale?" snapped the confused Jeffers.

"Alpha One, this is the Delta station. I can see them as well. Clydesdales are large horses bred in the Clyde valley of Scotland. They were used by the knights of the Middle Ages as the best mount to carry all the

weight of a man and his armor. Over," answered the
FBI agent.

"Horses? What does the don of all the Mafia bosses
want with twenty huge horses?"

"We have no idea sir. Over," came the replies from
observation posts Beta, Gamma, Delta, and even
Epsilon.

Four weeks later, sixty hard-eyed FBI agents all sat
in the same meeting room discussing the astounding
new developments of the Don Corollas Gambino
family.

A frustrated Jeffers looked over the field agents of
his command. These were the best men in the agency.
There was nothing they couldn't find out, which was
why Jeffers was so flustered.

"Gentlemen, for fifteen months we've been observ-
ing the Gambino family. In the past two months atypi-
cal behavior has been observed among the family
members and the compound. Something is happening,
and we need to know what it is to go in with due
authority and cause. I want your maximum effort on
this case. Carson, what do you have?" Jeffers steepled
his fingers and waited.

"Two weeks ago, two armored cars entered the
compound. We traced the vehicles back to their main
branch. When we interviewed the drivers, they tried
to tell us they couldn't divulge what was in their client's delivery."

The other agents burst into laughter at the thought
of mere security guards trying to keep information
from them.

Carson continued, "The trucks delivered two large
chests each—filled with thirty thousand gold coins
minted in Italy. Gold bars were delivered to the
foundry by agents of the Gambinos, and a minting
order was placed. The best in engraving talent went
into making the gold coins they produced. Side A has
the face of the old Don, Corollas Gambino. Side B
has the Gambino Italian family crest. Each coin is

worth approximately five hundred dollars in today's gold trading market."

There was a rumble among the men as each agent computed the worth of all that gold.

"Let's keep it moving, people; that's only part of this new puzzle," Jeffers said. "Agent Ackers, report from the observation posts."

"The younger members of the family have been taking riding lessons on those huge Clydesdales. The son, Corollas Gambino junior, is on his horse at least three hours a day. He's becoming quite accomplished, and we've noted he's grooming and even shoeing his mount." Akers took a deep breath before continuing. "We've also noted an increase in the family members moving into the compound. Tommy 'the Cooler' Gambino arrived last Friday; Cousin Dino Gambino and Uncle Artoro Gambino, two heads of muscle groups, arrived on Saturday of last week. Cousin Carlos Gambino, their main moneyman, came yesterday. All told, there are at least twenty new Gambino relatives living in the compound—and all of them are the young leaders of the family from here and from Italy. These men are all very important people in their organization, and there isn't one of them older than thirty."

"Curiouser and curiouser," Jeffers said. "Does anyone have anything else to report?"

Agent Breck stood up. "The Clydesdales were purchased from a breeding farm in Scotland. Fifteen are pregnant mares, the other five are high-quality stallions. They appear to be the best of that breed in the world. No expense was spared. The mares are worth fifty thousand each, and the studs one hundred thousand."

Agent James raised his hand.

"Yes," Jeffers recognized the agent.

"Thank you sir," James stood up. "For two and a half years now I've been tracking a pair of teachers coming in and out of the compound. One is an instructor in languages of the Middle Ages. The other is a fencing master who has been teaching the younger Corollas the saber and long sword."

Breck shifted in his seat and raised an eyebrow at James.

James continued: "At first, we speculated the language teacher was just showing the young Corollas the language of his ancestors—on some whim from the father. The swordsman? We figured he was just giving them a little exercise. Now I'm thinking there could be some strange tie between the horses, the gold, and those lessons. The fencing instructor has picked up his lesson times from once a week to three times a week now."

Jeffers's face turned redder as his level of frustration grew. There was something going on here, and he didn't know what it was. "Agent Theon, what about those black trucks?"

Theon was their best investigative officer. He had an outstanding ten-year record in drug enforcement, and had been brought to the unit to investigate the black trucks. "As you all know, for a year now at the beginning of every month black trucks have been making deliveries to the compound. Despite our surveillance cameras, it has been difficult to determine what they have been delivering. The observation posts report large crates coming out of the trucks. Intensive interrogation of the drivers reveals they don't know what's inside. Backtracking the trucks has revealed little. It's more than clear elaborate efforts were made to hide the crates' contents. The Gambinos know we're watching. And I have to believe that they know they're going down."

"And yet? What about those crates?" Jeffers motioned for Theon to keep going.

"After a great deal of effort, and with the help of my squad, we've discovered that more than half the trucks have been delivering power equipment. Heavy transformers and the like purchased from large companies here in the US. We also know that whatever the other materials are, they come from Germany. We have agents working there to backtrack the deliveries. I'll be going to Hanover myself tomorrow."

"Excellent work, Theon." Jeffers looked over his group, having just made a decision. "People, something big is perking at that compound. There's a full moon in two nights. We're going to hit that compound with everything we have then. I'm authorizing a hundred men to invade and discover whatever is happening there. This afternoon we'll go over the maps. We'll take down the Gambinos, and with luck we'll find enough goods to put them all away for a very long time. Dismissed."

The men left with smiles on their faces, Breck muttering that it was about time they'd be seeing some action on the case.

Two nights later, in a perfectly coordinated strike of helicopter and ground units, the Corollas Gambino Mafia compound filled to overflowing with law enforcement invaders. The power was cut as one hundred of America's best FBI agents went in.

But the lights never went out in the compound.

Agents came over the walls, crashed through the front gates, and rappelled down cords from five helicopters.

Reports came back to Alpha One from the squads. The horses and the equipment were gone from the stalls. It was noted that the horses hadn't left through the gates.

The house showed no sign of servants, and surveillance equipment confirmed that none of the family servants had left through the gates either.

"We're looking for a very large underground entrance, people!" Agent Jeffers shouted to his squad. "Those big horses are going to need a big entrance to walk through."

The investigation continued.

None of the rooms of the mansion revealed the large chests of gold.

Bedroom after bedroom was searched and found to be empty.

Reports back revealed clothes filled the closets and chests of drawers in those rooms; there was no evidence of things being packed up for a trip.

Not a single cousin, uncle, brother, or anyone else was found.

Until . . .

From five separate entrances, FBI men burst into the large ballroom of the mansion at the same moment. The bright lights of the chamber revealed the elder Don Corollas Gambino sitting in his wheelchair, smiling. Red lights dotted his chest as laser sights targeted the old man.

Beside him was a huge electronic device. Giant sparks of energy arched between two twenty-foot-tall transponder posts.

"What?" One of the agents blurted.

"I was too old to go," the Don said. "And that's fine."

"Go? Go where?" another agent asked.

"I wanted to have the last laugh on you Feds. You're too late!" raged the old man as he pressed a red button on a handheld unit in his lap.

Agents in the ballroom showed confused expressions. Those same expressions filled the faces of those stationed in the Alpha One outpost. "Too late for what?" the agents asked themselves.

Just then, the compound went up in a massive explosion heard three hundred miles away in the city of New York.

Six hundred and five years in the past, something a little different was happening at a large jousting tourney in the London of 1405.

"You are what kind of knight?" The head stooge

spat the words out as if they were unclean things leaving his mouth.

"I'm a knight of the family Gambino. I'm ot'ta the south side of Rome, Italy. You must'a heard of us?"

"I've heard of Yorkshire knights, of Templar knights, even knights of the unicorn. I've never heard of Gambino knights. If I haven't heard of these Gambinos, I daresay no one in all of England has heard of them," said the scowling stooge.

"Well, that's your loss to be sure, pally." Don Corollas Gambino tried to be polite under the circumstances. "See, this little shindig should change all that for me. Now sign me up for this clambake, and tell me where to pitch my tent."

"In due course, knight Gambin-e-o, in due course. Where are your squires, your armor, and other knightly equipment of note?" asked the Chamberlain of the tournament.

"Squires? I never use 'em," Don Corollas said with a grin. "Just let me sign the roster and get going. Okay, pally?" He slid his hand across the table and left five golden coins on the rough wood. His knowing wink spoke volumes about his true character and he suspected the gold coins would do the rest.

"Knight Gambino, you seem to have dropped these funds. No doubt all you have in the world. Squires are required for this tournament. Since you don't have one, you can't participate. I'm so very sorry." But the Chamberlain's face said he was clearly not sorry at all. "Better luck next year. Next in line please."

Seeing it would do no good to argue with this type of stiff on the stiff's home ground, the good "knight" wandered over to the other knights he'd seen rejected for various reasons. He walked up to the poorest-looking of them and bowed.

"So buddy, why wouldn't the lord high stuffed armorer over there let you play in his game?"

"My name is Tarlen, not Buddy, but no offense taken," replied the knight in a cheerful manner. "I didn't have the required funds to enter. It seems they've doubled the fees this year."

"Tell you what, sport," said Corollas, "I'm in need of a sort of squire-type guide to help me over the rough spots at this horse-lance-shield hoot enanny. I'll give you a thousand cool gold ones if you be my squire for the tournament. Wad'da say?"

"I say my name is Tarlen and the next time you make that naming mistake we will come to blows. However, I accept your offer if you prove to me that you can pay this sum," Tarlen replied.

"I likes a careful man. Come over here," the knight ordered, taking Tarlen to a small wagon. Inside were lots of chests and one contained many times the offered price in gold.

"Aren't you afraid of thieves and bandits? That's a lot of gold," Tarlen queried.

"We Gambinos don't take lightly to theft. I've a few cousins with me and more coming. Ten people have tried to get in'ta that chest. All ten are wearing stone overshoes in the middle of several rivers in the local area. Word gets around, if you know what I mean?"

"Well, yes, I see," Tarlen responded. "Shall we get you signed up for tomorrow's event?"

"Onward and upward, pal . . . err, Sir Tarlen," Don Gambino said with a sly and almost respectful smile.

Later that day, Sir Tarlen and his own squire set up Knight Gambino's tent.

"Sire, what did the strange knight call this darkly striped material the tent is fashioned from?" the squire asked.

Sir Tarlen held up the tent flap to the rays of the sun. "He called it pinstripe. I can't imagine why, there are no pins in it." Tarlen admired the material in the afternoon sun. "He also said his whole family had many tabards made of this material. Did you hear his last comment?"

"No, what did he say?" the squire asked.

"He said something about, 'seeing the lay of the land and getting the skinny on tomorrow's free-for-all.' I can't imagine what that means, can you?" Tarlen asked.

"No. I say, Sir Tarlen, come look at this Italian armor. It is astonishing." Wonder filled the young squire's voice.

The armor's surface displayed intricately engraved roses and grapevines. Covered in etchings and embossed images, each piece of armor was an artistic marvel.

"Where are the dents and tears? I've never seen jousting armor so perfect." asked the younger squire. "What are these stubby things in these holders?"

"They smell of sulfur and oil," Tarlen remarked. "Put them back; who knows what devilish things they are."

"Let's have no talk of devils, boys," Don Corollas interrupted.

The knight and squire leapt up from their examinations.

"We Gambinos are all good Catholics, and that's the way we likes it, see. Looking over the equipment, huh. Pretty good stuff, even if I do say so myself." The Don brushed his hand over the surface of his armor.

"We were just putting out your armor for the joust tomorrow. What are these odd clubs you have attached to carriers at your armor's hips?" Tarlen asked.

"Oh those . . . clubs . . . are a family tradition," the Don explained. "We call them tommy guns. They're named after my cousin, Tommy 'the Cooler' Gambino. He works the north side of Rome. That territory has become real quiet since he started carrying those. If you know what I mean. We never go into battle without them. They are kind'a like high-priced good luck charms. By the way, are there any Sullivan Acts against using missile weapons during the set-to tomorrow?"

"Sullivan Acts?" Knight Tarlen had no idea what his lord asked.

"If I may, Lord Tarlen," his squire interrupted. "I think he means are there any rules against using missile weapons during the joust." The squire smiled, getting into the swing of Knight Gambino's horrible use of English.

"Oh. Use of missile weapons is forbidden, unless the joust is to the death. In that case, only the most basic rules of chivalry apply. The more foolish knights sometimes charge an enemy in a fit of rage. This allows the defending knight to do whatever they wish. However, that hardly ever happens in jousts like these. A knight would have to be very angry to agree to a duel to the death," Tarlen answered.

"Gottcha in one, pal . . . err . . . Sir Tarlen," Gambino said with a knowing smile. "Well, let us get some shuteye, shall we? Tomorrow we have a great deal of business to transact."

It took several minutes for the two English knights to figure out what in the world Gambino said to them. They got the point when his loud snores filled the pinstripe tent. The younger squire went to take care of the horses, and soon all three were asleep.

"Why, I never, in all my years!" shouted someone outside their tent.

"That's right, pally. Youse never in all your years and you ain't gonna start now!" shouted another deeper voice.

The argument woke all three of them. Knight Gambino was up with a dagger in his hand and out of the tent before the others even sat up.

"Cousin Dino!" Knight Gambino sounded pleased.

"Don Gambino!"

The two English warriors opened the tent to see a huge, dark peasant type bending the knee to Gambino. The Master of the Lists fumed in anger beside the two as they hugged each other with joy.

"This serf laid hands on me!" declared the Master of the Lists.

"He was seriously checking out your war horse," cousin Dino said.

"Cousin Dino, we'll talk later." Knight Gambino pushed his cousin away from the area. "Scope the place for me while I deal with the help. What did you say your name was, bud?"

The elderly knight stood straight and glared at Don Gambino. "I am Lord Chesterfield. I am Master of the Lists and judge of this tournament. That lout needs to be beaten within an inch of his life!"

"Ya right," Corollas waved his hand in the general direction of the retreating cousin. "I'll take care of it to be sure. Why were you nosing around my horse?"

"There are a great many questions being asked about you and your right to enter this tournament," Lord Chesterfield replied.

"Sure. Well, you just send them all my way, and my squire, the Knight Tarlen, the English Knight Tarlen from castle Weyworth and third cousin to the king, will take care of 'em. Ain't that right, Sir Tarlen?"

"Lord Chesterfield, we are at your service," Tarlen said, a bit embarrassed because he couldn't hold back a smile at the lord's discomfiture. Tarlen's own squire actually made the mistake of laughing out loud.

It suddenly struck Tarlen that he hadn't told the good knight he came from Weyworth castle. How could Gambino have known that?

The Master of the Lists left in a huff.

"In the next day or two you're going to be seeing lots of my family in and around the joust," Knight Gambino advised the two squires. "They'll all be serfs, but treat them with respect. Although they ain't had my fine upbringing, they're family, capiche? I mean, do youse understand?"

"Will they all be as large as your cousin Dino?" asked Tarlen's squire.

"He's only a midsized muscle. Err, I mean in my family he isn't close to the largest cousin we have," Corollas answered. "Wait until youse gets a load of

Uncle Artoro. Now that's a Gambino to be proud of! Let's quit chitchatting and get me into some armor. What do you say, boys?"

They both heartily agreed and got straight away to work.

The day was perfect for jousting. London filled with people at the time of jousts. Just before mounting, yet another cousin appeared out of the packed crowd of onlookers.

"Cousin Carlos, it's great to see youse at last!" Corollas hugged this new cousin and kissed him on both sides of his face.

Carlos was a thin serf wearing that strange pinstriped tabard it appeared all the Gambino serfs wore. He bent at the knee and kissed the ring of Knight Gambino. Both men were clearly glad to see each other.

"How are the odds running?" Knight Gambino asked.

"You aren't even in the mix," answered the cousin. "I can get forty-to-one on you easy. The big fan favorite is a chump by the name of Lord Allen. He'll be the sparkler in white. He's an honor type of hit man. No amount of gold is going to get him to do anything. The real money is on this black knight fellow. He's a nasty one who likes closing and using a morning star to finish his marks. Keep your distance from him until you catch on to his style. The rest are just swells that you shouldn't have too much trouble with unless they gang up on you. They love doing that in this first free-for-all."

"I'm onto that," Corollas said not looking a bit worried. "Thanks for the bits of info. Lay a few thousand large on me for the finals. You know where the stash is."

"Indeed I do, pally mine. Indeed I do," came the smug reply from the cousin.

Cousin Carlos walked into the crowd singing to himself. It was a very strange song that went something like, "My kind of town, Rome is, my kind of town." He had a troubadour-quality voice.

"Sir Knight Gambino, I didn't understand more than three words of your cousin's speech," Tarlen said. "Is everything all right?"

"Couldn't be better, Sir Tarlen. Couldn't be better. Shall we get me to the joust?"

"Grand idea," Knight Tarlen's squire said.

CRASH!

Lucky lances met helmets and breastplates. Unlucky lances splintered on shields or just missed altogether. Two hundred of the best knights of England met one hundred and seventy-five of the not-so-best knights in mock combat on the open fields in front of the lists and galleries of Nottingham. The best knights were called the Inside Knights, as they were supposed to be protecting a special tent. The Outside Knights were supposed to tear down the tent. Not surprisingly, the better knights managed to unhorse more than a hundred of the poorer-quality knights.

Knight Gambino was not unhorsed.

In fact, in the next several sets of encounters he was able to take down seven of the better knights of England. His armor, shield, and lance took many blows that morning, but showed little of the effects of battle.

A number of armchair tacticians remarked on how strange it was that an unusual number of the knights, when given a choice, picked other targets than Knight Gambino.

Knight Tarlen's blood was high. He'd witnessed many fine passages of arms that day. His concentration on the tournament was broken, however, as suddenly there were several new cousins standing with them near the lists.

"More cousins," Tarlen observed. "Well met. I'm sorry to say you will have to move back behind the lists. Only squires are allowed in this area."

"You must be Knight Tarlen," one of the three large cousins observed. "We've heard of youse. Don't worry, the fix is in with the heavies among the field watchers. We laid a few hundred large on them, and they bent a few rules for us. How is the Don doing?"

"Don?"

"Gambino."

"Well, that's highly irregular, you standing here, but since you're clearly cousins by your garb, I will not quibble," Knight Tarlen answered back. "Knight Gambino is doing amazingly well considering the many foes matching against his lance this day. I estimate his ransoms could equal many thousands of gold pieces."

"No surprise there," another of the three cousins remarked. "He's had the best training money could buy. Now that you are a made man, I don't . . ."

"What's this 'made man' business?" Tarlen asked.

"Made man, you know, someone picked by the Don to help him," the third cousin remarked.

For the rest of the joust, Knight Tarlen grew more and more amazed as this new cousin told him how he had just become part of a huge Italian family. It seemed he joined the family not by marriage, but just by Don Gambino hiring his services as a squire. The knight wasn't at all pleased to learn the only way to leave the family was by dying. However, there was the list of benefits to consider, and even after the cousin described those in several different ways, the good knight still had no idea what the cousin was talking about.

Retirement plans, family death benefits, parcels of land in a place called the old country, pasta, the list soon became tiresomely endless, until Tarlen's mind was all a swirl trying to make something of each new concept.

Finally, the day's jousting was over. There were ten Inside Knights mounted, and only Knight Gambino from the Outside Knights still rode his exhausted war steed. The crowd cheered both sides, and Lord Chester-field gave the victory-of-the-day lance to the white knight.

"I say, that's a bit unfair considering the success of Knight Gambino," Tarlen observed.

"Don't worry," the tallest cousin said. "We figured the fix was in on this first day. The family will make its mark on the one-on-one fights tomorrow. Watch this now, the Don is a genius."

All the surviving knights wore mistletoe wreaths as tokens for the day's successes. The Don vaulted off his horse and walked over to the gallery. He laid his wreath at the feet of Lady Aster. The crowd went wild.

An enraged Black Knight couched his lance and charged Knight Gambino. It seems the Black Knight didn't like presents given to his lady.

The charge was a clear breach of knightly honor. Everyone in the stands knew Knight Gambino to be a dead man, as a ton of steel and horseflesh bore down on him.

Knight Gambino casually turned toward the charging steed, drew one of his war clubs from his holster, and the rest was explosive history.

PARSLEY SAGE, ROSEMARY, AND TIME

Jon L. Breen

It all started with a bet I had lost but was sure I should have won.

I was one of those wannabe writers determined to reach the shrinking ranks of willing-to-be readers, and for the past few years I had belonged to a writers' group that met every other Wednesday evening at the home of a member. The members ranged in age from late thirties to early seventies. Some, including me, were what's called pre-published, a vile euphemism that never raised my self esteem by a single degree. Others could lord it over the rest with a sale or two. A couple were so successful we wondered why they would bother with the group, maybe out of genuine altruism or maybe for relief from the built-in loneliness of the keyboard.

My chosen field was crime fiction, but no stories or novels by Justin Prince (classy byline, no?) had yet seen professional print. A recently acquired gig reviewing mystery novels for the local paper had raised my spirits, however.

The Wednesday after my first reviews appeared, we were meeting at Maisie Goldblatt's house, a quaintly cozy, fragilely feminine venue better suited to genteel romance than mean-streets violence. To sustain us through the evening, we had coffee (decaf only in these wimpy times), tea, and cookies; the readings were as mixed a bag as usual.

Our oldest member, retired math teacher Fred Bushworthy, had just finished reading his latest essay on the fine art of orchid growing.

Grace Needleman said, "Fred, that is just beautiful. I can just see those orchids. I feel like they're family." Grace invariably liked everything and encouraged everybody.

"Fred," I said, "your target market is a popular gardening magazine, right?"

"I hope so," he said cheerfully.

"Well, it's way too technical. Your weekend gardener is going to get lost in all that terminology." I glanced at the notes I'd made. "Like stigmatic depression and non-parasitic epiphyte."

"It's redundant anyway," said Maisie Goldblatt, who obviously understood the lingo better than I did. "Epiphytes are non-parasitic by definition."

"I think you need to either simplify it—"

"You can't write down to your readers," our perpetually gloomy poet Axel Gruber intoned. "Respect their intelligence. Don't treat them like children." It was his hobbyhorse, and variations on it were almost the only comments he made on other members' work.

I persisted. "Writing at a level they can understand isn't writing down. Fred, you're falling between two audiences. Either write it so the amateur can understand it or add some footnotes and send it to a professional journal."

Always cheerful in the face of criticism, Fred shrugged and said, "I get it. You're telling me this is another candidate for Fred's compost heap."

I shook my head in denial. Fred's compost heap, which we all swore would some day bring forth blossoms, was a running joke of the group.

Fred was and always would be a hobbyist who wrote to keep busy and didn't care greatly whether he sold.

Next to share was one of our successful pros. The latest chapter of Judy Klinger's cute-cat mystery in progress struck me as oversweet as the dessert recipe that accompanied it, but she was selling the damn things, so the group cooed over it.

"Isn't Itsy-poo just the darlingest pussy?" Grace enthused.

"Has there been a murder in this one?" Bill Wandsworth asked innocently.

"Three chapters ago," Maisie remembered.

"I'll get back to it," Judy assured us, "but you'll find when you've been at this as long as I have that your characters just take over and do whatever they feel like. I could no more tell Itsy-poo what to do than I could any other cat. And the people are just as intractable. Characters that really live and breathe can't be ordered around."

Preciously pernicious advice, but what could you say? She was a successful pro.

Next, Maisie treated us to a chapter of steamy romance that a few years ago would have been classified as soft-core porn.

"Can you get that graphic in a romance nowadays?" Charlie Wallace asked. Years in city journalism hadn't destroyed his ability to blush.

"You sure can," Maisie assured him. "I watch my market closely."

Bill Wandsworth, who was almost my age and thus younger than the rest of the group, had become a close friend. As usual, he regaled us with another case for his tough but unsold private eye Johnny Whiplash, who went through all the familiar paces, including taking on a beautiful but treacherous client and surviving another blow to the skull. This shamus had undergone enough concussions to retire half a dozen NFL quarterbacks, but he kept coming back for more.

"Bill," I said, "the pace is great and I liked some of your similes, but Johnny still seems to me like a forties character living in the twenty-first century."

"But don't you get it?" he said. "That's the whole point!"

There was no point, but I let it go. Not for the first time, I wondered if I was wasting my time taking these Wednesday sessions so seriously. Were we just spinning our wheels, making and not hearing the same comments, never getting any farther ahead? If not for my reviewing gig, the predictable course of the evening would have depressed me.

Now it was time once again to hear the newly revised first chapter of Grace Needleman's novel, a saga that would cover the whole rich canvas of twentieth-century American life. We all agreed it was getting better, the descriptions sharper, the writing tighter, the portents more portentous, but she'd been revising that first chapter for the past year. If she ever started chapter two, we'd have to break out the champagne.

We listened to Axel Gruber's latest poem, his usual surrealistic and impenetrable free verse.

"Axel," I said mildly, "have you ever tried writing a sonnet, I mean, as an exercise in self-discipline?" I wondered if he could, just as I wondered if abstract painters could draw a horse if they had to.

"I do not write sonnets," he intoned, voice dripping with disdain. "Nor limericks. Nor haikus. Nor clerihews. Real poetry, great poetry, doesn't color inside the lines; poetry isn't made by a cookie-cutter; poetry doesn't come with a set of printed rules like Scrabble. Poetry is the deepest expression of the self."

When no one seemed ready to add anything to that, I said, "Well, I guess it's my turn." Next to last on the evening's bill of fare, I regaled them with a new beginning on a suspense novel; I had a lot more beginnings than endings, but at least I offered a new one every week. Grace liked it; she always does. Judy made some grudging and patronizing remarks on my promise.

That brought us to the evening's last reader, our calming influence and the man whose unaccountably regular presence held the group together. Charlie Wallace, a columnist for the local paper and a thorough pro, read us one of his humorous essays. And as usual all we had to offer him was appreciative laughter. Why did he keep coming to the meetings? Maybe the silent appreciation of his readers wasn't enough. Maybe he was a frustrated stand-up. It was good to have Charlie as the last act, so to speak. If we ever let Axel go last, we'd all go out and kill ourselves.

The group's unwritten bylaw was that no adult beverages would be offered until the reading was over and the purely social part of the evening began. This time Maisie brought out a bottle of sub-Dom-Perignon-but-better-than-chainstore champagne, filled a flute for everybody, and offered a toast: "Here's to Justin's first sale."

Luckily, the group took the term sale rather loosely—what I was getting paid as a book reviewer was a little more than a free book but hardly enough to earn the exalted label of sale. It would have been more appropriately toasted with a boxed chardonnay. But I was pleased about it and happily accepted a round of congratulations. They all seemed to have read my first group of reviews and had nice things to say.

"It's so hard to review a mystery without giving too much away," Judy said. "So often, at least in my case, a reviewer will reveal something the reader should find out for herself. The people who write jacket copy are even worse. You hit just the right balance, Justin." She simpered coyly, and I caught a flickering glimpse of the pretty young woman in her years-old publicity photo. "Maybe you'll be reviewing me one day."

God, I hoped not. If the opportunity came, I'd quietly turn it down on conflict of interest grounds—I could claim Judy, whom I could barely stand, was too dear a friend for me to retain my objectivity.

All the comments were complimentary until Bill

said offhandedly, "You made one gaffe, though, you know."

I was wounded, of course. You'll always remember that single flotsam of rebuke in a sea of praise. "What do you mean?"

"When you were reviewing that mystery about the World War II home front, you said the use of the term 'shrink' was an anachronism."

"It was," I said. " 'Shrink' as slang for psychiatrist didn't come in until much later."

Charlie came to my aid. "Justin's right. I would say maybe in the late forties or early fifties, they started to use headshrinker as a slang term for psychiatrist or psychoanalyst. Eventually, this got shortened to shrink, but not before, I don't know, maybe late fifties, early sixties. For sure, early forties is too early."

Fred said, "Charlie's got it right. I'm older than anybody here, and I don't remember hearing shrink to mean shrink before the Kennedy administration."

"It's not a serious mistake, though," Maisie said. "It's not easy to keep track of period slang."

"I never said it was a serious mistake," I said, sounding more defensive than I intended. "I just mentioned it in passing in a damn favorable review. The author should be very happy with that review."

"Not the issue," Bill said. "You got it wrong, Justin, and the rest of you—well, all I can say is your memories are imperfect."

"Bill," Fred pointed out, "you're too young to remember when they said shrink or didn't say shrink. I was there."

"On the couch?" Charlie said. Fred grinned, and the tension lifted a little, but Bill wouldn't leave it alone.

"No, I wasn't there, but I read a lot from that period, and I'm sensitive to language. They did use shrink in that way at that time, and I can prove it."

"You can't because they didn't," I said, even while thinking we were making way too big a deal of this.

"I'll bet you ten bucks and a foofendorker I can prove it."

Ah, the dreaded foofendorker, our group's equivalent of the triple-dog-dare. Foofendorker had been the name of an alien race in a science fiction story by one of our former members. We were so hard on that story, we reduced her to tears one week, and to make amends and keep her in the group, we agreed to break our rule limiting members to one reading per meeting and awarded her an extra one at our next. She still drifted off, not getting the unalloyed praise she wanted except from Grace, and from that day forward the awarding of an extra reading was called a foofendorker, to much hilarity. If I awarded a foofendorker to another member through a wager, it would mean giving up my own turn to read that week.

"You're on," I said, confident I would win.

A couple of days later, Bill called me at work, asking me to meet him that afternoon at Liam's Irish Pub so he could collect his ten bucks.

"You haven't proved anything," I pointed out.

"I will. You know, of course, that I collect old pulp magazines."

"Right. It's a very positive influence on your writing." That last was sarcastic and he knew it. I liked the old pulps, too, but I hadn't moved in.

When we met after work at Liam's, we would normally stand at the bar, often arguing which of our office day jobs was the more exasperating and unfulfilling. Sometimes we would chat with the bartender, yet another wannabe writer who swore he would join our group if not for his working hours. But today was different. Bill insisted we repair to a booth in the most secluded back corner. He looked around with exaggerated furtiveness, then opened his briefcase and removed an old pulp magazine in a clear plastic slipcase. He could not have handled it more carefully if it had been an original Picasso or a vial of nitroglycerine.

He showed me the cover, which I peered at in the

barely adequate bar lighting. The magazine was called *Stunning Science Adventures*, dated January 1943, and its cover showed a classic bug-eyed monster wearing a Nazi armband menacing a voluptuous young woman in a see-through space suit, with a barren moonscape in the background, a recognizable Earth above the horizon. Then he carefully withdrew the magazine from its slipcase and opened its browning pages.

"This is from a story called 'Time Trampler' by Frank Paulsen. I'll read you some of the dialogue: 'I don't belong here. I belong in another place, another century, and I've been there. I want to go back.' 'Sophie, you need help. You need to talk to somebody. I can recommend a good shrink . . .' 'Sam, I'm not crazy!' " He looked up from the magazine with a complacent smile. "There it is. Ten bucks and a foofendorker."

"Let me see that," I said. He didn't like handing it over, but it was only fair letting me have a closer look and I took pains to handle the old magazine as carefully as he had. On the third page of the story, the dialogue appeared as he'd read it. It didn't take me long to decide I wasn't being hoaxed. A real sixty-year-old pulp would be almost impossible to fake convincingly, and even if it could be, it wouldn't be worth the bother for a ten-dollar bet, even with a foofendorker thrown in. I read a little more of the story in the dim light of the bar.

"Bill, this story is set in the year 2000," I said, knowing as I said it I was grasping at straws.

"Yeah? So?"

"In 2000, we *were* using 'shrink' for psychiatrist."

"Come on, Justin. Is that the best you can come up with? The story was written and published in 1943, and if you read it all the way through you'll see that in no way does it depict the 2000 we know. See any references to the Internet? Anybody sending anybody e-mail? And you'll notice everybody's tooling around the city in their personal flying machines, which if it's happened I haven't noticed. That story is not prophetic at all, and the characters talk just like people in 1943 talked. Old Frank Paulsen used the term shrink because that was a slang term in use at that time, not because he had some crystal ball for slang of our time. Now please pay up."

"Uh, sure, yeah, I will. I guess you've got me." I pulled out my wallet and handed over ten dollars. "You ever heard of this Frank Paulsen before?"

Bill shrugged. "I've seen the name once or twice, but I don't know anything about him. There were a lot of pulp writers. It might have been a pseudonym. He was no Max Brand or Carroll John Daly, not under that name anyway."

I wasn't satisfied. The ten dollars was no great loss, but something about this didn't make sense. I'm proud of my ear for language, and seeing that use of shrink in a 1943 story was as out of kilter to me as a reference to Britney Spears would have been. Something wasn't right, though I couldn't quite articulate my suspicions.

To begin with, I wanted to find out more about Frank Paulsen and at the very least read "Time Trampler" in its entirety. The next Saturday morning, I turned up at the special collections department of the local university library, which housed the biggest collection of pulp magazines in a several-thousand-mile radius. Access was closely controlled, and I had to fill out a lot of forms as well as surrender my driver's license. I think my status as a critic for the local paper turned the tide for me.

They had fully indexed their holdings in the library's online catalog, and I quickly found the Paulsen byline had appeared ten times in pulps held by the university. "Time Trampler" was the only one in a science fiction magazine. There was one in a sports pulp, one in a western pulp, the other seven in mystery magazines. I requested all ten, and they were brought to me in the huge, cold, and silent reading room, along with a whispered lecture about how fragile they were and how to turn the pages to prevent damage.

I was instructed I could take notes only in pencil, and I was glad the clerk stopped short of a full-body search to see if I was carrying a pen. Any request to photocopy, at a dollar per page, would have to be approved by the chief special collections librarian, and there would be a delay of a week before I would have the copies. A forbidding attendant sat at an elevated desk at the front of the room, watching me and my fellow researchers for any infractions of the rules.

The time travel gimmick in "Time Trampler" was a clever one but seemed familiar somehow. The present of the story was 2000. Time travel had been perfected, but characters were able to travel only for legitimate scholarly research, qualifying for which was nearly as tough as accessing the university library's special collections. Changing the present through accidentally tampering with the past didn't seem to be a big problem: the course of time would spring back into its normal track unless the change was major and deliberate, and that was the kind of catastrophe the hero, a sort of time cop with the all-American name Ted Armstrong, would be sent back in time to prevent.

The story had a romantic angle: on one of his trips to tidy up the past, he intended to make a side trip to win back an old girlfriend named Rosemary. The time travel was accomplished not via a time machine out of H.G. Wells but through more psychological means. Travelers would steep themselves in the surroundings and accoutrements of the time they wanted to visit—and once they were well enough steeped, they could walk out the door and there they were.

From "Time Trampler," I moved on to Paulsen's other efforts. He had a measure of that flair and readability essential to writers of popular fiction, but he seemed no better and no worse than dozens of his contemporaries. I was tempted to read some stories

by the real masters instead—there was a novelette by
Erle Stanley Gardner in one of the issues—but I stuck
with Paulsen. As I read through his stories, I was on
the lookout for more anachronisms, and I found a few
that seemed dubious but no smoking gun. I had almost
decided I must have been wrong about "shrink" when
I came across this in a 1944 sports pulp: "The Lions
batter looked glazed-eyed when he returned to the
dugout. 'What was that pitch, Skip?' he asked the
manager. The wily old man grinned and said, 'He calls
that his foofendorker. Don't worry, kid. Babe Ruth
couldn't hit it either.' "

Foofendorker! For a second, I felt lightheaded.
What was going on here? Take it easy, I told myself:
I didn't know every catchphrase that had become popular briefly and disappeared years before I was born.
Our former member must have heard the term foofendorker and appropriated it for her alien race. There
was nothing weird or paranormal going on here. On
the other hand, nobody else in the group seemed to
have heard it before, not even old Fred.

I noted the page and moved on to calming vistas
of pulp mystery clichés. But three stories later, I hit
something that blew all my calm reasoning up the
chimney and out of the water. The first-person private
eye narration ran thus: "The search for Flora sent me
to every garden supply store in the city. I got my first
clear lead at a place called Fred's Compost Heap."

That settled it for me. What was that old mystery
rule out of Sherlock Holmes? When you eliminate the
impossible, whatever remains must be the truth, something like that. Well for me, two coincidences became
the impossible, and what remained that had to be the
truth was simply this: Frank Paulsen was one of the
members of my writers' group and a time traveler.

I trolled through the pages for other clues. Were
there any letters to the editor commenting on Paulsen
stories? No. Were there any biographical notes on
Paulsen accompanying the stories or in the editors'

brag columns? No. I took down the names and ad-
dresses of the magazines' publishers—though the mags
were long out of business, the companies that put
them out might not be—and the names of the various
pulps' editors. Maybe I could find out something
through one of them, though it was a longshot any of
them would still be alive.

When I was sure I'd exhausted all possibilities, I
carried the magazines to the desk and made my photocopy order. I had decided to get copies of every
Paulsen story, even though it would cost me a couple
hundred dollars.

The attendant—I think a graduate student, not a
librarian—looked at me almost accusingly. "Do you
realize how rare and fragile these magazines are?"
he demanded.

I wanted to say, rarer than you know, and the life
we live is more fragile than you can imagine. Instead
I settled for, "I assume that's why you ask a buck a
page and an Act of Congress to get copies."

Events ground slowly from that point. By our next
Wednesday meeting, I had no copies yet and had
nothing to say to the group about my discovery. Our
venue this time was Fred Bushworthy's house, smaller
than Maisie's but somehow more comfortable and relaxed. The most prominent features of the room were
vases of flowers and a wall of gardening trophies. Mrs.
Bushworthy, a grandmotherly lady as cheerful as Fred,
popped in to say hello but stepped out to a movie
with some friends. Fred served us the traditional tea,
decaf, and cookies.

The meeting was much as usual. Bill had brought
only one piece to read but told the group a story by
somebody named Frank Paulsen had won him his bet
and reminded us all he expected to collect his foofendorker next time. I offered my sportsmanlike congratulations.

As the others read their stuff, my mind wandered
more than usual, and I had fewer comments to make.

I remember Maisie's romance had a figure-skating sequence. Grace, of course, said it was the most beautiful thing she'd ever heard. Charlie had a question about one of the jumps referred to, whether it was spelled axel or axle. Judy was pretty sure it was axel and asked our own Axel if there were any figure skaters in his family. He just looked disgusted. Grace said she'd once looked up the origin of axel, but before she could say what it was, Axel pointed out we were getting off subject and it was time to hear his latest impenetrable piece of free verse. Just a typical meeting, if even more useless than usual.

Throughout the evening, I wondered which of them, if my theory was correct, might be the time traveler. Frank Paulsen, who had written in predominately masculine genres, was probably a man. Bill himself seemed the most likely to want to travel back in time and make a name for himself in the pulps, but if he was Paulsen and didn't want it known, why would he make that bet with me? Fred's time on Earth actually overlapped Paulsen's, and maybe he wanted to travel out of a sense of nostalgia, but judging by his sincere and knowledgeable but ineptly written gardening nonfiction, I doubted he had the writing chops to produce Paulsen's output. Charlie clearly had the chops, but he didn't seem to relate to old popular fiction, and as for Axel, well, you couldn't tell about him, but his deadly serious commitment to inaccessible highbrow literature didn't fit with a pulp magazine sensibility.

Could Frank Paulsen be a woman? Certainly, but could he be one of *these* women? Maisie, with her calculatedly shocking patches of graphic romance, had a sort of toughness about her, along with the sense of humor that was implicit in Paulsen's career. Grace was certainly interested in the period, but she never finished anything in our time and it seemed doubtful she'd be turning out pulp stories if she lived sixty years ago. Judy seemed so doggedly (wrong word) devoted to her cute cat stories, she was disinclined to travel out of the state, let alone to 1943. The women just didn't fit.

Then another thought occurred to me, one that would accommodate a Paulsen of either gender. Maybe Paulsen was not a solo byline. Maybe my time traveler was collaborating on those pulp stories with somebody else native to that period.

A couple days later, I got my photocopies in the mail from the university and I was able to steep myself in Paulsen's work. Many of the plots seemed familiar, not in the general way of popular fiction formulae but in very specific ways, as if Paulsen were taking later writers' plots and recycling them (or do I mean precycling them?) point-by-point. Frank the preemptive plagiarist.

Between rereading the stories, I used my computer to Google all those editors, and for a while hit one dead end after another. Mostly all I could find were obituaries. Finally, though, I struck pay dirt. At least one of them was still living: C. Hardy Flint, editor of a whole string of pulps, including *Stunning Science Adventures*, was in fact resident of an assisted-living facility in this very city.

When I phoned to ask if I could arrange a visit with him, a pleasant-voiced woman assured me he'd love it. He didn't get that many visitors, and he'd welcome somebody to talk to. But what, I wondered, if all his memories were wiped clean by time and nature? I inquired delicately if the old fellow, who must be ninety plus, was all there.

"Very much all there," came the amused answer. "But—let me put it this way. Do you have a room in your house where you put everything you have no current use for but don't want to throw away?"

"Sure." I could have said my whole apartment was like that.

"You have an idea what's in the room, and once you find a particular item, you can put it to use. But you can't always remember exactly where it is, and you can't put your hand on it at any given moment—and when you can't, it frustrates you."

"I get it. You're telling me he's senile."

"I can see you're not afflicted with political correctness," she said. "No, he's not senile. He can often remember things from seventy or eighty years ago like they happened yesterday, but—oh, I think you understand my metaphor, don't you?"

"I'm a writer," I said.

"Are you? Oh, then I know he'll want to talk to you."

Having been warned of his cluttered attic, I figured it would be wise to prepare the old fellow in advance, so I wrote him a letter and enclosed a photocopy of "Time Trampler" before I went for a visit. When C. Hardy Flint met me in the cheery and spacious lobby of his building a week later, he was spiffily turned out in a three-piece suit. He told me almost immediately, with a mixture of pride and wonder, that he was ninety-four years old, and I assured him truthfully he didn't look a day over seventy. He had brought the copy I'd sent of "Time Trampler."

"This story brought back memories," he said when we were seated in the comfortable visiting area.

"Of Frank Paulsen?" I said hopefully.

"No. Just of that whole time in my life. To tell the truth, I can't call the fellow to mind. I worked with so many writers, you know. Sounds kind of familiar, but—what else did he write?"

"Everything, it seems. Mostly mystery, but some sports and westerns."

"For some reason, I think I should remember him." The old man shook his head in befuddlement, then brightened. "Now, the guy that did the illustration. I can tell you all about him. No signature, but I'd know that style anywhere." What he said about the black and white interior illustration's artist might have fascinated me at any other time, but I wanted to know about Paulsen.

"Do you remember the story at all?"

A smile came to his wrinkled face. "Oh, I remember the story all right. My memory's great, just get a little static now and then. Yes, indeed. But I'm pretty sure that story came in over the transom. I don't think I ever met Paulsen. As I recall, we changed the name of the hero. It wasn't Ted Armstrong originally. It was something else, some precious name like an Edwardian detective, what the hell was it? Percy something. Can you imagine a red-blooded pulp reader of the forties wanting to read about a hero with a sissified name like Percy?"

"No," I said, "unless he was the Scarlet Pimpernel on the side. What else can you remember about the story?"

"Well, of course, you can see it was derivative as hell. Most of them were. It may not even have struck me at the time, but when I was rereading the story you sent me, I could see where he stole his time travel gimmick. Two different sources actually."

"What were they?"

"Well, that whole business about time police and time snapping back into place if you didn't change it too much—that was Poul Anderson's. And the thing about sitting around in the atmosphere of a past time and soaking if up and just sort of thinking your way into it—you ever see *The Music Man*?"

"Sure."

"The guy selling the band instruments knew nothing about music, so he told the kids they'd have to learn to play by the 'think system.' That's what this time travel gimmick is: the think system."

"So he stole it from Meredith Willson?"

Flint looked at me disparagingly. "No, no. Your science fictional knowledge leaves something to be desired. It was in that book by Jack Finney. Some science fiction people hated it, but it was a great book. What was it called? *Time and Again*."

He said it with such confidence, I hoped I wouldn't upset him with what I said next. "Mr. Flint, I do know that book, but it came years later. Nobody in 1943 had ever heard of Poul Anderson or Jack Finney."

"Why, yes, I guess you're right. So did Anderson and Finney both read Frank Paulsen and borrow from him?" Flint looked lost in thought for a moment, then came to a decision. "There's something about this I should remember and I can't. We'll have to check my files."

"Your files?" I said, half hopeful and half dubious. I didn't think you could bring a bunch of old business files to a place like this.

He read my mind. "Oh, I don't have them here. My granddaughter's keeping them for me. Just until I check out." He smiled. We both knew he didn't mean check out of the assisted-living facility to move to his own place and reclaim the files. "She lives about a half hour drive from here, out in the suburbs, very nice place. If you could drive me out there, I might be able to help you a little bit more. How about it? I don't get out much, you know."

I was still dubious. Was he just stringing me along to get a rare trip off base? But if the files really existed, it would be great, and if not, I'd be doing a good deed for a nice old man.

"Will they let you go out?" I asked.

"Young fellow," he said with amused rebuke, "I am still a free man. No commitment papers have been signed."

So he called his granddaughter, told the front desk where he was going, and a few minutes later was sitting in the passenger seat of my aging Camry. He seemed to be enjoying himself so much, I decided not to mind if this turned out to be a wild goose chase.

His granddaughter's house was lovely, part of a tree-shaded upscale tract with enough individuality not to look like one. The granddaughter was lovely, too. Her name was Elizabeth, Flint had told me, with all diminutives and truncations (Eliza, Lizzie, Beth, Betty) firmly rejected. She had no children, no animals, and no husband (I got the impression she was divorced) and cheerfully pronounced the two-story house much too big for her. I had no logical reason to be interested in the granddaughter, but it's amazing what information you can pick up when you're besotted. Maybe I'd embark on a research project about the old pulps that would give me an excuse to visit her again. But for now, we'd concentrate on business. C. Hardy Flint's files were in half a dozen large filing cabinets that reduced the garage to single-vehicle capacity.

"You can't imagine what I went through to save these when the publisher went bust," he told me, as he looked through the files. "Everybody thought I was crazy. Nobody thought there'd be any interest in the history of the pulps, you see. When I die, they go to the university library. Until then, I can consult them. Elizabeth tells me I should write my memoirs. What do you think?"

"Absolutely."

"There'd be a market for them now. Some of the people I worked with became famous, and some of the ones that didn't were even more interesting. Ah, here we are." He pulled out a hanging file marked Frank Paulsen.

"Bring it inside, gramp," Elizabeth said. "I'll get some lemonade for you and Julian."

"Justin," I corrected. So she didn't share my besotment. Give her time.

Once Flint had the file in his hands, his memory was stoked. "Here's the original manuscript. Look at the title of the story!" He passed it over to me.

I got another shock. The title page proclaimed, "Parsley Sage, Rosemary, and Time."

"Parsley Sage!" Flint snorted. "That's an even sillier name than Percy whatever-I-said. Of course, the hero was looking for this girl named Rosemary, and the story did involve time travel, but still what kind of a title was that to pluck out of the air?" He pondered a moment. "Sounds familiar, though."

"It was a song," I said.

"Was it?"

"Simon and Garfunkel. 'Scarborough Fair.'"

Behind me, I heard a lovely soprano singing, "Are you going to Scarborough Fair? Parsley, sage, rosemary, and thyme."

"Of course," said Flint, smiling at his granddaughter, who had brought the lemonade. "But wait a minute. Didn't that song come much later?"

"Yes," I said. "Late sixties."

"Actually, yes and no," Elizabeth said. "Simon adapted the lyric from an old traditional English ballad. But I think the line 'Parsley, sage, rosemary, and thyme' was in the original."

"I'm relieved," Flint said. "This was all starting to feel a bit strange."

Tell me about it, I thought but didn't say.

Flint was shuffling through the correspondence. "Number of letters from Paulsen. Nothing to suggest we ever met face to face. Showed promise. I wonder what—oh, gosh, look at this."

He handed over a handwritten letter dated June 15, 1943.

"Dear Mr. Flint,

"I'm sorry to tell you that my tenant Mr. Frank Paulsen passed away yesterday. Thought he just had flu but it took him sudden. He never said much where he came from. I know of no kin or what to do with his things. If you can help me on this please let me know. If he was a good friend of yours I'm sorry for your loss. He was a nice fellow.

　　　"Yours very truly,

　　　"(Mrs.) Minnie Runcible"

"That's why there were no more stories," Flint said. "I knew there was something about Paulsen I should have remembered."

"That's just the sort of thing that would happen," I said, half to myself.

"What do you mean?"

"To a time traveler. If you traveled to another time, even fifty years ago, who knows what bugs might be around waiting to kill you, things that have been eradicated today, things we've lost our resistance to."

"Young fellow, I'm the one people take for senile, but you seem to be losing your grasp on what's fiction and what's real."

"I wish it were that simple," I said. "Do you think I could borrow this file on Frank Paulsen?" I looked over Flint's head and smiled at Elizabeth. "I'll bring it back in good condition."

"Sure, it can't hurt," he said.

As we bid goodbye at her door, I told Elizabeth I hoped I'd see her again, and at least she didn't wince at the prospect. I got her phone number, ostensibly so I could call her in advance when I wanted to return the file, and on the way home I suggested to Flint I might help him with his memoirs, not as a ghostwriter but as a legman.

Through all of this maneuvering, I felt a little guilty: here I was working on my social life and the problem of my time-traveling fellow writer had turned much more serious. He obviously hadn't yet made his trip into the past, or if he had, he'd become a fourth-dimensional commuter. And when he went back there again, his life would be cut off prematurely, blindsided by disease. I not only needed to find out which member of my writers' group was the time traveler, but I had to stop him from going. I could save a life here, and surely tampering with the literary career of Frank Paulsen wouldn't change history in a way it couldn't snap back from. But how could I do it?

That evening, I called Bill Wandsworth. "Bill, I have a favor to ask."

"Yeah?"

"Postpone your foofendorker one more meeting."

"Aw, Justin, I got two things ready to read, and they kind of work together."

"Trust me. It's important I read a story at this meeting."

"Why?"

"Something is going to happen, and I don't know when it's going to happen, and I want to stop it from happening."

"Oh, well, that really clarifies things," he said. "Sure, okay. If it's important, I'll take your word for it."

"One other thing. Don't say anything about 'Parsley Sage, Rosemary, and Time.' "

"What are you talking about?"

"I mean 'Time Trampler.' Don't say anything about 'Time Trampler.' "

"I mentioned it at the last meeting, though."

"You mentioned Frank Paulsen and a pulp story, but you didn't say anything about the theme of the story. Keep it that way."

"Okay, got it. Not a word."

What I wrote up for the meeting over the next couple of nights was something like what you're reading now, but it was shorter, read like fiction, and didn't have any specific references to the members of the writers' group. It did include the key point I wanted to make: the peril to a time traveler of unforeseen viruses.

We met at Judy Klinger's house, surprisingly catless and uncutesy, though she offered a rich chocolate fudge along with the traditional cookies. Throughout the evening, especially when I read my story, I kept an eye on one member of the group. By that time, I'd put a couple of things together and was pretty sure who my time traveler was. But I thought it would be better to have him come to me than for me to accuse him outright. When I finished reading, I told the group I wasn't sure how the story should end, and could anybody help me? Feel free to see me privately, if so. And, yes, someone took the bait, pulled me to one side as we were all going out to our cars, asked me to meet him at a nearby twenty-four-hour coffee shop. We both ordered coffee, the real stuff.

Now I was looking across the table at Frank Paulsen, and he told me his story.

"I hate the twenty-first century, you know. I'm not quite forty, but I feel that my century is over, and everything is downhill from here. I got to thinking, if only time travel were possible and I could go back to another, better time." He smiled. "Not to the Crusades or ancient Rome or the Middle Ages or Elizabethan England or anything like that. For one thing, I wouldn't be equipped to speak the language or follow the customs in a way to be seen as anything but a freak. For another, conditions of people, even the very rich, before the twentieth Century would seem unacceptably miserable to any of us, at least those lucky enough to be born middle class in the developed world. And although I didn't think to apply them to a time so recent, I did consider the medical aspects. I figured if I went back too far, some long-forgotten or long-defeated plague would get me as soon as I stepped out of my time machine."

Of course, I jumped on that. "Then there is a machine?"

He smiled slyly. "Figure of speech. I can't tell you exactly how it works, except to say the version in my story is seriously over-simplified. It started when I got into a talk with a physicist over at the university one evening. We hit it off and would get together for a drink occasionally. Over a period of time he started hinting and finally revealed to me that time travel existed, that he in fact had done it, that I could do it, too, if I really wanted to. He said getting back to the starting point had been the hardest part, and the uncertainty of being able to do that had kept him from further experiments. The guy has a family, and he likes the twenty-first century, can you imagine? I replied that I had no people, no real ties to the world we live in, and that I would not be coming back. If I keep my appointment with him, I guess I'll also be keeping that pledge, eh?"

"But you don't have to keep that appointment."

"And what happens if I don't?"

"Probably nothing terrible. I don't think you're suicidal, are you?"

"No, no, I do want to live. Just not in this time. Anyway, I've made all arrangements, packed my bags so to speak, and I'm expected to depart for World War II America a week from now. Tonight would be my last meeting of the writers' group, though obviously I was not about to say so."

"Why World War II? An odd period to choose."

He shrugged. "Safe enough on the home front, and at least I know we win. I would have to change my name, of course. Landing in America of the forties with the name Axel Gruber might draw some unwelcome attention, don't you think? I had my name all picked out, and that's why I was alarmed when that figure skating jump was mentioned at one of our meetings. Bill had said the author of the pulp story that won his bet was Frank Paulsen, and I didn't want Grace to tell everybody the axel was named after a Swedish skater named Axel Paulsen. I'd borrowed my pulp-writing surname from him and the forename Frank from a pulp-writing namesake of mine, though no relation that I know of, Frank Gruber." He looked at me humorously across the table. "You figured that out, didn't you?'

"Yes," I confessed. "I looked up axel in the dictionary after that meeting. It was a short jump—pardon the pun—to the Gruber part."

"I had always had some writing talent, though no one would know it from those dreadful poems I made you people suffer through. And I figured writing would be a sure way to make a living in another time without drawing too much attention to myself, at least at first. If I could do a little subtle plagiarism from writers who came later, it would help me sell my work, and I couldn't imagine it would really hurt them. When I heard about your writers' group, I thought I could gather some pointers, especially from you and Bill, who seemed to know the writing world I wanted to enter. But I wanted to reveal as little of myself as possible. I heard your group lacked a poet, and I thought that persona would be the easiest to fake. I used to act in college, and playing a role is fun for me, so I made Axel Gruber as obnoxious as possible. My scientist friend over at the university is understandably secretive, and I didn't want to the whole project to blow up in our faces, so to speak."

"Did you actually write those stories in 1943?"

"I haven't been there yet. But no, I've been stockpiling them to take with me, assuming that's possible. Since they got in print, I guess it is."

"Why the anachronisms?"

"Not intentional. 'Shrink' was just a slip."

"And the references to the group? Foofendorker and Fred's compost heap?"

"Just playfulness, like a message in a bottle in the timestream? Chances were you'd never come across it, and I'd be long gone from this time anyway."

"But you're not going now, are you?"

"Perhaps I have to. Perhaps I have no choice, having already made my mark on the past." He looked at me for a moment and shook his head. "No, I won't go. You've saved my life, Justin. Doomed me to live it in the twenty-first century, but saved it nonetheless. I'll call my scientist friend and tell him to find another guinea pig. What do you think the consequences will be, though? Will we wake up in the morning and find we lost World War II because the literary career of Frank Paulsen never happened?"

"I doubt it," I said.

"And what will we remember? What will the other people you've talked to about Frank Paulsen remember? Will the two of us even remember this conversation, or will our memories be erased?"

"We'll see," I said with a shrug.

"Or not," Axel said. "It's sort of like death. Either you wake up tomorrow with new insights, or everything disappears and it doesn't really matter."

As it turned out, I remembered everything (or I wouldn't have been able to tell this story) and I imagine Axel Gruber did, too, though he never mentioned it again. As for the others, the best way I can put it is that they all sort of remembered.

When I woke up the day after the meeting and found the file on Frank Paulsen was not on my desk where I'd left it, I didn't think for a moment it had been stolen or I'd mislaid it. I was sure the old pulpster's career was over, that is, had never happened.

C. Hardy Flint remembered our discussion of "Parsley Sage, Rosemary and Time," but only as a story idea I'd told him about, not as a real-time event. And he agreed to let me help him with his memoirs. When I called Elizabeth to arrange a time to come and search through his files, I said casually, "It's nice of you to store those for your grandfather. You probably have no interest in the old pulps."

After a pause, that musical voice said, "I think my favorites are Norbert Davis, Murray Leinster, and Fredric Brown."

Now I knew I was in love—but I'd better not introduce her to Bill Wandsworth.

Speaking of Bill, I had a call from him at work the day after my talk with Axel Gruber. "Okay, Justin," he said. "I'm licked. I'm ready to pay off that bet. I was sure I had a reference to 'shrink' in one of my pulps, but damned if I can find it. Meet me at Liam's and I'll pay you."

When he handed over the ten that evening, I pondered: was this the same ten I gave him when I thought I'd lost the bet, which meant I'd broken even? Or had I now never given him that ten, which meant I was ten dollars ahead? Another time travel paradox.

A BETTER PLACE

Linda P. Baker

"You're not really stupid, you know?"
     When Old Jerry said it, I was looking at the
lines and fractures of skin that surrounded his eyes.
Gram had an old bowl that she said had belonged to
her grandma, and it had lines like that in it. She called
it crazed, the lines that branches and connected, then
branched again. I had always liked to sit and look at
it, to try to follow one of those jaggedy lines to its end.
But even when I used my fingers to help my eyes along,
I never seemed to find an end.

Old Jerry turned his blue gaze on me. "You know?"
he repeated, forcing me to think about what he'd said,
instead of thinking about his crazed face.

"I guess," I said, turning my face to the sky. It was
a rare warm, almost windless day, and I could almost
see the sun through the clouds. It looked blue, like Old
Jerry's eyes. "Gram always said I caught to things
quick. It just don't seem to work the same here."

"It works just the same here, and don't you let nobody fool you into thinking different."

Gnash was gone the day I found Old Jerry lying in
the street, dying.

The old man was in the gutter, so still and blue at

126

first I thought he was dead. Dead ones were nothing unusual, but it was better not to go near them. Don't go near the dead ones. All kinds of things could come from the dead ones, bugs and disease and worst of all, dreams where the dead one's face chases you through a fog. But then Old Jerry groaned.

For a stupid, helpless moment, I stood looking down at the old man. Gnash wouldn't like it if I helped the old man, but then I remembered Old Jerry telling me I wasn't stupid.

Good thing Gnash was gone, then. Not gone on one of his mads, but gone to take care of some "bizness." When he said "biz-z-zness" with that particular whirr in his voice, it meant I didn't want to know what kind of business. And even if I had been bold enough to ask, all it would have got me was a slapping.

Old Jerry was dirty and cold, and when I turned him over, his eyes rolled back up his head. But he knew my name. He whispered it as I tried to get him up. He was one of the few who did know my name. Most just called me "girl," or "Gnash's girl." I never thought of myself as Gnash's. But it didn't hurt for others to think I was. He was sneaky and mean and he knew a lot of people's secrets. He got by, and so long as people thought I was Gnash's girl, I got by right alongside him.

Old Jerry roused enough to help me get him on his feet. Even with him helping, I didn't have the strength to get him up the stairs to our place on the third floor. I got tired of walking the stairs, but only a crazy would choose a ground-level squat. Too easy to break into. Too easy to wake up in the dark of night with some-one sitting on your chest, pressing a bottle dagger to your throat.

A few steps at a time, propping Old Jerry on the wall when he started to slide down, I got him into the first room on the bottom floor. It had once been many rooms, but now was just a big one with the bones showing. The walls had long been knocked down and burned for heat, the windows broken out for knives. The bars over the windows were still there, rusted over but still straight. The cloth on the floor was long gone, too, also burned, so that I had to let the old man slide down the wall and slump over on cold, hard concrete.

His coat, an old leather thing so worn that the filling showed through, was only on one arm. After a minute of struggling with him, I decided it would be easier to take it off than to get it all the way on, so I rolled him and shoved and pulled until it came loose. He was wearing a couple of old T-shirts beneath, the writing so faded on the top one I couldn't tell what it had once said. His arms were thinner than mine and soft, like rubbery sticks poking out of the thin black cotton. I wrapped the coat around him.

I risked leaving him alone long enough to run upstairs for a blanket and a tin can of water.

The old man had rolled over on his back by the time I got back to him. He clutched the old coat across his chest, and his breathing was labored and wet sounding. My boots grated on the floor as I moved, and the sound woke him. His eyes were blue, like my gram's, like the summer sky. I hadn't seen the sky blue much; it was mostly gray, or fuzzy white with rain, or pitch black at night.

He smiled at me as I shucked off my jacket and made a pillow of it for him. The shirt I had on underneath was a frilly thing with long ruffled sleeves, and it didn't keep out much of the cold.

I shivered as I helped him raise his head to take a couple of sips of water, but then he choked and fell back coughing. The sound was gurgly, and I realized what was wrong with him. He had the water sickness, Gram called it "new-something." I couldn't remember the word, just that Granpa Summerlin had died of it the year I turned twelve. Twasn't nothing to be done for it, although Gram said there used to be meds for it.

When he'd stopped coughing, Old Jerry reached out and caught my hand. His grip was stronger than it should have been for someone who sounded like he had mud in his chest. His voice was as spindly as his arms. "Came to . . . say . . . goodbye," he gasped, then let go of my hand and started coughing again.

"Shh-h-h-h . . ." I dipped the ruffled end of my sleeve in the water and wiped off the worst of the dirt on his forehead and cheeks and the spittle that had bubbled up on his lips. "Sh-h-h . . . don't talk so. You just need a rest out of the wind."

He paused in his coughing long enough to look at me with one of those piercing old-person expressions. The kind they use to tell you just how stupid a thing you just said was. "Want you to have my treasure," he said, his voice suddenly plain as could be. Then he closed his eyes and went to sleep.

"Treasure, girl, is in here," Old Jerry tapped his head, "or here," and then his heart.

We were sitting on a broken piece of concrete that had once been shaped like a long chair, looking at the street before us, a river of shiny, wet black that spilled off in four directions. A mangy-looking dog was sniffing through a pile of rubble across the way. I wondered how he'd managed to live this long without being eaten.

"There's those who think treasure's something to put in your pocket. A shiny trinket, or a sharp knife. But you know that ain't right."

Most of Old Jerry's talk was cryptic, filled with things long past, things long forgotten. Things he didn't remember that his parents or his grandparents had told him. But he understood the things I knew, about the land and wind and the mountains. Said he'd come down himself, after his wife died. Like me, he hadn't wanted to live up there alone. He understood when I said I couldn't bear to watch the trees die. So I'd come down out of the mountains, into the city, to see if I could find a better place.

I wrapped my arms around myself to keep warm while he slept. He didn't sleep easy. He kept waking himself up, coughing and mumbling words that I couldn't understand. I tried to talk to him, but he didn't know me, or even where he was.

I didn't know much about him, except that he was one of the ones who didn't put down a bedroll in any one spot for long. He kept moving from place to place, drifting, searching. I sorta understood it, but then I didn't. I'd come down out of the mountains searching, but from the tiny sliver of the world I'd seen, one place was much like the other, gray and dying. Some places were going slowly, some quietly, some with lots of shouting and bleeding, but all were dying, just the same. I wasn't happy here, just glad to be in a place where the dying was quieter.

I regretted now that I'd never asked him what he was searching for. "One more story," I whispered to him and stroked his hot forehead. It was what I used to say to my Gram, when she was trying to get me to settle and go to bed. "Just one more story and then you can sleep."

As the light outside turned the medium gray of afternoon, he seemed weaker. His coughing was harder, but it seemed to move him less, like his body was letting go of all that breathing and living stuff. His voice grew weedy, but easier to understand.

I could pick out words in the mumblings. "Green" and "the" and "scorpion." My name. And "treasure." Still he mumbled about his treasure. I supposed that what passed for treasure down under wouldn't be much. Dry boots. A tin of fish, maybe. Socks without holes.

I kept washing his face with my sleeve, thinking how mad Gnash would be if he caught me using precious rainwater for a dying old man. I wondered if I dared use a stick of our wood to start a fire.

There was a decrepit mattress, mostly rusty innards and bits of fluffy guts, in the room across the way. A couple of squatters had slept over there for a couple of nights before Gnash discovered them. If I brought it over and propped it against the window, it'd keep out the worst of the wind. But it would have also shut out the light. Funny, I'd never minded dark in the mountains, but I hated the stifling black of the city. Especially inside.

As the afternoon wore on, I did finally rip a pile of the stuffing out of the mattress and make another quick run upstairs for a light off our firestove. The stuff burned with a horrible smell, a cross between burning hair and melting plastic, but it warmed me through to the bone. Old Jerry paused in his rambling and coughing and turned toward it.

We were sitting by the pond, in a place that still bore a sign that had once said City Park. All but a piece of the y *and the* r *were gone, long ago salvaged to make someone a knife or a spear tip. The water in the pond was a dull green, the same as the sunlight, and skimmed over with an oily, fuzzy skin.*

I watched Old Jerry's hands sketch a story in the air. His fingers were long and pointed at the ends, except for the one that was missing after the second knuckle. The backs were as lined and cracked as his face, and one had a deep scar running along the back of it up into his sleeve. I imagined it crawling up his arm, coming out on his neck, snaking up his cheek to join the deep crater at the corner of his eye.

"You must be very old." The words popped out, interrupting his story of an adventure he'd had over on the carved mountain.

He'd glared at me, then grinned, showing a gap where a tooth was missing, and said "Big girl, you have

*no idea." He'd called me "big girl" for a long time,
until I told him my name, because I towered over him.
I towered over most people, even Gnash, who seemed
bigger because of the way he carried himself.*

Now I said it to Old Jerry again, smoothing my
fingers over his forehead. His skin felt slack, like the
man inside had melted down. "You must be very old."

"What the hell are you doing?!"

I jumped, knocking over the last of the water. I'd
been listening for Gnash, ever since the light started
to die. I'd thought I would hear him starting up the
stairs and have time to stomp the fire, go out into the
hallway and explain before he saw Old Jerry.

I scrambled to my feet, clumsy as I always was
around Gnash. "It's Old Jerry. He's sick."

Gnash pushed past me and killed my little fire with
one stomp of his big boots. "You stupid bitch! I
could see that fire for two blocks. You trying to get
killed?"

I didn't see any way that a fire no bigger than a cat
food tin could be seen out the window, but I didn't
argue. I dropped my gaze.

Gnash was a big bully. I'd known that only two
minutes after meeting him, but so long as I was careful
what I said, he didn't hit me.

"I found him outside. He's real sick. I think he's
dying." I took a quick breath, then held it to keep
myself from babbling more. Gnash didn't like it when
I babbled.

Gnash gave Old Jerry a rough shove with the toe
of his boot, leaving a smear of ash across the edge of
the blanket. "What'd you bring him in here for?
You're just gonna have to drag him out again. He'll
smell up the whole place, and the rats'll come out
for sure."

He reached down to grab Old Jerry by the collar
and the coat came loose in his hand. Gnash tossed it
aside and tried to tug the blanket off Old Jerry, but

it wouldn't come loose. Gnash shoved at him. "Stupid, using a blanket on a sick old coot. He might have something."

"He's got wet lungs. You can't catch it."

This made Gnash braver, and he shoved Old Jerry onto his back and tried to yank the blanket free, but the old man had twisted it up in his gnarled old hands, and he didn't let go easily.

"Don't!" I protested before I thought.

Gnash wheeled on me, his face red and his teeth bared. Any minute now, he'd be doing the thing that got him his name, gnashing his teeth in anger. Fists were never too far behind the grinding teeth.

I didn't like that he was between me and the door.

"Stupid bitch! Why not? It's my blanket. Who said you could bring anybody in here anyway? I never told you that you could." He kicked the empty can, exposing the telltale spot of wet on the concrete. His face got even redder. "You wasted water on him?!"

His voice was like a thunderclap. Worse than a thunderclap, because I knew thunder. This I didn't know how to handle. He'd taught me lots of things about surviving in the bricks, but not what to do to stop the yelling.

He took a step forward and I took one backward. I was taller than he, but when he was like this, I felt like I was three feet tall. I felt like he was burning up all the air in the room, sucking all the blood out of my muscles. He slapped me, open handed. If it had been his fist, my cheekbone would have split instead of just the skin over it. I fell, landing hard on my ass, but I didn't make a sound.

Gnash liked it better when he got a sound out of a blow. He was raising his fist when Old Jerry coughed, a terrible one that sounded like his lungs must be coming up, and he mumbled, "Treasure."

Gnash froze.

Shamed to the bone for what I was doing, I leaped at an excuse that would keep me from a beating.

"That's why I brought him in. He kept saying something about treasure. I knew you'd want to talk to him. I knew . . ." My voice ran down as I scrambled to figure out what I knew. What I could convince Gnash that I knew. "He was in the street outside. I was afraid somebody'd come along and hear him before you got back."

And then I ran out of "I knews" and of breath, and I sat there, gasping, waiting to see if my excuse was good enough. A trickle of blood dripped off my jaw and onto my shirt. I felt it, a blossom of warmth against my chest.

Gnash turned slowly to Old Jerry. Went to one knee and grabbed the old man by his shoulder. Shook him roughly and growled at him. "Treasure. What treasure, old man?"

"Don't." And when Gnash glared at me again, "You'll make him cough. He can't talk when he's coughing." But I was too late.

Old Jerry twitched as if he'd been hit in the gut and coughed so hard that snot and blood spewed out of his mouth. Gnash cursed and fell back onto his ass. I would have laughed if I hadn't been so horrified by the sounds Old Jerry was making, like bricks crashing against each other but with a sucking wet sound added.

I crawled to him and struggled to turn him onto his side.

The rest of the slime burbled out of Old Jerry's mouth onto the jacket under his face. My jacket. The whole mass was mostly blood shot through with streaks of yellow-green. I swallowed. I'd never be able to wear that again. It made my stomach churn to touch him and risk getting some of that slime on me. Since my jacket was ruined anyway, I teased one of the sleeves from under his chin and used it to wipe his face.

He mumbled something but the words were garbled.

"Ask him about the treasure," Gnash said, poking me in the back.

I wanted to tell him to ask himself, but I didn't want another slap. "Jerry, hey . . . Old man . . ." My shirt sleeve was barely damp now, but still cool. I patted his fevered face with it, careful not to get near his mouth. I didn't want any of that slime on me, any more than Gnash did. "Talk to me."

"Ask him," Gnash hissed.

Old Jerry opened his eyes. For a moment, I thought he was going to just come right out of his stupor and start talking. His gaze went to the cut on my face, or at least, I imagined it did. I raised my hand up to it, trying to cover the blood.

"Do you think there's a better place?"

We were at my favorite place in the city, at the edge of a field. It used to be called a "green," according to Old Jerry. The only green in the city now was the occasional weed poking up through the trash, and even then, it was more a sickly yellowish green.

"A better place than what, girl?"

I waved my hand all around us. "Than this. Gram said she was sure there a better place. That's why she told me to come down. But . . . I don't think this was what she meant."

Facing the green was a building with all its rooms showing. Its wall had fallen into a heap at its feet, leaving all the rooms inside showing. It looked like a bunch of little boxes, stacked one on top of the other. I liked imagining that each box had its own color, and furniture and pictures on the wall, just like the pictures in Gram's books.

In our box, Gram and I sat in a room painted the color of Old Jerry's eyes. Gram was clacking her knitting needles together, making a sweater with all the colors of the rainbow. I was sitting on the floor, surrounded by books. I loved books.

We'd had a few books, and I'd brought my two fa-
vorites with me when I came down. But Gnash had
burned them two hard, cold months ago last winter. I'd
grieved to see them go, but Gnash was right. Better
warm without books than dead with them. I could recite
them by rote, but it wasn't the same as it was to holding
the pages between my fingers, as smelling the papery,
dusty scent.

I came out of my reverie to find Old Jerry smiling at
me in a queer way. Like I'd just said something stupid.

"I'm sure your Gram must be right," was all he said.

Old Jerry looked up at me. His fingers moved,
creaky, like he wanted to reach out. But he just
croaked, "You know." Then his mouth twisted up,
and his eyes rolled up in his head and he gave one
last, long sigh. A horrible, gurgling one. Then he went
limp under my fingers.

Slowly, I closed his eyes. And my own. Hot tears
stung the backs of my eyelids. I tried to blink them
away. I hadn't cried since my Gram died, even with
all that had happened, and I'd promised myself I never
would again. Yet here I was crying over a crazy old
man, who hadn't even believed his own stories. How
could he say treasure didn't matter, then act like it
did in the end?

Gnash reached over me and poked Old Jerry, apparently brave enough to touch him now that there
was little chance of being spewed on. "Shit!"

He got up and dragged me to my feet by one arm.
He adjusted his fingers to a better grip and shook me.

There'd be finger-shaped bruises on the soft under-
side of my arm tomorrow.

"So what is this treasure? Where is it?" Gnash
demanded.

"I don't know."

Gnash shook me again, harder this time. "He said
you did."

I tried to pry his fingers off my arm. "He was crazy

out of his mind with fever. I don't know anything about any treasure." I reached down pulled the blanket up over Old Jerry's face.

Gnash was distracted enough that he didn't even protest.

I picked up the jacket Old Jerry had been wearing. It was a fair exchange, I guess. Maybe more than fair. The leather was worn, but it at least had a good thick padding. I could stick my finger through the holes in mine.

Gnash squeezed my arm again, leaving a new row of fingerprints on my forearm. "Don't bullshit me, stupid. I seen you talking to him lots of times."

"I talked to him. But he was like all the old ones. Always talking about the befores, you know, and—"

"The befores!" Gnash looked suddenly bright-eyed and avid. He let go of my arm. "Maybe he had a stash somewhere. Of old stuff."

It was a dream most people had . . . the fantasy of finding a stash of before stuff, cans of food and fancy stoves that ran on gassed air and shiny metal knives. Treasure. Always treasure.

I didn't think the idea held much water. "Old Jerry wouldn't have drifted in and out, lived down under, if he had better."

Gnash narrowed his eyes at my daring to question him, but I guess even he thought it made sense. I slipped the jacket on. Maybe its thick padding would protect my arms from Gnash's bruising grip.

I looked at the lump of leftover man covered in an old blanket and was shamed. There I stood, following along with Gnash's train of thought, admiring the jacket I'd salvaged, when its former owner lay dead at my feet.

I was determined to drag the body away somewhere and bury it. That's the least I could do for him. It was so cold, I didn't think the smell would bother us for a while. But it would draw dogs and cats, and worse, those on two legs looking for an easy meal, would come skulking around.

I swallowed. Death and feeding . . . that was all part of life. Someday, I'd be dead, too, and something would feed on me so that it could go on living. Even if Gnash bothered to bury me, even then it would be worms.

Somewhere there had to be something better. I'd thought that here would be better when I'd left the mountains. But I'd been wrong. It was different, but it wasn't better. In fact, it was maybe worse. In the mountains, I'd looked after myself. In the mountains, I knew what was safe and what wasn't. I hadn't needed anyone like Gnash to show me the ways of living and dying.

"You know . . . there's other places, girl. There's places where a smart girl like you could make her way."

I thought he was making fun of me, playing back at me the stuff I'd told him my gram had said. That had been right after the time I locked myself out of the building. Some smart girl that was. I'd set in the hall, blue with cold and shaking with hunger, for two days until Gnash came back.

"Maybe . . ." I said, but let my voice die away as I thought. Maybe . . .

"What?"

I jumped a little at Gnash's voice. I'd almost forgotten he was there. I wasn't used to him being interested in anything I had to say. "Maybe the treasure's in his stuff."

Gnash looked at me with what I now recognized as stupidity. Why'd I ever think this guy was smart? But he was smart. About how to stay alive. How to find stuff that other people wanted. How to make people beholden.

"In his stuff," I repeated. "Where he flops."

"Where does he flop?"

"He's a drifter," I cracked, exasperated. "Where do you think?"

Gnash didn't like that. He didn't like that one bit. His eyes narrowed and his punching fist clenched.

I backed away quickly and looked down. "Sorry."

Gnash didn't say anything, but his fist unclenched. "So?"

"Down under. He lived down under. I don't know . . . down under." I thought for a minute, chewing the inside of my cheek. "But I know some of his buds when I see them."

Gnash nodded slowly, thinking, his face pulled sideways like he was chewing on the inside of his cheek, too. "Okay," he said finally. "Let's do it."

Gnash went upstairs before we left. He came back carrying a bat. I knew what made the pocket of his coat look so bulky . . . ragged pieces of crete, slipped into the toe of a sock. I'd laughed to myself the first time I'd seen him pocket his special weapon, but then I'd seen him use it. I hadn't laughed afterwards.

The walk to the underground was different. I hadn't been outside at night since my first days in the city. Everything looked strange in the dark. Colder and bigger. The wind still slammed down the tunnel of the street, but it sounded different. Darker. At some intersections, we could see by fires set in drums. There were people dancing around them, or standing with their hands held out to the flames. Gnash walked quick, keeping to the middle of the street, only slowing a little when we moved into the pitch black away from the fires.

I'd never been down under before. I'd expected to have to go down. Instead we walked across a big empty space that was mostly lumps of black street pocked with holes where the red dirt showed through. One step, we were outside with a bit of moon showing through the clouds to light the way, the next we were inside, in the dark, like in a cave.

Gnash stopped just where the gray light turned to black, his breath hard and fast. For the first time since I'd met him, I saw he was as scared as me. I'd never seen it before. Maybe because I'd been so scared myself. Maybe he was scared all the time, just like I was.

He saw me staring at him, and he snarled, "What you looking at, stupid?"

And I heard Old Jerry's voice, saying, "You're not really stupid, you know." Only this time, it didn't sound so much like a question as he was telling me. I just shook my head at Gnash and stepped into dark.

There was only a little ways where we couldn't see where we were going, but it felt like a long ways. I put my hands out and slid my feet, just going little baby steps forward, and I could only have taken a few steps when I realized I could see again. Just a little at first, then I could see better.

Buildings. Well, not buildings exactly. More like . . . houses. Little houses, like the one Gram and me had lived in, shoved up against each other. Some still had signs above the doors. "Candy Kitchen" and "Souvenirs" and "Victoria's."

There were fires in barrels and laying bare on the ground, just like above, except down here, they left a smoky, sooty feel to the air. The smell made my head start to hurt. We edged around them, keeping to the shadows, away from the people hunched around the fires.

Then, we turned a corner, and we were facing a picture. A whole wall filled with pictures taller than my head. Like a picture in a book, only lots bigger. One showed a small mountain with black clouds rolling out of the top and across. The next one showed a bigger mountain with fire pouring out of it. The pictures were faded, but the fire still looked hot enough to burn.

"So how did it happen?"
Old Jerry had taken me way up top of one of the

*buildings. I was out of breath from all the climbing,
but tickled by the view. It was like being at Old Charlie's Bunion, except instead of bare dirt and scraggly
trees, I could see hills and paths made of crete. They
rolled up and down and snaked all around each other
until I got dizzy trying to follow one to its end.*

"Did what, girl?"

*I waved my hand all around us. "This? All this?
There's so many paths and roads . . . there must have
been lots more people here, before. What happened to
all of them? All my gram would ever say was it was
'man's inhumanity to man.' But I never knew what
that meant."*

*Old Jerry looked around. At the piles of rubble and
the couple of people we could see, walking along one
of the wide roads. On the top of a building a few streets
over, there were three or four young ones. You didn't
see young ones much anymore. They were beating on
a big pipe with sticks and yelling. Their skinny, young
voices echoed at us from a dozen directions.*

*Old Jerry said, "The way I heard it, it didn't start
with men being mean. A mountain blew up."*

*"A mountain blew up! I never seen no mountain
blow up."*

*He shrugged. "Me neither, but that's the way it was
told to me. A yellow mountain blew up. And then another mountain blew up. And then people started to
get mean. Hurting each other, killing each other over
treasures. And I don't reckon they've much learned
their lessons yet."*

Gnash prodded me with his bat. "What does it
say?"

I looked away from the picture to where he was
standing. At the bottom of the picture, there was writing. I read it, puzzling over a couple of words that
didn't make much sense. "On March 29, 2005, the
volcano under Yellowstone National Park, long
thought to be dormant, erupted, bleeding a river of

red hot lava and spewing clouds of ash and gas into the atmosphere."

"You can read."

The voice came from right behind me, and I jumped, wheeling so fast I knocked Gnash into the picture wall. He wheeled back, brandishing his bat.

The old man who stood facing me didn't seem too dangerous, but I wasn't any good at telling.

"Yes," I said slowly. Didn't seem like much point in saying no, since he'd heard me read it.

"Don't remember seeing anybody young as you in down under before." He smiled as he said it, but he was watching Gnash and the upraised bat.

He sounded like Old Jerry, like he just wanted to talk, but before I could say anything, Gnash stepped forward.

"We're looking for Old Jerry's flop." It was his mean voice. The one he used around people he wanted to scare.

The smile left the old man's face. His hand shifted to his hip, hovering near a knife on his belt. "I don't know you." His voice was a bit louder this time. There was two old men and an old woman several feet away, sitting on bedrolls. One of them climbed slowly to his feet.

Gnash shifted slightly on his feet, gave me an ungentle shove to the side, one of his hands moving toward his pocket.

I could tell something bad was about to happen. An old guy who probably had never done anything worse than steal food was going to get socked.

I could hear Gnash's teeth grinding against each other.

"Look," I took a step in, putting myself part way between them and Gnash. "Old Jerry's a friend of mine. He's—" I was about to tell them he was dead, but maybe they'd want to go through his stuff, too. "He told us we could stay down here tonight." I searched around, trying to salvage a thought in my brain, some excuse for what we were doing down here.

The old man squinted at me, like closing his eyes down would make him see better in the dark. "You're that mountain girl. Old Jerry talked about you."

A bit of the tension between my shoulders eased. At my back, I could feel Gnash relax a little, too. "Yes. Yes." I realized I sounded a bit too eager, so I took a breath and started over. "Yes, I came down from the mountains." I pointed. Silly. Like they could see outside to the hills.

Old Jerry's friend squinted at us again. There was a long quiet. The other man, the one who'd stood up, came ambling over. But I had the feeling he wasn't as easy as he looked. Just as he got close, the old man pointed toward a dark hole in the wall about twenty feet away. "Over there. And don't you go messing in Old Jerry's things. He's real particular about them."

I nodded. "Thank you, sir. We won't."

When I turned, Gnash was halfway there already.

I shrugged and smiled at the two old men, noticing how much they looked like Old Jerry. Leathery skin, faded eyes, stooped shoulders. Yet, just like him, they looked hard. Like that leather that had aged and toughened.

I could feel their eyes on my back as I hurried after Gnash. I had a scared thought, just as I slipped into the narrow space behind him. I was wearing Old Jerry's jacket. What if they recognized it? What if they thought to wonder why? They might think we'd killed Old Jerry for his treasure.

I peeked back out, but they'd gone back to their fire.

Gnash was already searching, pawing Old Jerry's bedroll aside to see if there was anything under it.

There wasn't much to Old Jerry's stuff. There was a box, made out of real wood, standing on its side, and it had books in it! I wondered how he'd kept them from burning it all. Two books and a piece of paper folded many times, with lots of writing and squiggles on it. It took me a minute to recall the name of it. A map. Maybe it was a map to a better place.

Except . . . if there was a better place, why was Old Jerry here? He'd talked about all his drifting. About the places he went, and they hadn't sounded any better than Lanta. Places like Columbus, the city where the man who discovered the States lived. And Birm, where if you had the right kind of trade goods, you could still get a real metal knife. And down into the Panhan, where you could eat as much fish as you wanted, if you could just catch them. But you had to eat a piece and wait a while to see if it made you sick. One of the other drifters hadn't listened to the locals and had gorged himself. He'd died of the fire sickness, with big pieces of his skin falling off wherever he touched himself.

Having as much to eat as you wanted had sounded pretty good to me, but then Old Jerry said fish was all they had. The plants there were dying, just like in the mountains. I asked why he drifted there, and he laughed and said for the tan, which didn't make any sense. But lots of Old Jerry's talk was like that.

A second bedroll stood on its end at the back of the little room. A pair of run-over shoes, crusted with red dirt, stood beside it. There were a couple of empty tins, large enough to hold a tiny fire. A cup with not enough water in it to even wet my lips.

Gnash grabbed the books, riffled their pages roughly, looking for something in between. He tossed the first one aside.

It hurt my heart to see it treated so rough, and I stepped over Gnash, sat down on the bedroll and rescued the book. I grabbed the second book before he could throw it and hugged them to my chest. These were treasure enough for me, and I'd be damned before I'd let Gnash burn them.

Gnash glared, then forgot me as he reached into the corners of the box. His eyes went big and round and white as polished river rocks. He drew out a piece of cloth. Even in the dim light, I could see it was as fine as anything I'd ever seen in my life. It was green, green as mountain grass, and it had a sheen to it like oil and a gold thread running through it.

I held my breath right along with Gnash as he unfolded the small square. I blinked my eyes, expecting whatever was inside would be as bright as the beautiful threads. But when he folded back the last corner of cloth, there was only brown. Little brown shapes with darker brown shapes like caps. My breath caught behind my heart.

Gnash cursed, as good a curse as any I'd ever heard, and stared at the small pile of brown shapes in the middle of the cloth. His lip curled. "What's this crap?"

I knew. I knew. My breath wouldn't go out past my throat. My fingernails were digging into my palms, and the books lay forgotten on my knees. "Nuts," I breathed. "They're from a tree."

Before I could stop him, he popped one into his mouth and bit down on it. It came out faster than it went in. He spat it onto Old Jerry's bed roll. "You trying to kill me, bitch?!"

"You don't eat them, silly. Well, you can, but they have to be cooked first."

I picked up the small ball, slick with spit. It was mangled. He'd bitten it in half, then chomped down on it. Ruined.

Gnash grabbed my hand, making me drop the ruined mass. "What did you call me?" His voice was low, more dangerous than it had been the night he'd beat the guy with the rock.

The breath I'd lost in excitement came whooshing

back out in fear. As if to remind me, my cheek throbbed.

"I didn't—" Before I could finish, fire exploded across the same place. The blow knocked me back onto the pallet. Gnash had moved so fast I hadn't even seen it coming. I could feel the skin around my eye pulling tight as blood rushed into it.

Gnash drew back to hit me again with one hand and flung the treasure at my face with the other.

Anger, hot as the fire in the picture, raced over me. It was like those little brown balls, hitting my face and my chest, had been sucked through my skin. Like they had lit a fire in my chest, stiffened my backbone. Gnash didn't see my fist coming, any more than I'd seen his.

Fire exploded over my knuckles as they smashed into his nose. It felt like I'd broken my hand. My eyes and my mouth watered with the pain.

He yelped and rocked back, the expression on his face almost funny as blood poured down over his mouth.

I wanted to moan, to cradle my hand and rock and cry. No one had ever told me it hurt so much to hit someone. Small wonder that Gnash preferred rocks and bats and such. But I couldn't afford to be weak and stupid now. I stood up and picked up his bat before he could think to do it. "You go. Go now," I said, and I could hear Gnash's meanness in my voice. Old Jerry had taught me more than I knew, and so had Gnash.

Fear slid across his face.

Joy and something I couldn't name, something hot and laughing, rushed into my chest like water pouring over rocks. The bat trembled in my hand.

Gnash stood up slowly. His hand slid toward his pocket.

I steadied the bat. "Go now. Before I call Old Jerry's friends."

For a minute, I was afraid he wasn't going to do

it. I was afraid he was going to fight me. I knew I couldn't beat him. I was taller, but he was stronger. I was clumsy and he was quick. He knew how to fight dirty, and I didn't know how to fight at all. But maybe my fiery new backbone would count for something. I wouldn't go down quietly, the way I had so many times before. Maybe he saw that in my face.

He made one snarling last attempt to save face. "You think those old coots gonna look after you like I do? What you gonna do now? Stay down here?"

I lifted the bat a little higher.

He backed away, gnashing so hard I could hear the bones of his teeth grinding together. Blood was still pouring out of his nose, and his voice was beginning to sound squashed. "I shoulda left you in the street. How long you think you're gonna live without me to protect you, stupid?"

"My name," I said slowly, "is Rosemary."

He reached down and snatched up the piece of fancy cloth, swiped at the blood on his face. He wheeled around and stomped away, flinging a few last words over his shoulder. "Don't come begging back tomorrow."

I started to shake. So hard that I had to sit down. The bat hit the floor only a little harder than my butt did. Then I snatched it up again, crawled to the edge of the room and snaked a quick look.

Gnash was way across the large room, beginning the trek back to above. He had one hand up to his face.

When I was sure he wasn't coming back, I crawled around the space, gathering Old Jerry's treasure. My treasure now.

My gram had loved the old oak trees above all other living things on this world, save for me. I'd thought the trees were dying, but somewhere, in one of Old Jerry's driftings, he'd found an oak tree that wasn't dying. Maybe that meant there were better places. Places where the earth was starting to live again. My gram had said there would be, if I just had the guts to go looking.

I'd only had pictures. In one of the books Gnash had burned, I'd even marked the page. If he'd ever bothered to look at it, he'd have known what Old Jerry's treasure was . . .

Acorns. Five precious acorns.

CHAOS THEORY

Stephen Leigh

"**P**rofessor?"

Damian glanced up from his laptop. "Oh, hey, Sarah. Come on in. Here . . ." He snatched the pile of books from the other chair in the small office and leaned them against the side of the desk. "Excuse the mess."

As she sat, he saw her glance move from the stacks of papers and folders on his desk to the haphazardly packed bookcase behind him, where the books lay in archeological layers. "Don't worry. I've seen the other professors' offices. Is it a rule that you all have to have to fill every available inch with paper and books?"

"It's a bit of an occupational hazard," he answered.

She laughed at the standard reply. "At least I see some science fiction and fantasy in among all that dry stuff. So I guess there's hope for you after all." She was sitting with her thighs pressed together inside the denim skirt that came to just above her knees, her lower legs splayed out to either side, her feet wrapped in low-heeled shoes. She had wonderful legs. Damian had noticed them before, since she generally sat in the front row of his class. Sarah was a nontraditional student, returning to school after some time away. Damian figured her to be in her late twenties; she was an excellent student, attentive and interested, unlike some of the seemingly bored regular students, just out of high school and enrolled in college simply because it was what they were expected to do. One hand was on her lap, the other on the arm of the chair: nails painted a cheerful red. Unlike most of the students, she had no backpack, only a copiously pocketed leather laptop bag such as a corporate manager might carry. She wore several rings, but there were none on the third finger of her left hand. In the small, cramped office, their knees nearly touched.

Unlike half the young women in his classes, who were either anemic in appearance or heavily overweight, Sarah had the appearance of someone who enjoyed food and good times, yet who kept herself in shape. He could imagine her jogging, or perhaps going to a gym a few times a week . . .

He kept his gaze on her face, though. It was safer. Sarah's was a pleasant face with an engaging smile, and eyes that were the color of the Mediterranean Sea in some travel brochure. Damian was certain she wore colored contacts; the blue was too saturated to be real. Her hair was dyed a blonde that verged on white, cropped too short for Damian's taste, the strands closest to her scalp just showing her natural brown. He told himself that the undistinguished hue of her roots would have suited him better.

He smiled at her as he closed the lid of his Powerbook and leaned back carefully on his desk chair; the mechanism was broken and would recline far enough to tip the chair if he wasn't careful. He'd have ordered a new one, but the Arts & Sciences budget, like every other college's budget in the university (but somehow not the athletic department's), had been trimmed to the bone—replacing office furniture was a low priority. "So what's up?" he asked her.

Now that she was sitting, she seemed nervous. One shoulder lifted in a shrug. She started to say something, then closed her mouth and started over. "I wanted to ask you—your lecture this morning . . . I'm curious. Is all that something you really believe?" Her head was cocked slightly to the side, and the smile had been replaced by a more serious expression. They'd had conversations before: she was one of the three or four students who generally lingered a few minutes after class to ask questions about the lecture or just talk, or who came early and chatted with him as he arranged his notes. But she'd never come to his office before.

"It's a hypothesis," he told her. "I'm open to persuasive arguments against it, of course, but yes, I think it's valid. It was the core of my thesis."

"It seems rather . . . cynical. You're what, thirty?"

"Thirty-one."

"I'm twenty-eight. So we're nearly the same age. But I don't think of myself as old—not yet, anyway." Her laugh was self-deprecating and soft. "What you were saying sounded so . . . cynical, and I suppose I equate that with age. You already think that history is written for you and you can't change it. I find that sad."

He was shaking his head. "You misunderstood what I was saying, Sarah. *My* history—or yours—isn't written, and neither is history in general. I'm only saying that the inertia of the past drives the present into the future, and that the momentum and 'weight'—if you don't mind my using that term for something that has no actual weight—of previous events doesn't allow for its course to be changed. It's too big for us to alter. We don't know where history's going, but even if we did we couldn't stop it no matter what we tried. I don't see any cynicism in that."

He stopped. Smiled tentatively. "Slipped into lecture mode there, didn't I? Sorry."

She nodded, returning the smile. She kept eye contact with him; every time he looked away and then back, her gaze was there. He'd noticed that about her in class; she watched him, kept her attention on him.

He found he liked that. They often made eye contact during his lectures. "You don't have to apologize. I've been trying to find an analogy," she said, and her gaze did drop for a moment, almost demurely, before those deepsea pupils returned to him again. "Something to use as a picture. I was thinking: a hurricane is huge, yet their paths can change. Sometimes quickly and radically."

"Sure, but what changes a hurricane's path?" As he often did in class, he answered his own question. "An equally huge force: a high pressure cell sitting in the Midwest, or shearing winds from the jet stream. But one of us . . . As a single person, we can't do anything to affect it. In fact, you could have *everyone* in the hurricane's path try to blow it away, all at once, to no effect. You could turn on every last fan on the entire coastline, and you're not going to change the path by even a foot."

She chuckled at the image he'd painted: a warm, throaty amusement. "So I guess having the Chinese jump up on command won't change the earth's orbit, either? Damn, another illusion gone." They both laughed. "All right, so hurricanes might be a lousy metaphor. But history's all about people. You said that going back in time to kill Hitler's parents before they conceive him wouldn't stop WWII or the Holocaust. How could it not?"

She inclined toward him, her elbows on the arms of the chair and hands cupping her chin. He could smell perfume: faint and floral and pleasant. He started to lean back in the chair, nearly overbalanced and had to bring himself forward abruptly. His face was suddenly a few bare inches from hers.

Her eyes widened, and he sat back quickly, embarrassed. He fiddled with the papers on his desk, rearranging them uselessly. "Sorry. This chair . . ."

"No problem. You were saying, about Hitler?"

"Ah, that . . . I'd argue that the Third Reich wasn't

the result of a person, but a social tsunami. Hitler's
rise was the consequence of political and social forces
at work in Europe and especially in Germany at the
time. If Adolf hadn't been there, someone else would
have been ridden the wave of that movement, someone with essentially the same attitudes and outlooks.
The Nazi Party, or something very much like it, would
still arise, with its dictatorship and imperialistic atti-
tude, and with its scorn and hatred of what it considered 'lesser races.' The same scenes would play out:
changed to some degree, yes, but not altered in any
truly significant manner. History would lumber on following the same path.''

He shifted in his seat and now his foot brushed hers
accidentally; they both moved back, both pretended
not to notice. "With all the standard 'alternate histories,' it's the same," he continued. "Look at the discovery of penicillin. Ernest Duchesne recognized its
antibiotic qualities way back in 1896, but the French
Institut Pasteur ignored the discovery—and even if
they hadn't, I'd contend, something else would have
intervened to keep the discovery quiet. It wasn't time
yet. Had Alexander Fleming failed to notice the penicillin in his lab in 1928, well, then the spores would
have wafted down to contaminate some other scientist's Petri dish—and we'd still get the vaccine. Same
way with more current events: if some circumstance
could somehow have stopped the planes from hitting
the World Trade Center, we'd just experience some
other seminal terrorist attack and still become em-
broiled in a Middle Eastern war. I've done the research, believe me. The currents of social, economic
and political trends are strong; they will sweep away
anything standing in their path. It's analogous to chaos
theory in physics: history as a system appears random
but—like the atmosphere and your hurricanes—is actually just immensely complex: a deterministic system
with no random parameters. If you want justification,

I can give you several references . . . " He started to turn to pull books from the case nearest the desk. Her voice stopped him.

"Lecture mode," she told him. The remonstration was gentle and amused. "You really need to watch that."

"Sorry," he told her. "Again."

"And you still don't need to apologize. I rather like how excited and passionate you sound when you get going. The thing is, you can't *prove* any of that." Her gaze held him, snared. "I mean, I do understand what you're saying and I can see why how you can make the argument and I'll even buy it, to some degree, but ultimately, you can't ever *know*. No one can put history in a cyclotron and break it down."

"No, I suppose we can't—and that's why I'm in the philosophy department, not physics. You're right, there's no experiment we can conduct to prove or disprove the theorem. At least not without a time machine—and even then it's not an experiment I think any rational person would care to make. If I'm right, nothing changes in any significant way. But if I'm *wrong*, then there are wholesale changes, changes we can't control. Of course, time travel isn't possible, so—"

"Actually, the physics department might disagree with that," she interrupted. "String theory." Grinned. "But go on . . ."

He found himself grinning back at her. "Yeah, I've read some of that too. But for now, it all remains a thought experiment."

Her hand brushed his thigh—the barest touch—and then withdrew. He could feel the heat of her skin through his jeans. "It still comes down to this," she said. "You believe in Capital-D Destiny. That story of Bradbury's that you mentioned in class . . ."

He nodded, still feeling the touch. He saw her glance at the bookcase, where *R Is For Rocket* adorned a spine. " 'A Sound of Thunder.' "

"Yes. You'd say that stepping on the butterfly back in the Cretaceous changes nothing. The 'inertia' of history is too great."

"Essentially."

"I don't agree. I think even a single person matters." She pressed her spine against the chair then, abruptly moving away from him, and he found himself sliding forward in response, as if their bodies were bound together with an unseen string.

"Of course you do," he told her. "We *all* want to believe that. Thinking that way comforts us. We all want to feel that we have some power, that we can make a difference, that our lives have some higher purpose and that actions we take can shake the very foundations of the reality around us. I understand that. I just don't believe it."

She leaned in again, and he didn't move. Their faces were very close. "But actually you *do* . . . " She stopped, then, her cheeks coloring as her gaze dropped.

"Go on," he told her.

She looked at him again, though the color heightened on her face. "This is so stupid . . . After class, oh, three weeks ago . . . I remember you joking about being married to the school, that you figured that's just the way it was supposed to be for you. That's why you'd never found someone to be with."

"I said that?" Damian frowned. He supposed it was possible; he vaguely remembered an after-class conversation with several students along those lines. "I don't think—"

Rose bloomed fully on her cheeks, and she laughed, a bit nervously. "The truth is, I didn't come here to talk about this morning. Well, I did in a way." She stopped. Her mouth was still slightly opened.

"What?" he prompted.

She nodded, as if to some inner argument. She bit her lower lip for a moment. "I enjoy talking with you. I like the way you start waving your hands when you're passionate about what you're saying. I like the gentleness I see in your face and your eyes. I like the sympathy I hear in your voice when someone doesn't understand you, and how you try to find a way to make it clear to them. All that tells me a lot about you."

"I . . . I'm not sure—"

"Yes, you are," she told him. "You know what I'm saying."

"Um, Sarah . . . " It wasn't the first time this had happened, that a student had propositioned him—he wasn't entirely unattractive, he knew, and if he was a bit shy around women, well, some women found that to be something they liked. But he'd never in his academic career overstepped the bounds. He'd always immediately squashed any hopes or expectations the student had.

He intended to do that now. "Sarah, I'm sorry, but—"

Her hand touched his. Lingered. He tried to move his hand away but the limb resisted as if it had a will of its own. "Look, I'm not a nineteen-year old, just-out-high-school girl with naïve ideas about life and love, Professor. I've been married and divorced. We're both adults. I don't have any illusions or even any expectations. You might not be interested in me at all, or be involved with someone else, or we might find after a few hours or a few dates that one or the other of us has changed our minds. I don't know. But it's a chance I'd be willing to take. As you said, we don't know what history holds for us."

"You're my student," he persisted, and watched her shake her head, her eyes never leaving his.

"Not any more. Check your class list," she said. "I withdrew this morning. And I won't be taking any other courses from you in the future."

"Sarah, you didn't need to do that . . ."

She smiled, sitting back again. "Yes, I did. I needed you to understand that I'm interested in having the chance to know you better, period. I needed to show you that I'm not hitting on you for a grade. I'm not stalking you. I'm not thinking I'm in love with you, either. I find you interesting, that's all. Nothing more. I think that feeling might be somewhat mutual, too." Her eyebrows raised slightly, her gaze moved from one side of his face to the other. "I'm not here at the university for any other reason than I want to expand my knowledge. I take classes where I think I might learn something interesting. I'm not here just to party or have a good time or get laid or find a husband." She grinned at that. "No matter what you might be thinking right now," she added. "So . . . "

Her hands spread apart. She rose in one lithe movement from the chair, brushing imaginary strands back from her face as she picked up her bag; he wondered how long ago she'd cut that hair. "So I've said what I came to say, finally. Sorry it took me so long, and thanks for the conversation—I enjoyed our talk. If you think that maybe you'd like to continue it, I'll be over at the Boarshead for the next few hours. If you happen to go there yourself to have a beer, I'll be in a booth back by the rear door. If you happen to stop by. Just to talk. I still want to hear your arguments about changing history."

She was already at the door, stepping out into the hallway.

"Sarah—"

She stopped, half-turned to look back at him.

"I think," he said, "I just might be a bit thirsty. I have some papers to grade, but . . ."

Her smile crinkled the corners of her eyes. "Good. You see, maybe one person *can* make a change in how things are supposed to go . . . "

His reading of the student papers was haphazard and rushed: they were for the 101 Intro course, which was all bullshit anyway. He kept smelling Sarah's perfume and hearing her laughter and her voice. He thought of her in the booth at the Boarshead, maybe checking her watch and wondering if she'd made a mistake, maybe getting up to go.

He set his blue Pilot pen aside and stuffed the papers in his briefcase. He told himself he'd get to them later tonight.

Maybe. Depending.

Damian was still thinking of Sarah and how he would meet her tonight and what they might say and what might happen afterward. He left his office, locked the door, and took the elevator down. He went out the main entrance of the building and started across the roadway to the faculty parking lot across the street.

Damian was generally a careful pedestrian. This afternoon, mulling over Sarah and their conversation, he was not.

He never saw the car.

THE MAN IN CELL 91

Gene DeWeese

In the Final Days, when the wretched Earth's population stumbled past fifteen billion and began its inevitable and precipitous descent, the nightmarish visions that had until then been confined to the dream-littered depths of night began to invade the day as well. The mounds of emaciated corpses, writhing and pleading wordlessly, were no longer banished by even the brightest sunlight, but flickered into being with every blink of an eye. The countless forms of death, ranging from suicide to mass murder, administered alternately with soulless savagery and with tearful compassion, with mindless fury and with emotionless indifference, increasingly blotted out the real world, which had not yet completed its plunge into those awful depths.

In that age of escalating misery and chaos, it was not surprising that few had the stamina to study the visions, nor the curiosity to seek out, their source and attempt to understand them.

Some, beaten down by generations of mundane misery, meekly accepted this new form of torture as their due.

Others believed—vainly hoped in some cases, feared in others—that the visions were simply the hand of God made manifest, delivering a stern and

159

final warning of the long-delayed Biblical retribution for sinful Man's betrayal of the stewardship he had been given over the planet: a long-drawn-out Armageddon unleavened by the promised Second Coming.

Still others believed that Nature itself had finally had enough and had set out to restore the balance by driving all men mad, thereby neutralizing the metastasizing cancer that humans had become.

Even so, there were those few who, despite the ongoing collapse of everything that had made Civilization possible, still contained enough hope, enough curiosity to attempt to understand what was happening. Instead of cowering or resisting, instead of shutting off their minds and trying to ride out the storm in a mental tornado cellar, they opened themselves to the visions, to the countless other minds that were also experiencing them—to *everything*.

And found themselves, disembodied, in the eye of a raging storm.

In an instant they felt their minds being splintered, their memories being set free, the boundaries of both space and time demolished.

And as those boundaries fragmented, so, too, did the sense of individuality. Suddenly the memories of one become the memories of all, their sources indistinguishable. They were no longer *they*. They were a single being, a gestalt, embedded in the greater mass of humanity that still remained isolated, resistant.

But once that gestalt formed, it could not be stopped. It was like dropping a tiny instantaneously seed of ice into a huge mass of supercooled water, transforming it into a solid. Just as instantaneously, the barriers that had kept those other billions separated were breached, and all minds became One.

And as this ephemeral but all-encompassing gestalt spread through both space and time, the reason for its brief and unnatural existence became glaringly obvious.

Mankind was being given—was giving itself?—a second chance.

Less immediately obvious was the nature of that chance, the nature of the actions that must be taken before that chance vanished into the mists of time from which it had emerged.

But then, as the billions upon billions of memories merged into one integrated whole, and the tangled, trillion-stranded path of mankind's history came into sharp focus, one clear turning point emerged. One and only one place, one and only one time at which the changing of one life could deflect Earth from its disastrous path.

Cautiously, then, like an army threading its way through a no-man's-land littered with mines and trip-wires, countless tendrils began inching their secret way back through time, seeking out and converging on that unique moment.

The lone occupant of Cell 91 lurched into consciousness, prodded by a sharp pain in his gut that a startled corner of his mind identified as hunger.

Ridiculous! that same corner of his mind insisted, even as his body responded with a sharply indrawn breath and a pained grimace. He had eaten his fill only hours ago. If anything, the source of the pain was indigestion, brought on by food richer than he was accustomed to, or perhaps by a nervous tension he wasn't controlling as completely as he had thought.

For a long moment he lay motionless except for his now carefully controlled breathing, his eyes tightly shut as he willed the pain to subside.

But it only became greater, more agonizing.

Surrendering, he opened his eyes.

And froze, the inexplicable hunger pangs driven from his consciousness as a chill swept over him and the hairs on the back of his neck snapped upright.

A man's face, emaciated and unshaven, shimmered

wraith-like in the shadowy darkness only inches from his own. For an instant he thought it was the face of one of the death camp inmates whose images had so tortured him after the revelations of Auschwitz and the other monuments to infinite cruelty. An involuntary moan filled his throat at this reminder that evil on such a scale could exist—*had* existed, not just in a distant, savage past but mere decades ago!

But then, as his rational mind regained control, he saw that he had been mistaken. For one thing, the face was Oriental, not Caucasian, and—

He shook his head violently. Why was he dreaming such madness as this? Had the prospect of all that he would face in the days and years to come completely unhinged his mind?

As if in answer, the face changed even as he watched it. Like a distant cloud being reshaped by the unseen fingers of the wind, it was transformed into the leathery and weatherbeaten face of a woman who could have been twenty or fifty.

Then it, too, was gone, replaced by a black man with a terrible scar across his ebony forehead.

His heart pounding so hard he could hear its beating, he closed his eyes and—

—froze.

The dimly lit room vanished with the closing of his eyes, but the ever-changing face remained, as if projected on the inside of his eyelids.

Gasping, he opened his eyes, bringing the real world back into view, but only as a shadowy backdrop to the ever-changing face, the transformations coming even faster, the images flickering and blending together until—

"Who—*what* are you? *What do you want from me?*"

Only after the words had emerged and reverberated throughout the tiny, spartan room did he realize they had come from his own lips.

For a long moment there was no answer, as the

images continued their eerie changeling dance, but then, suddenly, they stopped.

The death camp face returned, but would not stay still, as if it were being seen through the rippling surface of a lake.

And its lips moved.

Behold your legacy, it said, the words appearing soundlessly in his mind, accompanied by an astonishing mixture of feelings ranging from despair to hope, from deepest love to bitter hatred.

Abruptly, before he could regain control of his own voice, the face vanished, as did the bed on which he lay and the semi-darkened Cell 91 itself. After a dizzying moment of stomach-churning vertigo, his eyes were assaulted by blindingly harsh sunlight. And his stomach—

Suddenly the hunger pain returned, nearly doubling his body over with its intensity.

But it wasn't *his* body, he realized with a shock even more intense than the pain.

It was stick-thin, the muscles so weak he could barely stand.

And it was a woman's! A black woman's. Around him were dozens of other emaciated women, both black and white, and a similar number of men. And children, their stomachs already showing signs of starvation bloat.

Desperately he tried to understand what was happening to him. Was it God's hand or Satan's that had thrust him into this nightmare? Or was it merely his own madness?

But even as he cast about feverishly for a Sign, his very memory began to fade. His *life* began to fade, to take on a dream-like aura of unreality, as if it were something that had happened to someone else, someone he had once met, or perhaps only read about. At the same time, the harsh, sun-baked world of the nightmare became ever more real, as did the body he now . . . inhabited.

And her mind . . .

His memories, he realized in a shocking moment of clarity, were being replaced by *her* memories. Physically, he already *was* her, and soon his mind would be hers as well.

And then . . .

A hand touched Carlotta's shoulder, and she gathered the energy to look up. Her husband leaned over her, his anxious eyes peering into hers. The terrible scar on his forehead, a grim reminder of the last great food riot, seemed to pulse with each beat of his heart.

"There will be another plane," he said gently. "You will have food before the day is over."

"I know," she heard herself saying in an exhausted whisper, but even as she spoke, she knew it was not to be. The single parachute that had emerged from the last plane had wobbled to earth more than a mile distant, where others equally hungry had swarmed over it, only to have it wrested from them by an armed band. There would not be another plane, she knew, not today, probably not tomorrow or the day after. By then it would be too late.

She closed her eyes against the painful brightness of the sun, remembering.

When her mother had been a child, this now-barren patch of land had been an oasis of farmland, where a single tiny plot could keep three generations from starvation. But no more. The last remnants of the last planting were brown and shriveled. Survival now depended almost entirely on what the occasional relief agency plane dropped from the sky. Her parents and a small band of others had tried to leave, to search for land that would still accept seed, but they had been turned back from whatever oases they found by men with guns, men who laughed and snarled, who raped and killed, but who would not share even the driest morsel.

And now . . .

The intervals between food drops, irregular from

the start, were getting longer. The drops that *were* made were ever more likely to be snatched up by brigands from one or the other of the renegade army forts still in existence, or by one of the gangs that roamed the drought-stricken countryside.

She couldn't remember the last time her stomach had been full, the last time she had laughed or even smiled, the last time she hadn't been resigned to the possibility that her life would be ended before the day was out.

She had long been tired of fighting the inevitable, tired of hoping that the distant sound of a plane was real rather than just a product of her fevered imagination, tired of living without even the slightest hope that the constant misery would ever end.

But she had persevered.

Somehow, a day at a time, she had managed to hang on in the face of everything.

But no more, a small voice inside her said.

No more!

It was time.

Time to let go.

With that thought came a feeling of relief so intense it momentarily blocked out the resurgent pain in her shriveled stomach.

And she let go, her stick-thin body slumping to the ground.

For just an instant, as the world seemed to spin about her, a pang of fear gripped her. Suicide, she had been taught, was a sin and would bar her from heaven.

If such an unlikely place existed. And this was not suicide, this was simply letting go.

Letting go of an existence that had been a living hell from the first moment she could remember.

She relaxed and, to her surprise felt her consciousness begin to fade almost immediately, as if, exhausted, she was simply falling asleep.

The last thing she saw was her husband's scarred face as he leaned helplessly over her.

And in Cell 91, the first nightmare ended.

For a long moment, the man lay perfectly still, allowing his pounding heart to slow even as he tried vainly to fathom the meaning of the dream that had set it racing.

But even as his mind went back over those terrible, despairing minutes, it came to him that the dream was not like any he had ever had before.

For one thing, it had been so vivid, so realistic that, had it not been so outlandish, it would have been indistinguishable from reality.

For another, it remained crystal clear in his memory, not fading bit by bit, as all others had, until all he could remember was that he had a dream.

Even more disturbing, it was not only the few minutes of the dream itself that remained stuck in his mind but, he realized with new amazement, the entire life of the woman in the dream. He remembered her whole life as if it were his own, as if he himself had *lived* her every painful moment.

But that memory was nonsense, he told himself firmly, as all dreams are—but this one far more than most. He grimaced as the decades of memories darted through his mind, as if looking for a place to take firmer root. From what hidden corner of his mind had that nightmare world been dredged? A world in which the United States was nothing more than a loose collection of third-world-like fiefdoms, largely populated by roving gangs and tightly guarded military bases that provided only minor stability to those within their walls. And the rest of the world, that deceitful memory told him, was little better.

But then, as he struggled to make sense of the senseless, he felt the confines of Cell 91 melting away once again.

Within moments, he found himself once again inhabiting a body not his own, his mind overflowing with memories not his own.

A different—yet not different—body.

A different—yet not different—set of memories.

This time, in a starving body that could have been his own, he died somewhere in Europe, shot while he and a dozen others raided a food warehouse that was better defended than they had expected.

This time, Cell 91 barely flickered into existence at the moment of his death before it vanished once again, replaced by another sun-baked near-desert not unlike the first. But here he was surrounded not by dozens but by tens of thousands waiting with growing hopelessness for what was left of the world's governments to send food and water.

Then that life, too, was gone, flickering out of existence, leaving behind only its memories of a world that could no longer be saved. The shifting climate, the crop failures, the famines, the resulting wars at every level had already sent it into a downward spiral that wouldn't end until some new balance had been reached, a balance which, some said, could accommodate no more than one in ten, likely less.

The next life whose end he lived through was that of a missionary, not from a church but from an organization trying futilely to reverse or at least ameliorate the damage done by church missionaries and other zealots to whom the words "birth control" had been anathema, no matter the depths of misery that confronted them.

Then came a soldier in one of the myriad fragments of one-time massive armies. He died well-fed, but there was little else to differentiate his death from the others.

For another dozen deaths—or perhaps a hundred; he was no longer able to keep count—it was the same. The world, overburdened by humanity, was collapsing. Only China, which had been willing to employ truly draconian measures to maintain a stable population, had partially avoided the collapse that had overwhelmed the rest of the world. Despite the horrors that were each time loaded into his mind, he found he was becoming numb to it. The death of a single friend, he remembered someone saying, was a tragedy, but the death of a million in a faraway country is a statistic.

And so it went, until . . .

This time, as Cell 91 yet again flickered into and out of existence, he was suddenly overwhelmed by shame and guilt. Not his own, any more than the tortures those other lives had survived had been his own, but of whoever, this time, he had been thrust into.

Flinching, he felt his stomach lurch painfully at the horror of the alien memories as they flooded into his mind, growing stronger, clearer by the second. Suddenly, he longed for the moment when his own memories would fade from existence, replaced by those of this new host as they had been replaced by those of his previous hosts.

But this time they did *not* fade. If anything, his own sense of identity grew even stronger, which only deepened the sick horror of what he was seeing in his host's mind. What he was *remembering*!

Then, as he ceased his futile struggle to escape from this new nightmare and began to pay attention to what was happening *now* rather than on the remembered horrors of the past, he realized what was happening.

He realized that he was holding a gun.

And he was raising that gun.

Putting the trembling barrel in his mouth.

Crossing himself with his free hand.

And pulling the trigger.

As Cell 91 reappeared around him, he felt the nausea boiling up in his stomach. Lurching from the bed, he managed to reach the primitive chamber pot that came with each of the cells.

Shivering, he wiped his mouth and dropped back on the bed, too weak to stand or even sit up.

He was also too weak to thrust away the memories of this last host, no matter how much he longed to do so.

The man had been a priest.

And he had committed what he had always thought was the ultimate sin: the taking of his own life.

But in his case suicide had not been the worst sin he had ever committed. This man had committed worse sins—dozens, hundreds of times.

Until he had been found out.

Until some of the children had finally ignored his warnings and pleadings and told the truth to their parents.

Until his sins, no longer a secret of the confessional, had been broadcast to the world.

Until he could stand the guilt and the vilification and the shame no longer.

And now he was dead, by his own hand. But his sickening memories lived on in the occupant of Cell 91, to whom the worst knowledge was not that his host had killed himself. Nor was it what he had done to dozens of children. The worst, the knowledge that threatened to rip his heart from his chest, was the knowledge that such behavior was widespread and on-going. This host, the memories insisted, had been but one of many who had inflicted their moral carnage on the most innocent of their flocks, year after year, decade after decade.

A mixture of relief and terror gripped him as he realized the room was once again vanishing from around him. Relief that he might be able to escape those memories he already possessed, terror that he might be on his way to even worse memories, if such a thing were possible.

His stay in the new host was shorter than in any of the previous ones. He was at the wheel of a car, racing down an empty highway at breakneck speed. A hundred yards ahead loomed a concrete bridge abutment.

A quick glance in the rearview mirror told his latest host there were no vehicles behind him, no one who would be injured by his own selfish act, by his escape.

This time, in the two or three seconds he had, he

instinctively tried to control the host's hands, to force them to twist at the wheel and bring the speeding car back into the traffic lane.

But he was, as before, only a passenger.

As the car crumpled around his host, first crushing him, then literally tearing his body to pieces, the host's memories flooded his mind, and he found himself screaming at the walls of Cell 91, his whole body shaking.

This latest host, the new memories told him, had been one of the victims of the previous host. Unable to bring himself to tell anyone, even his parents, he had kept it all inside until, decades later, it had overwhelmed him.

Satan! he thought, shuddering. *These mad visions can come from no one but Satan!*

But why? What sins have I committed that make me subject to such punishments?

There was no answer, except for a renewed feeling of vertigo as Cell 91 once again wavered out of existence and he found himself in yet another body, another host.

But this one, he realized instantly, was different. This host was peacefully asleep and showed no signs of waking.

And the flood of memories he had come to expect and to dread did not come.

Instead, the only sensation he experienced was a muffled beeping that, he realized after a few seconds, or perhaps a few hours, matched his own pulse. His host's pulse.

Is this one in a coma? he wondered. *Is that why his memories have not been thrust upon me?*

He had no way of knowing how long he lay there, thankful for the respite, however long it lasted, be it seconds or hours.

Or forever.

As the ill-defined minutes drifted by, an unexpected and sourceless feeling of familiarity crept over him.

The same kind of gentle nostalgic feeling that washed over him whenever he returned to his boyhood home.

The feeling grew, slowly forcing out the apprehension and dread that he had felt as he waited for the merging with this new host.

Finally, the host's eyes opened.

The host looked around the hospital room, slowly. The beeping accelerated, and he wondered: *Is this it? Is it this host's time, as it had been the others'?*

But it wasn't, not yet.

The host, not strong enough to sit up unassisted, crossed himself as best he could with his palsied hand.

"Who is here?" The words themselves were slurred, but they were crystal clear in his mind.

Abruptly, he realized with absolute certainty who this host was, why the sense of familiarity had been so great.

It was himself, decades in his own future.

How long did I serve, he found himself wondering? Twenty years? Thirty?

And the answer came, appearing in his mind as the countless other memories had: *twenty-six*. Followed by the words themselves, slurred as the host's lips tried to form them.

As his own dying body tried to speak them.

Does this future self know the truth, he wondered? *Does he remember this night more than twenty-six years in his past? Is that why I am here, merging with that future self? To learn what the nightmares meant? Who had sent them? And why?*

Even as he silently asked the questions, the same voice that had spoken to him wordlessly moments before the first of the nightmares spoke again: *you are here to learn your destiny.*

And the memories flowed.

But not randomly, as they had flowed into his own mind during each incarnation. This time, as they flowed from his younger to his older self, they were organized, and both selves instantly recognized the starting point: Humanae Vitae, the document that his older self had upheld and defended zealously all these years. Its convoluted but meticulous logic, its carefully chosen words, its elaborately constructed arguments, its sometimes arcane references had not changed. Its conclusion was still, to them both, as obvious and irrefutable as ever.

Without warning, it was juxtaposed with the countless memories of war and famine and starvation, and the links between those catastrophes and the enforcement of the document's conclusions suddenly were made inescapably obvious by one memory after another.

Too many people, too few resources. A deadly combination.

Still, both selves resisted, convinced that it was nothing more than a Satanic trick, that Satan was indeed the source of these hideous visions. Surely the thoroughly reasoned and eloquent defense of God's law put forth in that sacred document could not have been the cause of such tribulations! Surely—

Abruptly, the memories of the last two hosts, the suicides, overwhelmed all the others.

The older self crumpled inwardly, shocked to his core not by the suicides alone but by what had driven them to it. By the hundreds of evils the one had inflicted on the other. By the knowledge that this one offender was not alone in his actions, but only one of many within the Church.

For an interminable moment it was as if his older self had ceased to exist, and he wondered if the end had come, if that terrible memory had utterly destroyed him.

But then his answer came.

I knew, but I did not believe, the older self's mind confessed, the unspoken words a cry of agony that assaulted the younger self's mind. *I was told, time and again, but I would not believe. I* could *not believe!.*

But now, suddenly and belatedly, he believed. They

both believed as the memories settled firmly into their minds, establishing their reality. And it was not just the abuse that they believed. They now knew that those terrible visions of starvation and war and cruelty and, most importantly, the relationship that had been revealed by the countless memories, were *not* the work of Satan. While they might not be directly from God Himself, they were most certainly a miracle—and a warning! They could both now see that they and countless others in the upper reaches of the Church hierarchy had been cruelly deceiving themselves. They had in their pride convinced themselves that their esoteric logic and eloquent words about respect and love and responsibility could truly bring about the Utopian marital relationships they desired and God demanded. They both knew that, despite their own memories of the death camps and a thousand other historical atrocities, they had not taken human nature with all its flaws sufficiently into account. And those flaws, like those of the abusive priests, had inevitably led to disaster.

And they both realized what must be done.

With that realization, the hospital room and his older self simply vanished, and he found himself back where his terrifying journey had begun: Cell 91, the room in the papal residence to which he and one other had been assigned while the elections were held and to which he had returned, alone, to spend the last night before his installation in solitary contemplation.

Resisting the totally impractical urge to rush from the room with the news of how his attempt at contemplation had been rewarded, he lay quietly, formulating his plans.

He might well fail, but at least he would have tried.

In his first act as pope, John Paul II startled the world by using the traditional speech following his installation to call for preparations for Vatican III, including a new and thorough examination of his predecessor's encyclical on the regulation of birth, the controversial Humanae Vitae. In the following months, he also earned—and gladly accepted—the nickname The Great Reformer, by exposing and waging relentless war against the child abuse that had been going on within the Church for decades. Already one of the most powerful popes in centuries as a result of his boundless energy and charisma, his series of major victories in that war gave him even more influence, so that when, at the conclusion of Vatican III, he issued a new encyclical in which birth control was not only accepted but encouraged. Objections were heard only from a minuscule and hidebound minority. From then on, birth control was no longer anathema but was promoted in all its forms around the world by this wildly popular and utterly fearless pope, who traveled and proseletyzed more widely than any previous pontiff.

And he succeeded.

By the end of the millennium, world population had leveled off and become stable, and abortions were at an all-time low. The specter of famine, while not entirely vanquished, was no longer the leading cause of death. He knew there were of course other problems, other disasters that would afflict humanity as long as it existed in all its imperfections, but at least irresponsible procreation, the worst of the self-inflicted disasters, was, for the time being, off the board. It would not be looming over everything, ready to multiply the effects of the natural disasters, the wars and all the rest.

Humanity still might some day succumb to the darker side of its nature, but now at least it had a chance.

OYER AND TERMINER

Joe Masdon

April 19, 1692

"**A**bigail Hobbs confessed to being a witch today before the court."

The sound of three slowly rocking chairs was the only noise on the porch for the next few minutes. Hands worked busily at patching small tears in shirts, knitting a small blanket, and shelling early season peas. A low whistle finally came from the youngest woman, and a hunting dog stood up from the steps and padded his way around the house. Pausing to sniff the air a few times, the dog raised his leg at a fence post, marked his territory, and finished his walk around the yard.

The old bloodhound had baggy eyes, and his tongue lolled from his mouth as he panted lightly. He stretched out near the corner of the house. It was early spring, and the New England air still held a chill in it. The bloodhound's spot was in the sun, and he closed his eyes as if to take a nap.

"No surprise about Abigail. The poor young girl would confess to being a butter churn if she thought it might shock those men." This came from the tall, rail-thin older woman who was shelling peas.

"She did certainly spend enough of her life being used as a butter churn—more like a butter churn than a witch by any account," came a muttered invective from a woman whose small gnarled hands were creating a baby blanket.

"Now, now, don't go being spiteful, Agnes. The poor dear has never been in her right mind, least not since . . . that business when she was younger." All three heads nodded briefly, sadly, at the truth behind the words of the youngest on the porch.

"Well, not the first to suffer such business, our young Abigail, nor will she suffer the last, I fear." Fingers flexed slowly, taking a break from the labor with the peas.

Repositioning the shirt, the youngest continued, "Even so, Constance, while it is the girl's nature to be inappropriate, I wonder at the things she claimed. Poor thing said she pinched those three young girls at the devil's bidding and flew on a witch's pole to dark meetings with others of the village."

Disapproving frowns and clucks came from the two older women. "Why didst she make such an outrageous claim, Ruth? I hope all in attendance did see her stories for the twisted yarns they were."

"I fear not, Constance. Judge Hathorne and Captain Sewall were most interested in her tale. It came as quite a shock to the gallery, let me tell you, when she talked of her parents being witches, too."

"That ungrateful child! Deliverance Hobbs, a witch? Foolishness!" Agnes scowled as she shook her head.

"They took much truth from her tales, as though she spoke gospel. Names were put to paper, and Sheriff Walcott didst hold the paper most solemnly when he was given it." Agnes snorted quietly as she heard this.

Agnes held up the blanket, examining it for some nonexistent flaw, "First Tituba, and now Abigail. How many others must falsely claim to be Satan's brides to appease these men?"

For a few minutes, there was no conversation on

the porch, just rocking. Peas were shelled with a bit more agitation, and stitches were made a little tighter. The sound of gentle rocking continued unabated.

"Stupid color-skinned Indian sow," Agnes spat.

"Her and her backwards voodoo talk. Got all those little girls all turned around with her words of fortune telling and bespelling men's hearts," Ruth agreed.

"Do not show pity too quickly on all those girls. I believe they have some knowledge of what they are doing. The contortions of young Parris and her cousin we all three knew as grain-fed when first we were told, despite *Dr.* Griggs being befuddled as a man on his wedding night."

Constance and Ruth nodded their agreement.

"But I do not see as anyone would have given them any of the purple rye since Tituba got jailed."

"I am most put out by Mercy Lewis, for I had hopes for her." Constance irritably threw an empty pod to the porch.

"It's the men I most hold in harm for this day. To follow the Book, and to try to do the Lord's work is one thing, but to let girls lead you astray when you ought know better is unconscionable." The baby blanket felt warm to Agnes' frail old hands.

"Aye, a problem not uncommon in Salem, is it; men acting unconscionably in the presence of girls, young and old." Constance was becoming agitated, and her voice started to rise. "Parris and his . . ."

A snuffling bark came from the corner of the yard. The gentle sounds of rocking returned, along with a subdued humming, halfway through a hymn.

"Good afternoon, ladies." A strong voice came from the front of the yard. "Might I come visit and share a bit?" The man held his hat, and absently patted the large bloodhound who had padded casually over to him.

"Well, of course, Mr. Samuel Wardwell." Constance's lined and weathered face smiled with genuine motherly warmth.

"You're very kind, ladies." The large hound followed him lazily and laid down at the steps when Wardwell joined the women on the porch.

"I hate to bear unpleasant news, but have you heard that Judge Hathorne pulled a confession of witchcraftery from Abigail Hobbs today?" If he found the news unpleasant, it was clear that he was nevertheless eager to be the one to make the delivery.

"My word, no!" Constance dropped her hands slowly, looking genuinely surprised.

"Goodness, Mr. Wardwell, what on earth did she say?" Agnes demurred.

"Well, ladies, I do hate to shock, but she claimed that she had pinched at poor Elizabeth Parris and her cousin Abigail Williams at the heed of the Devil. She confessed that she did fly by witch pole to a gathering right here in Salem Village, and that other witches are among us! I am just come from the court where she made her confession not thirty minutes ago!"

"My sakes, Mr. Wardwell, suren the child was being fanciful! I do hope the judges set a switch to her to see if the truth could be had." Constance and Ruth nodded agreement.

Samuel Wardwell pulled back at the notion. "I fear she spoke truth. She proclaimed with such recollection and detail that it chilled me as I sat. I daresay the room itself grew colder as she spoke. Further, all the while, poor Elizabeth and her cousin, the younger Abigail, were twisting and groaning in the court, in ways most unnatural. Such afflictions seemed only to stir the awful confession from the witch Abigail, as if she took devilish strength from their torment."

The three women sat stunned on the porch, shaking their heads. "Well, Mr. Wardwell, I am glad you have shared the truth of it with us. Without your direct account, we might not know the truth of it all." Constance said.

"Ladies, I fear our own neighbors might become revealed as doing the devil's work in this fine village.

I must return to Andover on the morrow, so my prayers are with you."

"Thank you, Mr. Wardwell, and ours with you," Ruth nodded as he left.

After Samuel Wardwell departed, pea pods and clothing remained untouched. The chill New England breeze carried Samuel Wardwell along to another porch where he hurried to deliver the ill tidings.

"What do we do?" Ruth asked.

One of the chairs began rocking slowly, and a baby blanket was picked back up, "We do nothing. You heard him. At the very suggestion that the girls might be dissembling, his own tendency was to make his memory more than it was. We do not speak against this. We are especially careful not to . . ."

A soft woof from the front yard was followed by the sound of three chairs gently rocking, and three kindly women humming hymns as they smiled and waved pleasantly to passing neighbors. Many stopped to discuss news of a second confession with the three kindly goodwives.

June 15, 1692

Their husbands walked ahead of the women under the pretense of discussing business while they returned from church. The women were also discussing business.

"Reverend Parris did go on from the pulpit today, did he not?" Ruth walked slowly to accommodate Agnes' pace and to maintain distance from their husbands. "Very Godly of him to try to save our souls from witchery, wouldn't you say?"

"Like they saved Bridget Bishop?" sniped Constance. "I still cannot believe that they hanged that woman."

"Serves her right. Always harsh with words and spiteful to others was our Bridget. Three husbands dead and never a nice word for anyone." The words came slowly, matching the pace of the small, fragile legs. "She hanged because hanging her was easier than not. She cavorted with men not her husband, and a great many of them. Such a woman gets no care from me, even when the rope draws tight. Standing before the magistrate is late for one to show courtesy and respect to others."

Chastised a bit, the youngest took the wisdom of the eldest's words. "Parris' daughter and the Putnam girl sat beside the judges as if they were lawyers themselves, and privileged to stand judgment."

"They are standing judgment. And we must all now fear these unbled girls as surely as if their displeasure was death itself." Agnes slowed to rest. A hawk flew far overhead. "They play with the lives of the people in this village as casually as they play in the churchyard."

"Again, my anger is for the men who hang on these girls' every word. For Putnam and Parris, it holds no surprise, as the little bitches are their own blood. But I feel an especial loathing of these men whom Governor Phips sent to oversee this Court of Oyer and Terminer. Judge Stoughton in particular has become a favorite of mine for . . ."

A distant screech from above went unheard by most.

". . . his tireless devotion to the Lord and his selfless pursuit to keep our village safe. May the Lord bless him," came the words a bit louder than they started.

"Ladies, my apologies, I did almost run over you." A girl in her late teens dashed out from behind a small hedge that the husbands had passed a few dozen steps before, nearly running into the trio of goodwives. She was a pretty girl, wearing poor clothes that marked her as a servant. She seemed a bit simple, but pleasant enough with a genuine smile.

"Mercy Lewis, dear, dear. Think nothing of it lass, for you stopped yourself before sending these old bones to the ground."

"You are kinder than any, Greatmother. I did hear you speak of Chief Justice Stoughton. I am most impressed with him as well. He is a most formidable magistrate, is he not?"

"Yes, dear, a powerful force for the Lord, to be sure. He blesses us all with his presence. We should be especially grateful that a man with such little experience and knowledge of law should come forth to help protect us from those who would seek to deceive us. And to have the esteemed Reverend Mather among us encouraging the judges to understand the value of spectral evidence in the absence of other proof has brought a tear to my old eye."

Constance and Ruth stiffened for the briefest of moments. The simple face of the young woman showed no sign that she heard anything other than glowing praise of the Chief Magistrate and the reverend who was advising four of the judges. "Yes, Greatmother, I would say we are blessed to have them. I must beg your leave. Ann and Abigail await me at the church."

"Good day to you, dear, and may God bless you." The other two echoed similar blessings as Mercy Lewis hurried along.

"She is a good-hearted child, for all her foolishness." Baited the youngest.

"If the sight of Bridget Bishop on Gallows Hill did not show her the cost of her foolishness, I fear she may lose what goodness is there," Agnes observed. "But then, suren the sight of wee Dorcas Good languishing in chains has not stirred her 'good heart,' so I misspeak to think an old whore hanging from a rope to shake her from this path."

"I fear you both overvalue the goodness in that child. While she has much potential for charity, there is much hurt and hardness at her core. Being orphaned as a child caused her less anguish than most believe," Constance said as they walked, "This child was not orphaned by accident or divine fate."

Agnes paused and looked back toward the churchyard, "Truly, Constance? You are confident in the child's now and past?"

Constance nodded.

Agnes resumed walking, "Then should we have the child . . ."

Constance interrupted, "Have you taken leave of all senses? Would you feed the wolf off your own throat?"

Ruth interrupted, "Is there else we should do at this time in light of Bridget Bishop's fate?"

"No, this is none of our dealing. One hateful old biddy hanged by a court led by outsiders who could see how despised she had made herself. It is not our business, and it will pass. And we are not as strong as once we were, so prudence is well considered."

Ruth self-consciously twisted the wedding band that still felt slightly out of place on her hand, and struggled meekly for words.

' "That was no admonition, child, merely a statement of fact," Agnes said, waving away Ruth's words.

"Truly, Ruth, Agnes speaks for me as well. We hold no ill will to you. You deprived yourself for longer than we could have asked. We must merely be cautious."

Accepting their words, Ruth nevertheless remained subdued. After a short time, she spoke quietly again, "Rebecca Nurse has been arrested."

Constance spoke, "She is not a despicable old crone. She is as kindly as any of us, and more so. She knows her scriptures and owes no one money or property, though she and her husband have quarreled with many over land in the past. She is as Godly a woman as this village knows. She has brought eight fine children into this village, more even than you, Agnes." Agnes cast a sidelong look to Constance at the mention of the delicate subject. Undaunted, Constance continued, "What is needed that we should see it our business?" The question was genuine, and full of unspoken pleading.

"Rebecca Nurse will not be found guilty. She is among the best of this village, and even Putnams cannot bring a jury to convict her. As to the rest, we keep to our own affairs, and go to Gallows Hill only to bear witness, not courtesy of Sheriff Walcott's buckboard. We owe these people nothing. What would Our Lord have us do? Perhaps this is His will after all." Agnes walked slowly up the steps to her home.

"I stand by your wisdom." Ruth said as she helped Agnes up the steps.

"As do I. As long as they only lead sheep to slaughter, I will abide. I am not a Shepherd, and should remember that. But if I see any of our backsides headed to Walcott's jail, I will act." A cold breeze blew through Salem Village. The eldest and youngest watched the strongest of their trio walk calmly away.

August 21, 1692

The heat of the day was fading. Three rocking chairs sat still on a freshly painted porch. A bloodhound lay snoring at the corner of the house. A lazy cat lay atop the hound, rising and falling with the hound's breath.

"I am glad you were not at Gallows Hill yesterday," said Ruth.

"I saw some of it." A blanket rested on old legs, despite the heat of the summer day. "But was unable to hear."

"George Burroughs recited the Lord's Prayer as perfectly as ever a minister has done it. Most were shocked. 'Clearly he cannot be a witch,' many cried. There was much uproar to see George Burroughs freed."

Constance rocked slowly. She had said nothing since she left Gallows Hill last night.

"But Reverend Cotton Mather stood forth, proclaiming it false, and stating that Reverend Burroughs had been given his day in court and had been found guilty, so guilty he would be. Before those assembled could refute him, he had the sheriff pull the cart, and all four hanged to death as we looked on."

"They no longer make pretense at following their own rules, no matter how falsely contrived." Coughing came from fragile lungs.

"Mather and Stoughton follow no rules. They are butchering the sheep," Constance's voice was calm, and she gently rocked her chair. "Rebecca Nurse was found innocent. Stoughton made the jury reverse its verdict. They hanged Rebecca Nurse and they hanged George Burroughs. I hold offense at those two deaths." The voice never wavered or rose in pitch. "Samuel Wardwell was taken from his Andover home earlier this month."

A mewling noise and a small, deep bark reached the porch. Sheriff Walcott walked down the street. "Ladies," he tipped his hat toward the porch and slowed to talk.

"Good eve, Sheriff Walcott. Could we entice you to a small bit of tea?" Gnarled old hands were already pouring a cup.

"Thank you, ladies." The Sheriff moved toward the porch amiably, noticing the dog and the cat as he approached. "I hope the Lord is treating you well this fine day."

"Yes, Sheriff Walcott, he is indeed. It is a beautiful day the Lord has made." Constance continued to look toward the setting sun. "We must thank you for the difficulties you have endured and the sacrifices you have made over the past few months, what with all this witch business. I do hope that the Chief Justice and the other judges feel that there is an end in sight to this work."

"Sadly, ladies, I am told that the devil may be more entrenched in our colony than first we feared. Reverend Mather is convinced that Salem is but the first. Lieutenant Governor Stoughton has already begun to make plans to expand the righteous crusade beyond

Andover all the way to Boston." The sheriff spoke with the weight of righteous conviction.

"I see. A man of vision, this William Stoughton." Dreadful calm betrayed no emotion from Constance.

"Indeed he is, ladies. He has said that he will root out all witches in Massachusetts, and he feels that the Lord guided his steps to Salem and to this crusade." John Walcott nodded his agreement before setting the cup down. "Good ladies, it has been my pleasure to share tea with you. I should be about my business, which regrettably involves one of you." He stood before Agnes, and read a list of charges, including forming nighttime specters and causing harmful agonies to young Ann Putnam. Some of his righteous fervor faded as he spoke, and he could not face the frail old woman.

Agnes never spoke. The sheriff had to help his prisoner stand, and she walked feebly from the porch. As he reached the bottom of the steps, he again noticed the cat resting on the sleeping dog. "This is a peculiar sight, if I say. A dog allowing a cat to share not just the yard, but a nap as well." He spoke casually, as if he had not just arrested someone they shared tea with.

Through her shock, Ruth managed to stammer. "Those two animals were pup and kit together, Sheriff, and were raised side-by-side to what they are today. Eight years they have been as brother and sister."

"Don't you fear that the hound might turn on the cat, and one day kill it?"

Still facing the sun, Constance spoke, "It's not in the hound's nature to turn on the brother or sister with which it was raised, John Walcott. It does not turn on its own, no matter that they have different forms. It could happen, but it is not his bent. Shame that all such animals do share that nature."

"And what of the cat?"

The taller woman smiled. "The cat is fickle. As long

as the hound does not bare his teeth, the cat is content to endure his friendship. It would be fair to say that she knows less loyalty than the dog."

"Well, I would not want to be the cat should the dog come to understand that the cat is meant to be his enemy."

"Sheriff. It is best that the dog go about his life and not make an enemy where he had none before."

August 23, 1692

"The Court of Oyer and Terminer meets today to hear evidence against Martha Corey and Mary Easty. They have been in jail for some time and I hear that Cotton Mather seeks to speed up the trials, as they have hundreds in the jails waiting to be examined." Ruth rocked slowly.

"Executed, not examined." Constance stood in the yard. Facing the rising sun.

"What can we do?"

"Much. I would attend today's examination of the court, and see for myself the evidence of these afflicted young girls."

"They are well rehearsed, Constance, and the room will be full of those seeking the entertainment of their performance. It may be that they appear struck dumb, or suffer paroxysms from unnatural torments, or have wailing fear of spectral visitations." She shook her head in sad disbelief.

"It will be spectral visitations."

"How do you know they plan to be tormented by specters today?"

"They do not."

August 23, 1682

The courtroom was full of people praying to God and discussing the atrocities of witchcraft. Many were speaking in slightly overloud voices, such that the judges and the afflicted girls could hear their praise. Constance sat quietly in the back, between neighbors who were always glad to see the kindly matron. A man had even surrendered his seat for the well-respected lady.

The trial went for some time, with Chief Justice Stoughton asking the same questions over and again, seeking to catch Mary Easty at deceit.

"You see these accuse you." Justice Stoughton looked to the group of young girls who sat as if struck dumb in her presence. "What have you done to these children?"

"I know nothing," was Mary's sincere reply.

"How can you say you know nothing? You see these tormented who accuse you. How far have you complied with Satan whereby he takes advantage against you?"

"Sir, I have never complied, but prayed against him all my days. I have no compliance with Satan in this. What would you have me do?" Mary held back her tears through fear.

"Confess if you be guilty." Stoughton was resolute, as if this were the first time such an idea had been placed before the accused.

"I will say it, if it was my last time, I am clear of this sin."

"Of what sin?"

"Of witchcraft."

"Are you certain this is the woman?" Justice Stoughton turned to the young girls, all seated at the side of the judges. Fits shook the girls, and many moved as if to speak, but strained as though some unseen force had stolen their voices.

A crying woman from the gallery, moved by the torment of the girls spoke out, "Oh, Goody Easty, say you are the woman, say you the one! Cease the torment of these poor children!" And others joined in the tearful plea against Mary Easty.

On the back row of the gallery, an old woman closed her eyes, and calmly located that razor's edge between love and hate. She quietly hummed a hymn.

Among the afflicted sat Mercy Lewis, wringing her hands and protesting her inability to speak, with fearful eyes and trembling hands. The older girl wailed her torment with soundless cries to the Lord Almighty, just as the other girls seated with her. Amidst the soundless performance, Mercy stopped abruptly, looking beyond the windows of the church. The other girls continued to rock and cry without words.

Suddenly, Mercy screamed.

It was not the writhing deep-breathed scream of groaning torment that had been so convincing to those willing to believe. It was a peal of sheer, undefined terror. Her eyes flew wide, and she pushed back against her chair, arms flailing, knocking herself and the girl behind her to the ground. All noise in the courtroom stopped, as many were startled to near panic at her cry. The girls in the box near her jumped in fear and pulled away from her, their soundless wailing forgotten. Mercy ignored them all as she clambered immediately to her feet, looking frantically about the room in abject fear. Her eyes found something near the judges that no one else saw, and she shrieked again as she turned to run. A constable reached to restrain her, but she tore from his grasp, looking behind her in irrational terror.

While other girls pulled away from Mercy in fear, Ann Putnam turned back toward the gallery and began to scream as well. The younger girl was shrieking as loudly as she could, but her performance had none of the raw truth to it that Mercy's terror did. Other girls began screaming as well, all in long, measured breaths. Betty Parris, among the youngest, simply slid down in the box and covered her ears, crying. Most of the gallery was stunned into silence.

None could reconcile what they were seeing.

Through it all, Mercy Lewis strained and screamed,

and finally broke free from the constable to run terrified from the courtroom. The justices were all too stunned to call for order. Slowly, in the wake of Mercy's flight, a frightened silence returned. All of the afflicted girls had ceased their screaming and many sat on the floor, sobbing quietly. Then, a scared little voice could be heard from behind the chairs.

"No, Uncle, please, no. Don't touch me there. Please, Uncle."

The other girls pulled away from a sobbing Abigail Williams, completely lost at what was happening. Others began to sob more deeply, and pulled away. Abigail, meanwhile, stared into space at something no one else in the room could see. None of the people in the gallery could see who was speaking, but all could hear what she said. Through sobs, little Abigail began to pull up her skirts, biting her lip and struggling to hold her sobs.

Ann Putnam began crying out and shaking her head, and she pulled her knees in tight as she covered her ears and squeezed as hard as she could to block out the sounds around her.

Mary Walcott, one of the oldest girls, scrambled across the scattered chairs and crying children to grab Abigail Williams in her arms. She pulled Abigail to her and covered her whimpering head, as she worked to pull the eleven-year-old's skirts back down, shushing the child and saying, "I know, I know," gently and protectively.

The tightly restrained silence exploded, and outrage and denial filled the courtroom as members of the gallery and the judges struggled to grasp what they had seen. One older woman, taller than most, stood quietly by, as surprised as any at what she had witnessed.

August 24, 1692

It was not yet midnight, and the summer breeze at Gallows Hill was warm and fresh with the scent of ripening grains. A woman stood alone by the elm tree, waiting.

From where she stood, she could see the man coming twenty minutes before he arrived. He was alone, so she remained.

Completely unafraid, Lieutenant Governor William Stoughton approached the elm. It was a cloudless night, and the moon showed his uncompromising face with its weak chin. This evening he walked with a cane, although he had no limp. He had come armed, though alone. He was early, and he looked around anxiously.

"William Stoughton, thank you for coming. We have something important to discuss."

To his credit, Stoughton only jumped slightly. The woman had been next to the tree, not really hiding. The woman was tall, and very thin. He estimated that she was close to his own age, though she wore the sixty years harder than he did.

"Yes, good woman, I am here. Now tell me what business you have that brings me out of my rooms at such an hour. Your letter promised to reveal proof of witchcraft in Salem Village. What is this proof? And be warned, I'll know if you lie."

The woman chuckled slightly, surprised by his choice of words. "Will you now? You can tell lies when you hear them? And does the truth sound like lies as well? Are you a witch, William Stoughton?" her tone light and full of humor.

Not liking her tone, Stoughton stood straighter, standing barely taller than the woman. "I will not tolerate such slander."

"My apologies then, William Stoughton, for I know you to be no witch. I know that you are a committed man of God, and you have no traffic with witches. I know that you come here to do what you see as the Lord's work, to find witches and see God's justice done."

Looking at the stern face of the woman before him,

he inquired, "Do I know you, good woman? What is your name?"

"No, William Stoughton. You do not know me. But you will."

A feeling of distant dread snuck up on Stoughton, but he held it down. Something here was making him uncomfortable, and it annoyed him. "You should know, woman, that I am emboldened by the Lord, and it does occur to me that you might not be a true woman of God, and you might think to do me harm. I will not hesitate to strike you down should you show signs of witchery. Additionally, I have placed the note you gave me in a secure place along with a letter explaining my purpose for coming out here. Should you seek to do me violence, it will go badly for you." Stoughton spoke with more confidence than he felt.

"Ah, yes. You mean these?" said the woman, pulling two folded parchments from her pocket.

Stoughton paled. "How did you . . ." Fear crept in again. He looked around the hill, not entirely comforted that he saw no one else lurking about. His anger began to rise. Who did this woman think she was to question him, and why was he tolerating it?

"I presume that you no longer have such faith in those girls and their spectral visitations? Or the wealthy patrons who house and entreat you? Half those girls have confessed to bearing false testimony, and will no longer approach the court."

"Woman, I am here doing the work of the Lord. I came to Salem to find its witches and see them purged from this village! I need no patron or girl to tell me when witchery is afoot! Words will not deceive me. Those girls were clearly bewitched and now claim falsely to being misled. I will go forth without their witness, and apply the vengeance of the Lord!"

"Do you know how to find a witch, William Stoughton?"

"Of course, woman! I have already found and put many of Satan's brood to the rope, and I will continue my mission!" Who was this woman, Stoughton wondered, and why was he continuing to suffer her questions? He was the magistrate here, not this wrinkled old crone. "I am tired of your games and questions. You will stand before me in court, and then you shall answer my questions! Then you shall tell me what you know of witches, old woman!"

"Fair enough." The woman's tone shifted. "But first, I must ask a favor of you, WIlliam Stoughton."

He was annoyed at this woman's use of his name, and eager to be away from her. He would no longer indulge her foolishness. It was most unlike him to meet her, but the events in yesterday's court had left him unsure of many things. To get away, he snapped: "What?"

"I ask that you take this paper, and this quill and ink. You are to write a letter that you were wrong to put innocents to death on the words of misguided, mistreated children. You will write that you prosecuted innocents in your blind zeal, pushed by the greed and spite of others. You will write that you abused your power and that you hanged people for witchcraft without any real proof."

Too outraged for words, Stoughton sputtered incredulously at the audacity of this woman.

"Oh, and then you will place that letter in your pocket. You will climb this tree, place that noose around your neck, and give value to your life by ending it."

Disbelief gave way to fear as the woman walked up to Stoughton. Giving in to the fear and outrage, he pulled back the cane he was carrying and started to bring it down on her, but found himself frozen by her gaze. There was no fear in her eyes, even though he was about to crush her skull. Fear made his arms tremble, and he could not deliver the blow.

"The truth of witches in Salem, William Stoughton? None of them, Stoughton. None of the people whose lives you ended were witches."

He whimpered. "What have you done to me?"

Ignoring him, she continued, "If it comforts you, realize that I am no better than you. I have heard your testimony, and in truth, I had already decided upon your guilt before you came before me."

"Why are you doing this?" he whispered as he moved toward the elm.

"Because you will not stop. And because it is the right thing to do. What you have done here is wrong. Your actions have served the cause of evil. And now I have to stop you from going any further. So now I must do what is right and serve the cause of good." The woman smiled a sad smile. "Again, you have brought me down to your level, William Stoughton. It seems we have both failed our Lords on this day."

William Stoughton tried to scream as he dipped the quill into the ink. In the distance, he heard a woman's voice reciting the Lord's Prayer.

Sheriff John Walcott walked nervously up to Gallows Hill. It was after midnight and clouds hid the moonlight. He saw a familiar face and walked purposefully toward her.

"Ah, John Walcott. Thank you for coming, we have much to discuss."

"What is this about?"

The old woman handed him a blank piece of paper and a quill. He caught a glimpse of movement behind her near the elm. His mouth fell in shock as he saw the limp body swinging. Next to the limp form were three dangling nooses.

"I must ask a favor of you, John Walcott."

September 23, 1692

"The funeral was lovely."

"Mm—hmm." The woman rocking on the porch nodded as she sewed an unfinished baby blanket.

"She was so frail at the end. She seemed to pass peacefully."

"Mm—hmm."

"And in her own bed."

The rocking slowed. "The governor was quick to clear the jails, wasn't he? A decent God-fearing man, our governor."

The bloodhound stretched out on the edge of the lawn, his head on his paws. A cat slept on the dog's back.

"I am glad that business is over. Four signed confessions of false prosecution from those men on Gallows Hill. Bad business." The younger woman sewed up a tear in a shirt.

The afternoon passed. Constance noted that Ruth worked slower than usual.

"Ruth, are you well?"

"I have been tired lately. And this morn, my stomach sent me from me from my breakfast again."

"Congratulations, dear!" the old woman said with a knowing smile. Two chairs rocked gently as hands worked industriously.

"I was thinking about the name Agnes. I believe it is a girl."

"That would be nice. What do you think, Mercy?"

Ruth started and looked up. Standing at the steps of the porch was Mercy Lewis. At her feet, the dog laid quietly, and the cat continued to sleep peacefully.

"I . . . I should think John or Samuel would be among the names to consider, not Agnes."

"Indeed." Constance nodded. Ruth looked at the two, and at the bloodhound that still lay quietly.

"May I . . . may I speak with you ladies?" the girl asked timidly.

"Of course, Mercy. We've been expecting you."

Mercy sat cautiously in the empty rocking chair. After a time she spoke: "I did not mean for it to go as it did. When Betty and Abigail began to have the fits, the doctor claimed witchcraft, not us. It was not our intent, but the story grew, and as we were in court, I feared for them if they were seen as lying."

"And when did you begin wanting very, very hard that all in the room should believe?"

Mercy sat with her mouth agape for only a moment. "Early. I first wanted Tituba to admit to witchcraft, and that others should believe her. And for all courts, I wanted with my heart that our lies not be turned on us. Then Abigail Hobbs claimed to be a witch, and that was not my doing. Then I had no part, and all believed despite me. Then I found that I wanted very, very much that people stop believing."

"But that did not happen, did it?"

Mercy shook her head, her eyes downcast.

"Once begun, you could not reverse the tide, could you?"

"No. I sat and prayed, and hoped and tried, but it was no use."

"No. Such persecution takes root easily in the minds of men, and grows like a fire," Constance said. "Is this the first of such misguided efforts, Mercy?"

Mercy shook her head. "No," she said very quietly. "My parents." Mercy began to cry. "Who never wronged me, not once."

"Well, what is done, is over." Constance resumed her work.

"But I have done wrong by others. My sins are terrible, and I do not know how to make them right!"

A maternal smile met the confession. "My dear, others have already died for your sins, because theirs were the greater sins."

"But does that truly forgive me?"

Smiles from both older women on the porch came to that question. "No, dear, none of us are forgiven, no matter how many others die."

Much later, at the sunset, Mercy spoke again. "May I join you ladies?"

"You already have, Mercy. You already have."

STANDING STILL

Donald J. Bingle

"**A**re you sure you wanna do this, doc?" The patrolman gestured across the lobby at the subject. "He's got some sort of a device, with a trigger of some kind duct-taped to his hand. S.W.A.T. says it's probably a dead-man switch."

Dr. Lefkowitz lowered his head to peer over the top of his glasses. The subject, a fit-looking Caucasian in his mid-thirties, sat on the floor, his back to an outside wall. Although his brow was furrowed and his eyes flicked about the room, intent, no doubt, on discerning any threat, he did not seem to be agitated. His hands were steady and his blue dress shirt was unstained by sweat, even under the arms.

"Well, sergeant, the fact is that I am going to do this, whether I want to or not. First, it's my job. Second, I've got my Kevlar vest on." Lefkowitz jerked his head toward the subject. "Notice that the top two buttons of his shirt are open?"

The cop shrugged. "Yeah."

"Obviously, our perpetrator is not wearing a vest. So, unless he is suicidal, I don't think he is going to blow up anyone, assuming . . ." He raised his eyebrows as he looked at the cop.

"Yeah?" said the cop.

". . . assuming the S.W.A.T. guys don't shoot him while I'm talking him down." He lowered his eyebrows. "It is a dead-man switch, after all."

The cop gave him a tense, crooked smile. "Don't worry, doc. I'll make sure the macho squad doesn't get trigger happy."

"Thanks, sergeant." He turned to leave, mumbling to himself as he began to move in slow, sure steps toward the fanatic-of-the-day. "Just another day at the office." He opened his palms and half-raised his hands, holding them away from his body, as he separated from the throng of police, onlookers, and emergency personnel watching the scene unfold, and continued to move toward the threat.

When he was about fifty feet away, he got the usual response.

"Stop," yelled the man with the trigger. "Stay where you are. There's a lot of people at risk here." The man waved the duct-tapped trigger toward Lefkowitz as he spoke.

"I'm not armed," said Lefkowitz in a calm, practiced voice. He moved his hands up and interlaced the fingers behind his head and did a slow turn in place. "No gun, no cuffs, not even a wire, as you can see." He completed his demonstration and faced the subject once again. "I could strip down to prove it, but I'd appreciate it if you didn't make me. It's a bit chilly in here, don't you think?"

The subject ignored his question and moved on to what was the typical next question according to the textbook on these things, a textbook that Dr. Lefkowitz had helped write. "Who are you and what do you want?"

"My name is Morris Lefkowitz and I'm a doctor, a crisis counselor of sorts. I work for the police department. My job is to keep everyone safe . . . including you."

The man bobbed his trigger-hand at Lefkowitz. "This is keeping me safe at the moment."

"I can see that. All of us can see that. What would happen if you were to let go of that trigger, if you don't mind me asking?"

"A lot of people might die, including you, maybe."

The doctor tilted his head to one side. "Including you, too."

"The world might be a better place without me," said the man. "Besides, that's a risk I'm willing to take."

Lefkowitz took a small step toward the man. "I see. I'd like to talk about why you feel that way, but I'd like to do it without shouting across the room. Can I come closer and we can sit and talk?"

The man's eyes flicked to a watch on his left wrist, the opposite hand from the one clutching the device. "Yeah, I guess. I've got some time to kill."

Lefkowitz started to walk toward the man.

"Not too close," cautioned the subject. "You stop ten, twelve feet away and sit on the floor." He seemed to consider something for a moment. "Cross-legged, with your palms on the floor at all times."

Lefkowitz nodded and did what he was told. "It's not a very comfortable position," he said lightly.

The man actually smiled. "Life sucks," he said. "And then you die." The smile faded. "Or maybe not."

"Bad things happen," agreed Lefkowitz as the cold from the floor began to cool his palms, "but I don't think life sucks just because some bad things happen, do you . . . I'm sorry . . . I don't know your name."

"That's right, doc. You don't know nothing about me or my life."

"Oh, I wouldn't go that far."

The subject's eyebrows popped up. "What could you possibly know about me? And don't give me any of that 'You've been hurt' crap."

Lefkowitz pursed his lips. "I know that you're not a lawyer."

Now the subject's eyebrows popped down in confusion and consternation. "How would you know that?"

Lefkowitz smiled. "My name is famous in legal circles. You didn't remark on it. Lawyers always do."

He was drawing the subject in. "You a famous defendant or witness or something?"

Lefkowitz shook his head. "No. But there's a famous legal case about someone with my name, from years and years ago. *Lefkowitz vs. Great Minneapolis Surplus Store.*" One of the methodologies utilized with people on the edge was to have a conversation that was as normal as possible, with all the asides and trivialities that entailed. He'd used this bit before with success. "The case is always taught in contracts class, so lawyers have always heard of it. Contracts is taught in the first year of law school, when everyone is their most compulsive, so they read and summarize and digest all the facts of the case and then, ten or twenty or even fifty years later, they remember the name Morris Lefkowitz." Now for the useful segue. "Funny how things in the past can affect us now, isn't it?"

The man said nothing.

"How about your name?"

"Edwin. You can call me Ed."

"I see," intoned Lefkowitz, "Can't say I've ever met an Edwin before. It has a nice, old-fashioned ring. What about your last name?"

"You won't have heard of me. I'm not famous and nobody with my name is famous either."

"Maybe not, but I'd still like to know who I'm talking to." Lefkowitz actually didn't care personally about Edwin's last name, but he knew the police were listening in from the sidelines. If they got a name, they could run the subject for priors or contact his doctor or his wife or somebody who could help talk the guy out of whatever it was he had planned. So he pressed the issue. "What's your last name, Ed?"

"You don't need to know. It won't do you any good

to know. Besides, it's against regulations and . . . despite all this . . . I do my best to follow regulations."

Lefkowitz was startled. He was expecting a lone crazy, saddened by the death of a loved one or pissed off at an employer in the building who fired him, not a military man on a mission. "Are you a soldier, Ed?"

Edwin glanced down for a second, but didn't respond. Lefkowitz sized him up. The guy was fit and strong, his hair relatively short. He had the look of a Marine.

"Are you a member of the Corps, Ed?" Edwin flinched at the word "Corps," but he still didn't respond.

"*Semper fi*," pressed Lefkowitz. Marines almost couldn't help but respond in kind when you said "*Semper fi*."

He almost grinned as Edwin started to respond, but the response killed the smile.

"Huh?" said Ed.

"It's the Marine Corps slogan, Ed," replied Lefkowitz. "There's not a military man in America who doesn't know that. There's probably not a lot of military men in the world who don't know that."

Edwin scrunched up his nose, but went back to silent-mode.

"You, Ed, have the look of a military man. And I could tell from your reaction, that you are a member of some corps, so how is it you don't know that?"

"I'm not supposed to tell you. Besides, you wouldn't believe me," answered Edwin in a world-weary tone.

Lefkowitz looked Edwin in the eye. "Are you supposed to be sitting here, threatening all these people?" He almost removed his palms from the floor to gesture at the distant crowd, but stifled the impulse.

It was almost fifteen seconds before Edwin responded. "No."

"I didn't think so," said Lefkowitz, secretly relieved that this didn't seem to be part of some military or terrorist plot. "So, as long as you're breaking the regulations, why don't you explain to me what military group you belong to and why you're doing this?"

"I told you, you wouldn't believe me . . . and it would be a problem if you did."

"I'm a psychiatrist, Ed. People tell me things I don't believe all the time. They tell me that they're Napoleon or Jesus Christ or that they're from another planet or that nobody in the world cares about them. I listen to them, but I don't believe them when they say those things. How about this? You tell me who you are and what's going on and, if you want, I'll promise not to believe you."

There was a long pause. "*Standing Still*," Edwin finally murmured.

"Huh?" said Lefkowitz, with less than professional aplomb.

"It's our motto, our *Semper fi*, the slogan of our corps," explained Ed, his voice low, his eyes darting about as if to see if someone was going to challenge him for what he had said or was about to say.

Lefkowitz tilted his head to one side. "I see, standing up against enemy fire, never surrendering, like at Masada."

Edwin shook his head, smiling wanly as he did. "No. Standing still, like unchanged . . . unmoving."

Maybe his subject didn't know the story of Masada. Lots of people didn't. So Lefkowitz tried to explain. "Right. Never retreating. The Jews held a fortress at Masada against overwhelming odds for . . ."

Edwin shook his head more vigorously. "No. Never retreating, but never progressing. Everything unchanged. That's what we try to do."

Lefkowitz's shoulders slumped in defeat. "I don't understand. Why would a military force have a slogan like that?"

"I told you, it's not a military force. It's . . ." Edwin pursed his lips and used his left hand to finger a gold ring on his right hand, turning it as he thought. "I'm from another time."

Lefkowitz had seen this before. He sighed. "Past or future?"

Edwin shrugged. "Both."

"Both?"

"The Dimensional Defense Corps, the organization I work for, is from the future, your future, everybody's future. It exists at the edge of time itself."

Lefkowitz said nothing.

"I was recruited from the past, your past, to help them with their mission," continued Edwin.

"Which is?" prompted Lefkowitz. A trained professional, he knew it was better just to let the subject run on when you got to this point.

"To make sure that things happen the way they originally happened."

Lefkowitz's eyebrows tilted inward and his brow crinkled. This was a new one. "And why wouldn't they happen the way they happened?"

Edwin stared out into the distance. "It's complicated and . . . more than you need to know. Let's just say that there are bad guys out there who try to change history in an effort to enslave and subjugate mankind. The Dimensional Defense Corps was formed to make sure that doesn't occur. They recruit people from the past to fix the changes the bad guys make before they can become permanent."

Now Lefkowitz was really confused. "But if time can be changed, then how can the changes become permanent?" He regretted the question almost as soon as he had blurted it out. It was dangerous to attack the internal logic of a delusion, at least in the field when the subject claimed to have a bomb. But the question didn't seem to faze Edwin.

"It takes a while for the change to propagate into the future. Once it has, no one remembers the way things first were. So the Corps, it has these emergency strike force teams that dash off into the past when a Corps historian in the future notices that a change has occurred in the history books that makes them different from what he knows actually occurred, to make sure the change is changed back."

"I see," mumbled Lefkowitz, noting to himself that the delusion was self-reinforcing. Whatever the subject did was justified by the fact that he believed that what he did was what had originally occurred. Kind of like believing in predestination. No individual responsibility for your actions. "And you've done this:"

"A great number of times. Usually it's pretty straightforward. You save the political leader from assassination by the enemy or you rally the troops to make sure the battle goes the way it should. Sometimes it can even be fun. Why, that whole 'Paul is dead' thing . . ." Edwin trailed off. "Sorry. I can't really talk about some things . . ."

"So, you save people, like a fireman."

"Yeah, just like that, at least at first. That was the best part."

Now we were getting somewhere. "But not now? What changed?"

"Different alterations of history require different types of responses to set history back on its original course. Sometimes you're not saving someone." Edwin's eye twitched twice before he continued, his voice low. "Let me tell you, nobody wants to be the guy on the grassy knoll. It can screw you up real bad."

Lefkowitz frowned for a moment, but let it slide. Edwin was obviously too young to have been in Dallas or anywhere else in November 1963. Best to drop that topic. He decided to ask a broader question, instead. "So sometimes the missions involve unpleasant tasks, even moral dilemmas?"

Edwin snorted. "It's not what I expected when I joined, that's for sure."

The two of them were silent for a few minutes. Edwin seemed depressed and Lefkowitz was uncertain how to proceed. Finally, he decided to press on the logic of the delusion a bit more.

"You know, Ed," he said in a calm, soothing tone.

"I don't know much about you. You said you were recruited from the past. When? Where?"

Edwin shot Lefkowitz a sharp, fearful look. "Don't ask that. Nobody asks that." But then his eyes softened a bit. "Sorry. You wouldn't know. In the Corps, no one would ever ask that. It's the rudest, most dangerous thing you can ask."

Lefkowitz wanted to scratch an itch on the side of his neck, but kept his hands on the floor. "Why is that?"

"If someone knows when and where you are from, they could betray you to the enemy. Your recruitment could be wiped out, wiping out every mission you had ever done. Recruiting is very important, but very secret."

"But," said Lefkowitz, "doesn't recruiting change history?"

Edwin smiled. "You're pretty smart, doc." He motioned with his left hand at the doctor. "You can take your palms off the floor, if you want. Just keep your hands where I can see 'em and don't move too fast."

Lefkowitz raised his palms off the floor in a slow, even movement, then satisfied the itch that had bothered him.

Edwin continued talking. "The Corps says it recruits some people that it has determined are so unimportant that the Corps knows their disappearance will have no impact on history." Edwin exhaled in a quick huff. "But, of course, they can't really know that, can they? The entire premise of the Dimensional Defense Corps is all about the unforeseeable and often unintended consequences of little things. The only time the Corps actually can be sure they're not changing history when they recruit people is when they enlist them right before they were going to die in real time and do it in a manner and or situation where they can leave another body behind and no one will be the wiser. Fires are good, drownings too. Especially before sophisticated DNA analysis."

Lefkowitz was chilled by the grisly turn of Edwin's explanation. Could this guy be a serial killer? He made sure to make eye contact with his subject before asking the next question. "You've recruited yourself, haven't you, Ed?"

"I can only wish."

It was not the answer Lefkowitz was expecting. "You haven't?" he pressed.

Edwin frowned. "Nah. I don't have the proclivity or whatever, they say. Emergency response, that's my job."

"That sounds satisfying," replied Lefkowitz, trying to reassure his subject of his value. Building self-esteem was always good for dissuading suicide bombers.

"It was for a while, but not now. Y'see the bad guys, doc, they figured out that the Corps recruits people who are about to die. The enemy may not be able to find out an individual recruit's time and place of recruitment, but they know where to go after them wholesale . . ."

"You mean . . ."

Edwin interrupted him. Lefkowitz could almost feel the pressure of the words that began to flow from the now agitated, delusional time traveler. "That's right, doc. They disrupt major disasters. You know what my last mission was, doc?" asked Edwin, before pushing on without even hesitating for a response. "The *Titanic*."

Lefkowitz was confused again. "A haunting tale. A good movie came out of it and a few major industrialists died with the others in the actual event, but I can't imagine it had that much impact on history as a whole."

Edwin's left hand darted out, waving away the response as if a triviality. "Sure it did, doc. The whole women and children first chivalry set the suffrage movement back years. Maritime regulations were changed because of the incident. And the sinking of the *Titanic* made the *New York Times* the preeminent newspaper in New York."

Lefkowitz's eyes went wide. "It did? How?"

Edwin gave him a half-smile. "When the first radio reports came in, they didn't say the boat had sunk. Everyone ran the same story about a collision at sea. But the *New York Times* ran a headline that the boat had sunk. Of course, they were guessing. They just wanted to sell more newspapers. But when it turned out they were right, suddenly the *Times* was the only news rag you could trust. One of those unforeseeable consequences, I guess. But all that's not the important part."

"No?"

"Don't you see, doc? Hundreds of people drowned on the *Titanic* and their bodies were never recovered. But the boat took *hours* to sink. It's the perfect recruiting ground for an organization like the Dimensional Defense Corps. All the enemy had to do was make sure the boat didn't sink and the Corps was screwed."

The color drained from Lefkowitz's face. This was one sick delusion. "So, that's where you came in?"

Edwin gave a curt nod. "My team had to make sure the *Titanic* sank. Of course, we suspected that those interfering with the timeline would slow the ship down and make it take a more southerly course, so we figured we would have to hole the ship with explosives."

"I see," mumbled Lefkowitz.

"But it was even worse than that. These guys had really disrupted the timeline. When we got on board, we found there were more lifeboats than should have existed. And there were regular lifeboat drills for the passengers and extra training for the crew on proper load capacity and lowering procedures. There was even a chatty radio operator on the *California*, a big ship that in real life was nearby during the sinking but didn't get the distress call. In altered time, the

California's radio man was in constant contact with the radio operator on the *Titanic*."

He didn't want to know, but he asked. "So what did you do?"

Edwin was agitated. His hands shook, his now loud voice quavered as he completed his crazed rant. "I did what I had to do, what I had been sent to do. Standing still. That's the motto." He spat on the floor. "My team wrecked most of the lifeboats so they wouldn't float. We killed the radio operator and re-placed him with one of our operatives. We faked an order to speed up the ship and send it further north and farther away from the *California*. We blew a hole on the ship and . . ." Edwin faltered.

"And what?" asked Lefkowitz, his voice barely a whisper.

"We had a list of, you know, who lived and who died and we . . . pennied people in their cabins."

Lefkowitz felt faint. He placed his hands back on the cool floor to steady himself. He had known rowdy students in his dorm, back in college, who had pennied people in their rooms. You took a penny or two and shoved them parallel to the door between the door and the door frame. The pressure against the door pressed the bolt tight against the housing and made it nigh-impossible to turn the bolt to open the door, trapping the person inside their room. It was danger-ous enough in a building where there could be a fire or other emergency requiring quick exit. In a sinking ship it was murder. Mass murder.

Of course, the story was utter nonsense. Edwin hadn't been alive when the *Titanic* sank. But stories, like dreams, have meanings, even if they are fabrica-tions. Edwin had obviously done this at some time to someone, with disastrous consequences to them and to Edwin's psyche. Lefkowitz looked at the S.W.A.T. members, growing uneasy in the distance. Their help might be needed yet. It was time to get to the point.

"Is that what you're here to do, today, Ed? Did someone tell you to make a lot of people die here today?"

Tears were flowing down Edwin's cheeks, but his hand still gripped the triggering device that had held S.W.A.T. at bay since before Lefkowitz had arrived.

"Yes," came the reply, almost too weak and high-pitched to hear.

"But you don't have to do what they say, Ed. You don't."

Edwin turned, apparently unwilling to face Lefkowitz. "I know that. Don't you think I already know that?"

"So, why don't you just disable whatever it is you're holding there and you and me and all these other people here, we can go about our business. No one has to die here today."

"God, I hope not," gasped Edwin. He turned finally to look Lefkowitz in the eye. "That's not what they say, you know. They say it changed history. It made us stronger, more united, more vigilant. It ushered in the governmental oversight of everything that was fundamental to the creation of the Corps."

The subject was losing it. He made less and less sense to Lefkowitz. But it was important to press the key point. This time, when Lefkowitz spoke, his tone was clear and firm, his voice loud, with an edge of command. He used the subject's formal name, like a parent would. "No one has to die here, today, Edwin. You don't have to complete your mission."

Edwin laughed, a crazed, sobbing laugh that scared Lefkowitz to the bone. "Don't you understand, doc? I've already not completed my mission. I betrayed my team—you'll hear about it on the news tonight, no doubt."

Lefkowitz tried to lighten the mood. "Could be. Mayoral election today. Election results tend to take up most of the coverage on days like today."

"It'll make the news. A bunch of arrests, all called

in by an anonymous tipster early, early this morning. There'll be another story later, about a dialysis machine, but you won't understand the connection. It's just insurance that what didn't happen today won't happen later."

The subject was babbling. None of it made sense to Lefkowitz. He decided to be direct. "Okay, Ed, if nothing's happening here today, what's that device you're holding with the trigger? What does it connect to and what will happen when you let go?"

Edwin looked at his hand and the trigger, as if he had forgotten about them. He smiled. "It's an anomaly field generator. It lets things out-of-time continue to exist for short periods in a limited space."

More delusions. "And what happens when you let go?"

Edwin studied the trigger. "Nothing . . . or really nothing."

From delusional to psychotic. "What does that mean, Ed? What happens when you let go of the trigger?"

The crazed look faded from Edwin's eyes, as he turned his head back to the doctor. "The anomaly field generator stops working. The protection from the time stream's history ends." He looked at his watch. "The wave has propagated by now. There's no time to send another team. They'll never even know what didn't happen."

Edwin's eyes flicked back to Lefkowitz to acknowledge the doctor's question, before he continued. "If the Corps still exists when the anomaly field generator is turned off, nothing happens. It will mean history did not change enough to wipe out the Corps. I'll still exist because the future still exists. You'll wave the guys with guns over and arrest me and tomorrow, you'll probably come to whatever psych ward they put me in and we'll chat about what was on the news tonight."

Lefkowitz's head had begun to throb, but he had to ask. "And if the Corps no longer exists?"

"It will mean that this had to happen for the world

to be what it was. And I will simply disappear. And you'll watch the news tonight and wish you had someone to talk to with about it tomorrow." The tears started to flow again, but Edwin made no move to stem them or wipe them away. "It will mean that I betrayed history, that I betrayed the Corps, and that all I now know is lost. Perhaps I'm just weak, but I couldn't do what they asked. I couldn't make history occur the way it originally happened. It's not right to ask. It's not what I signed up for."

Lefkowitz could tell he had pushed too hard. Something was about to happen. He tensed to signal the S.W.A.T. members to move in, but it was too late. Suddenly, Edwin raised the hand with the trigger, a serene calm coming over his face. He smiled at Lefkowitz.

"Before I was recruited," he said in a quiet, clear voice, "I *was* a fireman, back in the day. I save people. I don't kill them."

Lefkowitz flinched, throwing himself to the floor both from instinct and training as Edwin let go of the trigger. Those watching ducked behind their shields and a sniper shot rang out from the top of the escalators, ricocheting noisily off the floor, shattering a window behind and to the right of where Edwin had been standing.

And when Lefkowitz looked up, Edwin was no longer there. Instead, a bevy of S.W.A.T. members were frantically searching the premises and the area outside the shattered window, cursing and looking embarrassed.

It took a while before the debriefing was done and the search was called off, but Lefkowitz still had time to vote, so he started to hustle over to the nearby taxi stand. When he exited the building, he turned back to the scene of the day's bizarre events, where so much had happened, but really nothing had happened.

The twin towers of the World Trade Center gleamed bright and white against the blue sky of the crisp September day.

Standing still.

ONE RAINY DAY IN PARIS

Skip and Penny Williams

**Excerpt from Preliminary Report: Incident #6712514
—ATR 600120.346:**

The subject, one Kevin Bower, gained unauthorized access to a time travel apparatus at the University of Chicago through undetermined means—possibly via an arrangement known as "work-study." The subject left his own timeline sometime during the third week of April, 2006 CE (using the date from his own timeline) and traveled back 100 years, landing near a café in Paris. He seems to have had no appreciation of the potential for altering his own history, and the incident appears to have been entirely accidental.

Timecorps was immediately notified of the incident by Professor James Martinez, an authorized Timecorps researcher operating incognito from the University of Chicago's physics department. The professor had been preparing to cleanse the residual radioactivity from the site where Pierre Curie had lunched with several colleagues from the Association of Professors of the Science Faculties, in accordance with Directive D-6984, designed to minimize collateral effects from hazardous discoveries.

The view through the rain-streaked window revealed a wet, gray street where feeble gas lamps struggled against the failing afternoon light and the enveloping rain. A stream of sodden pedestrians strode past, bent against the damp wind. Kevin could see dozens of dripping umbrellas bobbing along, looking like the surface of a restless ocean. Occasionally, a slick, fluted umbrella top caught and reflected a faint ray from a gas lamp and gleamed like a breaker on a moonlit shore.

The whole scene reminded Kevin of the Impressionist paintings that had pulled him here, and he felt the urge to draw. He absently withdrew a pad and pencil from his jeans pocket and began to sketch the rainy street scene while his mind wandered back to the events leading up to his presence here.

It had been a night like any other. After a day of classes at the Art Institute of Chicago, he had headed for the University of Chicago's physics department, where he earned part of his tuition money by cleaning offices and laboratories. This evening, the door to Room 532b was open. *They must want it cleaned,* he thought. *There's probably six months' worth of old pop cans and candy wrappers in the wastebasket, 'cause that door's never open.* Inside, he caught a glimpse of a man dressed in gray overalls fussing with a satchel on a table. It was the machine beyond him that truly caught Kevin's eye, however.

It looked like one of those NMR units they had in the chemistry department, except that this one had some sort of viewfinder mounted near the controls. And prominently displayed on that screen was the corner of a building with a poster on it—a poster by his favorite artist.

"Oh, cool! Toulouse-Lautrec!" Kevin cried, rushing toward the machine. But the image was too small for him to make out any detail. "Where's the zoom button? Oh there it is!" He quickly jabbed a button with

an infinity symbol on it, just as the man at the table
turned around in alarm.

"Here now, young ma—," the gray-clad fellow said,
as a flash of brilliant light grabbed Kevin.

The next thing he knew, Kevin was standing on the
street corner he had seen in the viewfinder, in the
rain, staring at a worn-looking Toulouse-Lautrec
poster that had started to fray around the edges. People bustled past him on all sides, umbrellas shielding
their faces. Realizing that he had no protection from
the elements, he made his way to a cozy-looking café
across the street and took a seat.

Kevin was aware only of the scene outside the window and his pencil scratching on paper. He watched
the scurrying pedestrians, as well as freight wagons,
taxies, and buses, all drawn by horses.

He was out of Chicago all right. It seemed he was
also clear out of the twenty-first century! He knew he
should be concerned over what had happened. But
excitement overrode that. Cool!

The area looked like pictures he had seen of Paris
around the end of the nineteenth century. Toulouse-
Lautrec had been in his prime around then, hadn't
he? Kevin hadn't really paid much attention in his art
history classes, but he thought he remembered that all
his greatest paintings had been done around that time.

He thought back to the Toulouse-Lautrec exhibition
that the Art Institute had done in conjunction with
the National Gallery of Art the previous summer.
Kevin had won the local curator's goodwill with his
natural charm and gotten permission to help set up
and care for the display. Now that was a work-study
program! Not like being a janitor in the physics building, which was all that had been available after the
exhibition had moved on. What a grand time he had
had helping to set up that display! He had been careful not to damage either the museum's precious

Toulouse-Lautrec holdings or the paintings borrowed from other museums. In the process of arranging them and seeing to their daily upkeep, he had minutely examined each piece and developed an enduring passion for the artist's work. The man had been a genius! His use of color and his unique style had made him justly famous both in his own time and in posterity.

Kevin considered the possibilities of his current situation. If he really was in late-nineteenth-century Paris, then he should be able to find Toulouse-Lautrec and talk to him—maybe get some tips on his technique—before whatever source had zapped him here zapped him back home. And if he managed to catch the artist at the beginning of his career, maybe he could buy a painting or two really cheap and take them back to his own time, when they would be fabulously valuable undiscovered pieces. Very cool!

Kevin was so excited by the possibilities of the situation that he had no time to wonder exactly how he had managed to leave his native time and place, or even to worry about how he would get back.

Eventually, Kevin became aware that someone was speaking to him. Glancing up, he saw an annoyed-looking waiter in a stained white apron that suggested a busy lunch hour was just past. He understood what "Oui, monsieur?" meant, but the rest was a hopeless jumble. "Huh?" was all that Kevin could manage in response. He had studied French in high school, but, as with most of his school subjects, he had retained little of his previous knowledge.

Kevin squinted up at the frowning waiter and showed him his unfinished sketch. "Toulouse-Lautrec?" he asked hopefully. The impatient waiter pointed at a Toulouse-Lautrec poster on the wall, then spoke again in a tone that suggested he had no time to waste discussing art. "But where is he?" Kevin asked, then frowned as he realized that the waiter did not understand English.

Kevin stood, his mind desperately seeking some

French phrase or term associated with Toulouse-Lautrec. "Moulin Rouge?" he blurted out. A flicker of recognition crossed the waiter's face. Kevin thought harder, then snapped his fingers. "Montmartre? Maisons closes?" he said eagerly. The waiter's face flushed red, then purple. He spoke a few sharp words, and a second waiter appeared at Kevin's elbow.

"Jean, help me get this . . . this American . . . out of here before he ruins the reputation of the place," said the first waiter to the second in rapid-fire French. "Asking for brothels in the red-light district indeed! What kind of place do they think we run here?" Jean nodded his agreement, knowing well how most Americans viewed his native city.

Two pairs of rough hands grasped Kevin's upper arms, and he soon found himself standing outside in the rain once again. "I always knew French was a stupid language," he said to no one in particular. "People who speak it are crazy."

No closer to his new goal than he had been before, Kevin looked for a sign that said Moulin Rouge. But the only signs he saw were street signs that identified the corner where he stood as Pont Neuf and rue Dauphine, and signs over several shops. His shirt clung wetly to his body, and his soggy jeans hung heavily from his hips. Gathering his courage at last, he stepped in front of a pedestrian, who promptly collided with him.

"Excuse me," Kevin said, "but I need some help."

The thin, young man peered out from beneath his umbrella and ran his gaze over Kevin's jeans and T-shirt. Snorting once, the fellow mumbled something that sounded like an insult, then moved on. Kevin's attempts to speak with other pedestrians yielded no better results.

"There must be someone here who's willing to talk to a stranger," Kevin muttered to himself, shivering a bit as he peered through the crowd. A few feet ahead, an older man stepped out of a doorway, looked about somewhat distractedly, put up his umbrella, and began to limp toward the intersection. Deciding that he could at least delay the infirm gentleman long enough to say more than two words, Kevin stepped up and grasped the old gentleman's shoulder just as he was about to step into the street.

"Eh?" the man said, swiveling, then abruptly grabbing Kevin's arm in an attempt to steady himself after the sudden movement. Just then, a massive freight wagon drawn by a pair of towering bay horses thundered past, charging through the exact spot where the man had been about to step and spraying both men with mud.

"Sacré bleu!" The man's eyes widened in realization that this stranger had saved his life. He caught Kevin in a surprisingly strong hug and kissed both his cheeks, then stepped back and burst out in a stream of unintelligible French.

"Ex—excuse me, sir," Kevin interrupted at last, glancing down at the cracked and blackened fingers still clutching his arm, "but I thought perhaps you could help me." Wondering if the man had some terrible disease, Kevin briefly considered breaking the contact and fleeing, but just then, the fellow spoke—in English.

"Ah, you are Canadian then? One of my esteemed colleague Rutherford's adopted countrymen, perhaps?" His lilting French accent added music to his words. "I am so pleased to make your acquaintance! Please, call me Pierre. And you are?"

"My name is Kevin, and I'm an American."

"But of course, I should have realized!" Pierre slapped his forehead. "An American, yes indeed. Carrying on the fine tradition of . . . uh . . . oh yes, Franklin and Edison! But you have missed our luncheon meeting, my young friend."

"No, I . . . I didn't come for lunch," explained Kevin, wondering if the man was ever going to let go of his arm. "I need to find Montmartre. I'm looking for Toulouse-Lautrec. Can you help me?"

"Considering that you have just saved my life, I would be most happy to assist you in any way I can, Kevin. But Henri de Toulouse-Lautrec died a few years ago. Too much of the drink, you know?" He pantomimed raising a glass to his lips. "I am so sorry. Were you a friend of his?"

"No, just a fan," Kevin said, his dreams of gaining an undiscovered work of art fading abruptly.

"A . . . fan?" Pierre asked blankly.

"Um, an admirer. I'm an artist too."

"Ah, of course. You artists are so eccentric," said Pierre, glancing at Kevin's clothing with a smile. "Well, I cannot thank you enough for saving my life. May I offer you dinner at my home as a gesture of gratitude?"

"Er, no. I mean, thank you anyway, but I'd better see if I can figure out how to get home," said Kevin, as he finally realized the full enormity of his situation. "You see, I was working at the physics department when . . ."

"Physics?" interrupted Pierre. "So you are not just an artist! You are a true Renaissance man! Come then, my wife will be most pleased to meet you!"

"No, really," said Kevin, extricating himself at last from the man's grasp. "I really must be on my way. But thank you anyway. It's been a great pleasure to meet you."

Pierre sighed deeply. "Well, it cannot be helped, I suppose. But I am sorry you will not be able to join our colleagues at the table this evening. A fresh viewpoint always stirs the waters, you know. Here," he said, taking a small glowing vial from his breast pocket. "I would like you to have this—a bit of my life's work—as a gift for saving that life. Take it!"

"Wow! What a cool bottle!" Kevin took the vial almost reverently. "Thank you! How did you get it to glow like that?"

Pierre chuckled. "I never knew Americans had such a sense of humor. Well, I shall detain you no longer. Good luck in your research, young Kevin. Perhaps one day you shall join my wife and myself on the podium to accept the prize for the next great discovery."

With that, Pierre limped away, looking both ways this time before crossing the busy street. Kevin, still entranced by the glowing bottle, stood staring at it. Just as he was about to open it to sniff the contents, someone collided with him and uttered what sounded like a stream of French invective.

Deciding that he had best find a safer place to examine his prize, Kevin started to put the bottle into his jeans pocket, but stopped abruptly when a voice at his elbow startled him.

"I wouldn't do that if I were you," it said, "at least not if you ever want to have children."

"Wha—?" Kevin spun to see a short but rather nondescript man dressed in the same sort of gray overalls that the professor had been wearing back in the Physics Department. "Here, let me have that," said the man, extending a hand protected by a huge mitt made of some shiny material.

"No!" said Kevin, closing his fist around the bottle. "Pierre gave it to me!"

"He's given those to a lot of people," said the gray-clad man. "And if we didn't clean them up, half of Europe would be a radioactive wasteland by now."

"Radioactive?" said Kevin, opening his hand to look at the bottle's glow. "What is it?"

"Radium bromide," said the man cheerfully. "Pierre often carried some with him. It would have killed him eventually—and now I suppose it will, since you've prevented his death today. Now hand it over."

Kevin placed the bottle in the mitt and frantically wiped his hands on his jeans.

"That won't help," chuckled the man. "Come on, let's get you cleaned up."

Excerpt from Preliminary Report: Incident #6712514—ATR 600120.346

The subject Kevin Bower was removed from the past and returned to his own time and place after decontamination. It should be possible to convince him over time that the incident was only a dream, or at most, a metaphysical event involving astral travel or some such nonsense.

Though he altered the past by preventing the untimely death of Pierre Curie, the incident should not change the course of history overmuch, since the man cannot survive his advanced radiation sickness much longer anyway. He is certainly in no condition to make any further scientific discoveries. Thus, there is probably no need to reset history—let Pierre enjoy his last days with his family.

This incident dramatically illustrates, however, the importance of maintaining proper security on all time travel devices. Though the fluid nature of time is a natural aspect of the universe, those who do not understand it are apt to cause significant complications. Thus, complete lockdown and concealment of all such devices is necessary when they are unattended even for a moment.

A row of dun-colored tents huddled together in a dismal field somewhere in France. A persistent breeze caused the canvas to swell and billow, making the tents resemble great puffballs rising from the fields of mud and trampled grass. A few bored cows grazed along the field's fenced edges, where some skeletal trees offered a bit of protection from the wind, despite their leafless branches. Periodically, the wind brought with it a low rumble, like that of summer thunder. The cows didn't seem to notice.

Presently, a small car, well splattered with mud, turned off a nearby lane and bounced its way into the field. It screeched to a halt near one end of the row of tents, and a gaunt, middle-aged woman wearing a tattered alpaca coat climbed out. On one arm, she wore a white band with a red cross sewn on it. Her feet had barely touched the ground when a small crowd of men wearing shabby white coats over military uniforms appeared from the nearest tent. They walked smartly despite their haggard appearance.

"Welcome, Madame Curie," said one of the men, executing a low and unmilitary bow. "You and your X-ray equipment are most welcome indeed. We'll carry it from your car and set it up—under your direction, of course."

"Yes," said the woman rather sharply. "I am happy to provide peaceful aid to my adopted country in its war effort. I shall need only one man to show me a suitable place to set up. There's a generator to power the equipment in the car, and I have only so much cable." She fixed the man with a level stare. "Perhaps it would be best if I spoke to your chief surgeon before we begin."

"As you wish, madam."

Some time later, Marie Curie stood in a darkened tent with an eager surgeon who looked almost young enough to be her son—though not so young as the patient she had just X-rayed. Marie switched on an electric light and held up newly developed film. It clearly showed a leg bone with at least a dozen pieces of shrapnel embedded in it and in the tortured flesh around it. The bone was fractured, but perhaps an amputation could be avoided. The surgeon looked at it with admiration, then his face hardened. The picture was helpful, but where were the fragments, exactly? He tried to recall the exact position of the leg when the famed scientist had placed it in the machine.

Marie laid a reassuring hand on the doctor's forearm. "Don't worry. With a few simple calculations, I can give you the exact location of each fragment."

The doctor's jaw dropped as Marie told him exactly where to probe and cut to extract each fragment.

Marie made dozens of X-rays that day, working with all the surgeons at the field hospital. Some followed her instructions closely and performed some of the most brilliant operations of their careers. Others were skeptical, and neither they nor their patients did so well.

It was well after dusk before Marie could repack her equipment and prepare to leave. She was just closing up her car when the young surgeon came hurrying toward her. "I know you must leave, but there is another matter I must discuss with you." The surgeon hesitated a moment and cast a nervous glance at Marie's radiation-scarred hands. He shivered briefly, then silently rebuked himself for acting like a squeamish first-year student facing his initial cadaver.

"I have read your articles on the promise and the dangers of radiation with great interest, Madam Curie. I would now like to show you several cases I have here at the hospital whose symptoms bear some resemblance to those you have described for radiation sickness. These men are in the wing reserved for gas victims, but they were not gassed. While serving together, they endured a furious barrage that included a great many of what my military colleagues call 'air bursts.' These shells apparently contained some kind of powered blistering agent—similar to mustard gas, perhaps, but not a gas at all. In any case, it seems to have done some internal damage as well as burned their skin, though their uniforms were not damaged at all. Will you come?"

Marie's spine stiffened. "Of course," she said.

The ward was long, and dim, and much too damp and cold for Marie. It also held far too many young men. Why, she thought, had mankind not yet managed to find a way to settle disputes except through violence? Marie stopped at yet another hospital cot as an orderly held up a lamp. In the light, Marie saw the unmistakable signature of radiation at work, tearing apart a living body from the inside. A few questions to the emaciated young man brought the same answers she had heard before. The enemy shells had exploded overhead, showering the trenches with a dully gleaming black ash, like soot from a dirty chimney, or coal dust. The soldiers had hastily donned their gas masks, though not before some of them had inhaled the stuff. They had braced for an assault—the enemy usually followed up a gas attack that way—but none had come. They lived in their gas masks for days, walking about in the gritty ash the whole time, and feeling progressively weaker as they watched their skin develop sores and fissures. Finally, the rain came, and the black ash disappeared into the mud. And then came the assault.

Marie asked to see one of their uniforms and carefully scraped off a small sample of the black dust. Back at the tent that had served as her makeshift X-ray room, she examined the powder and ran several chemical tests. *Pitchblende!* thought Marie. *Those animals are filling artillery shells with pitchblende to make our soldiers sick! But it's more than just pitchblende ore— even weeks of exposure to that wouldn't make them so ill so fast. What could it be?*

Marie X-rayed the men, and the images confirmed her worst fears. Advanced radiation sickness, with bone deterioration and damage to the lungs, liver, heart, and kidneys, as well as the characteristic sores that she had seen on her husband's body and her own. But what could produce such results so fast?

Marie gathered a few fresh samples and packed them carefully for transport to her lab. There she ran test after test, feverishly trying to isolate the additional substance she believed was there. At last, she found it. *A remarkably simple molecule, really,* she thought. *But somehow it intensifies the natural emission of radiation from radioactive substances at least a thousand times. Most likely, it reduces the half-life considerably to do so. An elegant discovery, though it has been put to a highly immoral use. By grinding the pitchblende to a fine powder, they guaranteed that some of it would be taken into the body, either via ingestion or inhalation. Once radium and other radioactive substances are inside the body, they cannot be completely removed. And radiation emitted inside the body is far more potent than radiation originating outside it. Even so, however, it would normally take years for symptoms of this magnitude to occur. But this—this accelerator particle has greatly amplified the effect.*

The implications staggered Marie. Thousands— perhaps millions—of horrible deaths, just like her Pierre's. And not just soldiers—this material was in the land and the groundwater. For perhaps the first time in her life, the publicly stoic Marie Curie felt faint. When she recovered her equilibrium, she returned immediately to the field hospital and sought out the surgeon.

"These men will die, no matter what you do," she said. "It would be kinder to shoot them now than to let them suffer the agony that lies ahead. But I know you wish to do what you can for them, so I give you this advice. You must gather up everything these men have touched—particularly anything they carried or wore during the attacks—and bury it. Use staff people who have not attended these patients before. The furnishings and bedding in here might have to be discarded as well. I have brought some instruments with me that can determine the level of contamination. In the meantime, move the staff from this ward to other duties. No one should work in here for more than a few hours at a time."

She stared at the surgeon with the same intensity she had with the orderly many hours before. "If you don't have the authority to see to these requests, you must take me to someone who can. We stand on the brink of a new dark age!"

Excerpt from Ongoing Status Report: Incident #6712514—ATR 600120.346

By preventing the untimely death of Pierre Curie in April 1906, the subject Peter Bower set in motion an alternate timeline that was initially thought to be benign and of limited scope. Further examination, however, has demonstrated that the effects are more significant than expected.

Because Professor Curie did not die in a street accident, as he was meant to, his radiation sickness became progressively more advanced until medical science could no longer put the combination of unusual symptoms down to known maladies. X-rays of his bones showed extensive decay, and the blackened, hardened skin of his hands eventually succumbed to the necrosis as well. Most of his organs had suffered damage, and malignant tumors had formed throughout his body. Eventually his organs began to fail one by one, and in 1910, he finally died. Biopsies of his bones and skin revealed radioactivity. The conclusion was clear, even to Pierre and Marie, who had been blinded to the dangers by their passion for discovery— radioactivity was lethal. The medical community trumpeted the health hazard to the public, and legislation was quickly enacted to ensure that radium, thorium, polonium, uranium, and all other radioactive elements would be tightly controlled and available only to researchers who were properly protected against them. The "Radium Girls" incident in the United States in the 1920s and 1930s never occurred, and radium salts did not find widespread public use as medicinal substances.

However, the lethal properties of radioactive substances attracted great interest from warmongers, terrorists, and others with a penchant for killing large numbers of people. And though the refined radioactive elements were controlled, their naturally occurring source—pitchblende—the very ore from which the Curies had extracted radium and polonium in the first place—was not, nor could it be. Huge deposits still existed in Eastern Europe, and when World War I broke out, military scientists quickly developed a means to create dirty bombs by grinding pitchblende and mixing it with an accelerator substance that dramatically increased the decay rate of the component substances—as well as the production of radon gas. Millions of people died, and vast tracts of land in France and other countries were poisoned and rendered uninhabitable for the next thousand years.

Nuclear fission became a reality during the third term of American President Woodrow Wilson, and nuclear weaponry wasn't far behind. World War II commenced ten years earlier than it otherwise would have, and the death toll increased by a factor of one hundred. Other divergent events occurred as well. For example, the famed British-American collaboration that produced the first stockpiles of penicillin almost did not occur because the frantic effort to perfect bigger and deadlier nuclear bombs consumed most of each country's brainpower and funding. Only the efforts of an obscure young official in America (one Richard Nixon) salvaged anything from the drive to produce penicillin, and the wonder drug still was not available in large quantities until after the war.

Clearly, this timeline must be corrected.

But it seems that Marie Curie, already dying of radiation-induced organ damage, anemia, and perhaps leukemia, decided to take matters into her own hands. Wildly intelligent, she gained an understanding of time travel. However, since she does not know the deviation point and would not be likely to accept the need for her husband's early death anyway, intervention will be necessary to prevent an even larger divergence.

"Iréne, please hand me that rheostat." Marie turned from the machine she was working on to address her daughter.

"Mother, I still don't understand why you feel the need to test this machine on yourself before going public with our findings," said Iréne Joliot-Curie, picking up the requested component and handing it to Marie. "We've already proved that time travel is possible by using this machine to transport inanimate objects into the future and waiting for them to reappear. The applications of Mr. Einstein's theory are staggering—and we have your discoveries to thank for the necessary power to traverse time itself."

"I've told you before, Iréne," said Marie, picking up a wrench to tinker with the power generator system on the time machine, "mankind was clearly not ready for radioactivity so soon. Look at the devastation that our discovery has wrought."

"But why do you have to go back before your own discovery of polonium?" Iréne persisted. "You were always a reasonable woman with a good scientific head on your shoulders. Can't you just go back and convince yourself not to do it?"

Marie cursed under her breath as she worked at the circuit. "I do not necessarily subscribe to the theory that science fiction writers have put forward that having two of oneself in the same place and time will cause a disaster of epic proportions. But I do believe it would not accomplish our goal of delaying the inevitable discovery of radioactivity. If your father and I hadn't discovered those elements, someone else would have, and very quickly. I had to work like a demon to get those papers out before someone beat me to it, and Schmidt beat me by three weeks on one anyway. If the stage is set for a scientific discovery, someone will make it. No, the discovery that led to ours is the one that must be negated."

"You mean . . ." said Iréne, comprehension dawning in her eyes.

"That's right," said Marie crisply, straightening up and crossing to a locked cabinet. "Henri Becquerel must be prevented from making *his* discovery. That one was an accident anyway—he was working on something else entirely at the time." Marie withdrew a key from her sleeve and unlocked the cabinet, then reached in and took out a pistol. "Who knows how long it would have taken for someone else to make that discovery?" Placing the gun in her reticule, Marie returned to the time machine and began adjusting the dials.

"Ma chérie, you're not going to . . ."

"Don't be silly, Iréne. You know what a pacifist I am. This is just insurance. A person alone in a strange place and time needs some protection, after all." With that, Marie picked up the time transport unit, pressed the switch, and disappeared.

A moment later, Marie looked about. Yes, it was definitely a laboratory, and there on the desk was an open notebook with Becquerel's handwriting in it. She knew the hand well, from their periods of collaboration and the time they had jointly prepared the speech for the 1900 World's Fair.

Outside the window, the day was gray and cloudy. Henri would be abandoning his effort to induce X-ray generation by exposing uranium to sunlight for today. Now all she had to do was find a place to hide until he put the uranium and the covered photographic plate in the drawer, wait until he left, and put the plate out on the table. In the morning, Becquerel would think he had forgotten to put it in the drawer and continue his experiments. No more cloudy days should occur between now and the completion of his work. He would draw the wrong conclusion, fail to discover the existence of Becquerel rays, and radioactivity would not be discovered for some time to come.

Marie sighed as she mentally said goodbye to her own Nobel prizes. But this was for the good of mankind—and besides, if she didn't discover radium, she would not have to lose Pierre. Perhaps they both could live out full, normal lives. Some things were worth more than fame.

"Excuse me, Madame Curie," said a pleasant voice from behind her. Whirling, Marie beheld a lithe younger woman clad in gray overalls. "I can't tell you what a pleasure this is. I've studied your work for many years. You could say that you're my hero."

"Who—who are you?" stammered Marie. "And how did you know I was here?"

"Katrina Mason, Timecorps," the girl said.

"Timecorps?" Marie was only stunned for an instant. If she'd discovered time travel, certainly others could, too.

"Ma'am, I have to ask you . . . just what do you intend to do with that gun in your purse?"

"Probably nothing," replied Marie with a shrug.

"You don't intend to kill Becquerel, do you?"

"Well, I shouldn't have to. But I believe I would if it became necessary. Pierre never liked him anyway," said Marie matter-of-factly.

Katrina sighed. "I'm sorry, ma'am. I can't let you do this. The alteration to the timestream would be too fundamental."

"But don't you understand!" hissed Marie with a passion usually reserved for her work. "Mankind wasn't ready for radioactivity. Its discovery has to be delayed. And his discovery is the crucial point."

"No ma'am, it isn't," said Katrina. "Your husband's death is. Pierre was supposed to die in 1906, on that night when he came home and said a strange young man saved his life. That was the divergence point."

"Pierre?" said Marie faintly. "How could Pierre's earlier death prevent all the devastation that's happened?"

"Nothing can prevent wars," said Katrina gently, leading Marie to a chair. "Violent conflict is ingrained in the human species. But Pierre's death in 1906 would have lessened the overall death toll." As compassionately as she could, Katrina explained the divergence to Marie, counting on her scientific mind to make her understand.

"No," said Marie when the explanation was finished. "I won't relinquish my plans here. I understand how Pierre's death delayed the knowledge of radiation's power and thus its exploitation for war. But my solution would also provide that delay by ensuring that the discovery of radioactivity occurred at a later time, and it would save Pierre in the bargain. And you do not know," she continued, raising a finger to stop Katrina's attempted interruption, "that it would produce any negative result. Do you?"

Katrina averted her eyes from Marie's hard stare. "Well, no, ma'am," she admitted. "But a divergence of this magnitude generally does have unfortunate results."

Marie raised a hand dismissively and spoke with cold fury. "There is no scientific basis for assuming that what occurred by happenstance should produce any better or worse result than a planned alteration. In any case, I will not allow a solution that involves the loss of my Pierre, either in 1906 or in 1910. I want him to live a normal life. If you can accomplish that some other way, I will agree to your plan."

Katrina thought a moment. "Well, there might be a way," she said. "Let me contact headquarters." Taking a small rectangular object from her pocket, she pressed a number of keys, then spoke rapidly into it.

"All right," said Katrina as she put the object away. "We have a proposition for you—and for Pierre."

Rapidly she explained the plan. Marie considered it briefly, then smiled. "I believe we have a deal," she said.

"Great!" said Katrina. "Now let's get you out of here before Henri arrives."

"Don't worry about him," said Marie. "He never gets out of bed before ten anyway."

Excerpt from Final Status Report: Incident #6712514—ATR 600120.346

Agent Mason successfully prevented Marie Curie from altering Henri Becquerel's discovery of radioactivity and returned her to her own time. Two additional forays were needed to set up the conditions required for the agreement.

Pierre Curie was removed from the timestream in April 1906, two nights after Kevin Bower had saved his life. The cadaver substituted for him in the carriage accident was never questioned, since its head was crushed. The body was identified as Pierre Curie from the cards he carried and the bottle of radium bromide in his pocket. After decontamination, Pierre received cybernetic implants in his damaged legs and cybernetic replacements for his damaged organs.

In the last years of her life, Marie faded into obscurity as her illness began to take its toll. In 1934, she too was removed from the timestream and replaced by a specially constructed double, who wasted away and "died." The residual radiation in both her substituted corpse and Pierre's prevented any later attempts at autopsies. Marie also received cybernetic replacements for her damaged body parts, as well as synthetic bone marrow to correct her leukemia.

"The two of them should live to be a hundred," said the Timecorps doctor after completing the surgeries. "A little short by today's standards, but they're older models, after all."

Pierre and Marie Curie joined the Hazardous Discoveries Containment Division of Timecorps and have made exceptional progress in monitoring and managing scientific advances.

Kevin pushed his industrial-sized trash can through the darkened corridors of the physics department and wished he were elsewhere. "Hmmm, what's going on in 532b?" he murmured. "That room's almost never open. Maybe I can get in there and clean up the candy wrappers. Those guys never eat anything healthy."

Pushing open the door, Kevin saw Professor Martinez talking to a thin, older man clad in baggy gray overalls. Somehow the fellow seemed familiar. Creas-

ing his brow in concentration, Kevin tried to remember where he might have seen him before.

"Hey, didn't I meet you at that Toulouse-Lautrec
exhibit last summer?" Kevin charged through the door
to confront the gray-clad man.

"Er, no, young man, I'm afraid not," he replied in
a lilting French accent. "It must have been some
other Frenchman."

TRY AND TRY AGAIN

Pierce Askegren

When she came to our booth to take our order, the waitress did a double take, pausing in midstride and blinking in surprise. I didn't mind. She was pretty, with a good figure and red hair (rare where I come from) and freckles (even rarer). Anything that encouraged her to linger at our table was fine with me.

"Twins?" she said tentatively, looking at us.

"Hardly," said my lunch mate. His tone and expression said that she'd offended him with the question. Naturally, I found his offense offensive, but I tried not to let irritation show in my voice. The situation was already unstable enough and I figured it would be a good idea to defuse things.

"It's a long story," I told her, with what I hoped was my most winning smile. "But we could we have a moment?"

She nodded and flashed a dimpled grin, brief but real and directed just at me. "Just give a holler," she said. "I'm Mackenzie, by the way."

I could understand her confusion. Seated across from me, he looked like a distorted reflection: the same lantern jaw and same black hair, even if mine had picked up traces of silver and receded a bit. The gray eyes and high cheekbones matched, too. But his

232

nose had been broken at some point and not properly
set, and his teeth were much better than mine. Even
seated, he was nearly an inch taller than me and in
better shape, too; his belly didn't push out the way
mine does.

"She's just doing her job," I told my dining
companion.

"She's a subcitizen," he said. He spoke with the
matter-of-fact arrogance of someone who really hadn't
yet accomplished very much with his life but fully intended to.

I sighed. Laminated menus loomed vertically to either side of the table's napkin dispenser. I took two
and passed one to him. "Choose something to eat," I
said. "And don't use terms like 'subcitizen.' It's an
anachronism and it's offensive."

He glanced at me warily. Less than an hour had
passed since I had encountered him in the town
square, introduced myself, and invited him to lunch.
He still hadn't decided whether to trust me.

"It's not in common use," I amplified. "You'll call
attention to yourself, and I don't think you want to do
that just yet." I paused. "Look, what's your name?"

"You should know that," he said, still suspicious.

"I should, but I don't," I said. "Look, let's put it
another way. What do you want me to call you?"

"Mark," he said. "Mark was my grandfather's
name." For the first time, he smiled, however faintly,
and looked five years younger. Memory works like
that. A good memory can make you young again.

It wouldn't have worked with me, though. The
pleasant associations just weren't there. I never met
my grandfather and I never met my parents. Sometimes I even wondered if they'd ever met one ather.
My childhood memories were of crèche attendants
and instructor teams.

"That was my grandfather's name, too," I told him,
scanning the menu. It was nothing special and held no
surprises or mysteries that I could see, but he puzzled

over his like an instruction manual. It was easy to see that he'd never been in a place like this before.

Where we were was a small-town diner in southern Virginia, less than a mile off the Interstate and almost as close to a minor, but well-regarded, college. The eatery catered equally to truckers and students. Far from being a "subcitizen," whatever that was, Mackenzie looked to me like she was waiting tables to earn her tuition. The restaurant air was heavy with appetizing aromas and slightly thickened by cooking grease. We'd taken our seats at the tail-end of the lunch rush and the place was still busy, populated by people too occupied with their own business to care about ours. That was one reason I'd picked it.

Mark was still working his way through the menu, I saw. "What kind of place is this?" he asked. "Everything has meat in it."

"Not everything," I said, and pointed. "Here. Vegetarian."

Mackenzie came back. Mark ordered a salad but I opted for a roast beef sandwich, ignoring Mark's *tch* of disgust. If my eating meat was the biggest shock he had to put up with today, he could consider himself lucky.

"How long have you been here?" I asked as she moved away into the bustle her workaday world.

He looked at me but didn't say anything.

"It hasn't been long," I said, matter-of-factly. I had been in town for nearly a week, keeping an eye out for Mark or someone like him. He must have just arrived. "You still have that deer-in-the-headlights look."

"Huh?" he asked. My word choice had confused him.

I sighed. There was so much that people in our line of work need to know, but no one ever seems able to learn it all, at least not in advance. Local idioms were the hardest. "Shellshocked," I said again. "Confused.

Disoriented." I paused. "There's a lot to take in, Mark, and you're going to have to do it fast. They must have told you that."

Mackenzie brought our food. At my suggestion, Mark had ordered iced tea, but I'd selected beer, netting me more of his disdain. She'd brought a pitcher of iced water, too, and topped off our glasses.

"Let me know if you need anything more," she said, with a casual touch to my shoulder. I liked her. She was just friendly enough that I could pretend she was flirting, so I smiled, too. Courtship games were another thing that had taken some getting used to.

"She touched you," Mark said. Apparently, his personal boundaries were very different than mine.

"It's an old waitress trick," I said. "Casual contact almost always leads to bigger tips."

"Tips?"

I sighed again. He really did have a lot to learn. "How old are you?" I asked.

"That's not an easy question," he said. Once again, he smiled, however faintly. His sense of humor was like mine, too.

Food for thought, that.

"Work with me here," I said. Another bit of vernacular welled up in my mind, and I grinned. "If you can't trust me, who can you trust?" I asked.

Rather than answer, Mark picked up a fork and began to push food around on his plate, as if he'd misplaced something in the jumble of greens and vegetables. He speared a radish slice, eyed it skeptically, then popped it into his mouth. Loud crunching sounds followed, and his face lit with sheer delight as he continued to chew. It was easy to see that he'd never eaten genuine dirt-grown produce before.

The salad would likely keep him busy for a while, so I turned my attention to my own meal, thin slices of beef served open-face on whole wheat toast and awash in a sea of brown gravy. It was diner food, fast and cheap and loaded with more salt than could possibly be healthy. Even so, I made a great show of enjoying it. Mark's disdain still rankled.

Where I come from, animal flesh was a delicacy, scarce and expensive. I hadn't tasted beef until Graduation Day, when Academy classmates had convened a dinner to celebrate full citizenship. The serving I ate so casually now dwarfed what I'd been served then. Even the gravy I sopped with extra bread would have cost a day's credit.

Mark had paused. He eyed my plate skeptically, but this time, with a glimmer of interest. My enthusiasm had piqued his curiosity.

"How old?" I asked him again.

Sharing food tends to inspire trust, for some reason. Or fellowship, at least. "I don't suppose it makes any difference now," he said slowly. "I was born in '32. They sent me back in '52."

He was just a kid. The realization made me feel very old. "Who is 'they?'" I asked.

Whoever they were, they were getting desperate, I decided, sending a kid back on a job like this.

I hoped it had been the Academy. They weren't fun but they were familiar. I knew how the Academy worked and how Academy agents thought. Not so with the Cadre, though. As near as I could tell, those guys practiced a type of institutionalized anarchism and never did anything the same way twice. Any long term goals they held went beyond my understanding.

"The Imperium, of course," Mark said.

"The Imperium!?" I asked. I'd never heard of it before. "What the hell is the Imperium?"

If I'd offended him before, it had been with little things that really didn't matter very much to either of us. This was different. This time, I'd questioned the very bedrock of his life. Worse, I'd done so casually, even dismissively. He scowled at me and set down his fork with dramatic emphasis.

"Was Sizemore running things?" I asked. It was al-

most always Sizemore, at the Academy and the
Cadre alike.

"I know Sizemore," Mark said, seizing on the familiar name and relaxing. Familiar was good when you
found yourself in a new world. I knew that from
experience.

"Of course you do," I said, soothing. "We both
work for him. Now, tell me what you know about
the Imperium."

Because he really was just a kid, and one who'd
been trained to obey, he did. As we worked our way
through the meal, he offered up a brief history of
his Imperium.

None of it made a whole lot of sense. Apparently,
where Mark came from, the *Revolution Academe* had
never happened, let alone happened and prevailed,
and the French government had remained pretty much
intact until the end of the century. The revolt's absence meant that there had been no Academy, not
as I'd known it, and no Cadre, either. The Battle
of New Flanders had never happened, so the New
Monarchism had never been quashed. Thus, the Imperium.

The scenario was new to me, and not easy to accept.
I had no tears to shed for the Cadre, but I have to
admit that the complete nonexistence of the Academy,
even as a footnote, was a bit of a shock. Better the
devil you know than the one that you don't and all
that. And it sounded to me like Mark's outfit combined the worst elements of my people and the Cadre
both. The whole thing gave me pause, even though I
knew it didn't really matter.

"So things actually get worse," I said. I set down
my fork and reached for the beer Mackenzie had
brought with the food. Two gulps half-drained the bottle and made the world a slightly better place.

"It's not as bad as all that," he said. He was speaking
like a good citizen now. The only reason I didn't worry
about his being overheard was that what he was saying

would have made even less sense to eavesdroppers than it did to me. "Antarctica is nearly pacified, and the Biomass Affiance Protocols have been implemented. All we need is more time. In two generations—"

"Mark," I said, interrupting as gently as I could. "That's not going to happen. None of it. And Sizemore's never going to pull you back. He's gone, too."

I watched carefully to see how he responded, remembering my own reaction to his news about the Academy. Mark was ten years younger than me, and looked like he was in better shape. Depending on the nature of his assignment, he might be dangerous. It didn't seem likely that Sizemore would have armed him with a mumble-gun or a nerve-knife or any other technology that could cause long-range problems, but he had a fork in one hand and a knife in the other. A properly trained man in good condition could do a lot of damage with either. I knew that from experience, but I needn't have worried. He responded with confusion and surprise rather than violence, about the way I would have.

"What?" he said. "But Sizemore sent you—"

"*My* Sizemore. He's gone, too."

"But—"

"Just a moment," I said, raising my hand. Mackenzie was coming back to check on us. She seemed to have an excellent sense of timing. "Do you want dessert?" I asked Mark.

"Dessert?" It was as if he'd never heard the word.

I sighed. The Imperium sounded less and less like a place where I would want to live.

The waitress gathered up our plates, with the kind of efficiency and grace that comes only with practice. That was another reason I liked eating at places like the diner; it was always good to see someone do a job well and enjoy doing it.

"You didn't finish your sandwich," she said, in mild reproof. "It was okay?"

"It was fine," I said.

"How about you?" she asked Mark. He'd scoured his plate, but she still wanted to know. "How was the salad?"

"It was fine," he told her, parroting my words. He was learning.

"Anything else, then?" she asked. "We've got banana cream pie today."

"That sounds good, but I'll tell you what sounds better," I said. "Root beer floats. Two, with extra syrup and whipped cream."

"Good choice!" she said.

"Beer has alcohol, right?" Mark asked tentatively. He seemed relieved to have something else to talk about. "I don't drink alcohol. It's forbidden."

"It's root beer," I said. "Something different. You'll see."

He looked doubtful.

"Smile at her when she comes back," I said. "They like that. Make eye contact, too. It's polite."

"I don't think I need to learn the local mores."

"Yes, you do," I said. "Mark, you're going to be here a long time."

He shook his head doggedly. "No more than seventeen local hours," he said. "Then I go home."

Seventeen hours. I thought for a moment, then nodded. "You're here for the conference, aren't you?"

It was a college town. The local school was primarily a liberal arts operation, but the Dean of Mathematics had aspirations. He'd been able to justify and arrange a gathering of promising students from across the country, an invitation-only conclave complete with guest lecturers. In the here-and-now, it was nothing special, but I knew that it was precisely the type of event that loomed large in written histories. People would meet one another for the first time. Insights would be imparted, personal and professional relationships formed. Lives would be shaped. I tried to keep an eye out for events like the conference, and the announced topic had been particularly interesting.

Attending scholars were to present pro and con papers on the theoretical possibility of time travel.

That wasn't my primary concern, though, just an intriguing side-note. What worried me was that three founders of the movement that evolved into the *Revolution Academe* had been born in Virginia. I wondered if the history of Mark's Imperium was similar. I had to wonder if the attendance list included any future grandparents of interest.

"Registration starts tomorrow morning," I mused. "That's why you're here, isn't it, Mark? To see to it that someone misses a presentation, or never meets a mentor. Something like that."

He didn't say anything.

"How are you supposed to do it? Let the air out of tires on a parked car? Make a prank phone call?" I asked, then paused. "Tell me you're not supposed to kill someone."

He flinched and I knew I'd hit a nerve. Oddly, I found the reaction reassuring. Whatever the specifics of his assignment, he had his doubts. That was good.

Doubts made it easier. Doubts gave me something work with.

"You're not an assassin, Mark," I said gently. "If you try to do the job, you'll hate yourself. And if you succeed, you'll hate yourself even more."

"I can do what has to be done," he said doggedly. "Sizemore says that desperate times call for desperate measures. He says—"

"He says that expedience dictates morality," I said, interrupting again. "That the needs of the many outweigh the needs of the few, and that the survival of civilization is worth getting your hands dirty. What a bunch of hooey."

I'd heard it all before. Only Mark knew how his last experience with Sizemore had played out, but I remembered mine all too well. Fat-bellied and balding, the older man had been the closest thing to a father I ever knew and I guess in my own way I'd loved him. That hadn't made it easy to watch him labor over the chronal displacement unit's controls, lab coat spattered with blood from his wounds and breath coming in ragged gasps. All around us, laboratory lights had flickered and components smoldered while I waited anxiously inside the transit module's containment field. The machine's specific workings were a mystery to me, but I knew that I was the first text subject any larger than a neutron and the idea terrified me. The jumble of historical data and combat techniques he'd force-fed me with sleep tapes and deep conditioning hadn't helped my state of mind, either.

Sizemore hadn't cared about any of that, of course. He'd had his own priorities. "Just do what I told you and you can save us all," had been his final words to me. No good-byes, no benediction, just a last command as the door came down and the rebels swarmed into the lab.

The next thing I knew, I was huddled behind the bushes in a present-day public park, alone and confused, but still focused on a mission that didn't matter anymore.

"He told you that they were dead and dust, anyway, didn't he?" I continued. "That it was worth one more death, a century ago, if it saved the Academy."

Mackenzie came back with our desserts. They were huge, in tall, footed glasses cloudy with frost. Ice cream rose from them in smooth white domes topped with fluffy whipped cream. She set one in front of each of us, along with straws and long-shanked spoons. I felt better just looking at them. As far I was concerned, root beer floats were the best part of living in the past.

"Academy?" Mackenzie asked. I'd been speaking too loudly, and she'd overheard my last words. "You guys are here for the conference?"

"Sort of," I said, I said, and hazarded a guess. "You're attending?"

"Sort of," she said, echoing my words. "The dean said I could audit a session. I'm Engineering now, but

I might change my major. I always liked numbers."
She paused. "Hey, is everything okay?"

Everything wasn't. I felt as if the world was slipping
away a second time, and it must have been shown on
my face.

*Mackenzie was the reason that Sizemore had sent
Mark. By chance, I had brought them together!*

Even as I made the connection, he did, too. His
mouth opened and his cheeks went pale, and the boyish
cast of his features abruptly fled. He looked away from
Mackenzie, as if ashamed of what he was thinking.

"Everything's fine," I said slowly. Part of me wondered how many times I'd said those words. My whole
life seemed to be made up of things I had to do again
and again.

"How about you?" she asked, turning to Mark.
"You look like you just saw a ghost!"

Under the table, I prodded him with my foot, using
enough force to command his attention. "Manners,"
I said pointedly.

"I–I–Everything's great!" Mark said. Like I'd told
him to earlier, he made eye contact and even managed
a *pro forma* smile. "Really!"

"Well, okay," Mackenzie said, dubious. She set our
check on the table's Formica surface. "I can take this
for you, or you can pay up front. Maybe I'll see you
two at the conference?"

"Maybe you will," I told her. Once she was out of
earshot, I continued. "How about *that*, Mark? Isn't it
nice to have somebody pretty smile at you?"

"Shut up," he said, eyes narrowing.

"Mackenzie seems pretty bright and lively for someone who was dead and dust long before you were
born, doesn't she?"

"Shut up!" he said and I felt sorry for him. It's hard
enough to think about killing someone you've met, let
alone a pretty someone who's smiled and given you
food and asked how you felt.

Even so, I pressed the issue. "She's young and looks

healthy, Mark," I said. "Probably has a lot of years ahead of her. I wonder what she'll do with them?"

He slapped the tabletop hard enough to make the glassware dance, and looked away from me. "Shut up, I said! I don't want to hear it!"

I shut up. I shucked the paper wrapper from my plastic drinking straw and speared the root beer float. Melting ice cream had turned the soda thick and rich, and the bubbles tickled my tongue as I drank. Mark followed suit without prompting. Too shaken to light up the way he had with his first taste of fresh salad, he still obviously liked what he tasted. Long moments passed in silence that was broken only by the clink of metal spoons against glassware.

"What's the Academy?" he finally asked.

"Hmm?" I said, still eating. I may not have finished my sandwich, but I never, ever let good ice cream go to waste.

"The Academy. You said that Sizemore wanted to save the Academy."

"Of course he did. He was the Senior Professor of Applied Chronal Studies." I managed a snicker. "His job was on the line."

"Not my Sizemore," he said sadly. "His title was Duke of Trans-Temporal Physics."

My Sizemore. He'd figured it out.

"Uh-huh," I said.

"You're not me, are you?" he asked, plaintive now. "I thought at first you were a later me, that something else had happened and Sizemore sent me back again to help. But you're not."

"I'm not you," I agreed. "I could have been, though. Same genes. I was born in '48, and Sizemore sent me back in '73. I was born later than you and I came back further when I was older, but I could have been you. I've been here eight years, local time."

"Eight years," he said softly.

"It was supposed to be thirty-two hours at most," I said.

"What was your assignment?"

"Keep someone from being born."

"How?"

I hated that question. I always do. "Something bad," I said. "Something I'm ashamed of. But it didn't work. The kind of tailored changes Sizemore wants don't seem to be possible. There are just too many variables. And too many old patterns that reassert themselves."

"Oh." His straw gurgled as he drew down the last of the root beer.

I told him about my timeline, about the *Revolution Academe* and all the rest. The broad outlines were all that I offered up; the details didn't matter anymore. Besides, I'd forgotten most of the story. The only place that my specific past lived now was in my memories, and eight years is enough time to forget a lot.

"That doesn't make sense," he said when I finished, but the protest was half-hearted. He was nearly into the acceptance phase now. "It *can't* happen that way. That kind of socio-economic elitism—"

"It won't happen that way, but it *did*," I said. I wasn't in the mood for political rhetoric. "It seems to happen that way about half the time, but it happens other ways, too. Your Imperium, for example. And don't get me started on the Cadre."

"But you and I—"

"You and I are like the rest of the future. We happen a lot of ways, but we happen again and again. We're near-constants, the same bloodline expressed across multiple histories."

"That's a hell of a coincidence," he said.

I shrugged. Sometimes, shrugging is all you can do. "Sure, but it happens," I said. "Look at Sizemore. There's no such thing as fate, but there *are* patterns that play themselves out again and again. The Academy rises, dominates the world, then falls to be replaced by something worse. The Cadre does, too. The same thing, only different."

Eight years had been long enough to read a lot of

the local literature. Much of it was very good. One writer I particularly admired had likened the future to a booted foot, smashing down into an unprotected human face. He'd been right, but what he hadn't known was that the style of the boot would vary, even if the foot and the face stayed pretty much the same.

Mark continued. "But for our parents to meet over and over, and our grandparents, and—"

His words trailed off into silence, and I shrugged again. "It happens."

"What now?" he asked. "If I can't go home again, I mean."

"You can't. Home's gone, Mark, even if something almost exactly likes it happens instead." We were almost finished. I pushed my empty glass aside and reached for the slip Mackenzie had left. "And after a while, you'll be *glad* you can't go back," I said. "I sure am."

The diner was an old-fashioned place, even by the standards of the day, and the check was handwritten. Mackenzie had dotted the *i* in her name with a little cartoon heart. Mark watched as I added up the numbers in my head.

He really did have a lot to learn, but he'd manage.

"What am I going to *do*?" he asked, echoing my thoughts.

"Do? You'll do what I did. You make a place and a life for yourself," I said. "I can get you a new name and show you how the world works. I've done it before."

I left some bills on the table, enough money to cover the check and a healthy tip. With well-honed waitress skills, Mackenzie looked up from working another table and waved to us as we left. She really was a sweet girl. Mark waved back and I smiled; there was hope for him yet.

Even so, I have to admit that I was relieved when we stepped outside and those two were no longer in the same room.

By now, it was midafternoon. The sky was clear and the air was fresh and clean. I knew next to nothing about Mark's world, but this one had to be better, even if the seeds of the Academy and the Cadre and the Imperium were already sprouting. I was sure that Mark would come to agree. He already liked the food, which was a good start.

Life gets lived best lived in the present. The futures could take care of themselves.

"You'll like it here," I told him. "We always do."

"You keep referring to others," he said, as if he'd just realized it. "I'm not the first? After you, I mean."

Now that the hard part was over, now that I'd explained the situation and kept another me from making the same mistake that I had, I could manage a laugh.

"No," I said. "You're not the first. You're not even the first one this week."

YESHUA'S CHOICE

Nancy Virginia Varian

Old man, old man. Every joint and sinew groaned the words. Old man.

On the day of his leaving, Yeshua grunted when he bent to ladle water from the wide-mouthed clay jug; he couldn't help it, old men get thick in the belly, no matter if they eat modestly and they work all day. He was not very thick, but the leanness of youth had long ago become hidden. He lifted the ladle high, upending it, sighing with pleasure as the cool water poured over his head. It ran in rivulets through his silver hair, down his neck. It chased through the ugly channels of tortured flesh made by the old scars of an ancient scourging.

Again he bent, again he poured, and now he took up an old linen cloth and washed sweat and sawdust from his shoulders, arms, his thick chest and that old man's paunch.

Old Man Yeshua.

On this day of his leaving, he was older than most in his little village, younger than most of his storied line. Those people of David's house, men and women of legend who were said to have lived miraculous numbers of years.

By Adonai's grace, he thought, for they had been given miraculous deeds to perform.

As, once, I had been given.

Yeshua barely flinched when he thought that. His was the loss of the abandoned; the loss of the orphaned.

Only last night, a hot night when people of Natzeret did as they always did and went up to the rooftops to spread their bedding and sleep, one of Yeshua's neighbors heard a cry go up: *Eli! Eli! Sh'vak toni?*

My God, why have you abandoned me?

A child, suddenly wakened, called to her mother. Lying in silence, his own words still echoing in his mind, Yeshua heard the woman tell the little one that their carpenter dreamed and his dreams weren't for others to talk about.

"Now come here and sleep beside me, child . . ."

They were protective of Yeshua in that little town. He had grown up there, had traveled far and then come home to stay. For a time he had been their rabbi. He was now their carpenter, and a good man for all the strangeness of him.

This nightmare, as others before it, had been spurred by the terrible news being carried up and down the roads like the cawing of ravens.

But this dream had not left in the morning. It had lingered, and through the day he'd heard the words Yerushalayim, Yerushalayim. Yerushalayim!

He felt the words as a drumbeat, he recalled all he'd heard about the fate of Holy City, news brought by those who'd fled her gates. Murderers drove them out, and war drove them out; from both sides the people had reason to dread, and the latest word was that Titus the Roman had left the city in ruins, taking four thousand prisoners with him to be sold as slaves in Rome. Like wolves, factions of Jewish zealots had torn the city apart between them like beasts fighting over a corpse. When not one of those factions could triumph over another, the man Eleazar, descendant of a long line of rebels, took his folk by the hundreds out of the city to go and sit upon the rock that had once been the palace and fastness of Herod the Great—the place known now only as Masada, the Fortress.

"These are days," said the priests, "like the days of Babylon. These are the dark days before the storm."

It had been said that for a year a star shaped like a sword had hung over Yerushalayim. Few, it seemed, had seen that as an evil omen, most had thought it a sign of Adonai's protecting hand.

Only days after the blade star vanished, Titus and his legions had fallen upon the city.

As in the days of Babylon, now the Holy City, the great Temple, was a place where men were as butchers and dogs fed in the streets, the courtyards, in the gardens like wolves.

Some of Yeshua's neighbors, the ones who had heard the tale from their own fathers, recalled that thirty or more years ago their own carpenter had prophesied this terror.

But had it been prophecy, or had their carpenter cursed the city?

Some wondered, Yeshua saw it in their eyes now.

He wondered, too. In his dream last night he'd heard the sound of his own voice as it had been on a day long ago atop the Mount of Olives. He'd stood looking down at the city, the place where he was to die—and did not die—and said to men who had been his friends that the time was near when not one stone of the great Temple would stand upon another.

He had spoken as he always did, confident that what he said was true. How could it not be? Every breath he took, every word he spoke came into him from Eli, Adonai, Abba. His Father sat beside him when he spoke with his friends, stood at his shoulder when he addressed the multitudes; the breath in his lungs, the blood in his veins, the words in his mouth. Abba.

But Abba was gone now . . . he had long ago withdrawn his spirit and left but this mortal shell behind.

Yeshua snapped out the damp, grimy towel he'd used to wipe away the day's sweat, hung it on the window sill, then took a clean one from the basket near the door. This he folded neatly, smoothing the creases just so and set it upon the small table he'd today finished making.

Placing it, he heard in memory his foster-father's admonition when, adolescent and high-headed, he'd challenged the good old man for going against time-honored tradition by using a fresh towel.

"Yes, yes," Yosef had said. He'd spoken impatiently, for who is not often impatient with the youth who purports to know so much more than his elders? "I know the tradition, boy. Tradition says you place the towel you wipe off with. You offer the sweat of your labor as well as the product. Tell me—" He'd run his hands along the curve of the chest's lid. "—would you give this to the woman wanting it for her daughter's carefully woven dowry goods with the grime of your sweat and flecks of sawdust still clinging?"

He'd been a man to honor every tradition, had Yosef. Most he had honored in his own practical way.

And the boy Yeshua, moved by the image of a maiden weaving her dowry, perhaps gathering the lavender from her garden and braiding the slender stalks into fragrant wands to tuck between the linens, had come to follow this tradition in the same way his foster-father had.

He had never called Yosef "Abba," but his mother's husband had acted in all ways as a father and didn't seem to regret the name.

Now, on the day of his leaving, Yeshua touched the table, the cloth, then looked around his little shop. The tools he'd inherited from Yosef hung neatly upon pegs, the floor thick with sweet-smelling sawdust and fat curls of wood from the plane. All was well, as it should be.

When Rivka the smith's daughter came by in the morning to see the little table inside his workshop with the towel neatly folded and placed she would recognize the carpenter's simple message: the work is complete.

What she would have paid him, Yeshua hoped she would put to charitable use, for he would not be there to receive it.

On this day of his leaving Yeshua was bound for Yerushalayim, a city whose downfall he had foretold, the city he hadn't entered in more than thirty years.

No, he didn't know why he was going. He only knew he must go without delay.

The way from Natzeret took an old man's time to travel. Yeshua needed to rest often, and so he stopped whenever he could to take advantage of the shade of a cedar grove or the companionable overhang of stone.

Ah, but in his younger days it had been different, for he'd traveled the land on a journey to a fate ordained from birth.

No. Ordained from before birth. There had been the angel, the messenger sent to his mother from Abba.

Fear not.

"Thy will be done," the maiden Miryam had murmured.

So had Yeshua murmured, for much of his early life. When he left his family's home and began to teach, when the crowds came to follow him and name him Reb Yeshua, each night he'd lie down to sleep and murmur, "Thy will be done." When the lame walked and the dead awoke and tottered out of their tombs; when the multitude had been fed on a few loaves and fishes . . . he had said, "Father, thy will be done."

Saying so, he would feel Abba's presence, the spirit of his Father near.

When in Yerushalayim for the Passover of his thirty-third year, when his friends had deserted him and left him to the scourge and the mockery of a purple robe and a bloody crown of thorns, he'd murmured, "Abba, thy will be done."

And his Father was near, the breath in his lungs, the beat of his heart.

When he'd been bound like a thief and taken back and forth from the court of Pilate to the court of Herod and back to Pilate again, judge to judge, pillar to post, he'd accepted the will of his Father.

He'd been like a man who'd read a scroll bearing a verdict and learned the sentence before any other: this man will die, and it will be a terrible death.

Fear not.

And he hadn't been afraid. Abba would stand beside him in all his trials. Abba would see and he would judge the sacrifice of his son's life sufficient to the Redemption of the benighted race of men. And when he was dead he would do great deeds, flinging down the gates of Sheol and showing all the worthy the way to his Father's house of many mansions.

All this had been foretold since before the time of David.

Men would raise crosses upon the Mount of Skulls, two to bear thieves, one to bear Yeshua the Sacrifice, the Lamb of God. From Sheol the worthy dead would be called home at last.

But the Redemption had not happened that way. Redemption had not happened at all, and the gates of Sheol stood strong and unbreached.

By the will of a woman, freely given to her by her Maker, the race of mankind fell. By the will of a woman, freely used, the Son of the Father was born to redeem what had been lost with the sacrifice of his life.

By the will of a woman, the wife of Pontius Pilate, all that Abba and Yeshua's own mother and poor Chava herself had set in motion simply stopped.

Just . . . stopped, leaving him, the Lamb of God, the Word Made Flesh, to make do with a world he had not expected to live to see.

For if Chava could use her will freely and take fruit from the Serpent and give it to her weak and faltering husband, if his own mother Miryam could say yea or nay to Adonai's angel, so could a canny Roman matron exert all her will to convince her own weak and faltering husband to let Yeshua the Jew go, send him on his way.

"I have dreamed, and my dream tells me that the death of this man will bring about great sorrow and terrible change."

Pilate, who carried lightly the responsibilities of his office, certainly hadn't wanted to be responsible for that. His wife knew it, and she whispered, "If the crowds hunger for blood, give them a rebel or two. Give them Barabbas."

Pilate had, indeed, given the sometime-rebel, sometime-thief to the crowd. Yeshua had seen the crosses as he and his mother and a few friends had made their journey out of Yerushalayim. One of those crosses had been destined for him, until a woman willed otherwise. Upon that cross then had hung the man Barabbas.

The memory of those crosses haunted the old man's steps as he approached the broken walls of Yerushalayim. The sun was high; he judged it safe enough to enter.

He entered barely able to breathe for the stone in his breast, the stone of a lifetime of unshed tears.

He walked in the ruin of Yerushalayim's beauty, sometimes gasping for breath as he wound through the streets of a city beloved of Adonai, fallen now to rubble. An old man lay upon a heap of ashes, sleeping in the exhaustion of starvation. He passed others lying in the streets or fallen, their bodies half out the doors of their broken houses . . . sleeping forever.

In this way, slowly, his chest aching, his limbs growing more and more feeble, he ascended the roads of the city. Gardens had run to seed, those that had not been burned. Dogs ran in the streets, ears back, tails low. One had a large bone in its jaws; the gleaming bone that had once been the leg of a man or woman. The beast's prize had been stripped of flesh, but there would be rich marrow to dig out.

He found a stick to use for a staff; the road up was more than he could take unaided. Not all the buildings of the Holy City had been destroyed. During the Roman occupation some had been kept to quarter the legion and house their whores. Others stood empty, but untouched, their doors creaking on hinges in the quickening breeze. As he walked, Yeshua knew himself watched; no man lives so long and has not learned what the peculiar, persistent itch between his shoulder blades means.

Once he saw a hand move a ragged curtain at a window, then vanish. A pale hand, bony beneath a thin cloak of flesh. Another time, walking through streets that had once housed the wealthy of the Beloved City, he heard what sounded like a child wailing.

But no child lived in this places of ash and death, and the cat that had cried died soon enough in the jaws of a lean, black-eyed dog.

As he walked, Yeshua heard no other voice. The city, once home to thousands, rich and poor, Roman and Jew and traders of every nation, sat in bleak silence but for the snarling of dogs.

He had not seen Sheol, Abbadon; nor ever thrown down Sheol's gates, but Yeshua imagined that this city in her ruin might make up the landscape of that terrible place.

When he came at last to the temple mount, the sight of fallen towers and broken walls, of brazen doors flung down caused a sudden, painful easing of the stony lump in his chest. Gasping, he closed his eyes. Like small daggers, tears pricked behind his eyelids.

When he could bear to look again, he saw the Temple through a wash of running tears.

It was true what he'd said all those years ago about the stones of the Temple. Not one lay upon another, for the Romans had torn them apart after the fires cooled, looking for the gold that had melted.

He had foretold the destruction—and he had promised, with the words of his Father on his tongue, that he would rebuild the Temple within three days.

Three decades and more years than that had passed since that prophecy. The city had fallen, and it lay like a corpse rotting in the sun.

He wept all the long way down through the city, silently but to gasp now and then, for weeping took strength and he didn't have much of that.

The day was ending when he stood again beside the old man sleeping on his bed of ash. The poor creature in his rags seemed not to have moved in all the hours past.

Yeshua hesitated, for he was moved to take his cloak and spread it over the man, to give him warmth against the coming night. While he hesitated, the old man rolled onto his side and glared through narrowed eyes.

And the glitter in those eyes belied the white-haired, stringy appearance of the man. He might have been in his middle years . . . in another age.

"I've nothing to kill me for, old father, unless you want to sell my bones to the dogs."

"I don't want to kill you—"

The man laughed, then coughed. "—and the dogs can manage on their own, eh?" But when he saw Yeshua remove his cloak, he struggled to sit. He held out his hands as though warding off a blow. "No. For that fine cloak of yours anyone would kill me."

Yeshua winced, but he did as he was bid. He knelt beside the man and took food from the leather wallet at his belt, bread and cheese and dried, salted fish.

"Eat—" He shot a look around them as though expecting to see someone, man or beast, ready to pounce on the food. "Eat all you want."

The man shook his head.

"I am Natan ben Enosh, and I have not eaten in

many days. Nor had water to drink. I want none, and will not take yours for it will delay the day of my death." Then, strangely gentle, he said, "Though I thank you."

Natan waited, a discordant courtesy in this terrible place, to learn the name of his would-be benefactor. After a long moment, he heard it.

"I am Yeshua ben Yosef. I ask you, please, eat. Don't let the days Adonai has granted drift away. I'll take you from here and . . ."

The pain in Natan's eyes stopped him from saying more.

"You've eaten well, old father, I see it, and slept on good beds, tasted good wine. You don't know what it is like to count the hours until your death and know the last is still too far away." Natan sighed, a sound like a groan, and slumped to the ground. "Go. Find a better place to be. The city is for robbers, dogs, and the dying now. Go back home, tell your people what a dead city looks like.

"Or go where all the madmen have gone. You talk like a rabbi, so maybe you should go to the Fortress and see how the People of God make their last fight." He wheezed, it might have been laughter. "They will need a rabbi there. I think no rabbi survived what happened here to flee to the Fortress, and Eleazar and his thousand have decided to face down Flavius Silva and all his legions."

And so Yeshua knew he hadn't used all his tears that day. He sat for a while beside the silent man, prayed a prayer for the dying, the kind he'd known in the days when the people of Judea knew him as Reb Yeshua, when the people of Natzeret called him their rabbi. He left Natan ben Enosh, the man barely breathing, as chill twilight fell and he went out to the hills where it would be safer among the jackals than the robbers and the starving dogs now coming out of their holes in broken Yerushalayim.

But he would not go back home to tell a tale they already knew.

Laying himself down to sleep in the shelter of a hollow in the hills, ignoring the unkindness of stone to an old man's bones, Yeshua listened to faint cries echoing up from the ruined city. He did not know whether they were the cries of the ghosts of those who had died in the terrible battle for Yerushalayim, or those still left alive in the city the Romans, and after them the zealots and revolutionaries, had destroyed.

In the morning, he turned his face south and east. It was another day of leaving, another choice. It was not ordained, not commanded, not demanded.

It was a choice wholly his own.

Yeshua began the long walk to the Fortress, to Masada. It would be a journey of weeks. As he had for too many years, he walked alone with no friend at his side or Father to guide him.

Of the two Romans at the approach to the wall, the younger looked at the old man with barely concealed boredom.

"What are you, one of their holy men? A priest?"

Yeshua shook his head. "I'm not. Once I was a teacher, a rabbi." He paused, then stated what must be obvious. The youngster looked on edge. "I'm not armed."

He'd been searched twice before, then waved on to these two at the wall surrounding the foot of the high hill. On it stood a walled fortress, which itself surrounded a walled palace and temple.

Herod the Great had earned many enemies, and so he'd built many walls, upon which sprouted many towers; all of them but this one on the ground at the foot of the high hill where Herod's great fortress, Masada, stood.

And yet, the Romans had done damage to the outermost wall, battered it with siege engines and built embankments and ramps high enough so that archers would make it hard for any defender from with the Fortress to so much as put up his head.

"Why do you want to go there?" the elder of the two solider asked. "Don't you know they're all mad up on that hill?"

"I've heard it said."

The solider snorted. "Do you have a calling to death, old one?"

I'd heard it said.

"No. I have a calling to this place."

"Another one of their mad prophets," said the young man to his companion. "He's unarmed, he might try to pray us away, but I'm not worried about that. Their god hasn't been paying too much attention to prayers lately. Let him go, he will find plenty of company among the madmen."

The other thought for a moment. Two roads went out from the Fortress, one from the top of the hill led to the lake and it was a trader's route for bringing supplies into the city. The other had been known always as Snake, the brutal, winding path leading up the hill from the east.

Grinning, the elder soldier nodded toward the winding way.

"There's your road, old man. Go if you will."

But the younger stopped him before he could take a step. He thrust a leather bottle into Yeshua's hand. "The day is hot. Take it."

A moment later, the young soldier appeared ashamed before his companion, muttering about not wanting to be the one to have to go kick the corpse off the side of the road when the old man fell down dead. Still, he didn't withdraw the water, and Yeshua was glad to have it.

Yeshua thought the road might better have been named Anvil, for it was hard as iron underfoot and heat rippled before and behind, even off to the sides where the drop was so deep he could not see to the bottom. He went with great care, letting his staff feel the way before him, for the road had long lain in disrepair and the edges crumbled easily. In some places, he must go one foot in front of the other.

But he came to where he wanted to be, and he had little trouble gaining admittance. No one thought such an old man could be a danger to the well-fortified multitude sitting now in old Herod's ancient fastness.

Certainly Eleazar the Zealot didn't think so. With less interest than the Roman soldiers below, he looked up from where he sat among a cohort of a dozen men, all hard-eyed and lean. He glanced at the newcomer and then looked away. As though the looking away were a signal, a small woman left a covey of others and came to greet Yeshua.

"Adonai be with you, old father," she said. White teeth flashed in a face fine-boned and brown as a nut. "I'm Marta bat Yakov, and the wife of Eleazar there. If you have only come up the hill, you have come a long way to be here among the besieged. Though I think you have come farther. Have you eaten? Are you thirsty?"

Yeshua glanced around the compound at the men, the women and the children going about the task of a warrior's encampment. The place felt like the hour before a storm. He declined her offer of food and drink, and he too gave his name—said he was Yeshua ben Yosef, a rabbi come to see if all they said about this place was true.

"Well, if they say we are all mad here, they could be right. If they say we are the last of the Jews, they are probably right about that." Marta drew a breath and let it out softly. "If they say my husband leads an army of a thousand—they are wrong about that. You cannot count the children; not the little ones. Most of us are farmers and shopkeepers, but we can fight when we have to. We don't lack for weapons. Just as we don't lack for all else.

"The old king had such an armory that no one here need worry about running out of spears and swords. Water still fills the wells, for there are springs in the caves below this fortress and the water is always fresh. His granary was as fat as he used to be. He laid by figs and dates and olives. By some miracle or the quality of the air so high up, much of his provisions remain edible."

Marta nodded toward a line of low buildings. "There is where we are quartered. We have room for you, Reb Yeshua, if you wish. Rest, refresh yourself and when you are able, tell us what news you have heard in the world outside of here."

She showed him to a cool chamber, windowless and protected from the sun in the shadow of one of the inner wall's great towers. She gave him a pile of thick blankets to lie upon and left a jug of cool water.

"I'm glad to have a rabbi among us," Marta said. "A man of sense and learning."

She said no more. And as he lay down to sleep, Yeshua thought that in Marta's eyes, he saw storm coming.

In the hour before dawn, he woke to shouts of glee and cries of triumph. Yeshua ran from his chamber to see that a storm had indeed come—a firestorm.

Fire lit the sky as though the firmament itself had been set ablaze. Yeshua saw dark figures running through the compound, women after their children, men and boys for their weapons. He found Marta at once, and she herded all her frightened flock toward him and went to look for more. He, in his turn, hurried them to the nearest well.

One or two brave boys scrambled up ladders to see where the greatest danger lay. No one had expected to hear their hoots of derision and scornful laughter.

"Adonai wills!" one shouted, turning to yell the news into the compound. "The Romans forgot to check where the wind felt like traveling!"

Indeed, the fire the Romans had set ran before the north wind, which turned the flames back upon their makers. A great cry of dismay arose from below as Flavius Silva's soldiers ran desperately here and there trying to move their wooden siege engines.

At the well, Yeshua saw no joy in the frightened children. Smoke and shouting and a sky turned red by fire left them all trembling and the smallest crying. Old joints creaking, he sat on his haunches and took the smallest into his arms, told the older ones to stand look out.

"For Romans," one said, somewhere between bravado and terror.

"No." He ruffled the boy's hair and turned him to face outward. "For Marta. She will want to know where we are."

Nor was it long before Eleazar's wife came to the well, trailed by women searching for their lost ones. Low voices murmured, "Thank you, Rabbi; Adonai bless you, Reb Yeshua," as each mother claimed her child from the well to bring them to safety on the other side of the fort, far from the fire.

Yeshua didn't go with them. He watched as one after another, men and boys climbed to the towers and onto the walls to jeer at the Romans and watch them run before the fire. And so he was there when the wind turned, the fire ran back to the fortress wall and the cries of the watchers on the wall became cries of anger, terror, and despair.

Yeshua joined the water line, taking his place behind a brawny youth pulling buckets from the well. One after another, he passed the brimming containers and saw them go man to man in the frantic endeavor to save the wall.

Old man, he thought each time his muscles groaned or his joints cried out in pain. Old man, old man. Old Man Yeshua, what are you doing here?

Fear not . . .

The words settled like a balm on his soul. An old

phrase from another time, he thought, and made his aching arms swing another brimming bucket to waiting hands.

When the fire was out, the women and children and the men of Eleazar's army were black with soot and streaked with sweat. Reb Yeshua stumbled back to a pallet of blankets. He lay in a stupor of exhaustion, and he heard a long, howling cry winding out of the darkness.

Eleazar the Zealot, he who'd led his people out of Yerushalayim and to this fastness, walked through the fortress, like ghost wailing.

"We are the abandoned of God!"

Too weary to give voice, Yeshua could only move his lips to frame words before he fell asleep.

Fear not . . .

When he woke again, he heard Eleazar holding forth not far from the door of his chamber. The zealot's words of despair had hardened into something else, something like stone rushing down a hillside plowing all before it.

Yeshua went out into the morning and found all the nine hundred sixty who had for long months of siege lived in the ghost of King Herod's fortress. Upon the faces of all but the infants suckling or sleeping in their mothers' arms, Eleazar had painted dread with his words.

"Hear me," Eleazar shouted. "We are deprived by Adonai himself of all hope of deliverance. That fire which was driven upon our enemies and of its own accord turned back upon our wall—this was Adonai's anger against us for our sins. We have been arrogant, insolent, changed ourselves into the enemies of our countrymen!"

Yeshua stepped out from the shade of the wall, into the sunlight.

"Eleazar," he said. The words came gentle into the heat of the morning. So they used to do, in the past. "Eleazar, you mistake Adonai's will if you think a north wind turning south is such a thing of wonder that no one has seen it happen before."

The crowd's silence rustled and became muttering. A child sobbed, another wailed. Eleazar turned as though stung, his bloodshot eyes like two red coals. Here was a man counting the dead, though they had not yet died.

"The rabbi. And what do you know of Adonai's will? What have you seen of it?"

Yeshua smiled. "I have seen more of it than you, enough to say to you that—"

Eleazar turned away, already exhorting the crowd as he did.

"We are guilty of such sins that we *deserve* what punishment is ordained. We know this, for Adonai would not mete out punishment unjustly. And so I say let us not take our just deserts at the hand of the Romans—let them not be Adonai's executioners!"

The crowd came closer, and some on the edges began to murmur in agreement, though Yeshua could see they weren't sure what they agreed to. Others shook their heads in confusion.

"Eleazar," Yeshua said, "how do you know the will of Adonai? Has he spoken with you?"

He asked so seriously that none dared laugh.

"Do I know the will of Adonai? No! I am his humble servant. And I say that we have earned his wrath, for he would not visit it upon us if we hadn't." Swift, like a snake, his fervor took another path, as it did, he turned to his people again. "My friends, I can only tell you what I have seen. I have seen how the Romans treat captives, how they use our women, how they use our men for sport in their arenas, feeding them to wild beasts."

Now the men among them grew loud in their agreement, though Yeshua wondered how many had seen what Eleazar claimed to have seen.

"Listen! We will not let the Romans do Adonai's work!"

The crowd held it's breath, and storm came creeping nearer.

"We will do it ourselves!"

From that moment, Eleazar spoke madness, telling them that each man must take his wife children aside and embrace them, kiss them, and in the next swift moment become their executioner.

"For we will not let the Romans have them! We must not!"

Then fell the storm, fed by the winds of madness and fear.

Many in the crowd took up his cry as though it were a battle shout: "We must not! We must not! We will not!" Women wept, children sobbed, and Yeshua murmured, "Fear not."

To whom? He didn't know, perhaps only to himself as he waded into the crowd.

They parted for him, so many knew him as the rabbi who had sheltered their children and helped put out the fire.

"Now," he said, and he spoke in the voice of his youth. "Hear me. Adonai has declared no doom here. He has asked for no blood. My Father," he said, "would weep to see the murder of children at the hands of their parents."

Abba! Beside him, Abba stood; Abba, the breath in his lungs, the beat of his heart.

"Each man put up your knife and look into the face of your wife! Kiss the cheek of your child! Find your wit and your heart there and think of what this man asks you to do."

Like a pillar of white fire, Eleazar raged. He threw in front of their eyes the most horrific images he could summon. Some had heard of the terrors in Yerushalayim, the killings, the rapes, and the torture. Others had been there and did not need imagination to summon what Eleazar wanted them to see. As fire had spread in the night, so did fear now.

They shouted down the words of the strange rabbi.

"Yes!" Eleazar shouted. "Why fear death? We do not fear sleep. Death is no worse, only more! Am I speaking to brave men who will protect their wives and sisters, their children? Or am I speaking to cowards?"

Knives glinted in the sunlight.

Fear not . . .

In his heart, Yeshua cried, Abba! Abba! They will slaughter the lambs!

Fear not, my Son.

The voice of his Father was the beat of his heart.

Yeshua turned and found Marta nearby. He waded through the crowd, trying to get to her. She met him, her fine-boned face changed into that of a warrior. Such a face must have been D'vorah's, she who led the armies of the Israelites in the age of the Judges, tear-streaked and sobbing. Around them grew a storm of shouting and weeping, and suddenly came the smell of blood.

"Listen," Yeshua said. He took her by the shoulders. "Take what children you can and bring them to the caves in the place where the water feeds the wells. Hide there. Hide until this madness is over."

Fire had not bellowed as this crowd now did, and yet around the two a calm settled. Marta clung to his hands. "Come with us. Reb Yeshua, come!"

Abba, the blood singing in his veins: *Fear not!*

Abba beside him, Yeshua shook his head. "Go. I am where I must be."

She hung on her heel, then ran, leaving him, leaving her husband. Yeshua saw her grab the hand of another woman and saw them snatch what children they could, their own and a few others.

He watched them vanish into the crowd, and when he looked back into the compound, he saw that the storm of exhortation had ended. Women sat on the bricks of the dusty courtyard, they stood their children in front of them. Men came and knelt beside them. Some took their babies in their arms, others kissed their wives, and tears rolled down their cheeks.

In his heart, Yeshua said: Abba, make it stop!

But his Father did not answer but to say that the will freely given to all mankind is not to be gainsaid by the Giver.

Fear not . . .

Abba!

Fear not. Go among them.

And so he did, for it had been always what he'd been destined to do. Go among men, minister to them, help them, teach them.

Eleazar, too, walked among the people, quiet now, and sometimes he touched the dark curls on the head of a child, or the shoulder of a father while, here and there, like small silver flames, light danced on the blades of knives.

And where Eleazar walked, Yeshua came after, his eyes the last a weeping mother saw, his step the last a grieving father heard when he ended his own life.

They walked, the two, Eleazar and Yeshua, each aware of the other, until all the deed was done but one part. The last of his people left alive, Eleazar took a sword and wiped it clean.

"Rabbi," he said from across the vast, bloody courtyard. "Help me."

Yeshua shook his head. "You know the law as well as I know it: I shall not kill."

"And you will not defend yourself."

"No. If you do this, you do it of your own will."

The man walked away, his sword clean of all the day's blood, and Yeshua, weary, weary, took himself to the pallet of blankets and lay himself down.

He didn't hear Eleazar die, but he felt it.

Like the draining of my own life, Abba, my own blood seeping away.

"And I don't know what it has all been for. I have

saved no one, redeemed nothing. I was, for a while, filled with your Spirit. And then . . ."

And then, My Beloved Son, you were not. For a woman worked her will upon her husband, and the promise I made to all of mankind that their will would be free has been kept. If I had not kept that promise, what worth the promise of Redemption?

Sickening in the reek of smoke and blood, Yeshua said, "But there was no Redemption. All is as it was."

It is true that all is not as it would have been with the world had you died Barabbas' death. Yet all is not as it would have been here, had you not come. Five children live, and two women. Can you tell me, Yeshua, what will come from those seeds in ten years, a hundred, more?

The last chance of Redemption has not passed, for the promise has not been fulfilled. The time will come again, one day. And we shall see again what may happen.

Rest.

No more did Abba say, but weariness became something else, something sweeter, like the assurance of peaceful sleep.

Old man, old man. Yeshua stood and took a blanket from the pile that had been his bed. He folded it carefully, making sure the creases were even and straight. Then he went and put it at the threshold, laying out the old message.

The work is complete.

THREE POWER PLAY

Wes Nicholson

Present day:

"**I**t's not right," the hooded and cloaked figure said to no one in particular, as it watched the events unfolding on a screen. "It shows that the Japanese attacked Pearl Harbor, and the Americans built the atom bomb. It wasn't supposed to be that way."

A clawed hand reached out from beneath the cloak and twisted a dial. The movement on the screen slowed, stopped, and began rewinding—faster and faster. The clawed hand reached out again and brought the screen to a stop. A small counter on the bottom read: "local date, June 6, 1941." The picture on the screen was of a tranquil palace, definitely oriental in origin but otherwise not remarkable.

The figure did something inside its cloak and then flowed from its chair and into the screen. A shimmering something slid silently through the gardens of the palace and flowed into a spot in midair.

A moment later the cloaked figure reappeared in front of the screen. The counter now read: "local date, June 7, 1941."

"Now then, let's see how that looks," the voice

rasped, and the clawed hand reached out to turn the dial forward, just a little.

June 9, 1941:

The Imperial Japanese War Cabinet was meeting to discuss Japan's options with the war in Europe and Africa.

Should they stay out of it?

Should they take the opportunity to subjugate China while the rest of the world was otherwise occupied?

Should they enter the war on one side or the other?

One of the cabinet members, an admiral, spoke his mind. "The time is right for the sons of Nippon to take our rightful place in the Pacific. We must kick the western influences out of our waters, beginning with the Americans in Hawaii. A strike on their fleet in Pearl Harbor will make any entry into the war on the part of the United States almost impossible."

There was much discussion about the wisdom of attacking a country that had so far shown no inclination to join the war, and was weighing options about which side to come in on—if it came in at all. After some debate, the cabinet members turned to the Emperor Hirohito.

"I had a vision of the fires of destruction that will come of this action," the Emperor said. "You should not send the Imperial Navy to Hawaii; there is a better way. Send the ships to Singapore and Malaya, and take those countries in the name of the Chrysanthemum Throne. The Americans will leave Hawaii soon enough, and then you may send the Navy there to take control."

The cabinet began making plans to invade Malaya and Singapore, and remove the British and Australian forces from those countries.

Meanwhile, in the United States, debate raged about whether supporting the British in their struggle against Hitler was a good thing. For now, most accepted that the debt being built up by Britain was worth the effort—the economy was still recovering from a terrible recession, and anything that got money flowing and people working had to have at least some good points. In the press and on the radio, the far right argued that Hitler's Aryan policies were correct and that the United States should be joining with the Germans to ethnically cleanse the country of all the inferior races.

In the desert of Nevada, a group of American scientists worked alongside Jewish scientists who had fled Europe just before Hitler's jackboots ground their homeland into submission.

In Britain, the war cabinet struggled to come up with a plan that would rock Hitler back on his heels, and the people of Britain worked long and hard just to stay alive. Those who could left the big cities and went to the rural areas where the bombings didn't happen every night. In the moors of Scotland, a group of scientists worked around the clock on weapons and technology that might defeat the Axis powers.

Present day:

"Hmm, better" the voice croaked. "Let's look a bit further." The dial got a sharp twist, and then wound back until the counter stopped at . . .

December 7, 1941:

The Imperial Japanese fleet was well in place to support the land forces in the subjugation of Malaya, the first stop in the conquest of Southeast Asia. In the economic powerhouses of the eastern United States, opinion was swinging more and more in favor of Hitler and Mussolini, and if not for the huge debt being run up by Britain, the war supplies carried by ships would be curtailed.

Present day:

"Ah, now it's looking like it's supposed to." The hand gave the dial another sharp twist, stopping the display at . . .

January 18, 1942:

Singapore had fallen to Japan three days earlier, and now the sights turned south toward Indonesia, Papua/New Guinea, and Australia. A few concerned voices in New York and Washington were howled down when they pointed out that Japan now controlled most of the world's supply of rubber and tin. More voices joined the growing chorus of calls for the US to join with Germany. The Irish-Americans were among the loudest supporters, their historical hatred of all things British fueling their desire to see Britain crushed once and for all.

In the desert of Nevada, the scientists still labored to uncover the secrets of the atom, but their Jewish coworkers had long since fled to Canada, Mexico, and Brazil.

In the wilds of Scotland, the British scientists and their Jewish counterparts worked around the clock, convinced the secret to Hitler's defeat lay in their work.

In Berlin, Hitler's advisers informed the Fuhrer that there were suitable facilities in Sweden for the development and testing of heavy water, a necessary part of building the atom bomb.

In Russia, the people struggled to survive the last of winter and looked forward to the spring thaw.

Present day:

The hand twisted the dial to the right once more, until it read:

June 3, 1943:

The pressure from the media, and through it the public, finally pushed an ailing U.S. President to sign a declaration of war against Great Britain and her allies. The U.S.-Canadian border was formally closed, although in reality it had been a "no-go" zone for some months, and the Canadians moved a sizeable number of troops to each of the known border crossings. The U.S. Navy bases on the Atlantic seaboard were a hive of activity as the officers and men put the last touches to their ships before setting sail for Europe. Around the country, at airfields where new airplanes were being tested, work stepped up a notch to get the latest instruments of war ready for action. America was going to war with the British—again.

In Tokyo, the Imperial War Cabinet laid plans before the Emperor to invade Northern Australia and take control of the mineral resources there. The Emperor liked what he saw, and with Indonesia and Papua/New Guinea already under Japanese control, he saw no reason to halt the expansion of the Rising Sun. He gave his approval of the plans and then retired for the night.

Present day:

"No, no, no." The voice was totally devoid of emotion as it wound the dial back a day, and the view of the palace garden once again filled the screen. Once more the figure fidgeted inside its cloak, and once more it flowed into the screen, disappearing as it touched the grass. A few hours later, the screen shimmered and the cloaked figure reemerged.

Then the dial wound forward one day and the screen focused on the Imperial War Cabinet meeting with the Emperor.

June 3, 1943:

The Emperor nodded at the plans and smiled, but the smile did not pass his lips. His eyes were as hard as granite.

"No. To invade Australia at this time would not be wise. Better to consolidate our position in the region, and secure our supply lines. If the Imperial Navy can cut off shipping to the west coast of Australia, there will be no need to invade. The weakling Australians will come to us, begging to surrender."

While it was plain that not all the Imperial War Cabinet agreed with this strategy, none dared argue with the Emperor, and so it was that the plans for the invasion of Australia were shelved—for now at least.

In the desert of Nevada, the scientists made a breakthrough and begun constructing a device to test their new theory. If it worked, this new war with Britain would be over in a matter of weeks.

In the Scottish moors, the scientists loaded a crate onto a nondescript truck in the dead of night and drove it to an abandoned coal mine, where they unloaded it and hauled it into the mine on an ore car. If the night had not been so dark, a curious onlooker might have wondered why an abandoned mine didn't have rusted rails. But there was only one curious onlooker, and it knew the answer. A thin laugh escaped from beneath the hood as it watched events unfold.

*   *   *

In Russia, the warm weather was matched by warm smiles from many of the workers in the fields. Only the ones dressed in one-piece gray outfits were not smiling, and that was because they were German POWs being forced into slave labor. A few managed the occasional wry grin, as they realized their lot was better than that of the Jews who were on "holiday" in Germany.

June 4, 1943:

In Scotland and Northern England, all the wireless sets suddenly stopped working at 6 AM.

In Scandinavia, people felt the earth tremble and wondered if an avalanche was coming.

In the British Isles, people felt the tremor and looked out their windows, expecting to see a long line of tanks or heavy vehicles passing by. But there was none to see, and the people got on with their lives as best they could—each doing his or her bit to keep Britain's war effort going.

Present day:

The claw turned the dial to the right again, and the display read:

June 6, 1944:

For a year now the British had stood almost alone against the might of the Third Reich, and the American Navy was making sure almost no supplies got through from Canada. It was clear the Germans were massing troops on the beaches of Normandy in preparation for an invasion of England and Wales. The skies were filled with German and American fighter planes, and although the Spitfires and Hurricanes gave as good as they got, the enemy was simply too numerous.

It was only going to be a matter of weeks, if that, before Winston Churchill would be forced to eat his claim that Britain "will never surrender."

Japan had a solid grip on Southeast Asia and China, and the Imperial War Cabinet again raised the possibility of invading Australia. Admiral Kogetashi pointed out to his lord and master that Australia had sufficient resources of its own that the lack of supply from outside was an inconvenience, not a stranglehold that would bring the country to its knees. But the Emperor would not be swayed. That evening, the admiral committed seppuku to atone for his temerity.

In the Nevada desert, the scientists showed the Army and Air Force generals what it was they had been working on these past four years—a bomb, about the size of the one-thousand-pound ones that had been raining on Britain the past twelve months. The generals were disbelieving when told that this bomb was over ten thousand times more powerful than a conventional bomb the same size. The scientists had known would happen, and so had prepared a little demonstration for their high-ranking visitors. At 6 AM the next day, they would show the generals what all the fuss, and funds, had been about.

In France, and throughout occupied Europe, the leaders of the Resistance movement were quietly contacted and told to get their people out of Berlin—within twenty-four hours. For some, this was not going to be possible, but they did their best. None knew why such an instruction would come from the French leaders in England, but there was surely some important reason for it.

In Moscow, the Russian commanders received a coded message from London that it was time to end this war—one way or the other. This was the signal they had been waiting for, and they quickly dispatched messages to their field commanders to prepare to march on Germany.

June 7, 1944:

In the desert of Nevada, as the sun rose over the Rocky Mountains, there was a rumbling sound from beneath the earth and a bright flash at the base of the mountains. Where the day before there had been a moderate-sized town nestled at the base of the mountain range, now there was nothing but a huge cloud of dust thrown up when the earth heaved. The doubting generals doubted no longer, and inquired as to how long it would take to get these bombs into production. When the scientists said it would take another year, the generals said it was wartime, and they had six months to get the job done.

On the Russian front, the German forces were getting nervous. It was clear the Russians were up to something, but the superior German equipment and training had so far kept the Russians from mounting an attack. If not for the Russians being so well dug-in, the Germans would have overrun them last summer. They had learned the lesson of Russian winters, and would not repeat that mistake. But summer was a different matter.

In London, Prime Minister Winston Churchill sent a message to Berlin, and another to Washington, inviting Hitler and Roosevelt to contact him to discuss surrender terms. With Britain on her knees, it did not occur to any of Churchill's staff, nor Hitler's, nor Roosevelt's, to wonder why the Prime Minister had not explicitly stated whose surrender it was to be.

In the north of Scotland, far from the nearest town or farmhouse, at a secret airfield, six planes were

loaded with a single bomb each, and every spare cubic
inch of space on four of them was taken up with extra
fuel tanks. The planes were wheeled into separate
hangars, all of them disguised with peat moss to look
like another hillock on the moors. As soon as darkness
fell, four of the planes would be on their way, the
other two following around dawn. The flying fuel cans
would make a stop at Port au Choix for refuel before
heading to their final destinations.

In Tokyo, the Imperial War Cabinet met to discuss
their options. Japan had taken all of Southeast Asia,
had effective control of China, and the warlords
wanted more. But, with the disgrace of Admiral Kogetashi fresh in their minds, they had no suggestions
as to how to expand the empire further.

June 8, 1944:

Washington, DC. 4 AM. The air raid sirens started
their banshee wail as the fighter planes scrambled to
find the enemy planes that had caused the alarm.
None of the American fighter pilots had yet seen action, as the United States had not been attacked. It
could only be the Canadians, but what were they
thinking? Once the British surrendered, it would be a
formality for Canada to do the same, and become a
part of the U.S. Why would they attack, when the war
was all but over? Their confusion wasn't eased at all
when the fighters found only two bombers, flying a
little apart from each other, coming from the direction
of Newfoundland. There were no enemy fighters visi-
ble, which did nothing to settle the nerves of the un-
tested American pilots. Still, they had their orders,
and they moved to engage the bombers.

The dogfight did not last long—perhaps thirty seconds from start to finish. One of the enemy bombers
was hit in a wing-tank within a few seconds, and it
exploded in a ball of fire that engulfed three of the

attacking American fighter planes. The remaining fighters kept back from the other bomber, making it harder to target accurately, but ensuring they would not be caught in any fireball. It was still only a short time before one of the fighter pilots got lucky, and his bullets shredded the bomber cockpit canopy, the instruments, and the enemy pilots. As the invading bomber's nose dipped, a single bomb fell from the bomb bay.

Less than a minute later, the bomb struck and a bright flash, brighter than the midday sun, lit up the night sky. Within seconds, the American fighter planes' engines died and the pilots survived only a few seconds more as the shock wave from the blast picked up their planes as a child picks up a toy, and tossed them carelessly away, to fall out of control to the earth. The fighter pilots did not live long enough to see the mushroom cloud forming over what had been the American capital.

In New York, just before sunrise, the scene of devastation was worse. Two bombers managed to release their deadly cargoes before they fell out of control. The center of U.S. economic might was a smouldering ruin, with poisonous dust filling the air and fires burning unheeded across the rubble of the city.

Berlin, 10 AM. Two bombers flew over Berlin, unnoticed in the crowded skies. The British had seemingly put every aircraft they had up today, and the Luftwaffe was busy shooting them down as quickly as possible. But it was inevitable that some would get through, and the two special planes did. They dropped their bombs and turned for home, one of them with flames licking at the tail. The bombs exploded in the air above Berlin, and hell on earth followed. Cars, trucks, trams, all came to a shuddering halt. In the skies, the planes closest to the explosions were vaporized, while farther away the engines simply stopped and would not start again. Then came the shock wave, which hurled man and machine alike in all directions.

June 9, 1944:

What was left of the German and American high commands scrambled to surrender to the British, lest any more of the hell bombs be used against them.

In New York, those who survived—and who up until yesterday had been the rich and powerful—quietly packed up their most treasured belongings and headed for Mexico and South America.

On the Russian front, the German troops stopped wondering what was going on, as their Russian opponents had their orders rapidly changed from invading German territory to accepting the surrender of the German army.

In Tokyo, the Imperial War Cabinet abandoned the plans to invade Australia. It was still a part of the British Commonwealth, and whatever weapon the British had developed was not one the War Cabinet wanted to face.

November 11, 1944:

In London, Prime Minister Churchill greeted his guests and showed them to comfortable, overstuffed armchairs. An exquisite Oriental tea service was laid out on a sideboard, with a Japanese woman hovering over it. She served a cup to Emperor Hirohito before retiring to the background. At the other end of the sideboard, a glass and silver tea service was set out, a wisp of steam drifting lazily from the spout of the teapot. Josef Stalin served himself a cup of the jet black brew—not for him the trappings of servants. Churchill poured himself a cup of tea from a Wedgwood teapot into a matching cup, added some milk and sugar, and sat to face his visitors.

"Gentlemen, it seems the world has changed quite a bit these past few months. Though it's a clichéd term, I venture to suggest things will never be the same again, and we three must decide where we go from here."

It took several days and much talking among the functionaries each of the leaders had brought to the meeting. But the three leaders eventually hammered out an agreement.

Eastern Europe would be ruled by Moscow.

The Africa nations would remain as they were—governed by various Western European capitals or in a few cases ruling themselves.

Western Europe was now free of Hitler's yoke and would be allowed to recover and choose its own destiny.

Asia would be governed from Tokyo.

Britain would reclaim her recalcitrant North American "colony."

South America would be left to its own devices, as none of the victorious leaders wanted to contend with mother nature in the jungles down there.

There would be combined efforts to find a way to clean up the mess that had been Berlin, as well as Washington and New York.

And a few visionaries among the delegations suggested that the technology which had helped end the war might be useful in sending a rocket to the moon.

Present day:

The claw reached out and turned the dial to the right again, slowing it down in the early 1990s.

The figure saw that in the fashion houses of Paris, the latest designs were being shown to an appreciative audience. The financial capital of Western Europe had grown stronger in the past forty-five years. French was now the official language of Europe, and the franc its official currency. Many of the other Romance languages were still spoken, but the Germanic languages were forbidden.

In the center of what had been Germany, the figure noted that a sheet of black glass absorbed the sun's rays. Underneath the glass were the remains of old Berlin, but only twenty kilometers away (Europe was definitely a metric society) another city had been built. New Berlin was a hive of industry, and the hub of the aeronautical industry in Europe.

In the northeast of what had been the United States—and what was now known as New Britain—a two-hundred-square mile (the British Empire refused to adopt metric measurements) nature park sprawled where once New York reached for the sky. Two hundred miles to the south, the governor of New Britain built a grand city on the ruins of an old one. He'd had to wait twenty years for the environmental engineers to figure out how to clean up the mess, and then do it, but it had been worth the wait.

In Tokyo, the Emperor was getting very old and frail, but his son stood ready to take over the reins. Japan had found ways of making their expanded empire very productive, and had taken the lead in developing an electronics industry that continued to amaze the rest of the world with their "what will they think of next" ideas.

In Eastern Europe, much of the land was being used for farming. Advances in fertilizers and growing methods had led to a threefold increase in output. Famine was a thing of the past. In the cold wastes of Siberia, people who had been forgotten by all but their closest families dug mineral ores from the earth using electric jackhammers and loaded the ore into mine carts that were hauled to the surface by remote-controled electric locomotives.

Everywhere in the world, people drove to work in their cars, rode pushbikes, walked, took the train, or rode in buses. All motor vehicles were hydrogen or electric-powered; the air in even the largest cities was clean and crisp. Even aircraft used hydrogen fuel cells to get them off the ground, and solar cells covered their wings to power the plane in flight.

In the deserts of Africa, locals and Europeans worked at reclaiming the land from the sands. Progress had been slow to begin with, but at last the results were beginning to show. As more and more land was reclaimed and put to use growing crops, or the ever-important trees, the climate was beginning to shift away from the harsh extremes to a more temperate one.

In the heart of Australia, a concrete tarmac led to a gantry system. In the low buildings all around, workers made ready for the next launch of the Aerospatiale-Boeing orbital vehicle. It was the only vehicle on the planet that still used hydrocarbon fuel, and the scientists were working on a more efficient fuel cell to replace the polluting technology. They just hadn't got it right yet.

On the moon, the scientific research station housed two hundred and thirty-six people from all the nations of Earth. They studied the moon's structure and tested the soil and the very thin atmosphere. Terraforming the moon was still a pipe dream, but it might not always be so.

In the jungles of South America, the children and grandchildren of those once-powerful Americans conducted research of their own, into the properties of the juices of the many plants they had to choose from all around them. The answers might not come in their lifetime, or in their children's, but one day their descendants would use the biological agents they were developing. They would strike at the descendants of those who had murdered their parents and grandparents, and they would claim their rightful place as leaders of the modern world.

In the darkness, the clawed hand withdrew from the dial. "Must keep an eye on the South Americans, and not let them get too far too quickly."

A few feet away, another clawed hand reached toward a similar screen and twisted a dial hard to the left. "Now, about this Genghis Khan . . ."

ONE TIME AROUND?

John Helfers

The man shimmered into existence at the end of Oak Street on a beautiful summer afternoon in July. His instant, incredible appearance went completely unnoticed on the sleepy suburban street—except by a dog. Lying in the sunlight in the front yard of the house on the corner, the animal raised its head for a moment at this new intruder.

He checked himself over, making sure that nothing was missing, his movements hesitant and unsure as he verified that he was in one piece. With a sigh of relief, he realized that he was breathing fresh, clean air. And he filled his lungs with as much as they could hold before letting it out in a slow whoosh that deflated his chest, exulting in the untainted oxygen around him.

He gazed at his surroundings in rapt awe, taking in the squat, wide-roofed bungalows that were already a few decades old in this northern Minnesota town. Trees that would be towering and stately in fifty years—and dead in a century—were just new saplings now, barely able to shade the grass around them, much less the street. Blocky, stocky cars dotted the suburban landscape; curved fenders and large shadows were cast by Fords and Packards and Chevrolets and what would be the last of the Studebakers. There wasn't a car in every driveway—not yet—but here and there, for those who could afford them. Everywhere the man looked he could feel a sense of anticipation—a sense that the time of troubles was over, and that a golden age was about to begin.

And that was exactly why he was here—to ensure that one person in particular would share in that golden age. Studying each house intently, he began strolling down the street.

"Would someone please turn that damn klaxon off?" David Melchior barely managed to get the words out before a violent fit of coughing doubled him over. He knew better than to try and stop it, but instead just let it run its course until the hacking spasms stopped, leaving him bent over his control panel, sweating and exhausted.

The woman next to him, a tall, Nordic-looking blonde with thick eyeglasses and snow-white, almost translucent skin, stabbed several buttons on her keyboard while pushing a thick, plastic bottle of water over to him. The hooting, deafening alarm stopped as quickly as it had turned on, making her raised voice echo in the silence. "David, please, take a drink."

He managed a feeble grin in response, running a hand through his close cropped, thinning brown hair. "No—thanks, Irena, I'm all right. Besides, I've used up my ration for today—no need to waste yours on me too. Besides, we have to figure out what happened before the good general comes down here and sticks his nose in our business. I—"

Another coughing burst cut off his speech, and the woman gently pressed the bottle into his hand while studying her bulky analog screens with a practiced eye. "Everything looks normal—wait. I'm reading traces of residual activity in the temporal displacement chamber."

David nearly choked on his water. "What? That can't be—we have no tests scheduled for today, nothing until tomorrow morning."

"Maybe Jack has an idea as to what might have happened—" Irena looked around, a frown crossing her normally calm face. "Hey—where is he?"

David put aside his thoughts of taking another gulp of Irena's water as the unsaid implication of her words hit him. "There's no way out of here until our shift is done—unless he went into the chamber—Oh my God . . ." Fingers made clumsy by sudden fear stabbed buttons that seemed ludicrously small. "Come on, come on, scan, damn you."

The old DVD-R drive ground to a stop, and David's finger jabbed the green *Play* button.

The two scientists' heads drew close as they watched the flickering image on the small, black-and-white monitor. Jack Hollister, their partner and coinventor of the temporal displacement chamber, as it was officially referred to in all top secret government documents, stepped into their time machine and disappeared in the space between two seconds.

Jack walked down the street in a daze, numb with the idea that their machine could actually transport a human being back in time. But the scientist's part of his mind chided him. *Twelve minutes left, Jack, better hurry.*

Shaking his head, Jack squinted up at the sun and the impossibly blue sky over his head—did people really live with all this light a century ago? *Apparently so,* he thought, and quickened his pace, scanning the houses on both sides of the street. Five buildings down, he found the one he was looking for.

It was nearly indistinguishable from the rest on the block, a low-eaved, brown brick two-story home with an open porch and steps that led up to the recessed front door. Jack almost started marching up the sidewalk, then realized his folly with his very first step. *Yeah, and what am I going to say to them? "Hi, I'm from the future, and I'm here to talk to your foster child for a few minutes?"* He wasn't even sure how she would react upon seeing him, especially dressed the way he was.

Jack shook his head. He had tried to pick a time when the young girl might have been outside, but the stress of planning the unauthorized trip in the first place—not to mention the completely unknown effect of spatial and temporal dilation on time travel in the first place—had made positing an exact time nearly impossible. But if he didn't see her in the next eleven minutes, everything he had sacrificed—his career, his life, such as it was back home, would have been for nothing.

But isn't that exactly what you're going to be sacrificing in a few minutes, everything you know, everything you've ever done? The sound of a slamming screen door broke Jack's train of thought, and he looked up to see her come bounding down the steps.

"Attention!"

Instead of his spine imperceptibly straightening at the armed guard's clipped command, David's shoulders slumped. *Oh God, not now.*

The thick, duty-gray permasteel doors rumbled open, and in walked General Anthony "Razor" Steele. Unlike the frail and weak scientists, his body was a perfect example of the developed human specimen, honed by years of military training and selected experiments to ensure that every soldier was in peak condition. Bulging muscles flexed and relaxed as he crossed the room to the two scientists, tossing off a casual salute to the guard at the door as he passed.

"Doctor Melchior, Doctor—" The General's eyes darted to her chest for a second "—Marikova." As he did every time the General greeted them, David squelched the urge to punch the other man out, as ludicrous as that sounded. He shook off the brief fantasy of himself standing over the general lying prone on the floor, to hear the end of Steele's sentence.

"—thought there weren't any tests scheduled for today?"

David stared at the taller man helplessly as he realized he didn't have the faintest idea of what the general was talking about. Just as he was about to stammer a reply, he felt his airway closing, and he erupted in another coughing fit, all the while thinking, *Thank God.*

"Is he all right, Doctor?" The expression on the general's face was solicitous enough, but he made no move to help David either.

Irena shoved her water bottle into his hand again as she addressed the general. "Yes, there was a power surge in the room, and no, we did not have any tests scheduled for today, general."

David grabbed the bottle and gulped more tepid water to soothe his aching throat. *Did he see the surge from the displacement himself? I'm surprised he even knew what it was.*

"I see." Steele looked around. "Something's different here. Aren't there usually three scientists in this room?"

David lowered the bottle before he sprayed droplets all over Irena and Steele. Coming from the general, that simple sentence was the equivalent of any other person saying that they had figured out a way to travel faster than light speed. A side effect of the treatments that had been performed on General Steele was that he had also been given the perfect military mind to go along with his very competent military body—able to accept commands from his superiors without question, and fearless—or stupid, as David suspected—enough to go charging into the mouth of hell itself if so ordered. Such esoteric things as time-travel were light-years beyond him, although apparently the simple math classes he had studied as a boy had stuck with him.

"As Doctor Marikova said, there weren't any tests scheduled for today. And you are correct, General, there usually are three scientists in this room. However, unfortunately, Doctor Hollister has—left."

"Left?" the General's face wrinkled in puzzlement. "But he can't leave—none of you can leave this room until your shift is over."

"Again, you are correct, sir, but Doctor Hollister didn't leave through the door—he went into the displacement chamber. That was the power surge you registered upstairs."

"Ah—so where is he?"

David and Irena exchanged glances, then both shook their heads in resignation. "The question, sir, is not where he is, but *when*. And we're working on figuring that out right now."

"So an unauthorized displacement has occurred in this room, and has involved a human being—correct me if I'm wrong, but the first human being to undergo this sort of journey, right?"

David grudgingly revised his estimation of the general up a notch—he knew many smarter men who would have had a hard time grasping the implications of what had just occurred. "Yes, sir."

And the general's next words surprised him even more. "All right, so what do we do now?"

Jack stared at the little girl holding her doll as she walked down the steps, the expression on her face serious, as if she had already seen too much of the bad parts of life in her eleven years on this planet. She did not walk with the carefree joy of a young girl, but quietly, as if, even out here, she was worried about making a noise that would bring someone's wrath upon her.

A fair assumption, given how she was raised, Jack thought. Even so, he had chosen this age to contact her, in the hopes that perhaps all of her childhood innocence hadn't been stripped away yet, before the rigid mindset of a teenager—any and all teenagers— set in. Still, from what he knew of her, it was possible that he had come back too late.

A shadow fell across his feet, and Jack looked up

to see her staring at him from a few yards away. He glanced down at his clothes—the form-fitting nylon jumpsuit, stained and wrinkled from too many hurried meals and countless days sleeping in his chair before and after his shift. His eyes came up again, and he took in her shabby, brown plaid dress, scuffed Buster Brown shoes, and falling-down, dingy white socks. Her dark brown hair hung limp around her face. "Guess I must look pretty strange to you, huh, Lana?"

Her brows knitted in puzzlement, and Jack continued before he frightened her away. "Yes, I know your name—you could say that I know a whole lot of things about you, even though you've never seen me before."

The little girl cocked her head, the frown now warring with a bit of curiosity. Jack pressed on. "I'm from somewhere very far away, and I know a great deal about you. For example, I know that the people who are raising you here are not your real parents. They are Gloria and Dean Tavermeier. I know that Mr. Tavermeier loves you very much, but Mrs. Tavermeier, well, I'll bet she can be very strict sometimes, isn't she?"

The little girl looked back at the house, the doll clutched tightly to her chest. Jack looked up as well, scanning the house for a form at the curtains, or the door cracked open so someone might be able to hear outside. Nothing moved in the late afternoon sun, and the house remained silent, motionless.

Jack looked down to see the little girl had now halfway turned back toward the steps, as if she was about to bolt for the relative safety of the home. He willed himself not to move, as if she were a doe, and any sudden motion on his part would frighten her off, never to be seen again. Even his breath caught in his throat as he waited to see what her decision would be.

Lana turned back toward the bungalow one more time, then back to Jack, nodding her head once in response to his question as she did so.

Jack let out the breath he had been holding in a

whoosh, once again aware of the incredible pureness of the air around him. "It's all right, Lana. I wouldn't hurt you, not for anything in the world. In fact—" He smiled, and knelt down so that his head was on the same level as hers. "I'm here to help you."

David rocked back and forth on his heels, wondering how to explain everything so that the general would understand it all. "Now? Well, we don't really know, sir. I mean, the chamber has been tested first with inanimate objects, then with programmable, remote-controlled vehicles that recorded what they saw, so we were able to prove that indeed they had traveled through time."

He paused for a valuable breath, and Irena took over the summation. "We had only recently begun testing by sending animals through, but all initial tests seemed to indicate that they had adjusted to the process with little or no short-term effects. Long-term ramifications are unrecognizable, since there hasn't been enough time to really study the effect of time-travel on living beings."

"Fine, fine, but that isn't my point. What are the ramifications of Doctor Hollister going back in time?"

David and Irena exchanged helpless glances. "Frankly, sir, we have no idea. Even though we've been studying it for almost two years, time travel is such a theoretical field that the data gathered is difficult, if not impossible, to quantify. It is possible that Jack going back might have already changed things in the future. But how would we know? After all, this isn't like the movies where we would see big sweeping changes around us."

Irena spoke up again, and David was glad for the respite. "Alternatively—again, this is just hypothetical—there is a theory that every decision made by a person creates a separate reality—an infinite number of them, given the millions of decisions that are made throughout the world on a daily basis—and so therefore we would be faced with trillions upon trillions of separate timelines, each one representing the culmination of millions of separate choices made by people. As for what effect Jack's travel will have on this timeline, I guess it depends on whether there is only one timeline, or many divergent ones."

"What about sending someone back to find him?" the general asked.

Irena shrugged. "Well, we do know that he went to just after the post-World War II period, about 1948, but we don't know exactly where on the planet he went to. When he set the longitude and latitude for his jump, he programmed the computer to erase the numbers after the trip was made."

"Even if we knew where he was, we couldn't make another jump for about an hour, and by then he should be back here, given the trip's standard duration of fifteen minutes," David said. "All we theoretically have to do is wait for him—assuming that he is in the exact spot he was transported to when he traveled to that time in the first place."

The general's brow raised. "Why is that?"

"Well, sir, the one thing that we have figured out is that the universe does strive toward a semblance of order." David stared at the displacement chamber as he spoke, wondering what his friend was doing at that exact moment. "If something—or someone—is out of place chronologically, then after approximately fifteen minutes, a second timehole opens up back to that person or item's originating time period, and they can go back through. It's the only way we've been able to get any data back. Jack stumbled upon the phenomenon accidentally when he piloted one of our drones back through the rift. In approximately ten minutes— assuming he wants to come back—Jack should reappear in the chamber. His condition—well, that may be another story, since we have no idea if a thinking life form can survive the trip with their faculties intact yet."

"Maybe so, but who knows what havoc he's wreaking back there. Nineteen forty-eight—did he go back to assassinate Stalin? Truman, God forbid? What is he planning to do? Why did he risk everything to go back?"

Only silence answered the general's question.

"How?" the girl's first word was so quiet Jack almost didn't hear it. "How are you going to help me?"

A myriad of answers flashed through Jack's mind—all things he knew about this girl. *That she would be abused by a seventeen-year old boy in the next foster home she would go to. That she would slink through high school, never working up the nerve to be able to talk to the boy she liked there, and never getting the chance to go to college, which was her dream. That she would end up marrying not one, but two deadbeat husbands that would slowly drain the life and the spirit out of her, emotionally and physically abusing her throughout both relationships. That she would have three children, a daughter from her first marriage who would carry on a tradition of ignorance and small-mindedness, and two sons, whom she would live for, simply because there would be nothing else in her life. That she would end up living in a small apartment, alone, waiting to die, her only accomplishments being her two sons, and leaving behind a life of struggle, heartbreak, and loneliness.*

"Even though you've never seen me before, as I said, I know all about you. I want to tell you about three men that you need to stay away from when—*and if*, he thought—you meet them later on in your life." As much as Jack wanted to, he couldn't bring himself to tell her what the first guy would do, but he described him clearly, and also where and when she might meet him, and described him in an ominous-enough tone that he was sure she got the point. He also told her about the two potential husbands, giving her their names and where she might meet them. "And never, ever give up on your dream of going to college." Her eyes widened, and he kept going, hoping that his words would imprint on her, and somehow stay with her through the years. "You can do it, even though it will be difficult at times. But I know you can succeed, and become a nurse, just like you've always dreamed of doing."

Lana's mouth hung open, and Jack smiled, as he was sure that she might not have even thought about what she wanted to do at this age. "If you take anything away with you after this, know that out there somewhere is a man who always believes in you, no matter where you are, or what you are doing. Most of all, be true to yourself, and don't let anyone tell you how you should think or what you should do, unless you agree with them. Only you can possibly ever know what's best for yourself. Understand?"

Lana nodded, just as the screen door creaked open. An iron-haired, stern-faced woman appeared in the doorway. "Lana, you come in this house right now!"

The girl turned to go, but looked back at Jack one last time.

"Remember what I said, Lana, and trust in yourself. You can do it!"

She lifted her hand in a shy wave, and then ran up the steps to where the woman waited, her hand on her hip. "What have I told you about talking to strangers?" she scolded as she ushered the girl inside, giving Jack an icy glare as she closed the door.

Well, at least she's teaching her that much right away, I suppose. The encounter had gone faster than Jack had expected, and he actually had a little time left to himself. *Time to do what—walk around this world that had no idea of what lay ahead of it—Korea, the Cold War, Vietnam, the Gulf War, Iraq, Iran, the Sino-Chinese War, and a world brought to the brink of destruction less than seventy-five years from now? Is that any kind of world to leave to one's children?*

He turned and began walking down the street, back to his starting point. *But by doing this, have I truly*

*made any kind of difference at all? I don't even know
if she will take my words to heart and change the path
she is on—she might just chalk it up to the ramblings
of a strange old man who accosted her outside her
house one summer afternoon.*

The sound of a window opening behind him made
Jack turn his head to look behind him. The window
of the lone upstairs dormer in the Tavermeier home,
which he could have sworn had been closed, was now
open, its curtains fluttering softly in the breeze. And
there, framed in the window, was Lana, waving
good-bye.

Jack raised his hand and waved back, a faint smile
ghosting across his mouth. *Then again, maybe she will
be better off.* He continued on down the street. He
had lost track of how many minutes he had left in
this time, but figured that the return hole would be
appearing very soon. *Which begs the next question: am
I going back?*

In all their research at the military redoubt deep in
Cheyenne Mountain, they had never been able to answer the age-old questions of time-travel paradox.
Jack knew that if he did go back, he would face a
swift trial for unauthorized use of military equipment
during a time of war, and most likely be accused of
treason and anything else the government could
cook up.

Perhaps I will be able to stay here, he thought, even
as the logical part of his mind figured that would be
impossible, especially if Irena's theory was correct,
and that the laws of the universe tended toward order.
As a man displaced out of the time he should be in,
that left a whole lot of unknowns that possibly might
come crashing down on him. *I could end up disappearing for good, vanishing from the universe forever.
I could explode in a burst of complete cellular disinte-
gration. I could—just end up staying here, trapped forever in the past.*

A spark of white light across the street caught his

attention, and Jack walked toward it, knowing that the return timehole was opening, growing to form a rift in the continuum that would enable him to enter it, if he desired. On its edge, he hesitated for a moment, taking one last look around, particularly at the house halfway down the block. He thought of the little girl who lived there . . . and what she might accomplish in the hopefully new future that stretched out before her.

Goodbye, Mom.

"I hope you both realize the jeopardy that your colleague has placed us in with this hazardous and incredibly foolish stunt," the general said. "Yes, we were certainly hoping that this program could be used to change the past, to divert the timeline of crucial events so that our world wouldn't be nearly destroyed in the War against China. In time, we had hoped to send people back to accomplish certain—missions—to ensure that the war never happens in the first place. But now, thanks to Doctor Hollister's egocentric little jaunt, all of that is possibly in very real danger."

David's jaw dropped, mirroring Irena's shocked expression. "Sir, have you even given a thought to what you're saying? The consequences of trying to alter the time continuum could be disastrous, even catastrophic. We don't know if it is even possible to do what you're suggesting."

"Well, I guess we're about to find out," the general said. "Just by going back in time, Doctor Hollister has already altered events, even it he does nothing, correct?"

"Yes, the very fact that he is there could potentially alter time, and change the future. However, as we've already said, we won't know about it, since the reality we exist in is occurring right now, already around us, created every second."

"But does that mean he will shift that time stream over to another, different path?"

"I think we're about to find out," David said, waving them over to the monitor that showed the time displacement chamber, now containing a blinding white glow that was spreading to every corner of the room. "The return cycle is starting."

Jack shielded his eyes enough to block most of the glare from the dazzling light that appeared in front of him. But he couldn't help watching as other things began to appear in the incision between the two time periods.

He saw Lana going to school, then entering college as he had hoped, then graduating with her degree and going to medical school—

But then a different scene appeared, and he watched Lana under very different circumstances, pregnant and alone in what looked like a grimy third-story walk-up apartment building, with tears running down her face as she sat at a battered kitchen table—

What's going on here? he wondered, just as another view of her appeared, this time in a corporate boardroom. His mother, looking about forty years older, was dressed in a tailored pantsuit and presenting some kind of make-up line to the people seated in the room. Above her head was a company logo: *Striver Cosmetics*—

The scene changed again, and he saw Lana dressed in a black robe and with her right hand raised and her left hand on a Bible, taking some kind of oath of office—

As Jack watched, he saw hundreds, then thousands of alternate Lanas, each one following a new path to a varying conclusion. Some of the different versions of his mother were cut down by accidents or disease, some were the victims of crime or poverty, and many went on to accomplish careers, marry and raise a family, or, in some of the best cases, both. The images flowed over and around each other, like hundreds of thousands of different life paths that his mother could take, branching off from this moment—

—*Including the same one she might have continued*

on after I spoke to her, Jack thought. *Irena was right after all; it doesn't matter whether any of us go back in time to try and change things; all that does is create a new, separate reality, in which that choice is played out, and all of the other, different decisions after that.*

So if every choice creates a different line, then there are billions—no an infinite number—of alternate worlds being created every second of every day.

But what will happen to me now that I've stepped out of my timeline and changed things? I mean, I still exist, because somewhere in all of these infinite timelines, she met and married my father, and apparently still had at least one child—I think. So I will not disappear like a figment of so many fevered pulp writers' imaginations. But would I still go back to that moment—would I still exist in that future?

Before he could even ponder the ramifications of answering his own question, Jack stepped into the glowing white rift and blinked out of existence from Oak Street in Duluth, Minnesota, in July, 1948.

"The universe moves toward order," Irena whispered under her breath as the white light faded, revealing Jack standing in the middle of the displacement chamber, looking around with a satisfied expression on his face.

The general unsnapped the flap covering his pistol. "Guard! I want you to arrest that man—"

David limped forward. "Wait, general, consider what you are doing right now. Jack Hollister is the only human being to have successfully traveled through time—assuming that the man in there is indeed Jack. If you lock him up now, years, perhaps decades of research will be lost to us, and we would be no closer to seeing if your goal is even possible."

The general glared at David, his hand hovering over his pistol, then motioned the guard back to his position. "You get everything out of him you can, and then he's mine, understand?"

"Perfectly, sir."

*   *   *

Jack opened his eyes to find himself in a vast forest, with a small, bustling town composed of dozens of clapboard building that ringed a large, frenetic port on the shore of Lake Superior.

The sound of whuffling horses and creaking wagon wheels made him turn to see a buckboard and team pull to a stop nearby. A man in a homespun shirt and well-worn canvas pants regarded him. "Wherever did you come from? I would have sworn this road was empty a moment ago."

Jack regarded him with a frown. "That would be almost impossible to tell you, sir, so I'll just say I come from a very, very far away place. Mind if I get a ride into town?"

"Ayuh, hop on up here. I can take you to the mill on the outskirts, then you're on your own."

Jack looked around with a smile. "That sounds just fine."

The white glow faded, and Jack found himself back on Oak Street, everything around him unchanged. For a moment he thought about going back to see his mother, then he shook his head, turned around, and began walking down the street in the opposite direction.

Jack winked into existence in a thick forest, and stumbled around just long enough to attract the attention of a hungry cave bear that stalked, killed, and ate him in 1948 BC.

Jack . . .

ABOUT THE AUTHORS

Kevin J. Anderson has more than sixteen million books in print in thirty languages. Of his more than eighty published novels, thirty-three have appeared on the bestseller lists. He has penned many popular Star Wars and X-Files novels, as well as numerous internationally bestselling prequel novels to Dune written with Frank Herbert's son Brian. His original work has appeared on numerous "Best-of" and awards lists, including a *New York Times* Notable Book of the Year. In 1998, he set the Guinness World Record for Largest Single-Author Book Signing. His recent novels include *Of Fire and Night* and *Scattered Suns* (in the Seven Suns series), and *The Martian War*, as well as a collaboration with Dean Koontz, *Frankenstein: Prodigal Son*. With his wife, Rebecca Moesta, he is writing an original young-adult fantasy series, Crystal Doors.

Pierce Askegren Born in Pennsylvania and one of four children, he lives in Virginia these days. Humble and fuzzy yet strangely loveable, Pierce is the author of eleven novels, three of them in collaboration, eight based on media properties such as Marvel comics and TV's *Alias*. His most recent books are *After Image*, featuring Buffy the Vampire Slayer, and *Exit Strategy*,

the third of a well-received original science fiction series set on the moon in the not-too-far distant future.
Pierce's short stories have appeared in such anthologies as *The Chick is in the Mail* and *Historical
Hauntings*. He's currently at work on his next book,
but he's not sure just what it will be.

Linda P. Baker is the author of *The Irda* and *Tears
of the Night Sky*, with Nancy Varian Berberick. Her
short fiction has been published in several Dragonlance anthologies as well as *First Contact, The New
Amazons, Wizard Fantastic,* and *Earth, Air, Fire,
Water: Tales from the Eternal Archives.* In her nonfiction guise, Linda is a researcher and writes brochures
and software guides. Linda dedicates her story to her
sister Laneta and brother-in-law Garland. As survivors
of Hurricane Katrina who chose to view their loss as
a chance to make their move to a better place, they
serve as role models for their family and friends. Linda
and her husband, Larry, live in Mobile, AL, and are
always on the look-out for a good antique auction.
They have found their better place in Ireland, and
hope someday to live there.

Donald J. Bingle is a frequent contributor to short
story anthologies in the science fiction, fantasy, horror,
and comedy genres, including the DAW anthologies
*Civil War Fantastic, Historical Hauntings, Sol's Chil-
dren, Renaissance Faire, All Hell Breaking Loose,* and
Slipstreams. He is also the author of *Forced Conver-
sion*, a science fiction novel set in the near future,
when everyone can have heaven, any heaven they
want, but some people don't want to go. His latest
novel, *GREENSWORD*, is a darkly comedic eco-
thriller about a group of misfit environmentalists who
are about to save the world from global warming, but
don't want to get caught doing it. He and his lovely
wife, Linda, currently co-habit with two dogs: Makai
and Mauka. Don is also a frequent author and coauthor

of adventures and tournaments for the TimeMaster role-playing game. He can be reached at www.orphyte.com/donaldjbingle.

Jon L. Breen has contributed stories to *Isaac Asimov's Science Fiction Magazine* and *Fantasy Book* and belongs to Science Fiction and Fantasy Writers of America, but he is best known in the mystery field. He has won two Edgar Awards for critical writings and is the author of seven novels and nearly a hundred short stories. His most recent books are the collection *Kill the Umpire: The Calls of Ed Gorgon* and the novel *Eye of God*. Retired as a librarian and professor of English, Breen lives in Fountain Valley, California, with his wife Rita.

Since 1984, **Jackie Cassada** has written the science fiction/fantasy review column for *Library Journal*, giving her the perfect excuse to read a lot of imaginative fiction and call it "work." She has also authored "The Year in Science Fiction and Fantasy" for the *Dictionary of Literary Biography Yearbooks 2000, 2001* and *2002*. Her published fiction includes the now out-of-print Immortal Eyes trilogy (*The Toybox, Shadows on the Hill, Court of All Kings*) of novels for White Wolf's Changeling role-playing game and has contributed short stories to the White Wolf anthologies *Death and Damnation, Truth Until Paradox, City of Darkness: Unseen, Splendour Falls* and *Dark Tyrants*. She spends her days as a member of the support staff of the Asheville-Buncombe Library System in western North Carolina. Jackie shares a house with her longtime partner, five cats, and a Plott hound. In her spare time she reads, plays role-playing games, crochets, and dreams of founding a haven for geriatric animals.

Author of forty science fiction, mystery, and fantasy novels, **Gene DeWeese** was, once upon a time, a technical writer who did manuals for B-52 navigation systems and intuitive programmed instruction texts on orbital mechanics for NASA's Apollo program. He's lived in Milwaukee the past forty-five years with his multitasking wife Beverly and assorted single-minded cats. His most recent books are a Star Trek novel, *Engines of Destiny*, and a small-town-sheriff mystery, *Murder in the Blood*.

John Helfers is an author and editor currently living in Green Bay, Wisconsin. He has published more than thirty short stories in anthologies such as *The Sorcerer's Academy*, *Faerie Tales*, *Alien Pets*, and *Apprentice Fantastic* (DAW Books). His media tie-in fiction has appeared in anthologies for the *Dragonlance* and *Transformers* universes, among others. He has written both fiction and nonfiction books, including a comprehensive history of the United States Navy. His most recent novel is *Shadowrun: Aftershock*, co-authored by Jean Rabe.

Stephen Leigh has published twenty-some novels and a few dozen short stories, under both his own name and pseudonymously. His fiction has won several awards within the science fiction and fantasy fields. He also teaches creative writing courses at a local university. His other interests and avocations include music, Aikido (in which he holds the rank of Nidan), art (he has a bachelor's degree in fine art), history, language and sociology, prowling the Web (he has a site at www.farrellworlds.com and a Livejournal account) and finding spare bits of free time.

He is married to his best friend and favorite first reader, Denise Parsley Leigh; they have two children who are growing impossibly old.

Joe Masdon lives in Elon, North Carolina, with his wife Sherrie and their two sons, Jonathan and Robert. He has written numerous horror and fantasy short stories that have never left his hard drive and a few that saw publication in books that very few people read. He writes fantasy as a way to apologize for being an accountant.

Wes Nicholson is a born-and-bred Australian who has always had a fascination for technology. He never really decided what he wanted to do when he grew up and has several trade and university qualifications to show what he's tried. He began his writing career in the role-playing industry, and has several published credits for the Advanced Dungeons & Dragons and Shadowrun games, and has had short fiction published in the Forgotten Realms setting. A world traveler, he lives in Canberra with his wife and three children and teaches karate when he's not writing or role-playing.

Chris Pierson has been a writer since he was a kid up in Canada. He has written seven novels for the Dragonlance series: *Spirit of the Wind, Dezra's Quest,* the Kingpriest trilogy (*Chosen of the Gods, Divine Hammer,* and *Sacred Fire*), and the Taladas trilogy (*Blades of the Tiger* and *Trail of the Black Wyrm*). He is currently working on the third Taladas book *Shadow of the Flame*. In addition, he has been published in Dragon Magazine and in the anthologies *The Dragons At War, Dragons of Chaos,* and *Rebels & Tyrants*. During the day, Chris works as a game designer for Turbine, and has been involved in the Asheron's Call series, Dungeons & Dragons Online: Stormreach, and Lord of the Rings Online: Shadows of Angmar; he also writes and edits other game material. He lives in Boston with his wife and fellow movie addict, Rebekah.

Harry Turtledove is a Caltech flunkout who perplexed everyone, including himself, by ending up with a doctorate in Byzantine history from UCLA. This suited him for telling lies for a living, which is what he mostly does now. His novels include *The Guns of the South,*

Ruled Britannia, In the Presence of Mine Enemies, The Case of the Toxic Spell Dump, and *Every Inch a King.* He has won a Hugo, two Sidewise awards, and the Hal Clement award for YA fiction. He is married to Laura Frankos, also a historian and also a writer. Of his three daughters, the two in college are both history majors. Environment or genetics, do you suppose?

Robert E. Vardeman has been interested in Nikolai Tesla and his fabulous inventions since doing a grade school book report in a prior century. Other than "The Power and the Glory," Vardeman has written several dozen short stories and more than seventy science fiction, fantasy, and mystery novels. He currently lives in Albuquerque, NM, with his teenaged son, Chris, and a cat. Two out of three of them enjoy the high-tech hobby of geocaching.

Nancy Virginia Varian is the not-so-secret identity of Nancy Varian Berberick. While N.V.B'.s work has long been known to Dragonlance fans and those who enjoy reading short stories (and the occasional novel) with a distinctly Norse or Old English flavor, **N.V.V.** has only recently popped her head up over the parapet. "Yeshua's Choice" marks her second short story, the first being "The Oaths of Gods" in *Lords of Swords,* an anthology of sword & sorcery stories.

James M. Ward has been a successful author and game designer since 1974. He created the first science fiction role playing game in Metamorphosis Alpha. He's written for Marvel, DC Comics, DAW, Random House, Del Rey, Bantam, Tor, and Western Publishing. Voted into the Game Designer's Hall of Fame, he also received the best game of the year award for Gamma World. His novels have been on the bestselling lists of Waldens, B. Dalton's, and Locus. His game credits include work with *Charlie Brown, Sesame Street, He-Man, Conan, Indiana Jones, Dragon Ball Z,*

Marvel, DC comics, Worlds of Wonder, Robert Jordan's *Wheel of Time*, Joss Whedon's *Firefly & Buffy*, and Wizards of the Coast/Hasbro. He designed the smash hit card game *Dragon Ball Z* that's been breaking sales records since 2001. He lives in the Midwest with his wife. He's taken up fencing and this hobby constantly pits him against younger, faster people, just like in the game business.

Skip and Penny Williams profess a love of old things, such as silly old movies, the century-old farmhouse they share, and each other—though not necessarily in that order. Penny has degrees in chemistry and Russian and dozens of editorial credits in the role-playing game industry. Skip co-authored the Dungeons & Dragons 3rd edition game and has numerous other role-playing game credits. This short story is Skip and Penny's first published piece of fiction.

When not exploring alternate histories, Skip putters in his vegetable garden (which keeps many deer and rabbits fed); works to reclaim the fields around the farmhouse from the (thus far) implacable weeds that blanket them; and paints toy soldiers. Penny enjoys many different crafts, puts up jam, and works as a substitute teacher in all subjects.

CJ Cherryh
Classic Series in New Omnibus Editions

THE DREAMING TREE
Contains the complete duology *The Dreamstone* and *The Tree of Swords and Jewels.*   0-88677-782-8

THE FADED SUN TRILOGY
Contains the complete novels *Kesrith*, *Shon'jir*, and *Kutath.*   0-88677-836-0

THE MORGAINE SAGA
Contains the complete novels *Gate of Ivrel*, *Well of Shiuan*, and *Fires of Azeroth.*   0-88677-877-8

THE CHANUR SAGA
Contains the complete novels *The Pride of Chanur*, *Chanur's Venture* and *The Kif Strike Back.*
0-88677-930-8

ALTERNATE REALITIES
Contains the complete novels *Port Eterntiy*, *Voyager in Night*, and *Wave Without a Shore*   0-88677-946-4

AT THE EDGE OF SPACE
Contains the complete novels *Brothers of Earth* and *Hunter of Worlds.*   0-7564-0160-7

To Order Call: 1-800-788-6262

Julie E. Czerneda

Web Shifters

"A great adventure following an engaging character across a divertingly varied series of worlds."—*Locus*

Esen is a shapeshifter, one of the last of an ancient race. Only one Human knows her true nature—but those who suspect are determined to destroy her!

BEHOLDER'S EYE
0-88677-818-2
CHANGING VISION
0-88677-815-8
HIDDEN IN SIGHT
0-7564-0139-9

Also by Julie E. Czerneda:
IN THE COMPANY OF OTHERS
0-88677-999-7
"An exhilarating science fiction thriller"
—*Romantic Times*

To Order Call: 1-800-788-6262

C.S. Friedman

The Best in Science Fiction

C.S. Friedman

The Coldfire Trilogy

"A feast for those who like their fantasies dark, and as
  emotionally heady as a rich red wine." —*Locus*

Centuries after being stranded on the planet
Erna, humans have achieved an uneasy stale-
mate with the fae, a terrifying natural force with
the power to prey upon people's minds. Damien
Vryce, the warrior priest, and Gerald Tarrant, the
undead sorcerer must join together in an uneasy
alliance confront a power that threatens the very
essence of the human spirit, in a battle which
could cost them not only their lives, but the soul
of all mankind.

BLACK SUN RISING   0-88677-527-2
WHEN TRUE NIGHT FALLS   0-88677-615-5
CROWN OF SHADOWS   0-88677-717-8

To Order Call: 1-800-788-6262

DAW 18

OTHERLAND

TAD WILLIAMS

"The Otherland books are a major accomplishment."
–Publishers Weekly

"It will captivate you."
–Cinescape

In many ways it is humankind's most stunning achievement. This most exclusive of places is also one of the world's best-kept secrets, but somehow, bit by bit, it is claiming Earth's most valuable resource: its children.

CITY OF GOLDEN SHADOW (Vol. One)
0-88677-763-1

RIVER OF BLUE FIRE (Vol. Two)
0-88677-844-1

MOUNTAIN OF BLACK GLASS (Vol. Three)
0-88677-906-5

SEA OF SILVER LIGHT (Vol. Four)
0-75640-030-9

To Order Call: 1-800-788-6262

DAW 44